Catch and Keep

HORSE DOCTOR ADVENTURES

ELIZABETH WOOLSEY

ELIZABETH WOOLSEY HORSE DOCTOR PRESS

HORSE
DOCTOR
PRESS

Chapter 1

Previously

Maggie Kincaid was retired from her career as an equine veterinarian, and despite her children's warnings and displeasure, returned to her birth country and bought a log cabin. She planned to ride horses, fish for trout, and write books.

Mission accomplished. Despite the murder-suicide in her log cabin, several years before her purchase, Maggie was living her best life. Then a young deaf boy came and asked for work. This connection and her eligibility as a single mature woman brought her to the attention of an aging film star, Colin Chandler, and a multimillionaire, Charlie McLeod.

She narrowly escaped from a kidnapping, and then her prime candidate for marital bliss was killed in a plane crash. Life became too much, and Maggie withdrew from the social scene. Amid depression, Maggie spent several weeks in bed as winter loomed.

Colin Chandler rescued her from the blues and offered to take her fishing in the Southern Hemisphere—a destination unknown. Despite her reluctance to get out of bed, she went, and upon entering a remote fishing lodge, found that her former love interest was not dead and was hiding from his co-conspirators awaiting trials where he would give evidence. Or was he hiding from the authorities?

With two rivals for her affection, Maggie decided to look for salvation and left the men at the lodge to go fishing.

Chapter 1

I was in a fog. The light was streaming into an unfamiliar room as I attempted to orient myself. I could hear distant banging. The pounding of a fist on a door brought me to attention.

"Maggie, it's almost lunchtime, and it's time to get up. I want to go fishing. If you aren't out of bed with your gear on in fifteen minutes, I'll be coming in and dressing you personally."

I looked at my watch. Holy shit, it's eleven a.m. I drank way too much, way, way too much. I didn't even make it to my room. What was I thinking? That's it, I'm never drinking again. I don't think the boys even know I was sleeping on the couch all night in the lodge. Oh well, live and learn. One of my dear friends was banging on the door of my cabin thinking I was in there. But I wasn't. I was on the couch, inside the main building of this remote fishing lodge. Oh, my aching head. I got up and walked to the veranda door, and thankfully it was only Colin who saw me.

"Aren't you a sore sight for old eyes?" He shook his head.

I smiled weakly. "Give me twenty, Collie. I need a cup of coffee too." I was still in the same clothes I wore last night and almost fell off the veranda when I descended the lodge's steps heading to my cabin. Colin caught me and took me by the shoulders. "Fishing can wait. You need something to eat. Get in the shower, and I'll cook something for you."

"In the shower?" I teased him, and he swatted at me as he let me go but missed. "You'll have to be a bit quicker if you want to catch me, old man." With that, he reached out and took my hand, and spun me around.

"You mean like that? Get going. I need to fish. I do my best thinking with a rod in my hand, you know." Colin was mocking me.

I laughed, remembering that I had said the exact same thing yesterday. When I said it, I hadn't a clue what that might mean coming from a man. It was true, though. I almost had a religious experience with fly fishing. I studied nature and the biology of insects. I calculated aerodynamics, and then I prayed a lot while trying to coax a fish onto my line. Who was I kidding? I was an amateur in all aspects of the biology of fish.

Last night was going to be a pivotal night. Sadly, and probably thankfully, alcohol got in the way. Here I was in New Zealand with two eligible bachelors. My fishing partner, Colin Chandler, was eighty but still as robust as a man half his age. As an aging film star, he was so unaffected by fortune and fame, I could barely keep up.

On the other hand, my host, Charlie McLeod, or now as he wanted to be called, Todd Mulholland, was a few years younger than me. Until he went into witness protection after surviving an unsurvivable plane crash, which incidentally never happened, Charlie McLeod was physically much older than me. In truth, he was five or more years younger. I was reminded that birth order was relative at our age.

Thankfully, I was sixty-nine going on forty. Well, that's what I told myself. But after last night, make that sixty-nine going on CTD, or "circling the drain," which is often used in veterinary medicine to denote a very sick and potentially soon to die animal. That was me, CTD for sure, after last night. I'm sure the eighteen-hour plane trip didn't help. The shock of finding out that the man I thought I loved was not dead, was involved in the drug trade, and played a hand in almost killing me didn't help.

My name is Margaret Kincaid, and I am a once-a-year alcoholic. The good news was it was mid-December, and I only had a few weeks before I could repeat this act of debauchery (not).

I went to my room, showered, and dressed in shorts and a long-sleeved fishing shirt. I had gloves that I wore to protect me from the bite of sandflies. Still, I'd forgotten them last night, and my hands were already swollen and itchy from my adventure the previous evening. There was a cup of coffee on the kitchen counter and a piece of toast.

"Thanks, Collie. Sorry about that. I'm swearing off all forms of mind-altering medicinals for the rest of the year."

Colin shook his head and nodded. "Me, too, but only tonight. Any joy last night?"

"A strike. I was too slow. The fish got away."

"Are you talking about the fish or someone near and dear?"

"The fish. I'm swearing off nears and dears as well." I drank the bitter coffee, took the cup to the sink, and refilled it with water.

"We'll see. Have you got your waders? It's warm out today, but I'm guessing the water is cold, and I want to be prepared to cross when we want. If you complain or whine, I'll bring you back, and you won't go again."

"Yep, got any anti-whining drugs?"

Colin shook his head in dismay. "I saw some Tylenol in the pantry." He got up, opened the door, and threw a bottle at me. Thankfully, I caught it. Colin announced, "Charlie, I mean Todd, is up in his gallery painting. He asked us to be back by five, so we can eat and maybe take a tour of your property."

I'd forgotten that Charlie, I mean Todd, had given me this lodge. I guessed it was so he could remain anonymous with the government. "Not mine. Maybe ours, but not mine alone."

"You had enough? Ready to hit the river, Maggie?"

Chapter 2

Of course, Colin had the first fish, then the second, and the third. He pursed his lips, shook his head at me, and simply said, "Let's get you educated." We walked down the river and saw a large trout darting in and out of a bubble line. It was actively feeding. Colin stayed up on the high bank to monitor the fish and sent me downstream. I quietly waded out into the water a few feet, and Colin silently pointed to a clump of grass where I was to land a fly above the feeding fish. Colin opened his arms, indicating that I should let the fly land two feet from the bank.

I'm not an expert at fishing, but one thing I was good at was placing a fly in a sweet spot. It was a crapshoot after that. I rarely visualized a fish take a fly unless I had a gigantic fly strike indicator. Strike indicators come in many forms. They might be the fly itself, or a bubble of florescent floating gum-like material, or yarn that is attached to the line. It drops below the water's surface if a trout takes a submerged fly or the fly hits on the riverbed causing the line to hang for a second.

I performed two false casts where I let my line out, and then I went for the gold. The fly landed perfectly. The fish rose, and I could see by Colin's actions that I was close. Colin rolled his wrist, indicating I should repeat my cast, and once again, the fish rose but didn't take the fly.

Colin raised a finger, indicating that I should try one more time. I did, and then the same thing happened. Colin then walked back behind me and motioned me to take my line and flick it to him. For an old geezer, he still could tie a fly quickly. All he did was add a nymph to the dry fly, and using this drop shot rig, he asked me to wait until he was back on the bank and able to see the feeding fish. Colin held his hand up and indicated I should wait.

From my perspective, I was fishing blind. I watched Colin lower his polarized glasses and cup the sides of his head to help him see the fish. He finally smiled and turned to me, holding up two fingers. There must be two fish now. He finally nodded, and I did a single false cast and let the fly and nymph sail away from the area where the fish were feeding. I knew it would take extra effort to land the flies ahead of the fish, and I didn't want to blow it and scare away the fish.

Colin nodded and then pointed to where he wanted the flies to land. I longed to impress him, and I was so nervous, but with all that I had in me, I did a single false cast again and then sent the line out two feet in front of the trout. Even I saw the indicator drop. I raised the tip of my rod and hooked the trout.

"Fish on, darlin'." Colin quickly came back to join me down at the water's edge. I would like to say it was an epic battle, but the fish gave up rather quickly, and Colin walked into the water and netted the hen. "Nice, Maggot."

I was pleased. I didn't mind Colin calling me Maggot. Despite what it sounded like, it was a term of affection when my sister called me that, and I knew it was the same with Colin. He pulled out his camera and took a picture. I hadn't charged mine last night, and I didn't bring it when we left to come down to the river. "I'm sorry I didn't get any with you and your fish, Collie."

"They'll be plenty more, but let's see if we can get all three of us in a picture for Luke." Colin stood behind me and held the camera out while I held up the fish.

"Won't that make him jealous and sad?"

"With any luck. Yeah, with any luck." Colin returned the fish to the river. We decided that we would take one fish home tonight for dinner, and we had at least another hour or two of fishing before we needed to return to the lodge.

"You miss him, don't you?"

Colin didn't respond. He put his fishing glasses on and pointed to the far bank. "Let's cross here. Grab my belt." We each took hold of the belts behind our backs that we wore around our waders. Colin had his walking stick, and we slowly waded out into the stream. The rocks were only slightly slippery, and the current wasn't too strong, but we were up to my waist and Colin's upper thigh. Holding on to one another is a safe way to negotiate a crossing. With more contact points while crossing a riverbed, the better chance a person has of not slipping and falling.

"Hang on, Maggie. I won't be impressed if you fall and take me with you."

"Likewise, old man."

"I'd be careful of that 'old man' talk. He let go of my belt, and for a second, I felt myself slipping and going down. He quickly retook my belt and caught me.

"I mean, kind sir." Lesson learned—no more "old man" talk. *Yikes.*

When we got to the shallow water, he took my hand, and we walked a short way upstream and then climbed up the bank. We continued to hold hands for a moment, and we both knew it was for a different kind of stability. Neither of us said anything or acknowledged this gesture. I was not an innocent recipient of this token. I liked the feel of his hand. He said nothing, and we walked on for several minutes.

I was hungry again and needed water for my dehydrated, post-alcoholic condition. "Shall we stop and have a bite to eat?" Colin took off his backpack and stared at me without comment.

"Sounds good to me. There's grass over there, or we can sit on the log. Your choice."

"If I lie down, I might not be able to get up." Colin stared at me for a second longer than was comfortable.

"I'll help you if you help me." Who was I kidding? Even at sixty-nine, getting up off the ground was difficult.

I watched Colin sit down on the log and slide down onto the grass. He rifled in his backpack and pulled out cut apples, cheese, and bread. He handed me a water bottle, and we ate while we watched the river. Neither of us spoke. Had a line been crossed? Maybe I put more into it than was there. He was like a brother, and yet he was more.

Colin sat up and put his finger to his lips. He saw or heard something. I waited, and then a magnificent buck walked down to the river and drank. Deer had been farmed all over New Zealand. Many deer had escaped captivity and became part of the habitat in the mountains, with some saying they were almost as important as trout to the tourist industry. Still, they were considered unwanted pests to many New Zealanders. We watched the buck cross the river and jump up to the other side. No other deer followed.

"He must be the top dog." Colin smiled. I suspected a hunting trip was the next thing on his agenda. We watched the stag move off. His antlers suggested he was old. I thought about Colin. He was like this old buck—alone and waiting out his time.

"Well, I was wondering." Colin paused, and my heart leaped, thinking what his following words would be. "Wondering what you thought."

"You mean about all of this and Charlie?"

"You meant to say, Todd?" Colin laughed.

"It's a nice name. I like Todd." I knew what he meant, but I couldn't let the chance to tease him go. "I know what you mean. I don't know. Charlie's kind, and he's smart. He's trying, and I know he loves you, Collie."

"And I love him like a brother, but who do you love, Maggie?"

There it was. Who do I love? I tried to think of a way to answer this without answering.

"Collie. If Helen called you and asked you to come home, live out your life with her and Luke and forsake all others, how fast would you be out of here?" He didn't answer. That summed up things pretty well. "And if Linda showed up tomorrow, how fast would we both be kicked out of here?"

Colin laughed. "Well, you'd be kicked to the curb, but I'd be allowed to stay. But here's the thing, darlin', Linda isn't coming back, and neither is Helen. We all have past loves and lives, and we all have our get-out-of-life cards. Who would make you want to leave?"

I smiled and nodded. "That's easy, Robert Redford." I gently punched Colin on the shoulder.

He grabbed me and pulled me over his lap. He was laughing so hard I was able to escape. "That old codger? He's five years older than me.

Now I know I'm in with a chance." He was laughing so hard he was crying. He finally peered at me while squinting, and in a severe tone, asked if I wanted to meet Bob.

"If I could've met him twenty-five years ago, yes. Not now."

"And if you hadn't met me, would you want to meet me?"

"Probably not. I'm not normally attracted to good-looking, virile, generally nice men. I seem to be attracted to serial killers and general assholes."

"Are you making an exception in my case?" He stared at me and waited for my response.

"Can I answer that when you get me back across the river?"

"Help an old man up, and let's fish that bend over there." Colin pointed his rod upstream to a bend in the river. "Let's catch dinner and head back. The jetlag's catching up with me."

We fished the bend. This time I stood on a bank above the deep pool. I saw several fish and decided that one sitting inside a bubble line would be nice. I pointed to the fish from the bank, and Colin stepped out from below and quickly let out some line and, without a single false cast, landed his fly over the fish. It landed softly on the water and drifted a foot down the bubble line. With a single mend, once again, Colin had a fish on his line.

I jumped down from the bank and came over, reached up to his shoulders, and took the net attached to his backpack. I took the phone from his pocket and waited for Colin to play the fish. This one fought for what seemed like an hour. I took several pictures of Colin and then waded out to net the tired fish. I took two pictures of Colin holding the enormous fish. Then he asked me to take one of him and me together.

"Is this to make Luke or Helen jealous?"

"It's for me, darlin'." I stood in front and tried to hold the camera and get us both in the picture, but my arm wasn't long enough, so we switched, and I held the fish. Colin took several, and I asked to see what it looked like. I flipped through the images and realized there were maybe thirty of me alone. Many were not even with me fishing. He saw me and shrugged. My face reddened, and I turned away, pretending to get into the shade. There were even some of me riding Digger, Colin's horse that he'd given me when I helped his grandson. I closed the camera and handed it back without comment.

As we approached the riverbank where we were going to ford the river, we saw Charlie or Todd approach. We both waved, and I pointed to Colin and yelled, "Dinner is in the bag." We each held the other's belt as we crossed the river. When we got to the other side, Todd extended his hand and pulled me up onto the riverbank and then turned and did the same for Colin. Colin said he would have a nap, and I asked to use Todd or Charlie's phone, so I could call my son and give him my plans for the next few—weeks, months, or years?

Chapter 2

Of course, Colin had the first fish, then the second, and the third. He pursed his lips, shook his head at me, and simply said, "Let's get you educated." We walked down the river and saw a large trout darting in and out of a bubble line. It was actively feeding. Colin stayed up on the high bank to monitor the fish and sent me downstream. I quietly waded out into the water a few feet, and Colin silently pointed to a clump of grass where I was to land a fly above the feeding fish. Colin opened his arms, indicating that I should let the fly land two feet from the bank.

I'm not an expert at fishing, but one thing I was good at was placing a fly in a sweet spot. It was a crapshoot after that. I rarely visualized a fish take a fly unless I had a gigantic fly strike indicator. Strike indicators come in many forms. They might be the fly itself, or a bubble of florescent floating gum-like material, or yarn that is attached to the line. It drops below the water's surface if a trout takes a submerged fly or the fly hits on the riverbed causing the line to hang for a second.

I performed two false casts where I let my line out, and then I went for the gold. The fly landed perfectly. The fish rose, and I could see by Colin's actions that I was close. Colin rolled his wrist, indicating I should repeat my cast, and once again, the fish rose but didn't take the fly.

Colin raised a finger, indicating that I should try one more time. I did, and then the same thing happened. Colin then walked back behind me and motioned me to take my line and flick it to him. For an old geezer, he still could tie a fly quickly. All he did was add a nymph to the dry fly, and using this drop shot rig, he asked me to wait until he was back on the bank and able to see the feeding fish. Colin held his hand up and indicated I should wait.

From my perspective, I was fishing blind. I watched Colin lower his polarized glasses and cup the sides of his head to help him see the fish. He finally smiled and turned to me, holding up two fingers. There must be two fish now. He finally nodded, and I did a single false cast and let the fly and nymph sail away from the area where the fish were feeding. I knew it would take extra effort to land the flies ahead of the fish, and I didn't want to blow it and scare away the fish.

Colin nodded and then pointed to where he wanted the flies to land. I longed to impress him, and I was so nervous, but with all that I had in me, I did a single false cast again and then sent the line out two feet in front of the trout. Even I saw the indicator drop. I raised the tip of my rod and hooked the trout.

"Fish on, darlin'." Colin quickly came back to join me down at the water's edge. I would like to say it was an epic battle, but the fish gave up rather quickly, and Colin walked into the water and netted the hen. "Nice, Maggot."

I was pleased. I didn't mind Colin calling me Maggot. Despite what it sounded like, it was a term of affection when my sister called me that, and I knew it was the same with Colin. He pulled out his camera and took a picture. I hadn't charged mine last night, and I didn't bring it when we left to come down to the river. "I'm sorry I didn't get any with you and your fish, Collie."

"They'll be plenty more, but let's see if we can get all three of us in a picture for Luke." Colin stood behind me and held the camera out while I held up the fish.

"Won't that make him jealous and sad?"

"With any luck. Yeah, with any luck." Colin returned the fish to the river. We decided that we would take one fish home tonight for dinner, and we had at least another hour or two of fishing before we needed to return to the lodge.

"You miss him, don't you?"

Colin didn't respond. He put his fishing glasses on and pointed to the far bank. "Let's cross here. Grab my belt." We each took hold of the belts behind our backs that we wore around our waders. Colin had his walking stick, and we slowly waded out into the stream. The rocks were only slightly slippery, and the current wasn't too strong, but we were up to my waist and Colin's upper thigh. Holding on to one another is a safe way to negotiate a crossing. With more contact points while crossing a riverbed, the better chance a person has of not slipping and falling.

"Hang on, Maggie. I won't be impressed if you fall and take me with you."

"Likewise, old man."

"I'd be careful of that 'old man' talk. He let go of my belt, and for a second, I felt myself slipping and going down. He quickly retook my belt and caught me.

"I mean, kind sir." Lesson learned—no more "old man" talk. Yikes.

When we got to the shallow water, he took my hand, and we walked a short way upstream and then climbed up the bank. We continued to hold hands for a moment, and we both knew it was for a different kind of stability. Neither of us said anything or acknowledged this gesture. I was not an innocent recipient of this token. I liked the feel of his hand. He said nothing, and we walked on for several minutes.

I was hungry again and needed water for my dehydrated, post-alcoholic condition. "Shall we stop and have a bite to eat?" Colin took off his backpack and stared at me without comment.

"Sounds good to me. There's grass over there, or we can sit on the log. Your choice."

"If I lie down, I might not be able to get up." Colin stared at me for a second longer than was comfortable.

"I'll help you if you help me." Who was I kidding? Even at sixty-nine, getting up off the ground was difficult.

I watched Colin sit down on the log and slide down onto the grass. He rifled in his backpack and pulled out cut apples, cheese, and bread. He handed me a water bottle, and we ate while we watched the river. Neither of us spoke. Had a line been crossed? Maybe I put more into it than was there. He was like a brother, and yet he was more.

Colin sat up and put his finger to his lips. He saw or heard something. I waited, and then a magnificent buck walked down to the river and drank. Deer had been farmed all over New Zealand. Many deer had escaped captivity and became part of the habitat in the mountains, with some saying they were almost as important as trout to the tourist industry. Still, they were considered unwanted pests to many New Zealanders. We watched the buck cross the river and jump up to the other side. No other deer followed.

"He must be the top dog." Colin smiled. I suspected a hunting trip was the next thing on his agenda. We watched the stag move off. His antlers suggested he was old. I thought about Colin. He was like this old buck—alone and waiting out his time.

"Well, I was wondering." Colin paused, and my heart leaped, thinking what his following words would be. "Wondering what you thought."

"You mean about all of this and Charlie?"

"You meant to say, Todd?" Colin laughed.

"It's a nice name. I like Todd." I knew what he meant, but I couldn't let the chance to tease him go. "I know what you mean. I don't know. Charlie's kind, and he's smart. He's trying, and I know he loves you, Collie."

"And I love him like a brother, but who do you love, Maggie?"

There it was. Who do I love? I tried to think of a way to answer this without answering.

"Collie. If Helen called you and asked you to come home, live out your life with her and Luke and forsake all others, how fast would you be out of here?" He didn't answer. That summed up things pretty well. "And if Linda showed up tomorrow, how fast would we both be kicked out of here?"

Colin laughed. "Well, you'd be kicked to the curb, but I'd be allowed to stay. But here's the thing, darlin', Linda isn't coming back, and neither is Helen. We all have past loves and lives, and we all have our get-out-of-life cards. Who would make you want to leave?"

I smiled and nodded. "That's easy, Robert Redford." I gently punched Colin on the shoulder.

He grabbed me and pulled me over his lap. He was laughing so hard I was able to escape. "That old codger? He's five years older than me.

Now I know I'm in with a chance." He was laughing so hard he was crying. He finally peered at me while squinting, and in a severe tone, asked if I wanted to meet Bob.

"If I could've met him twenty-five years ago, yes. Not now."

"And if you hadn't met me, would you want to meet me?"

"Probably not. I'm not normally attracted to good-looking, virile, generally nice men. I seem to be attracted to serial killers and general assholes."

"Are you making an exception in my case?" He stared at me and waited for my response.

"Can I answer that when you get me back across the river?"

"Help an old man up, and let's fish that bend over there." Colin pointed his rod upstream to a bend in the river. "Let's catch dinner and head back. The jetlag's catching up with me."

We fished the bend. This time I stood on a bank above the deep pool. I saw several fish and decided that one sitting inside a bubble line would be nice. I pointed to the fish from the bank, and Colin stepped out from below and quickly let out some line and, without a single false cast, landed his fly over the fish. It landed softly on the water and drifted a foot down the bubble line. With a single mend, once again, Colin had a fish on his line.

I jumped down from the bank and came over, reached up to his shoulders, and took the net attached to his backpack. I took the phone from his pocket and waited for Colin to play the fish. This one fought for what seemed like an hour. I took several pictures of Colin and then waded out to net the tired fish. I took two pictures of Colin holding the enormous fish. Then he asked me to take one of him and me together.

"Is this to make Luke or Helen jealous?"

"It's for me, darlin'." I stood in front and tried to hold the camera and get us both in the picture, but my arm wasn't long enough, so we switched, and I held the fish. Colin took several, and I asked to see what it looked like. I flipped through the images and realized there were maybe thirty of me alone. Many were not even with me fishing. He saw me and shrugged. My face reddened, and I turned away, pretending to get into the shade. There were even some of me riding Digger, Colin's horse that he'd given me when I helped his grandson. I closed the camera and handed it back without comment.

As we approached the riverbank where we were going to ford the river, we saw Charlie or Todd approach. We both waved, and I pointed to Colin and yelled, "Dinner is in the bag." We each held the other's belt as we crossed the river. When we got to the other side, Todd extended his hand and pulled me up onto the riverbank and then turned and did the same for Colin. Colin said he would have a nap, and I asked to use Todd or Charlie's phone, so I could call my son and give him my plans for the next few—weeks, months, or years?

Chapter 3

While Colin napped, Charlie or Todd gave me a tour of the property. He showed me a map and pointed to features that I would recognize when I walked out to see the land. It was all native timber. Pine plantations were typical in New Zealand, but this property had never been cultivated. Old, native trees covered much of the land. There were only a few paddocks near the barn that required some upkeep. A few sheep or a tractor with a mower would make that easy. An old road was the only access to the property. Grocery deliveries were made and left at a locked gate. The direct access for guests had been by helicopter. This lodge had been for elite clients who wanted exclusive access to actual wild rivers and fish that were unaccustomed to human intervention.

The barn was old, and inside was a tractor. It had seen better days but appeared to be usable. A mower was attached. "Does it start?" I hadn't driven a tractor in years.

"I started it last week. I need more diesel, though." Todd took me through the barn and then out the other side to the back of the cabins, where he had an extensive, well-cared-for vegetable garden. There were fruit trees heavily bearing peaches, pears, apricots, and apples. "They should be ready to pick next month." We picked up an onion and more lettuce for dinner.

"Charlie, I mean Todd, in the remote chance I stay here, do you have jars for canning the fruit?"

"So, there's a chance?"

"Remote. There are a few details." I remembered the reference to details when I purchased my cabin. Details that included a murder-suicide in the house I bought. I knew the nature of the deaths in my cabin years before I purchased it was still hotly debated among the locals.

My phone was charged, and I took the only sim card and walked up until I began to see that I had a strong signal. I FaceTimed my son, Brandon, and told him I was in New Zealand on a fishing trip and how I was essentially unreachable. I didn't give the exact location, and I said I was with Colin Chandler fishing. Brandon knew about Charlie McLeod and his passing. I may have forgotten to mention that he was still alive. My children didn't know that Charlie was the man who orchestrated my kidnapping and release.

Brandon was the child that made you want to have more. "Mum, whatever makes you happy. Colin Chandler's kind of old, though, isn't he? Can't you find someone who is more age-appropriate?"

That made me laugh. "Age-appropriate is only a factor if I begin to date men thirty years younger than me. Or when you were a teen and wanted to date a thirty-year-old."

"Mum, she was only twenty, and I was sixteen. It worked out pretty well, though. We've been married eight years this March."

"Brandon, will you let everyone know I'm fine and having the time of my life?"

"Yes, but are you burning through our inheritance? That's what Trev and Colleen will want to know."

"I'm here at the pleasure of the king, and it's a gift."

"Can we come and see you?"

"Sure, anytime." That was easy. In a million years, they would never come. If I had said no, I'm sure one of them would come down here and try to find and rescue me—problem solved. I hung up and emailed my sister, Christy, and told her Colin and I were at a remote fishing lodge and probably wouldn't be back until the snow was gone.

I checked my emails, and there was nothing from the FBI or my agent. I was free to enjoy myself. Several emails went to my unknown sender junk file. They were probably ads for things I had no use for, such as erectile dysfunction or breast enhancement. I'd look at them later. I returned to the lodge where Colin and "Oh my God, how was I ever going to make the transition to the name Todd," were sitting on the veranda drinking a beer. Todd offered me one, but I said I was on the wagon until next year. "What's the date?"

"December eighteenth. A week before Christmas." Todd turned to Colin. "I hope you're both staying?"

Colin was quick to respond. "Helen's meeting the kids and grand-children in LA for the week. She's meeting up with her husband's family, who are flying in. That's why I agreed to come. I'm not allowed to join them." I could see the hurt and disappointment on his face. I went over and hugged him. He didn't offer any resistance. He patted my arm. "I'm losing my filter. I would never have let anyone know I was upset before. I blame you two."

"I'll stay too. Not sure about the long-term, but I can't think of anyone with who I would rather share Christmas than you two. Well, one old geezer aside."

This made Colin laugh, and Todd looked at us both and shook his head. "I must be out of the loop."

Colin turned to Todd and asked him who he would abandon us for if he could be with anyone? "They have to be alive. Maggot's choice is that old geezer, Bob Redford."

"Sandra Bullock. And how about you?" I waited to hear Colin's response. I knew it was Helen, but he wouldn't say it.

He didn't hesitate. "Maggie. So, no need for an out. You name the others, and I've met them—thanks, but no thanks."

I could see Todd wasn't amused. Colin won round one for my heart that evening. Todd cooked a fantastic meal with trout, fresh vegetables, and an excellent New Zealand wine. I only tasted it to be polite, and Todd won round two. I could almost enjoy this.

I was jet-lagged and exhausted from my debauchery last night with the alcohol and fishing with Colin today. "Sorry gentlemen, I'm bailing out for the evening."

Charlie asked, "Maggie, have you got everything you need in your room? I'm going to make an order tomorrow for supplies. Let me know what you need to add to the list. I'm kind of out of practice with female needs. Sweet dreams."

"Char... I mean, Todd, I have everything I need right here. Thanks, and thanks for everything. Really, in ten years, I may forgive you for your past sins, but for now, I am one lucky girl, and having you both with me now is almost as good as having the 'old geezer.' Are there baseball gloves and a ball?" I laughed and left them. I was not ready for goodnight kisses.

As I walked out of the lodge, I thought about the Christmas dinner. I yelled, "Hey, can we have a turkey for Christmas?"

I returned to my cabin. I didn't have the sim card and no internet access, so checking was pointless. I did open my phone. Colin had airdropped the pictures from his phone to mine. He included some of the photos he'd taken of me when Digger was ill, and I nursed him. There were pictures of Luke and me, and of course, the pictures of Colin and me with today's catches.

I thought about the day and the river crossing. It felt good to have a strong man holding me. I'd been on my own for twenty years. My happiness and purpose in life were derived from my new and old occupation. Having a life partner was not a consideration. I didn't need human companionship to lead a fulfilling life—but it felt good.

I opened the mail app on my phone to ensure I had no missed emails from close family and friends. I went down the long list to one from an unknown address. I'd already binned ten or more junk emails, but this one appeared from a legitimate source, and it may have been an old client or a fan. I went down the list and found no other emails that might be worth saving. I returned to this one that only had the subject title "help."

I opened it and realized it was a genuine email. It was from Colin's grandson, Luke. The body of the email only said:

Please call me. Please, please, please.

Don't tell Grandpa.

Luke

I sat up and reread the email again. Doug Cameron, who worked part-time for Colin, had taken my dog up to stay with Luke while I was gone. Maybe Baxter was sick or injured. I was sure Luke was happy, enjoying school and his life with his grandmother. What could be the problem? It was probably nothing important. Kids overdramatize the most trivial things. I would borrow the sim card and head up the mountain in the morning.

Chapter 4

"Todd" was in the lodge when I walked over in the morning. There was a slight drizzle, making fishing less than desirable, and so Colin had taken a gun and gone hunting.

"By himself? You let Collie go by himself?" I shook my head.

"Have you ever told Colin he can't do something?" Charlie smiled, knowing the answer.

I poured a cup of coffee and sat down at the table where Charlie, or Todd, was eating and reading a book. "Uh, no. I haven't. Do you think he'll be safe on his own?"

"No. I'm worried sick."

"Did you ask to go with him?"

"I wanted some time alone with you. I can see you're unhappy with me, and I want to talk to you. I'm not sure I'll ever be able to make it up to you for what's happened, but I want to try."

I sipped my coffee without replying. Charlie continued. "Maggie, I risked your life, and it was wrong on many levels. I know I almost got you killed. I'll never let anyone hurt you or let anything like that ever happen again."

"Charlie, and bloody hell, I'm not calling you 'Todd' again until I'm in public. A line was crossed. I trusted you with my life, and I'm not sure I can do that again. If I knew you were alive when Colin asked me to come with him to go fishing, I don't think I would have come.

"I only came because I thought Collie needed company. The FBI and the government did a pretty good job convincing me and many others that you were dead. That's almost worse than risking my life. I was falling in love with you, but who was the man I was in love with?"

I could see the pain etched on his face. "I don't know how to fix this, but I'm going to try."

"I don't know either. I wasn't born when I moved back to the States. I had a life, and I have history, including a prior love and loss. I thought I knew my husband, but I really didn't. I was fooled, or was I a fool? I didn't have time to, nor did I want to, explore or worry about how I ended up in a foreign country with three small children and no support. I had to survive and raise those children on my own. I was lucky that I had a career that allowed me to do it all. That left no time for introspection, and frankly, I didn't want to waste time on the past. I survived, but since then, I've been wary of anyone wanting to get into my inner sanctum, as I like to call it." I smiled and went to the kitchen to get more coffee and toast.

"If I had told you about what was coming, I felt I would put you in jeopardy. I had to hide my other life for the last few years. Since Linda's illness and our trip to Mexico, I've had a double life. Even Linda was unaware of what I was doing. I thought Colin might have guessed, but now I know he was as unaware as you were."

"You fooled us both, and in our grief, we have become closer. You must see that."

"I have a rival, don't I?"

"Not sure about that, Charlie. He still loves Helen, and like you and Linda, I'm your fallback and not the primary interest. Neither one of you is my primary interest anyway."

"You care to explain?"

"My tire-changing guy? Did you forget him? Just kidding, but I bet that made you think. Right now, I'm mad, and I'm wondering why I'm here, and at the same time, I don't want to be with anyone but you two. If the truth be told, I love you both, but not sure if I love you both more than I love my horse and dog. Which reminds me I need to make a phone call. Can I borrow your phone?"

"You have to be careful when you make calls using my phone. I don't know if it has a tap on it."

"I'll use your sim card, and then I'll use my phone and my calling app, and that should be okay, shouldn't it? Can you order me a sim card when you make the order today? We could go up to the reception area together if you want. Do you think we would hear a gun go off if Colin shot something?"

"I don't know. Collie went downstream. He knows I was going up on the mountain to make an order."

"I'll go get dressed, and we can leave if that's okay."

"You're wrong about Linda. It took a while, but I'm ready to move on."

I doubted that, but I wasn't going to shoot myself in the foot. "I'll be back in ten if you're ready." I took my toast and more coffee and returned to my cabin. The rain had lifted, and the sun was out. I hadn't noticed when I walked over to the lodge earlier, but a small vase with some flowers was sitting on the table. I was amazed at how it gave me pleasure to see this small gesture. I thanked Charlie for the flowers when I returned. I saw his face fall, and instantly, I realized they must be from Colin.

"I need to lift my game. Is that what you say over here?" I could see the wheels turning in his mind. "I give you a fishing lodge, and he gives you flowers. Two can play this game."

"You might want to think about what really makes a woman happy. I can be bought, you know. I'm guessing there's no more CLM philanthropy going on, but there are other ways I can be bought."

"I can't open a school for indigenous locals."

"Could you teach at one?"

"I'm not allowed to show my face to anyone. I'm essentially a prisoner in my own jail. I'll be giving evidence at the upcoming trials, but that won't be for months and maybe longer. Until then, I'm dead to the world, and I may have to remain dead after that anyway."

Immediately, we heard the sound of a gun. "The great white hunter may have scored our dinner." I thought about yesterday while Colin and I sat and watched the buck with the enormous antler rack. I secretly hoped it was a younger animal.

As we climbed up the hill to make the phone calls, Charlie fell back behind me. "Let's stop for a second. I need to catch my breath."

I was alarmed. Was Charlie so out of shape that he couldn't climb to the top of the hill? The mountains were a lower elevation than where we lived back home.

"Are you okay?"

"Turn around." He took my shoulders and spun me. I gazed down on the lodge and cabins. In the distance were the river and the barn and paddocks. It was a beautiful sight. There were two buildings I hadn't noticed before, and I pointed to the compound.

"Charlie, is that where you paint?"

"One is mine, and the other I've set up for Colin or for you to use to get away. Are you going to start writing again?"

"Not sure what I want to do. This is all so new. You must realize I've had a shock, and I'm considering my options."

We walked up to the top of the mountain, and Charlie's phone began to ping. He stopped and opened the phone and checked his messages. I wondered who they were from. What if Charlie was lying and still part of the cartel and hiding from the FBI? How would Colin or I know for sure? I didn't want to ask him outright. I thought it was best to discuss that possibility with Colin first. I waited and let Charlie talk to someone for several minutes. I couldn't hear, but when he returned, he was already removing the sim card for me to use.

"I ordered a hunting license for Collie and fishing licenses for you here at the lodge. They'll be in the next delivery. A car will be left at the gate for you and Colin to go to town when they deliver the groceries and gas tomorrow."

I didn't ask about this arrangement. I wanted Colin to be present when we asked any dicey questions. I needed his perspective on this situation. For the second time, I wondered if Charlie was a good guy or a bad guy. I suspected Colin was wondering this before me, and that was the point of his question yesterday when we ate our lunch.

I told Charlie I needed to make a private call. He didn't ask why, and I suspected he thought I might be calling the FBI or my contacts back in the States. He looked at me, and I could see his concern. "I'm not dobbing you in." He looked at me, and I smirked. "Snitching." He relaxed somewhat.

I dialed the number for Luke and waited. There was no answer. I tried once more, and he answered right away. "Hello?"

"It's me, Luke. What's going on? Is everyone okay? Does your grandmother know you called me?"

"Maggie, I want to come and see you. I don't want to go to LA. I hate my step-grandfather."

"Why?"

"All he talks about is how bad Grandpa is, and how Grandma needs to forget Grandpa and how she needs to take care of her current husband and not spend so much time with me."

"Luke, I don't know what to say. Your grandmother is a wonderful person. Are you sure this is what he means? I didn't get that impression from anyone before."

"Grandma says I need to go and behave. She said you and Grandpa are having a short vacation, and when you get back, I can come and visit. I asked her if I could come down and see you for Christmas, and she said you were in South America fishing, and you'd be back in a month or two, but I want to come now. I know Grandpa would only do what Grandma says, and so I thought I would ask you."

"Uh, not buying this, Lukey Boy. Is your grandmother around? Does she know you're talking with me?" I was not going to interfere with this family dynamic. No, sir.

"Luke, let me talk to your grandmother."

"I can't." He sounded like he was about to cry. I looked over at Charlie, standing out of earshot, holding binoculars.

"Luke, can't or won't?"

There was a pause. "Don't hang up, Maggie. Please?"

"I won't." I waited for a few seconds, and then I heard Helen's voice shouting on the line.

"Maggie? Is that you? If you can hear me, I want you to know I'm so sorry about this."

"Helen, I can hear you. You don't need to shout. Is everything okay? I'm getting a story from Luke. I prefer to deal with the responsible parties if you get my drift."

"Loud and clear, Maggie. And that's why I love you." There was a pause while I could hear Helen asking Luke to leave the room.

"Luke asked to come down here and join Collie and me. He says he doesn't want to go to LA with you and Roberto?"

"I'll admit, it hasn't been as good of a fit as I had planned. I love having Luke, but Roberto doesn't exactly love this arrangement. I'm assessing my options, Maggie. You know, maybe a break would be a good thing? Would you mind if he came down to stay with you? I'd never have thought to ask. How's the boy, by the way? Have you two found each other? You know you aren't getting any younger. A good man is not easy to find at your age."

How that made me smile. Helen and Colin were both ten years older than me. They were sharp and acted so young. Still, I couldn't tell her that Charlie had resurfaced. "Helen, I'm still on the fence. I'm struggling to keep up with him, but it's early days. I suppose having Luke here would put a damper on anything romantic, but maybe that's a good thing. At my age, I need to pace myself. Collie's already outfished me on our first day out together."

"That would be right. I'm glad you both enjoy fishing. I could never get interested in killing anything but my cattle. So, what would it take for me to send Luke down to be with you while I sort out my personal life?"

"Do you promise to consider coming back and rejoining Collie?"

"Too late, darling. We discussed it. He's in love with you. He told me he's taking you down to sort out a few things, and then he's planning a full-on assault on your heart."

I groaned. "Okay, well, Luke will definitely be a fly in the ointment. Can you get him to Auckland? I can take over from there. When do you go to LA? Can you put him on a flight from LA direct to Auckland?"

"What's your email? I'll send you a confirmation." We exchanged email addresses, and I hung up. I might need to live away from the lodge. I wasn't sure if Charlie would go ballistic, and if that was the case, I would get a place to stay near the fishing lodge, and Luke and I would stay there until he was to return to Helen. I also considered what Helen said about Colin's feelings for me. I decided to talk to Colin before I broached the plans with Charlie.

We turned to go. "Everything okay?" I could see Charlie was worried about who I was talking to. I stopped and realized I had the perfect answer to this problem. "Charlie, I need to make one more call."

He handed me the sim card one more time. "Maggie?"

"No, it's fine. Start on down the hill. I'll catch up. I won't betray you. You have to believe me."

I walked up to where I had a signal and redialed the number. Luke answered immediately. "Are you changing your mind? Please, Maggie, I miss you."

"No, Luke. I need to ask you an important question, and I need an honest answer. Okay?"

"Sure."

"I know this is tough, but I need to ask you. All I want is a yes or no answer. Nothing more. Agreed?"

"I think so."

"Luke, you're pretty good at keeping secrets, aren't you? Yes or no."

"Yes, I think so."

"Did you see your mother die, and do you know who killed her? So sorry to ask this."

There was a long pause. "Yes."

"And you've never told anyone, have you?

"No."

"Okay, see you when I see you. Bring your waders. I have fishing needs."

"Love you, Maggie."

"You too, Lukey Boy. You too."

Chapter 5

We walked back to the lodge, and Colin had already returned and was up at the barn dressing a small buck. He'd carried it back to the compound on his own. We shook our heads, and Charlie was obviously impressed. "I'm going to have to do some weight training to keep up with you, old man."

Colin looked over his shoulder at us as we watched him eviscerate his buck. "Todd, happy to help you get in shape. We can start with a jog down to the river and back after lunch?"

I laughed. "And I'll watch you two old men from the porch. I'm going fishing after lunch."

I left them and returned to my cabin. I opened my laptop. I was starting to get the urge to create once again. The funk was lifting, and I was considering my options. I was courted by two men who I had loved or did love. I was in a beautiful location with access to trout. My favorite adopted grandchild was on his way to join us, and I would surprise both Colin and Charlie later this week when I would retrieve Luke from Auckland. Christmas was a week away, but something was missing. I needed a horse to ride. I needed female companionship, and I needed a purpose. A woman does not live by trout alone.

We sat down in front of the fireplace after lunch and talked. I told Colin that I was reverting to calling our host by his proper name.

Colin was glad. He personally detested the name. He mentioned he'd worked with Todd Hunter, and he found the guy too nice and too good-looking. "He made me feel inadequate."

The car would arrive tomorrow, and I would take it into town and do some retail therapy. I could get my hair done, although the boys said the gray was not horrible. I'd only brought clothes for a short fishing trip and needed more if I was going to stay for a while. There was a hot tub which Charlie said worked, and I needed a suit. Both men protested that idea, but I reminded them I was sixty-nine. Any actual eye-to-skin contact might result in permanent visual impairment.

I left to fish on my own. I didn't take my waders, and I planned to fish downstream this time. I spent an hour studying the various pools and currents. I spotted two fish in the third pool, decided to walk around downstream, and wade in below so I wouldn't scare the fish by a poor fly presentation. I still had on the double-rigged fly with a dropped nymph. The sky was cloudless, and only a hint of wind made the water appear challenging to visualize. I cast out away from my target to wake up my muscle memory and then cast out over the target. The fly drifted past with no takers. I recast, and despite a poor cast, I saw the fish rise and look at the floating fly.

As I was retrieving what I thought was an unsuccessful cast, I felt a tug and quickly jerked and set the hook as I retrieved it. It was pure luck. I played the fish that gave me a good fight, and then, as he was tiring, I reached back for my net and realized I'd forgotten it. Colin walked down to the stream with his net and quickly scooped up the trout. I looked over sheepishly. "How long have you been watching?"

"Not long. I had the net in my room, and I knew you would need it. I decided to bring it to you. Nice fush." He was mimicking the New Zealand accent.

"Very. Did you bring your phone?"

Colin lifted the net and examined the handle, which displayed a weighted scale. "Nope. Sorry. The scale says almost nine pounds. These fish are monsters."

"I didn't ask, but how was the hunting?"

"All right. It was hunting. I used to love it, but now I can probably take or leave it. I wanted to give you some time with Charlie."

"Yeah, thanks." I turned to set the fish in the water, and then I walked over and sat in a clump of grass. "Collie, did it ever occur to you that Charlie might be lying, and it's the FBI he's hiding from?"

"I've been wondering about that too." Colin took my rod and walked over to the river and cast my line a few times. His reach was far longer than mine. I was in awe.

"I wish I had your strength." I knew it was more than strength, but I didn't want to admit it.

"Come up here, kid, and let me give you a lesson in casting." I stood up, and he handed me the rod and told me to try to cast to the far bank of the river. I was short by about two feet. He told me to hold my rod with my thumb straight up and stop bending with my cast. I did as he said, and I was only one foot short of the mark.

"Close." I smiled.

"Close, but no cigar." Colin came up behind me and took hold of my arm and wrapped his arm around me and took the line. Together we did several false casts, and then he said, "On three. One, two, three." We both let the line go, and the fly landed on the far bank. He stepped away and told me to repeat my cast. I did, and again it was short of the bank. He came up behind me, and we cast together once again. The line went to the far bank. Colin stepped away again as I sent the line across the river and onto the grass of the riverbank.

I turned to thank him, but he was already walking up toward the lodge. I heard him mumble, "So much to teach you, and so little time." How often had I said that to young vets who worked for me? We never finished our conversation about Charlie and what side of the law he really was on. It would only be speculation anyway.

I stayed down at the river until I thought it was time for dinner. So far, no one has asked me to cook. I suspected the men were conscious of asking me to assume the traditional female role. I thought we should take turns, and I planned to offer to cook the turkey for sure. I didn't want to start a pattern of me cooking every meal.

After dinner, we sat outside and talked about our youth. I'd heard about Charlie's story and his lack of parental support. I mentioned I had the traditional television family history. Two loving parents who, while not exceptional, had done the best they could to get me and my siblings all educated and raised. I had not heard Colin's story.

He described growing up in Texas and playing high school sports. He was above average in all his pursuits. He admitted he had the looks and personality to date any girl in his class. He was not a scholar and never planned to attend college. Still, he received a sports scholarship and went to the local college. He decided the most straightforward path was to get into the arts.

He was chosen for a minor role in *West Side Story* and then the lead in an avant-garde production. Colin mentioned he was noticed by an actor who had returned to watch his own daughter in the play. The daughter was Helen. "I didn't know Helen well at that stage, but her father invited me to come to LA for Thanksgiving, and that was it. I was smitten, and it never ended."

I thought about what Helen said on the phone. She mentioned Colin was over her. *Note to self. Apparently, that wasn't the case.* I took a deep breath and asked a few polite questions. I was stung. I tried not to show it. I then questioned Charlie about his baseball days. After he described the rise and fall of his career, I said I was tired, and I was going to do some writing and head to bed. I planned to take the car down to town in the morning and be away most of the day.

I went to my room, and after a few minutes, there was a knock on the door. It was Charlie asking if I was okay and if I needed anything. He stood in the doorway. "You can come in. I'm only half-naked." He slowly opened the door, either fearing or hoping I was serious. These men were such prudes.

"I guess I was wondering who you were calling this morning. I think you can guess that my presence here needs to remain a secret."

"Helen. I was talking to Helen. Luke was upset and wanted to talk to me. It seems all is not what it should be in paradise, and Luke wanted to talk, but I didn't want to talk to him unless Helen was happy. Charlie, I would prefer to keep that among ourselves. I don't want to upset Colin."

"Does he need to return and take care of things? I'd understand."

"Well, I wouldn't. Collie gave me one of the greatest lessons in fly casting I've ever received. I don't want him leaving until he teaches me all he knows."

"Oh, well, a guy can dream."

"Are you worried you have a rival for my affections?" There it was, out in the open.

"Yes." And back at me.

"Obviously, you weren't listening. Collie said he was smitten with Helen, and it never ended. As I told you, I'm not interested in being Plan B. In fact, I'm pretty darn happy with things as they are. I have no complaints."

"Well, you wouldn't be Plan B with me, and I hope to show you that. The car and delivery should be here by lunchtime. I didn't order sim cards. You can get them when you go to town. Pleasant dreams, Maggie."

"You too, Charlie." He closed the door, and I was alone, but not for long.

"Maggie, can I come in?"

"Come in, oh great fishing instructor."

"Glad you found the lesson useful. I wanted to clarify something I said tonight."

"No need to clarify anything, Collie. I'm happy with this little adventure. I'm having the time of my life."

"It has ended." He walked in and stood at the end of the bed. I was in bed and only had a T-shirt on. I wasn't prepared for staying in a five-star lodge and only had minimal clothes.

"Okay, and what might that be?" I knew exactly what he meant. He meant his love for Helen, but I tried to appear to haven't heard him this evening. He sat down on the opposite side of the bed, leaned forward and put his elbows on his knees, and cupped his face in his hands. "I think you know. I'd love to go to town with you, but it would attract too much attention, and I don't want to jeopardize anything for Charlie or Todd." This made us both laugh.

I reached forward and patted his back. I decided the most prudent plan was to say nothing. "Don't worry, I'll only be gone for a few hours, and I promise to come back. Is there anything I can get for you?"

"No, not really." He sat there holding his face, and I could see he struggled with something.

"Cat got your tongue?" I felt he wanted to say more.

"Probably. I need time to think about things. I'm not sure if I can believe Charlie, and to be honest, what can I believe about you?" Colin stood up and looked at me. I was shocked. What had I said that made him suspicious?

"This is what you can believe about me. I am confused and wondering if I should drive out of this place, catch a plane back to Australia and give up on my dream to fade away gracefully. My plan was to ride, write, fish, and repeat. I didn't want or require any human emotional attachments, and then this little kid came along, and he stole my heart. Then I met some wonderful townsfolk who were my kind of people. Carol, Hal, Sylvia, Trent, and then add in Baxter and Digger. It all became so much more than I ever thought I would want or need. Sadly, that wasn't all. I met a movie star, a billionaire, and let's not forget my serial-killing tire-changing guy...

"Now I have new interests and new demands on my life and heart. Most of the time, I want to run away, but then someone gives me a fly-fishing lesson, and once again, I'm hooked. I need time to sort out my feelings and ensure I don't fall for someone like my ex-husband. God knows I am a pathetic judge of character. And that's what you can believe. Now get the heck out of here so I can sleep. I have retail therapy tomorrow, and I need to be rested."

Colin stood and smiled. "Pleasant dreams, old girl."

"Sweet dreams, beautiful boy."

"It's flattery, but I'll take it tonight."

"Just stating the facts."

Chapter 6

The delivery arrived, but there was no automobile. There was a note to say that the car had been delayed and would not be here until tomorrow. The men were not disappointed, but I certainly was. Charlie, Colin, and I decided a property tour would be an excellent way to pass the time. We unloaded the groceries, and Colin and I borrowed Charlie's sim card. The first place on our journey was to the top of the mountain to retrieve our communications.

Colin didn't have anything. I received a message from my son to say that it would be hard for him or his brother and sister to come to New Zealand at this time, and they were thinking of me this Christmas. Sadly, no surprise, but that was a relief that true to form, my kids were well and indeed launched.

There was an email from Helen giving me the flight and arrival time for Luke. He was flying to Christchurch instead of Auckland, arriving late on December twenty-third. I planned to drive to Christchurch and pick him up. I would ask Colin to go as well, and then we would go back to the lodge to have Christmas with Charlie. I was confident Luke would keep a secret, but I had to ensure Charlie would be safe and agree to this idea.

I wanted it to be a surprise for Colin. It was going to be a great Christmas. Tomorrow I will purchase small presents for all three boys for Christmas day. I was "funkless." I was out of the fog. I began to sing along with my phone music. The guys even sang with me. Our favorite was "Walk Like a Man."

In a few days, I would ask Colin to take me to Christchurch. I needed to think of a reason to take Colin, but I was sure he would agree to go. The sad part was leaving Charlie. I hated to hurt his feelings. I couldn't think of a good reason, but it needed to be done. I started to watch an earthquake website. I didn't want to get into one. I'd been to Christchurch shortly before and then a few years after the big quake decimated the city.

I walked to the gate with Charlie, and we found a brand-new SUV parked there the following morning. The booklet was sitting in the driver's seat, and the registration papers were tucked inside. The registration was also in my name. I turned to Charlie, who was already walking back toward the lodge. "Drive carefully, Maggie."

"Yes, sir, and thanks. Oh, I may be back after New Year, but no promises." The car was gray with a leather interior and had all the bells and whistles. The narrow dirt lane leading out of the lodge went for about ten kilometers and wound alongside a creek. It eventually merged onto a well-graded dirt road that took several more kilometers. The internal GPS took me down out of a mountainous area with dense foliage and into a paved, what the Kiwis and Australians called bitumen, road. From there, it was an hour's drive to town.

In town, I was nervous driving a new car and parked in a protected area far from any other vehicles. I went to a shopping district and found an art supply shop, and bought paints that Charlie requested. I also knew that Colin liked watercolors, and the shop owner gave me some paints, brushes, paper, and a few canvases for them both.

Next, I went to the bookstore and found books about native New Zealand trees and birds. Charlie seemed to like to paint natural scenes. His trout paintings were exquisite and accurate. Colin hadn't painted anything yet, but the ones in his house tended to be sports, horses, and family portraits. I had a feeling he would leave soon. I hoped to have Luke here, so Colin would stick around longer.

I picked up a few novels and saw one of my books on the shelf. As I was browsing books that might interest Luke, someone tapped me on the shoulder. I turned and immediately recognized Mackenzie

Williams. "Mac, what the heck? I thought you went back to the States after you left Australia?"

"There and back, Magster. Do you remember Kerry Penfield? She worked at the practice in Newcastle. She and I got together and decided to come over here. We worked for a guy who eventually sold us his practice, and we're happy as hogs in heaven."

"Well, this is great. If I need a horse fix, I'll call you. Is it a mixed practice, or only horses that you treat?"

"We do them all, but there aren't many horses here. I sure could have used your opinion last week. We had a killer colic. The owner wouldn't let go, and we had to see the old girl die a prolonged death. Are you here for a while? I'd love to have you come and visit the clinic. I heard you retired. Are you ready to come back to work yet?"

"Not a chance, sister. I'm staying up at a lodge about three hours from here. I'm with friends, and we're kind of on the lam from life. I don't know how long I'll be down here, but give me your number, and I'll call you after Christmas. Would that be okay?"

"I can hardly wait to tell Kerry. What's your number, and we will call you?"

"I'm off the grid, but you can leave a message. I check my messages every other day. I'd love to catch up with you."

I was excited to make contact with Mac. She was a great American vet who worked for me ten years or more ago. Like most young vets I'd encountered, Mac wanted to get some overseas experience, and return to family and friends and then commit to a life as a vet. I'd lost track of her, and I looked forward to catching up and spending some time with her and Kerry. New Zealand was looking more promising.

Mac reminded me of an experience when she and I went out at night and got the vet truck stuck in the mud. Some unsavory characters came and rescued us. We both were scared shitless, so we decided to let them think we were lovers, and we hoped any ideas of payment for their help would be made with money. It turned out that they were lovers too, and we bonded in our mutual alternative lifestyles. We didn't fool them, and they let us know as we drove off. I still cringed, remembering that story. "See you soon, darling." Mac waved as we parted. She laughed, and I knew she was remembering the same encounter.

"You too, lover girl."

I purchased a few more small gifts. I walked to the fishing and hunting store to check out the latest and greatest in apparel and anything that would enhance my fish-catching endeavors. I found shoes, sweaters, and neoprene socks that would be easier than waders to wear on warm days. I was introduced to some new flies that were working well this season. As I was finishing my purchases, I noticed a familiar face. He smiled and waved. *How did I know this man?*

"Maggie!" The robust man came over and hugged me. I was embarrassed as I could not remember his name. When he hugged me, I smelled his aftershave, Old Spice. Bingo!

"Ned Schaeffer, how are you? How's the world treating you? How's Donna?" Ned was a fishing guide who also owned a small fishing lodge where I'd stayed several years ago. He and his wife were beginning to take in anglers like me after retiring from teaching. Their last child had flown the coop, and they were determined to live off the tourism boom and keep their retirement funds for when they were too old to work.

"I'm sorry. I guess I haven't kept up. Donna passed two years ago. She had a stroke."

"Oh, Ned, I'm so sorry to hear that." We'd exchanged Christmas letters, but like many people, when I didn't hear from them at Christmas, I thought they had decided to save the planet and stop sending letters. They never did get into emails or computers at all. They built their reputation on Ned's skills and Donna's hospitality to build their clientele.

"Maggie, I can't say it's been easy, but my son came back for a while and helped out, and I stopped guiding. I still have the lodge, but it's only a bed and breakfast now."

"Ned, I'm so, so sorry. You're here, though." I waved my hand around the store. "Are you fishing then, or are you back guiding?"

"I work here." He picked up a set of glasses from the counter. "Madam, can I interest you on this fine set of magical glasses. Put them on, and you will see fish where they were previously invisible."

"I'll take two, thank you. Got any magical sandfly repellent? Not sure if my hands can take any more bites." The flies had taken their toll on my hands. Their bites made my hands swell, and they were always itchy. I had to be careful not to scratch them too much, as my skin was now prone to petechial surface bleeding of old age, and I would look like I was bruised or had a bleeding disorder.

"The hook's been set, Maggie. Now let's head over to the register while I reel you in." He smiled and had a delighted look on his face. "So, can I keep you, or is this a catch and release moment? Where are you staying?"

"It's a bit of both. I'm staying down south with friends, and I may be here a while. I've retired and moved back to the States. I'm over here dodging winter. I'm probably a short-timer, but who knows. I better get going. Are these glasses really any good?"

"No better than any others, but they're new and guaranteed to remain scratch-free for six months or your money back."

"I'll take three, thank you. That reminds me. I need a rod, reel, and some gear for a twelve-year-old. Let's go shopping, Ned."

An hour later, I was headed back to the lodge with a car full of fishing gear, clothes, presents, and food for the entire Christmas holiday. Things were looking up. I'd planned to have my first white Christmas at my cabin when I initially moved in, back in the States. I'd even picked out a Christmas tree I planned to use. Then, when I thought Charlie was dead, it all seemed pointless. The Christmas spirit was once again invading my body. No snow, but it would be a happy occasion if it killed me.

Chapter 7

I returned late that evening to two grumpy old men. Colin was particularly cranky. "So, did you go to Australia today? You were gone long enough."

"No, just to Fiji. Sheesh, I was gone less than I planned. I'm guessing you missed me."

Colin looked up from a book he was reading. "There was no one to fight over. Was your trip successful?"

"Very, and that's all I'm going to say. I have many things that you're not allowed to see until Christmas day, so you two stay up here while I put it in my cabin. Have you both had dinner? Anything left for a poor starving girl?"

Charlie got up and said there would be heated leftovers when I returned. I'd driven the car and parked it near the cabins. I instructed the men to stay inside, and I returned to my cabin to hide the presents. I then drove the car up to the main building and brought in the first of the groceries. Colin came out and helped with the remaining bags.

"Nice wheels."

"Yes, very. I have a proposition for you. I'll tell you both about it in a minute." I brought several magazines that I thought the men would enjoy. I spread them out on the table. There was fishing, New Zealand lifestyle, and financial magazines.

Charlie poured me a glass of wine and set out a plate of lasagna, garlic bread, and more garden salad. He perused the magazines and newspapers and asked general questions about the town and what was happening in the world.

I told the men about meeting a colleague and my commitment to visiting her veterinary practice sometime in the new year. I also talked to them about meeting my former fishing guide, Ned, and his turn of events. Finally, I informed them I had received a message from my daughter-in-law.

I explained I was going to meet her on the twenty-third in Christchurch. She was coming over with the two older grandchildren, and I would meet them at the airport before they caught a plane to Queenstown. I planned to drive over to see them, leaving early on the twenty-third, and be back on the twenty-fourth for Christmas. My family planned to meet friends. Christchurch was only a stopover, and I would see them at the airport. I couldn't pass up the chance to visit.

I didn't mention my plan to take Colin to spell me in the driving. It would be six or so hours each way. I hoped Colin would come to my rescue and offer to drive with me. Colin only remained anonymous so he didn't attract any unusual interest that might threaten Charlie's need for privacy.

It was beginning to rain, and I decided to put the car in the barn. I drove it up and in through the barn door. As I closed the door in the driving rain, I caught my pants on a nail near the barn door. It tore the fabric, and I suspected it also tore my calf. I could feel blood running down my leg. I swore and hobbled down to the lodge. I knew I didn't have anything to bandage the leg. I was soaked from the rain, and my leg was drenched in blood as I limped up the steps.

Without saying a word, I slipped inside the door to the kitchen and finally asked Charlie if he had any bandages. I was on the other side of the kitchen island, and neither man got up. Both were engrossed in their magazines. Charlie mentioned a first aid kit in the second drawer below the knives and forks.

I opened the drawer and found a small box with adhesive strips. I hadn't even looked at the wound, but the blood flow had slowed down considerably. If either Colin or Charlie had looked over, they would have seen a trail of blood on the tiled floor. This wasn't going to work. I pulled my pants up and realized this was a stitch job. I immediately felt faint. Without saying a word, I sat down on the floor.

"I think I'm going to need more than adhesive tape, guys." Charlie got up and came around the corner.

"Oh, my God. Collie, call an ambulance."

"Charlie, it's not an ambulance job. Is there anything more in the house? How about a clean towel?"

Colin jumped up, came around the counter, and knelt down. "You're going to need stitches. I'll go up and get the car."

"Let's wait until morning. If I can have some soap and water and a clean towel, I can drive in tomorrow morning and get it checked out."

"No way. I'm taking you down now."

"Trust me, I'm a vet. It can wait. If I was a horse, I would say it needed to be stitched now, but if I wrap it tightly and keep it clean, waiting until morning won't be a problem. I won't die."

Charlie took some towels, and Colin found some "female protection" pads, and we eventually wrapped it up. The boys helped me to my room. I wouldn't let them inside, and despite their protests, they allowed me to leave them at the door. I slept on top of the bed with several towels to protect the linens from blood.

I went to the kitchen and made bacon, eggs, and coffee before the men were awake the following day. I wrote a note to say I was heading into town and hopefully would be back by the early afternoon. I retrieved the keys I had placed on the table by the couch, but they weren't there. I searched around but was unable to locate them. A few minutes later, Colin walked in, holding the keys. "Your chariot awaits." He'd brought the car down to the lodge.

"Oh, thanks. I made you and Charlie breakfast. Hopefully, I won't be too long."

"I don't think so. I'm driving you. Get in, or I think we both know what the alternative is."

"Have you driven on the left side of the road?"

"Maggot, I'm eighty years old. I've been to New Zealand many times. I spent a year in Australia making a documentary and two years in England making a movie. Now, get in."

Charlie came up behind me, tapped me on the shoulder, and pointed to the car's passenger side. "I think you understand the implications of resistance to authority, don't you?"

I pursed my lips and reluctantly got into the passenger seat. When we left the lodge and locked the gate, I rolled down my car seat and tried not to watch. I was scared to death. I was driving on a narrow road with an eighty-year-old man with a known need for speed. In all the time I had known the famous Colin Chandler, I'd never driven with him. True to all reports, he drove like a maniac—a skilled maniac, but he had a requirement for speed.

When we got down to where the road was straight, he reached into the console and pulled out one of the financial magazines. He handed me the magazine. "Page eighty-three."

"What's it about?" I turned to a page titled 'What happened to CLM?'

"Jesus, is it good or bad?"

"Good, I think, or maybe not. I don't think Charlie saw it."

"Collie, I'm the vomit queen. I get carsick. What does it say?"

"The article says that CLM's been found to be trading with known drug cartels for the last few years, and the only reason the founders are not being sought for prosecution is that both Charles and Linda McLeod are dead. The assets are slowly being sold off, and the money is being held in trust until the federal government can decide what to do with the remaining assets."

"What's good about that? It seems to me Charlie could still be lying."

"Maybe. I've known Charlie for twenty years, and I believe him." Colin swerved to avoid a limb that had fallen on the road.

Colin's driving was excellent, despite the speeding. "I wish I could know for sure. I'd feel pretty bad about hiding out with a known criminal. Do you think we could get prosecuted?" I was another kind of sick, thinking about the ramifications of consorting with a criminal.

"Yeah, maybe. Maggie, turn on your phone and get me to the local emergency clinic."

Two stitches, a tetanus shot, a stop at the chemists for antibiotics and bandages for any subsequent injury, and we were on our way home. The best part was that the doctor said I shouldn't use the leg too much for a few days. Happily, Colin said he would drive me to Christchurch to see my grandkids.

When I was getting my stitches, Colin stepped out of the room, and I checked my phone for an email from Helen. Luke was set to jet, literally, and would arrive at seven in the evening. He was flying as an unaccompanied minor and would be in business class. The airlines would assign someone to take him from gate to gate. He would be in safe hands.

We had ample time to assess whether we took Luke to the new lodge or if he and Colin went and stayed somewhere else. I knew Luke would remain silent about it all, and he would never betray Charlie. In the end, it would not be my call. I hoped Charlie and Colin felt the same. I'd know about Colin's view tomorrow night. Either way, I knew Colin would be pleased to have Luke with him. Colin was worried about the boy's safety. When we were leaving the town, Colin mentioned that he had talked to Helen. "I hear you talked to Luke."

"I didn't want to worry you, Collie. He was upset, and he asked to speak to me. I wanted to speak to Helen before I got involved."

"She said you calmed him down and that everything is all right now. I'm disappointed that you didn't tell me—bloody disappointed. I would never do that to you. He's not your grandson, you know."

I was shocked and hurt. I knew that tomorrow, Colin's anger would be replaced by joy, but I wasn't going to let that surprise slip prematurely. "I'm truly sorry, Collie. I really am. I thought if you knew, you might leave, and I didn't want that to happen." I hoped this small lie would quell his anger. It did.

Colin reached over and patted my hand. "Maggie, you're one in a million. How did I get so lucky to have you as a neighbor? I'm sorry, but if you do that again, there will be hell to pay."

"Acknowledged and noted, sir." I was relieved. The lie appeared to work. The problem was it wasn't a lie.

Chapter 8

It's beginning to look a lot like Christmas. When we returned, Charlie had decorated the lodge. He found a few boxes of ornaments in the basement and brought in a native pine tree he had encountered before we arrived. I was relegated to the couch and pampered the rest of the day. It was nice, but I wanted to help. "Not going to happen, darling." Charlie was in command mode. He even had Colin scouring for items to make the lodge appear festive. It was like we were a bunch of kids.

Charlie had no issues about Colin and me going to Christchurch to see my grandchildren. He was sorry he wouldn't get to meet them and mentioned that in a year or two, he would hopefully be free from his five-star prison. We ate more venison, which Charlie had marinaded. He asked if we could stop at a bookstore in Christchurch that he knew about and see if a cookbook was written about using native fauna.

Colin looked at me and smiled. "Are you trying to kill us, old man?"

"No, I'm trying to keep from killing you, Dad." Charlie pointed at Colin and smirked.

"Boys, boys, boys. Do I have to send you two to your rooms?"

After dinner, which I must say was superb, I left for the evening. I had presents to wrap. As I was going, I noticed Charlie was reading the magazine that Colin had returned to the coffee table. I wondered if he would comment on the article.

The next day my leg was swollen and bruised, but I knew there was no infection. I walked down to the river with my rod before the men were awake, and I practiced the casting technique that Colin had taught me. As I cast in the mist emanating from the river, I saw the old stag come out of the woods. He saw me but didn't appear alarmed. He walked downstream and drank from the river, and as he raised his head, water dripped from his muzzle. He stood, and we watched each other. As he paused, a doe and two fawns trotted out and went down to the river where the doe drank as well. She gazed up and saw me. She didn't move, but her attention made the fawns look as well.

While the buck continued to drink, the doe and fawns skittered off back into the woods. The buck shook his head in my direction in a challenging motion. He stood for what seemed like an eternity and then slowly turned and followed the doe.

I returned to the lodge and prepared French toast and bacon for my fellow lodge mates. Charlie was the first to appear. He came around and hugged me. "Merry Christmas a few days early. Are you sure you'll be back in time?"

"Scout's honor. Charlie, have you seen the buck with the massive rack? I saw him down at the river this morning."

"Not sure. There are a few with racks. There's a six-pointer who often comes down to the river below our cabins. Were you down at the river this morning? I thought the doctor told you not to use your leg if it wasn't necessary."

"And surely by now, you realize that fishing is a necessary function?"

"Hmm, not sure that was what the doctor was thinking."

Colin came in and was ready to leave as soon as we could. He wanted to do some last-minute shopping. He had on a disguise that made me do a double-take. "Well, hello stranger. New in town? You could fool me." His hair was almost black, and his clothes were very businesslike.

Charlie whistled and admitted it was a great disguise. "I'm guessing you could pick up some younger women in that outfit."

"I aim to. I want to meet Maggie's grandkids." Colin did a little jig.

"Very dapper, I totally approve. Now I'll have to dress up to meet the new standards. Good thing I bought an evening gown when I was in town." Both men looked at me.

"You own a dress? I need to see the evidence." Charlie was serious.

"I'm saving it for a special occasion. My funeral."

"Or a wedding?" Colin was playing along.

"Okay, before this gets out of hand, yes, I own dresses, and on rare occasions, I wear them, but I do not have a dress for fishing and general hanging out at a lodge. Sorry boys, but breakfast is served."

After breakfast, I returned to my cabin and changed into some three-quarter length pants and a new shirt I'd bought in town. I was excited to visit Christchurch and see how the post-earthquake renovations had progressed. Before I climbed into the car, Charlie took me in his arms and hugged me, and wished me a swift return. Colin objected, but Charlie said Colin had me all day and he would be here alone.

"Colin, I can go alone. My leg's fine. You two can hang out together. I promise not to be jealous." Charlie swatted me and said no thanks. He would be happy to have some time to finish his Christmas presents.

When we'd been on the road to Christchurch, and the road was straighter, I rechecked my emails and then Googled CLM Enterprises. *Forbes* had a report as well. It was not as favorable in the possibility that Charlie was innocent.

"OMG, Collie, listen to this. 'Flying under the Radar can be Lethal: How Charles McLeod got away with drug running for years and then flew one degree too low.'"

"Can you read it and not vomit?"

"From the looks, I couldn't read it if I was sitting down in the house and not vomit."

"Do you want to drive and let me read it?" Colin turned to me and pulled over.

I handed him my phone. He read in silence and then set the phone down. "Either he's fooled the entire United States government and us, or he's a brilliant saint." Colin pulled the car out onto the road and drove toward our destination. I picked up the phone and read it to myself.

The article suggested that Charles McLeod was a wolf in sheep's clothing. He made his money in illegal drug importations. Then he took the money and used it to benefit the needy, allowing him to mask his wealth accumulation by his acts of charity. It listed many charities but curiously didn't mention my friend, Sandy, or her school for underprivileged aspiring Southern students. The article discussed how he risked the life of his fiancé and then was killed coming back from the penultimate deal in Texas where his associates were arrested. The FBI would neither confirm nor deny that he was the head of the cartel and was killed when flying low in an attempt to escape the radar. The article concluded: "The Robin Hood of the corporate world is dead."

"So, is he, or isn't he? Collie, do you think he's seen this? Did you show him the other article about him and CLM?"

"You know I did. I didn't want a big confrontation, so I waited until you went to bed. Charlie laughed, and his only comment was that he was happy, and his plan was working like a charm. Let's give him a chance. When Christmas is over, you and I may urgently need to return home, and we can figure it out from there. He loves you, and in his own way, I'm the brother he never had. I know we're safe for now."

"Or the father he never had. Since the lodge is in my name, maybe we could kick him out." That remark got me a punch in the arm.

"Ouch." I feigned pain, but I groaned inwardly. How will Luke's presence change things? I desperately wanted to surprise Colin with Luke instead of meeting my grandchildren at the airport. Still, was I putting Luke in harm's way? Would Charlie accept the presence of Luke at the lodge? Maybe I should go back to the fishing lodge alone and leave Luke and Colin to fly back immediately. I didn't want to put either Colin or Luke in any danger. Perhaps if Charlie and I were alone, I could ascertain the truth. *Earth, open up and swallow me.*

"So, were you officially engaged?"

"We discussed a merger, but as you know, there was no ring or anything official. I won't deny it was in the cards, but it was early days. By the way, how's the divorce coming?"

"Ouch, back at ya. Heidi's cunning and demanding. It's a work in progress."

We made excellent time. Despite the crowded streets and traffic, we found a place to park, so Colin and I did a tour of the renovated downtown and booked a room at an airport motel. I smiled and wagged my finger at him.

"What?" He tried to hide a sheepish grin.

"I'll take the double, and you can have the king." Might as well set the rules early. It would make sense once we picked up Luke.

Colin stared at the beds. "I hate making extra work for the maid." I shook my head. Colin was trying.

"I'll leave a big tip. Glad we used my card, and the motel staff didn't recognize the handsome spunk I'm traveling with. I'm guessing they think I'm a cougar now."

Colin began to sing, "I'm Just a Gigolo." And I surprised him by singing the following two verses. "Louie Prima, baby."

"You continue to amaze me." He opened the door, and we headed for the car and more shopping.

You have no idea. "Collie, I was not born yesterday. I have history."

"Get in the car, Maggot. I have shopping needs. I'm supposed to shop for Charlie and me. You know it's Christmas. It kills me, but he asked."

We returned to downtown Christchurch. Colin sent me to the museum, and he took off for parts unknown. I had all the gifts I wanted and had no interest in shopping. I stopped in the museum café and had a cup of coffee. I searched for more information on Charlie, but there was nothing more that I could find. I was sick. I'm sure Colin would understand that I had no idea about this when I agreed to take Luke. Helen would get some of the blame as well.

I received a message from Colin that he was finished and asked me to meet him back at the car. We drove to the airport, and Colin rolled back the seat, and we both slept for a short time before the plane was to land. We woke with a start and realized we only had a few minutes until the plane landed. There were several aircraft coming in at the same time. Fortunately, the one from LA was coming in a few minutes after another from Sydney. There was a god. Colin would be fooled right up to the last second. I was so excited to view the reunion. I had my phone ready to capture the moment.

The passengers would all go through security, and so we had at least fifteen minutes before Luke would emerge. We hadn't eaten, and I'd told Colin I hoped we could have a meal in the airport, and I could see the grandkids before they caught their second plane to Queenstown.

We found seating near the gate where the passengers emerged. I began to search for Luke. A few passengers started to walk through the gates, and then a woman with two teenage children walked out. Colin grabbed my hand and pointed.

"Nope, not them." I was becoming nervous. Many people were now walking out of the customs area, and it was difficult to see everyone. I stood and watched for what seemed like a lifetime. I checked my phone in case there had been a delay or a change of Luke's flight. Colin was trying to calm me and continued to hold my hand. I was glad for the support. Finally, an airline attendant emerged with Luke. The crowd had dispersed, and he recognized me immediately. He ran to me and hugged me. Colin searched for a family and didn't notice Luke until he greeted me. Luke didn't recognize his grandfather with his disguise.

As Luke let me go, Colin looked down and realized what had happened. Luke stared at the stranger who accompanied me and then went and hugged his grandfather. I signed some paperwork as the two men hugged one another. Both had tears which made me teary as well. The attendant then said she was sure we were the correct people to hand over her charge and thanked Luke for the trip and the drawings, and she left.

Colin looked at me, shook his head, and wagged his finger. "You have some 'splainin' to do, young lady." He hugged me and kissed me on the cheek. "So, so in trouble."

"Grandpa, don't be mad at Maggie. Grandma organized it."

"Luke, I only hope you get as lucky as me in the female department. I am one fortunate man." Colin hugged me once more. "I guess we can let the hotel maid earn her keep tomorrow." Luke didn't understand, but I smiled and nodded.

Chapter 9

Luke wanted to get take out. He rarely was given the opportunity in Helen's rural homestead. He was keen to experience the hamburgers and a shake. Colin wasn't that keen, but I didn't care. We headed back to the hotel, and as we entered the room, Luke asked if he could sleep in the queen bed, and Colin and I could take the king. I smiled and looked at Colin, who said, "Great idea, sport."

"Uh, no. Not going to happen, guys. Luke, you and your grandfather, are sleeping in the queen, and I'm taking the king." I headed over toward the king bed, and Colin grabbed me around the waist and marched me to the queen bed. Luke was in bed and asleep in minutes. Colin and I stepped out to the patio off the room. In my best Gomer Pile accent, I said, "Surprise, surprise, surprise."

Colin followed with, "A decoy, shazam." We sat down on the cold metal chairs as Colin fought back the tears. "How do I thank you?"

"You can thank me by telling me how this is going to work. How are we going to get Charlie not to blow his top and kick us out?"

"Funny, you should say that. When you were gone, Charlie and I talked about our losses. I mentioned how this was the first Christmas in many years that I would not be with my kids, or at least Luke, and he intimated that if he could find a way to bring Luke over, he would."

"You're kidding? Do you know how I've agonized about this? I've been apoplectic, worrying how Charlie would react. You know I even put Luke to the test. He can be trusted not to talk. I asked him if he knew who killed his mother, and he said he did. Collie, I think he'll go to his grave with that secret."

Colin sat without responding. It was warm outside, and he and I sat without talking. He took my hand and held it. I didn't resist. His hand felt comfortable and reassuring, and I had a surge of pleasure that I hadn't had since the tire-changing serial killer guy shook my hand. We sat for several minutes, and then Colin stood and said he was going to bed. He wanted to get an early start. "Maggie, I don't deserve you. Thank you." He bent over and kissed me lightly on the lips and went inside.

In the morning, Luke climbed into bed with me. He whispered his grandfather was making too much noise. I found Colin to be a relatively quiet sleeper. I put a pillow between us and told Luke to go back to sleep, and if he crossed the line, there would be hell to pay. One more hour, and then we would be on our way. I woke up when both Luke and Colin were loading the car. I yawned, stretched, and headed to the bathroom. When I emerged, Colin was sitting on the edge of the bed. "So, you realize he's jail bait."

"Jealous?"

"Yes, very. I want to get some presents for Luke while we're here. Do you mind?"

"Not at all, but I already shopped and have lots of things for him. I think I have it covered."

"Maggie, how can I thank you?"

"Just enjoy the time you two have together."

"I'm not going to die anytime soon." He was serious.

"Collie, Luke is a short-timer here in New Zealand. Do you know when you're leaving? I sure don't, and relative to his life, neither you nor I will be in his life that long. I wished it had been my grandkids getting off the plane too, but they have wonderful parents, and their other grandparents are all active in their lives. Maybe next year, one of them will be old enough to visit me, and then I can corrupt them. I hope we both live long enough to give Luke the stability he needs. Did you talk to Helen about what's happening with her? From the sounds of things, she may be available soon."

"Well, she did say something to that effect. She doesn't know anything about Charlie, you know. I guess I'll have to go back with Luke sometime after Christmas. He'll have to go back to school, but I doubt it will be with Helen again. Mind you that doesn't break my heart. What about you? When are you coming back?"

"Unknown quantity, Collie." I didn't want to broach the subject, but if Helen's marriage broke down, I guessed I would be kicked to the curb. I wasn't going to allow myself to fall in love with Colin Chandler, no, sir. Anyway, not going to happen. So why was the news about Helen possibly reentering Colin's life so depressing?

The trip to the lodge was long. I sat in the back and allowed Luke the chance to see all the sights as Colin was still playing chauffeur. I reminded him several times that this was my car, and he better slow down. We now had precious cargo.

"Yes, we do. I finally have some decent whiskey. Luke, am I driving too fast for you?"

"Nope. I'm going to drive just like you when I grow up, Grandpa."

I couldn't help myself. "That's if we survive today and our return."

"And our return" was not lost on Colin. We both were concerned about how Charlie would react to having a new guest. "Charlie is going to be so happy to see you, son. Maybe we can all play catch again."

"Sorry, Grandpa, I didn't bring my glove."

"Luke, you and your grandpa will be out fishing and hunting all day. You won't have time to play ball."

I jumped out, unlocked the gate, and relocked it when we had entered the property. Colin asked us to get out and walk up to the lodge, so he could get some presents sorted before we arrived at the house. He nodded to me, and I knew he would go ahead and warn Charlie. I knew Colin expected me to do the same with Luke regarding Charlie's resurrection. The subsequent conversations were going to be difficult for everyone. I took Luke off the road and headed up the hill to see the lodge and river. Luke gazed around and smiled. "Maggie, thanks for letting me come."

"Lukey, I wouldn't have it any other way. If it wasn't here, it would be home with me. You can always stay with me."

"I like it when you call me Lukey. You know my mother called me that."

"Oh really. Then, Lukey, it is. Along those lines. I have an important request. I need you to man up and do for me what you did for yourself. You know I asked you if you know who killed your mother?" Luke nodded, and I observed his face darken. "I would never ask you what you know. I understand you have reasons not to tell me, but I have to ask you to keep another secret. Can you do that? It's just as important."

Luke put out his little finger, and we pinky promised. "Is this about how you love Grandpa?"

"What? No, and don't even think that. I'm guessing he and your grandmother will be together fairly soon. It's way more complicated." I then told him about Charlie and how he is alive and waiting to testify against the bad guys. Luke had seen enough FBI movies and television shows since his encounter with the FBI men handling my abduction that he was all over it. He promised not to tell anyone, including his grandmother.

"Let's pinky promise again, Maggie."

We did. "You're wrong about Grandpa. He loves you, and I can see you love him."

"I only have room for one man in my life, Lukey."

"Oh, thanks. I'm happy to share you."

"Did you think it was you? Nope, my beautiful horse Digger is my main and only squeeze, Lukey Boy."

Luke tried to imitate Colin's voice. "Not buying that darlin'."

I cuffed him and told him to march. I would find out how the other end of this hiccup in our adventure went in a minute.

Chapter 10

Luke and I walked up to the lodge. Both Charlie and Colin were sitting on the porch with sandwiches. Charlie stood up and extended his arms. "Best Christmas present ever. Welcome, Luke. So glad you can join this motley crew."

Luke walked up the steps and onto the veranda. He hugged Charlie, and for an instant, I thought he was going to cry. Indeed, Charlie was teary as well. I stood down on the driveway and watched Colin, who glanced over in my direction and gave me the thumbs-up. I returned the gesture and grinned like a fool. It was a second before Charlie regained his composure. "Are ya hungry, mate?"

"A little." Luke was overwhelmed. "I need to go."

"Okay, let's take you to your cabin. We each have a cabin. Do you want your own, or do you want to share?" Charlie put his arm over Luke's shoulder and walked him toward the cabins next to the lodge.

"I'll sleep with Maggie."

Instantly all three of us said "No." Simultaneously. We each had our reasons, and I'm sure that Colin and Charlie's reasons were less than honorable. I knew each night one or the other hoped to be invited to stay in the inner sanctum. I heard Colin mention that when they discussed my room.

"No one goes in there until after tomorrow for sure." Luke decided to try a night on his own. His only other option was Colin, and I could see Colin was relieved. There were two cabins for families, and each had two bedrooms and a shared room. If Luke decided he wanted to be with someone at night, there was that option. Colin took Luke up to the fourth cabin and left him there. As we were waiting, I looked at Charlie, and he smiled. "Really, this is the best present Collie and I could receive. Thanks for organizing this."

"Well, now you know what I was really doing, Charlie. I hope you can trust me now."

"I'm sorry I doubted you. My life is kind of crazy, you know."

I nodded. "Luke won't tell on you. You can take it to the bank. It's me and Collie you have to worry about."

"Especially after those reports about CLM and me are surfacing."

"Especially," Colin added.

"You know they aren't true." Charlie stared at us, waiting for Colin or me to confirm his affirmation.

"I do, thousands don't, so we remain here in purgatory." I patted Charlie's hand.

"Is purgatory this nice?" Colin observed me comforting Charlie.

I gazed skyward. "Don't know, never been."

"Here he comes." Luke changed from his traveling clothes to shorts. He'd grown taller in the last few months. Not only had he grown taller, but his voice was cracking.

"What would you like to eat, Luke?" Charlie was heading into the kitchen. Luke followed him while Colin and I sat and quietly high-fived each other.

"One in a million darlin', one in a million." Colin smiled, and I nodded.

"Mission accomplished. I'll be expecting some more tuition on fly casting, Collie."

"You're a demanding soul, aren't you? Not as expensive to please as my, hopefully, soon-to-be ex, but demanding nonetheless."

"I can be bought. Ask Charlie." I knew Colin was present when Charlie had made the assertion. I guessed Charlie had told Colin that I asked him to consider charitable donations to Sandy's organization.

"There are whores, and there are whores. Hopefully, you're a bit of both. I don't mind either way." He smiled as he stared at me.

"Mr. Chandler, enough of that talk," I smirked as Luke emerged carrying plates and sandwiches. "Are you two going to hit the river this afternoon? I need to get some things ready for the turkey tomorrow."

"Can we, Grandpa?"

"I can't think of anything I would rather do, Luke. Trout for dinner tonight? Want to join us, Charlie?"

"I'm going to be up in my studio. I need to finish a few things. You guys enjoy yourselves."

We ate, and Luke told us about his school and living with Helen. He didn't mention his step-grandfather or the dramas at home, so Charlie was oblivious to Helen's marriage issues. Colin must not have discussed this with Charlie.

Charlie began to pick up the plates. "So, Luke, you got a girlfriend yet?"

I was a bit surprised that Charlie would ask such a question and even more surprised when Luke said, "Yes."

Both Colin and I shot forward in our seats. "Mate, you're holding back. When were we going to hear about this?" I cuffed him, and he ducked.

"Her name is Tiffany, and she likes to ride, and she's really smart. Would you like to see a picture?"

Colin sat forward and circled his hand. "You know you're going to make Maggie jealous."

Luke brought out his phone and showed us a picture of a slightly chubby girl with a sweet smile standing next to a horse. Colin slapped him on his back. "Well, you're following in the family tradition. Maybe we need to have a few man-to-man talks while you're here."

"Lukey, don't listen to them. Let me help you. I can advise you on how to treat a woman and what might...." I almost said, 'turn her on,' but instead said, "Might be a good way to make her happy."

My intention was not lost on the men and, hopefully, went over Luke's head. Nope. "I was hoping you were going to tell me how I could get her to kiss me."

I was glad to hear he hadn't gotten to first base. He was still only twelve. "Lukey, early days, and my suggestion is to pay attention to her horse. The rest will follow, but maybe wait a year or four."

"Listen to your grandmother, Luke. She knows how to string a guy or two along and enjoy the ride. Let's go 'fushing,' as they say over here. I might have a different perspective on that advice."

"You all get out of here. I have culinary needs, and I'll clean up. So glad you're here, and maybe I can help you avoid any bad advice these two men might give you. I'll be back in fifteen." I headed for the cabin. "Power nap, gentlemen. Do you want to use my rod?"

Colin shook his head and grinned. "No, I like the feel of my own." I got the double entendre from my original statement about doing my best thinking while holding my rod. Charlie had to keep a napkin over his face to hide his mirth from Luke.

Everyone was gone when I returned to the kitchen. I made sure the turkey was thawing and began to make the stuffing, and prepared some almonds for tomorrow. I'd soaked and peeled the almonds a few days before, as my grandmother had taught me, and then left them to dry. I heated some oil and then cooked the almonds in oil until they were a light brown. I removed them, drained most of the oil, and salted them. I left a few on a tray and put the rest away for tomorrow. When the stuffing was prepared, I placed it in the refrigerator, sat down in the main room, and picked up a book.

I was restless, and I decided to go up to the mountain and call my kids. It was too late to call my sister in the States. As I walked up to the area, I realized Charlie was up making a call. I hated myself, but I needed to know what the truth about Charlie McLeod was. I could easily hear him shouting into his phone. "I don't care what the hell you say. I need this sorted. You know I can blow this whole thing, and you guys will be up a creek. I want to know by next week. I need you to protect these people. Am I clear?" There was a pause. "Well, you better. They're starting to ask questions, and I don't blame them. If I don't have an answer by the twenty-seventh, then the deal's off."

I quickly retreated and hid as he descended from the mountain top. I waited for several minutes, skirted around him, and returned to the lodge before he arrived. I was sitting on the sofa when he entered. "I'm ready for tomorrow. How about you?"

He looked upset, but he smiled and said he came to get a drink and returned to the studio. He asked me if I needed anything and then asked me to take a walk after dinner. I nervously agreed. "Sure. Sounds like a plan. I think I'll head up to the mountain and try and call my kids. I'll be back, and then if the boys get some trout, I'll cook the dinner."

"Two dinners in a row, Maggie. Can we afford to take the risk?"

I stood up, walked over, and hugged him. I was trying to hide my concerns. "It's a risk you are going to have to get used to, my friend." I walked out and reminded him I hadn't killed anyone yet with my cooking.

I turned on my phone and heard the ping signaling reception. I sent an email with a picture of Luke and Colin to Helen and thanked her for making the arrangements. I then called my children, and all three answered, and Brandon decided to set up a four-way teleconference. The presents I'd sent had arrived weeks ago, and they were all sending things to the States, and all would be delayed. *No surprise there.* We talked for thirty minutes, and all the grandchildren got on the line and wished me a happy Christmas.

I told them I was still in New Zealand with Colin. They asked what he was like, and if I was helping the "old geezer" get around and down to the river. "More like the other way around." He was an excellent guide, and he taught me how to get some distance with my cast.

"Is he teaching you anything else?"

"I wish. Nope, Colin's grandson's here with us now, so any chances for other lessons have been abandoned."

"Mum, he's a player. At least he was a player, according to the magazines. You aren't seriously interested in him?"

"Not a chance. He's married, and I am simply his neighbor who likes to fish."

"Mum, be careful. We don't want you flying too close to the sun. These people aren't like us. They don't care about anything but fame, fortune, and getting laid. Although at his age, you could probably take that off the table. How old is he?"

"Eighty, and yes, you can take that off the table. We are friends. That is it."

We tearfully hung up, and I returned to the lodge. Luke was standing behind the kitchen island, and when I entered, he presented a beautiful trout.

"Well done, Lukey. Did your grandfather teach you to clean fish?"

Charlie and I went up to the barn before dinner. Colin decided the risk of me cooking was too great, and he and Luke would prepare the dinner. Charlie and I went to the barn and examined the new car.

"Is it what you want? You don't have to keep it, you know. I can replace it."

"It's a great vehicle Charlie. I know this is all in my name, but you're the owner. I have no expectations that this is anything other than a ruse to keep your resurrection hidden."

"No, you're wrong. I chose New Zealand, and I chose this place for you. I'm trying to win you back. I love you, Maggie, and I know I blew it. I wish you could see that. I will go to my grave regretting getting involved with these people and all that has transpired since then."

"Charlie, I don't promise anything, and you need to understand, I'm not in love with you. I thought I was, but that love was for a man who didn't exist. When the FBI told me what you were up to, I was appalled on every level."

"Wait a minute, they told you?"

"Charlie, I heard one of the men at the meeting in your house. He was the same man I heard in the cave. You tell me. What was I to think? Then you died in a plane crash. Did you expect me to think that you were alive? The FBI then told me I was safe and to go home and live like nothing ever happened. I mourned the death of the man I thought I was falling in love with, and I mourned the man who helped so many people, but I didn't mourn what the world now thinks of you."

"You have to believe me. I'm not that man. I'm not a drug dealer, and I never want to hurt anyone. I was only doing what the FBI told me to do. They had me over a barrel. Can you imagine what it would have done to Linda when we thought she might beat her cancer if I went to jail for smuggling heroin into the country?"

"What would she say now? I hadn't forgotten you saw other women when she was still alive. I could forgive you for your past transgressions, but while I know your life's in danger. You'll eventually be free from your prison once you testify. How will I know if the man I am looking at is the same person I thought I knew?" I made sure Charlie thought I believed his story. I didn't know what to believe. I didn't want to jeopardize Luke and Colin's welfare and safety by having a confrontation about our concerns regarding which side of the law Charlie was on.

"May I kiss you?"

I didn't want to. Now I really did feel like a whore. "Yes, but no promises. You're going to need to do more than give me things before I can trust you again."

"Are you in love with Collie?" I shook my head. "Charlie, I love him like a brother. I don't care what anyone says. He's in love with Helen. To be honest, if I thought otherwise, I'd be gone in a flash. You wouldn't stand a chance. Just as I know, if Linda was alive, I wouldn't stand a chance with you either. In truth, I love you both, but I need to know it's returned, and it's the kind of love that you would lay down your life for."

"I'll take a chance," and he put his arms around me and kissed me. I tried to reciprocate, but I don't think I fooled him. I didn't fool myself. It wasn't a kiss from the socially awkward man I had loved. It was from a stranger. When it ended, he thanked me, and we walked back to the lodge and dinner. He held my hand, but he realized I was not reciprocating, and he let my hand go. "I'll make it all good, I promise."

After dinner, everyone retired to their cabins. I was still wrapping a few articles when Luke knocked on my door. "Can I come in?"

"No. I'll come out."

He whispered. "Grandma gave me presents for you and Grandpa, but I don't have anything for Charlie."

"Go back to your room, and I have something for you to give him. Give me a second." I searched through the pile of wrapped presents and found the cookbook wrapped and already labeled to Charlie from Luke. I knocked on his door, and he let me in. His room didn't have as many paintings as ours, but it was still very nice. "You all right in here?"

"Yes, and thanks for letting me come. I missed you and Grandpa. I think I might be moving back."

"Wait and see how it goes. You know all relationships have their rough patches. If you came back, you would probably lose your new girlfriend."

"Maybe she would come too."

"Luke, get real. You know that wouldn't happen. Your grandmother loves you, and I know she would be sad to lose you. I'll see you in the morning. Sweet dreams, Lukey Boy."

"You too, Maggot."

I turned to him and pointed my finger. "I have my limits, mister."

As I walked past Colin's room, the door was open. "Sweet dreams, beautiful boy."

He was asleep and didn't hear me. I shut his door and returned to my room. I waited for several minutes and then took my presents to the lodge. It took three trips, but Santa was done.

Chapter 11

I thought I would beat everyone to the main building and begin breakfast. I planned eggs, bacon, and pancakes. I was wrong. I was the last one up, breakfast was already prepared, and the boys were waiting for me. I still had on my new pajamas and robe. They were dressed. The floor was covered in presents, and there were four easels draped with white sheets.

"Merry Christmas, Maggie." Luke came over and hugged me. He was followed by Charlie, who gave me real champagne. He kissed me on the forehead as he handed me my glass of bubbly. Colin, who had washed out the hair dye, stood behind the kitchen counter cooking and raised his glass. "Merry Christmas, darlin'. Ready for eggs Benedict?"

"Whoa, seriously. You guys sure got the jump on me. I'll just go quickly change."

That was greeted by a chorus of noes.

Luke protested. "Can we eat first? And I want to open presents."

"Okay, but no pictures."

Colin was in command mode. "You don't get to make the rules today. How's your leg?"

I'd forgotten about it in the excitement. I patted it. "Still attached to my body."

We sat down on the veranda, and I was served the eggs and then toast and more champagne. "Slow it down, Charlie. I'm a cheap drunk."

"More the better," and he tipped the last of the contents from the bottle into my glass.

"So, what time do you want your turkey? If I get drunk, I'll only sleep. I need to start cooking in an hour."

Colin reached over and took my glass. He drank the contents in one gulp. "As nice as it would be to see you drunk and maybe even letting your hair down, I think I'd rather have my turkey on time."

Charlie nodded, and we finished our breakfast. Luke cleared the table while Colin washed the dishes. Luke looked at the pile of colorfully wrapped boxes under the tree and turned to me. "Can we open our presents now?"

I looked at Charlie, who shrugged. "It's Maggie's lodge. She gets to decide."

"I'm going to shower. I'll be back in half an hour."

A wail erupted from all three. I smirked and shook my head. "All right, kids, go for it."

The first presents opened were for Luke. He received a new rod and reel and a fishing vest from his grandfather. He was thrilled, and he went over and hugged him. Colin looked over Luke's shoulder and winked and mouthed, "Thank you." I nodded in return and glanced over at Charlie, who was either teary or slightly drunk.

The next present was for Charlie from Luke. It was a book of native New Zealand animals with fauna and an identification guide. Charlie hugged Luke, who also turned and thanked me. The next present was for Colin from me. It was a box of watercolor paints, paper, brushes, and two palettes for his colors. He smiled and thanked me as well. Then Charlie stood and, with great effort, walked over to the easels and removed the first covering. It was for Colin. It was a painting of the old buck. It was just as I had seen him two mornings ago down at the river. Behind him was a doe with a tiny fawn. The detail and the richness of the painting were exquisite. "When did you do this?"

"Last month when you agreed to come and visit me. I can't look at that buck and not see you, Collie."

Colin stood up, and he appeared to be slightly inebriated as well. He hugged Charlie, and they patted each other's back. Luke stood next to the painting and saw the two men's interaction. I hoped he understood that this was what good friends did for one another. I swallowed hard. I knew Charlie couldn't go shopping.

The following picture for Colin was one of Luke and Colin fishing. I recognized it from our fishing trip on Colin's birthday. I'd taken it from behind and near the helicopter when Colin showed Luke how to cast. The sun was on their backs, and they stood out from the river and surroundings. I thought the pictures were lost when I was kidnapped. I was so happy that I didn't ponder why he had the photograph. Had I shared it with Colin before I lost my phone when kidnapped?

Luke received practical presents, including a rain slicker, some hiking boots, and a hiking stick like his grandfather's. He thanked us all as I'd put all of our names on the card. Luke gave me a framed photograph of Baxter and him sitting together on an old tree that had fallen many years ago. In the package was a drawing of the picture. I loved it. I got up and hugged Luke and then asked if anyone wanted more coffee. I made the rounds and returned to my seat.

Charlie removed the cloth coverings of the two remaining paintings. One was of Digger and me standing by Saddleback Lake near my home. I was holding the reins and looking down into my fly box.

"How?" I had no idea how he had the picture.

"I'll tell you someday." Charlie beamed.

Colin stood up and examined it closely. "Forget the wealth accumulation, sport. You need to concentrate on this talent. You can be anonymous, and I'll be your agent."

The other painting was of me sitting on my bedroom deck, writing on my computer. I never mentioned I did this, and I never thought anyone had ever observed me. Charlie had to have been spying on me. I glanced up and nodded. "Drone?"

"Something like that." Charlie didn't appear to care that he'd been caught spying on me. He removed the painting, and behind it was a scene that we all recognized. It was of the four of us playing ball on the grass at Colin's ranch. We all loved it, and it had been intended for Colin, but there was no argument when Luke asked if he could have it.

"Be back in a minute." I quickly got up and went to my cabin. I knew the men thought I was overcome and wanted to let my emotions go in the privacy of my cottage. It was true, and I did have a quiet cry, but

I also retrieved five packages from under the bed: four identical boxes and one elongated box. I returned to the lodge and handed each of the boys a box and the elongated one for Luke. "You go first, Lukey."

He opened both. One contained a baseball glove and a ball, and the other held a bat. I nodded to Charlie and Colin, who opened theirs, and each found a glove and a ball. I then opened mine, which also had a glove. As they put on their gloves, they each found a small card with a message from me. "Here's to a continuation of the best summer evening a girl could ever ask for."

Luke was the first to come and hug me. He was crying. Colin and Charlie got in line, and I stood up, and each hugged me. "Well, are you going to stand around like a bunch of babies? Let's play ball. But first, I'm going to get showered and get the turkey in the oven. Now get the heck out of here."

Luke asked his grandfather if they could play catch by themselves for a minute. Charlie and I put our arms around each other and then looked at the paper strewn all over the floor. "You go, I'll get this. Collie gets fifteen minutes, and then I'm stepping in. I don't want Luke learning any bad habits."

I returned to my room and dressed for the morning activities. It was warm, and I had shorts and a top to get dirty when I prepared the turkey. I watched the boys sorting out how we would play on the sloping lawn. It needed mowing. I would have to purchase a lawnmower if I were here for any length of time. As I showered, I thought about Charlie's phone call I'd overheard on the mountain yesterday. How did Charlie have access to photos I'd taken on my phone that I thought I'd lost after being abducted? Some questions needed answers. I hadn't had a chance to speak privately with Colin. It was Christmas, and I had baseball needs.

Chapter 12

We played ball, ate turkey, and Colin helped Luke with his fishing gear. I had purchased boxes with flies that Ned had suggested. I forgot to give Colin and Luke their fishing glasses, and I brought those out at our Christmas dinner.

The good news was I cooked a beautiful turkey dinner, and no one was poisoned. I'd dressed in a nice shirt and pants, and despite protests that it was not a dress, I was complimented on my food and attire. Colin beamed and poked me. "You're a heck of a catch, young lady."

"Thanks, but not looking to get caught. Playing the field is too much fun."

We played more baseball until Colin and Charlie sat down on the lounge and fell asleep. Luke and I decided to walk down to the river without any intention of fishing. The backs of his hands were becoming itchy. I brought out Ned's special sandfly repellent. We sat on a rock and watched the river. We both had on our new polarized glasses, and we observed two trout rising to a hatch. "Will you remember this day for the rest of your life, Lukey?"

"Yeah, and I'll tell my kids about it too. Maggie, promise me you won't die or leave until I'm grown. Will you?"

"No promises, but I'll try."

"If things don't work out for Grandma, can I come and stay with you or Grandpa?"

"No, on second thought, I think your grandfather is keen to have you back, and I'll be living next door. You can have us both."

"All right, but I sure wish you could love my grandfather. I know he loves you."

"You never know, but I'm happy with the way things are now. No need to change it."

"Are you coming back with us?"

I was alarmed. I wasn't going to discuss this any further with Luke. Did Colin say he was going back soon? I pointed to the riverbank, and there was the old buck. I put my finger to my lips, and we watched him walk into the water and drink. A younger buck came to the riverbank, as well. The younger one appeared to be challenging the older one. There was some snorting and pawing, but the older buck shook his head, and the challenge did not proceed.

"Time to get back. Aren't you tired? It's late where you're supposed to be."

"No, not at all," but then he yawned. "Maybe a little."

We headed back to the lodge. Both men were reading the books that I had purchased for them. They looked up and smiled. "Would you like a brandy?"

"Oh, that sounds perfect. Luke's getting ready for bed. Does anyone want to do the honors?"

"That would be me." Colin stood up and went to the kitchen and returned with a glass of brandy and then bid us goodnight.

Charlie stood, and they hugged. "Can't thank you enough for all you've done, brother. Can you imagine me here alone at Christmas? I barely got through any of the Christmases since Linda died, let alone spending it by myself."

"Yeah, I hated that first Christmas when Helen left."

That was telling. Both men were slightly intoxicated, and here they were talking about past loves. I think it was time to realize that I was second to two other women. For Luke's sake, I hoped Colin and Helen would get back together. I was sure I would die as a single woman, which had been my plan for the last twenty years—no sense in getting wound up for two old geezers who are in love with past loves.

"Charlie, I love my pictures, but I'm trying to remember how you would have the photos to make the paintings." I wanted him to think and not answer, so I asked, "Where did you learn to paint like this?"

He might be glad for the deflection. "Oh, from the Crackerjacks box."

"Oh, really? Your technique reminds me of someone. And here I thought it was paint-by-numbers. In all seriousness, I'm totally impressed. Thank you."

"I had an aunt who painted. She taught me."

"You have more talent than half the artists I've met. It's too bad you can't show them and sell them."

"I'm happy if you and Collie appreciate them. I don't need any publicity."

"I guess not. Especially now. Any word on when you can come out of hiding?" We'd just had this conversation, but that was pre-alcohol. Maybe his lips were loosened.

"I talked to them yesterday, and they said it would be a while."

"I'm so sorry, Charlie. You deserve better. I think I'll head to bed. Thanks for a wonderful day, and thanks for everything. This has been a perfect Christmas. It's one of the best ever. Don't get up." I came over and kissed him on the top of his head.

As I walked out the door, he shouted, "I'd still like to try for a better grade." He referred to our first real kiss after my abduction, in which I gave him a B.

"You never know your luck."

I went to my cabin and was in bed when there was a knock at the door. "May I come in?"

"Sure. What's up, Collie?"

Colin entered and smiled. "Thanks for today, Maggot. It was a day to remember forever. Can we plan on a repeat next year?"

"Maybe. Luke and I'll check our calendars and see if we can fit you in."

"I have one more present for you, Maggie."

I sat up straighter. I was in my nightgown and wanted to be careful. Colin pulled out a small jewelry case and handed it to me. Inside was a necklace with a trout made of gold. It was like my ring. I'd removed my beautiful ring when I arrived in New Zealand, and while I had it with me, I hadn't worn it around Charlie.

"Oh, Collie. You saved the best for last. I love it." I took it out and examined it. I knew it would hang down out of sight. I could wear it, and only Colin would realize I had it on. I attempted to put it on, but Colin took it from me.

"Turn around. Let me help you." He draped the necklace over my head. His hands rested on my neck while I held my hair out of the way. "There now, let's see how it looks." I turned, and his hands stayed on the necklace, and he lifted it away and examined it. "Beautiful, and so is the necklace."

A surge of pleasure went through me. "You certainly know how to make an old woman feel good."

He kissed me full on the lips, and this time it felt like I had hoped. "Oh, Helen, how I've..." He caught himself. "Did I just say what I think I just said?"

"Yep, you did." I knew he was embarrassed and disappointed, but I laughed it off and kissed him one more time, but the feeling had gone. "Repeat after me, Margaret, Maggie, Magster, darlin' or Maggot. I respond to any of those. Just kidding, darlin'. I know your intentions. Maybe you should examine your heart. I'm not going anywhere, Collie. It's not me that has to work out where my heart resides." He stood to go. He was disappointed and still embarrassed.

"Sweet dreams, beautiful boy."

"Pleasant dreams, Margaret, Maggie, Magster, Maggot, darlin'. Did I forget one? You flatter an old man."

"Just stating the facts, sir. Just the facts."

He shut the door as I fingered the beautiful necklace. I planned to leave. This arrangement was doing me no good. I would go down and stay at Ned's bed and breakfast and spend some time with my colleagues. Recalculating route. There was no way I would ever be the love of either man's life. I didn't want to be the fallback to anyone. I was happy in my shoes and didn't need a man or anyone to—complete me. Gag me. These men were way too complicated for me. Way too....

Chapter 13

Ah, my old friend insomnia came to visit. I asked him to leave, but he persisted. Not only did he stay all night, but he brought a headache as a parting gift in the morning. I needed coffee. I headed to the kitchen early and made the coffee for everyone, and then sat out on the porch to watch the dawn. I gazed at the mountains behind the river and watched as the sunlight descended to the river itself. My headache was receding following the second cup of coffee. Luke came up behind me and pounced on me with a bear hug.

"Want to play some catch?"

No, I didn't want to do anything. "Sure. Do you want some breakfast first? Oh, by the way, Happy Boxing Day. We're still in holiday mode, Lukey." I then explained the traditional British convention of a second day free from work. Over the last few years, many places in Australia opened for post-Christmas sales. I didn't know if it was the same in New Zealand, but it didn't matter. Every day at the lodge was a holiday.

We played catch, and still, the men didn't emerge from their cabins. "I promised your grandmother that I would make sure you called today. You know it's officially Christmas over there. Do you want to call her with your grandfather or with me?"

Luke appeared to consider this. "What time is it there now?"

"I don't know for sure. It would be on your phone, but I know it's after lunch."

"I'll wait. Grandma said they were going to have dinner in the afternoon. Can we go up around lunchtime? Grandpa said he would take me down to the river this morning, and I could practice with the new rod he gave me."

"Okay, well, let's make those laggards some breakfast."

"Can you show me how so I can learn? I might need to know how to cook if I see Tiffany again." I rolled my eyes and suggested that any idea of seeing a girlfriend for breakfast at his age was a no-go in my house. "Grandma said it was okay."

"Oh, really? Want to put some money on that?"

Just then, both Charlie and Colin walked in. *Fake it until you make it.*

"Anyone for coffee?" Did I sound too cheerful?

"Yes, please. Are those pancakes?"

"Yes, sir, and Luke made them. He says he's practicing for Tiffany."

Colin came around the corner, avoiding my gaze. "Can't start too soon about learning the way to a woman's heart. Wouldn't you say, Margaret, Maggie, Magster, Maggot, darlin'?"

"Grandpa?"

Charlie looked perplexed. "Can I have stuffing for breakfast? I know there're some leftovers."

Colin chimed in. "Yeah, me too. Best stuffing ever. Love those pine nuts."

I pointed to the fridge. "Just a few bites, boys. We need some for leftovers tonight."

Colin opened the fridge. "Dinner is on Luke and me tonight. You don't look so good. Bad night?"

"Slept like a baby." *Gee, I was getting good at lying.* "Sorry if I'm not movie-star perfect this morning. By the way, Luke needs to call Helen. He wanted to wait, but he should call before it becomes too late. I need to make a call too. I promised my sister and brother I would call them on Christmas."

Charlie could see the tension, and I knew he wondered what had happened. Despite it all, I knew he was still concerned and probably hoping that I would see the light and fall back in love with him. Neither man suspected I would go visit an old friend next week.

"I'll head up now and do my calls, then you two can do yours. Sorry, Charlie. I wish you could call someone too." I did feel sorry for him. Yes, he was still in love with someone else, but he would never call her. It was tragic. I left the boys and headed up to the top of the mountain.

"Christy, it's me, your favorite sister."

"Is there another? I sure wish I had one. I was so looking forward to spending the next few Christmases with my baby sister, but alas, she dumped me so she could go fishing with a movie star. How's that working out, Maggot?"

"Great. All systems go. Luke has joined us as well. We're staying at a lodge, and it's a dream come true. Really." I was crying, but I don't think my sister could tell.

"Well, when you get back, will you come and join us lowly, poor, regular people? We miss you." She went on to tell me about her kids and grandkids. Sadly, they were in Tahoe skiing. We weren't that different.

I called my brother Bill but only got an answering machine. I left a message with my overseas number and waited for a few minutes to see if he would call back. While I waited, I checked my messages and emails. My vet friend, Mackenzie, had left a message. She wanted to remind me that I was invited to stay with her and hang out. She said she knew I was missing veterinary medicine. She indicated that she had some interesting cases, and she would kill for a second opinion.

I texted her back, "Is January second soon enough?" She replied immediately. She had the gin and would have my bed waiting. She wrote, "Can't wait for my sister in crime."

I called Ned and asked if there was room in the inn. He said he was booked up until the fourth of January, and after that, he would be excited to have me. We confirmed that I would stay until the ninth, and to be polite, I gave him my credit card details.

As I walked back to the house, I met Colin and Luke. "Howdy, strangers. New in town?"

"Yes, ma'am. Know where a fellow can get lodging and a good meal?"

"Well, you've come to the right place. Now you mosey down the hill when you've finished your business, and we can get you all settled in."

Luke gazed at us like we were crazy. "Maggie, did you say 'hi' to Bill and Miles for me?"

"Sure did, Lukey Boy. They said to say Merry Christmas, and if you're home next summer, they're going fishing with you again and making some more pools in my little creek for fish to hang out."

Colin put his hand on Luke's shoulder. "We'll be back in a flash, and we want you to go fishing with us."

"Gee, I was going to do my hair and nails today. I'll let you know when you get back." I fingered the necklace, which was not lost on Colin, who smiled.

"Nice Christmas, huh?"

I pointed to Luke. "The best."

I was sitting in a comfortable chair outside my cabin when Luke ran up and asked why I wasn't ready. I opened my eyes. "I thought maybe you and your grandfather might want to have some guy time."

"No. I want some Maggie time. So does Grandpa. Come on, Maggie."

"If you insist. Where's your grandfather?"

"I left him. He's still talking to Grandma. He told me to get you and go down to the river. He would come after he finished talking to her. I think they wanted to be alone."

"Okay, give me five. Do you think you could make some turkey sandwiches while I get ready?" There were enough leftovers to feed a small army, and I was determined that it was not wasted.

Luke was in his new waders and ready to go fishing. "Okay, but hurry."

When I emerged with my waders on, Luke had three sandwiches, bottled water, and apples. We walked down to the river. I wondered where Charlie was, but I assumed he was back in his studio creating another masterpiece. I had a feeling I'd seen his artwork somewhere else. But where?

We stopped and stared at the river for several minutes. We both had on our new glasses, and it only took Luke a minute to spot a fish in a quiet stretch of water near the riverbank. He pointed to me, but I shook my head, and he smiled, realizing he was free to have a go at hooking the fish. His grandfather had taught him well. He quietly sidled into the water downstream and began to let out the fishing line. I stood above the fish and watched it. It was feeding and darting in and out of the nearby riffle. Luke's cast was terrible, but for some reason, it didn't bother the fish, and I circled my wrist, indicating he should try again.

Luke let out more line and did several false casts, and then landed the fly in front of the feeding trout. In a flash, the fish took the fly, and I yelled, "Fish on." Luke's reaction time was quick, and he began to play the fish as it darted in and out of the current. Luke fell in the water as I came down to help him net the fish. He kept his rod tip up and somehow managed to stand and keep the fish on the line. "It's a beauty, Lukey. Stay with him." It took another minute for Luke to bring him up to me, and I netted the large brown trout. "It's at least eight pounds. Good job, Lukey Boy."

Luke beamed with pride. "Do you have your phone, Maggie? I want to show Grandpa."

"No need, Luke, I'm right here." Colin stepped away from a tree and walked toward us. He brought out his phone and took several pictures. He insisted on one with Luke and me together with the fish.

"Nice fush." Colin could mimic the New Zealand accent perfectly.

I nodded. "Very."

"Shall we go over to the other river today? Charlie says it's a forty-minute walk, but we should see what it's like." Colin seemed particularly happy this afternoon. I studied his face and thought he certainly had some good news.

"Everything okay?" My guess was that Helen was moving home, which would be the best outcome for all concerned.

"I'll tell you later, Margaret, Maggie, Maggot, whatever the hell the other names are."

I hummed the girl scout tune, *Make New Friends, but Keep the Old. One is silver and the other, gold.* Colin knew it and hummed along. We took hold of each other's belts and, with me in the middle, forded the river. This time there was no continued handholding. We then followed a path that must have been made by the previous lodge owners. I could barely keep up with Colin and Luke, who talked a blue streak with his grandfather. Twice they stopped to allow me to catch up.

"Eighty going on forty, Collie?" I was so out of shape—two months of lying in bed while grieving had not done me any good.

"I can carry you if you need to rest." He winked at Luke, and I side-kicked him. Colin caught my foot, and I almost went down. He steadied me, and we continued to climb over a rise and stared down on the wild river. There were deep aqua pools and rapids that appeared like white foam from a distance.

The scene made my heart race. It was like something out of a travel book. We all grinned like kids and began our descent to the river. There were plenty of places for us all to fish. Colin spotted a fish and wanted me to step up, but I waited and indicated that this day was for Luke. I could tell he was pleased I would sacrifice my pleasure for his grandson's. It was seconds before Luke attempted to land a small but recalcitrant trout. It was a rainbow, and the obligatory photo was taken before the fish was released.

"Now it's your other grandmother's turn." He turned to me, and Luke said, "Go get 'em, Grandma." I gave them both a look that indicated that calling me a grandma, while endearing, might not be the best choice. I stepped up to the riverbank and then walked out onto a rock protruding a foot into the river. Colin pointed to a deep pool above us. I'd already changed my fly to a weighted nymph. I waited for a gust of wind to subside and then cast out into the pool. I watched Colin clench his hand a bring them to his abdomen. He mouthed, "So close." I waited again and then recast, and it felt like a microsecond, and I knew I had a fish on my line.

Luke whooped, and he and Colin went down to the shore to help me retrieve the fish. I was in heaven. It was a nice fat fish, and with the beautiful pool and surrounding forest, I could die a happy woman at that moment. Colin took the obligatory picture, and he went out to fish in the same deep pool. He moved down to the other end and brought in a nice rainbow.

Colin turned to us. "Shall we have our sandwiches?" I gazed at the river and saw several more fish. "Let's let them settle while we rest for a few minutes."

I ate my sandwich, had some water, and then made the error of reclining on a bed of nearby grass. Colin shook my arm and told me it was time to go. I was dead to the world, and it took me several seconds to realize I may have extended my power nap. "Wake up, beautiful girl. It's almost five. We have a fished-out boy to feed."

"It can't be. Can it?"

"Sure is, Margaret, Maggie...,"

I kicked him and said one of those names would be enough. "I need to talk to you while Luke has one more go at the river. Luke turned and began to walk over.

"Maybe later, darlin'. Is that okay if I still call you darlin', darlin'?"

"Silver or gold?"

Luke was behind Colin, who was down kneeling beside me. Colin pulled me up and dusted my back. He lingered on my 'no-go' area and said, "Lead, for as much as it took me to get you up."

We returned to the lodge and planned to come back tomorrow. I felt guilty leaving anyone behind, and I hoped Charlie would join us. I had yet to tell anyone of my plans for next week. My guess was Helen and Colin had made plans to reunite, and therefore, Luke would be back at Colin's when they returned to the States. The question was, when would that be?

As we walked back toward the lodge, I swatted his butt. "That's for the 'lead' comment, mister." I knew where I stood. I was a close second in his life. I could be happy with that. I had no need to be anyone's number one, my horse and dog aside. The inner sanctum was safe for the foreseeable future.

While the sequence was different, the next few days were deliciously repetitive—play catch, hike, fish, and repeat. Colin didn't tell Luke or me what had transpired on the phone regarding his conversation with Helen. Charlie joined us for the hiking, but it was clear he wasn't up to long hikes and steep terrain. Charlie stopped hiking altogether and spent hours in his studio. It was clear he didn't want us invading his own inner sanctum either.

Colin went to the second studio, where he dabbled in his watercolors. Still, he never stayed for long and would come out and occasionally take Luke for man-to-man journeys into the New Zealand wilderness. While they were gone, I wrote and prepared for my time with my homies.

I told the boys during dinner that I needed some estrogen and planned to go visit my colleagues for a week. I knew Colin would leave soon with Luke. He still didn't tell me his plan. From his mood, I suspected it included a return of Helen to the marital property. I would be their good friend and confidant, and when they needed to attend events in LA, I would be the almost live-in babysitter. I didn't ask.

"Maggie, please don't leave me here. Can't I go with you? I still want to be a vet." Luke searched his grandfather, who shrugged. Charlie sat forward, and I could see he was alarmed. "I'll be gone a week at most, and you guys can run naked and pee on the trees. I promise I'll be back. Pinky promise."

"Take the car, Maggie. It's yours, anyway." Charlie seemed resigned to me leaving and was grateful that I didn't say it was for good.

Colin didn't respond other than to nod and wish me well. Tomorrow was New Year's Eve, and we planned to stay up to greet the new year with Luke if it killed us. It just about did.

Chapter 14

We turned on all the lodge lights and tried to play ball until clouds came over, and then rain halted all outdoor activities. We played some board games, and Colin and Charlie each took turns singing or telling tales of their adventures together. At midnight, we toasted the New Year. I headed for bed, but the boys remained in the lodge. The rain, thunder, and lightning decreased, but despite the rain, it was hot, and I was sleeping in a T-shirt and undies. So, when there was a knock on the door, I had to get my dressing gown.

"May I come in?" Colin sounded slightly inebriated.

"Will I be safe?"

"No promises on that, my dear." Definitely drunk.

"Enter at your own risk. I'm armed and dangerous."

He entered and searched around. "Do you have a gun hidden in here?"

I pulled out a straw. We'd had a competition to see how far we could stab a straw into a potato earlier in the evening.

Colin put up his hands, palms forward, and said, "Whoa, I promise not to go near you."

"That's probably safest."

"Gold." He cocked his head, knowing I wouldn't understand.

"Huh?"

"You're gold. You know the song about making new friends? Silver or gold, and I'm here to report that you're gold, well really platinum, but that isn't very romantic, is it?"

"It could be if it was a brick. That might be a real turn-on."

"Turn-on aside, I had a talk with Helen. We've decided to make some changes." He paused, and my heart fell, and my stomach rose to about the level of my throat.

"Oh, great, you're getting back together? I could tell when you came back from talking to her. Congratulations, Luke's going to be so happy."

"Margaret, Maggie, Magster, Maggot, darlin', wrong, wrong, wrong. You are clueless on so many levels, and if I wasn't madly..." Colin didn't finish.

Without betraying my feelings, I simply said, "Go on. I'm listening."

"I told Helen how I called you by her name and how I wanted the earth to swallow me at that moment."

"What did she say?"

"She thought it was funny—hysterical, actually. She said I called her the names of my costars throughout our marriage, and she knew it didn't mean anything. She told me to get back up on the horse and get going because at her and my age, we don't have much time to enjoy the small things, let alone the big things. This is a big thing. She told me that if we did join forces..." Again, he paused. "Well, you, being so much younger, you might be around longer for Luke. So, will you consider my request to maybe forge an alliance? I know I'm old, and God knows things don't always work like they used to, but I think we make a good team. One way or another, I want you in my life."

I was dumbfounded. I was caught so far off guard that I couldn't even think of a reply. "Oh, Charlie." I stopped and waited for a second. His mouth opened, and I could see he appeared crestfallen. I then looked up and said, "Back at you." He realized I was teasing him, and he walked over, pulled me into his arms, and kissed me once again. "I know I need to sort out a few things, and I'm hoping you can wait for me," he paused and gazed skyward, "to free myself from some entanglements. Will you consider this and wait for me?"

"Does Charlie know?"

"Helen is the only one who knows, and she's your biggest fan. Do you want me to talk to him? Are you still leaving tomorrow?"

"Yes. Mac and Kerry expect me, and you can keep Charlie happy while I'm gone. Let's wait until you're free for sure. I think it's best not to tell Luke either. I would hate to get his hopes up and then have things not work out. I'm guessing you won't throw the baby out with the bathwater and capitulate on your ex's divorce demands? I can't keep you in the style that you're used to. There won't be any first-class flights or heli fishing if I'm paying. I don't mind supporting you, but there will have to be some sacrifices." We held each other for a minute, and then Colin said he better get in his cabin before bed inspection.

"Collie, thanks, and you must know how I feel about you." I didn't finish the sentence. He bent down and kissed me one more time.

"No more pretending, Margaret, Maggie, Magster, Maggot, darlin' for either of us. Maybe we should keep it a secret for the outside world, but not between us."

I emerged in the morning with packed bags. I would play one more game of catch with Luke, walk with Charlie to the garden and check for weeds and bugs, but Colin and I remained aloof. We both knew this was going to break Charlie's heart. There was no chance for Charlie and me to get back to where we'd previously been. He'd betrayed me, and it was rare anyone got more than one shot at me.

As I drove out, I waved to everyone and said I would see them next week. I regretted my decision to leave, but I knew the time was coming in which we all would leave Charlie. I guessed he knew it as well. When I reached the main road, I turned on the GPS and noted it would be an hour and a half to the veterinary clinic, where I would meet my host for the next two days. Vet-girl time here I come. Let the fun begin.

   is one once a year."

Chapter 15

I arrived at the veterinary clinic mid-morning. It was a mixed practice, with the small animal portion only slightly more significant than the food animals and horses. It was jointly owned by Mackenzie and Kerry. Mac did most of the large animals, and Kerry did the smallies, but they interchanged as needed. They'd recently renovated their old clinic, and it was bright, practical, and had a grooming component as well as a retail section.

Kerry was still the same as I remembered. She was athletic, and only the gray hair gave away her age. Neither of the partners was married or had children. They shared a house, and Mac took me to drop off my car and clothes.

"Nice wheels. How'd you score that from a rental company? You must be paying a fortune."

"Oh, the company gave me a deal." I hate lying. "This place is nice. Do you guys own it, or do you rent?"

"We bought it a few years ago." Mac stopped and stared at me.

"What?" I knew I was being assessed.

"You don't know, do you?"

"Know what?" As I said that, I instantly knew where this was going. She didn't have to explain. "I feel like a fool. Nope, not a clue. Were you?"

Mac interrupted me. "Yes and no. I was bi, but now I'm married to the woman of my dreams."

"Yep, totally clueless." My gaydar let me down once again. I think I'll toss it out the window.

"Does it make a difference?" Mac stared as she waited for a reply.

"Only if you have a thing against card-carrying straight women. I can't believe I missed the clues. Weren't you dating John Sutton when you worked for me?"

"We all have our pasts... How about you? Are you dating now that you aren't married to your work?"

"I have a friend. He's old enough to be my older brother."

"Whoa, that old." I threatened to kick her.

"The big six-nine a few months ago. And I still have the immaturity gene, thank you very much." I swiped at my hair in the fashion of a beauty queen.

"If you say so." She rolled her eyes. "Is he continent? Does he have any of his original teeth? Does he know who you are when you visit him in the home?"

"Yes, to all. He's at the lodge with his grandson. He's fishing and hunting while I'm down here hoping to play vet with you two."

"Shall we get the show on the road? I'm dying to show you one case this afternoon."

"Lead the way."

We made sandwiches which we took to the clinic. We ate in the back room. Kerry finally finished her morning consults and came into the staff kitchen. Kerry assessed me and glanced at Mac, who smiled and shook her head. "You're right, not a clue."

"Okay, pay up." Kerry extended her hand, and Mac laid five dollars in her palm.

"You had a bet on me?"

"Mac said you were savvy and knew what was going on. I was confident you didn't." Kerry took the ends of the fiver and snapped it. Just then, a tall skinny man walked into the kitchen and announced the kennels were done, and he was going home to fish. That got my attention. Kerry noticed and introduced me to their kennel man, Lennard.

He immediately corrected the pronunciation. "I'm Lennard. Like Leonardo Davinci, only without the 'o'." He held his curved hand upward like a ballet star with an emphasis on the ARD. "Lennard Mitchell at your service."

I extended my hand. "Pleased to meet you, Mr. Mitchell. What kind of fishing do you do?"

"You're not from here, are you?"

"No sir, but I often come here to fly fish, though." With that, he took me by the arm and said he would bring me back later. He only let me go when Mac howled and told him he would be fired if he stole me to go fishing. We chatted, and then Mac and I went to her truck and headed out to Anthea Hira's farm to see her pony.

"The pony is thirteen and is a hellion. It's almost impossible to even get a needle in him. He cow kicks like a mule. He has a tumor on his sheath that I have removed several times, and it keeps on coming back."

"Did you submit it for histopath?"

"It came back as a sarcoid. I thought it was gone, but it returned, and it's growing larger each time."

I could hardly wait to see this. (Not.) I had retired because of cases like this. As I aged, I had slowed down. No one saw it except one of my nurses and me. She encouraged me to retire several years ago, but I hung in for a while longer, then a bit longer, and then one more year, while my staff spent their days keeping me safe. I successfully retired before I was seriously injured, thanks to my nurses, who "took a bullet" for me almost daily. I'd kill to have one with me now.

"What have you got in the way of sedation?" Fingers crossed she had something substantial.

"I've got the usual. We had detomidine gel, but it's been on backorder for months."

"Do you have the injectable form?" Please say yes, please say yes.

"Yes, we do. Have you used it orally?"

There is a god. "Daily. It's the bomb for taming a terrorist."

We climbed a long, rough driveway to an old shed on a hillside property. The horse owner, Anthea, was half European and half Māori. She was probably in her fifties, and there were children everywhere. She and her husband were foster parents. There were three ponies in small pens constructed from old tree limbs. I was surprised they held the ponies.

Anthea greeted us and offered us a drink before we examined the pony.

Mac declined, and we went over to see the little monster. The mass was not typical of a sarcoid tumor and didn't have a wart-like appearance.

Anthea pointed to the other two ponies. "I've meant to ask, Mac. Is this catchy? The other pony seems to have one, and so does the yearling."

Oh great, three terrorists. I turned to Mac. "Good luck. I'll be in the car. We oldies need our naps."

"Not a chance, Maggot." She firmly took my arm and headed up to the next pen. This pony had a similar mass at the commissure of the lips and a larger lesion under the halter. The third young pony had one in the groin.

"When was he castrated?"

"Last month. Oh, Jesus. It's not a return of the sarcoid. Is it?"

"Never say never, but can you spell 'habronema'?"

"I'm an idiot." Mac was embarrassed.

"I want you to remember this moment. I missed the same diagnosis as well many years ago. I had the embarrassment of sending one of my cases to a local surgeon who made me look like a fool to the client." I quietly turned to Anthea. "You are one lucky woman. Mac asked me to confirm that this isn't a tumor anymore, and she was suspicious that it is a parasite transmitted by flies. Not saying for sure because they look like tumors, but I concur with her assessment. Keep in mind, I've been wrong before. I think we will take that drink if it's still on offer, and we want to sedate all three, and then while the sedation is making them sleepy, we can have a talk about management."

We loaded three syringes with the detomidine and, with a carrot, were able to place some in the worst one's mouth and then some in the other two. Mac observed me doing all of this from the other side of the fence. "I'm a total chicken. I prefer to live another day to fight again. Learn from me sister, I want to keep you around. I need a base when I come to fish in your beautiful country."

"Worth your weight in gold, Maggot."

"Or horse poop. Let's go hear about Anthea's story. And maggot may be the operative word here."

We were given tea. I detested tea, but this had a pleasant taste. When I asked about the brand, Anthea mentioned it was sweetened with manuka honey. I almost spit it out. "Yikes, isn't that expensive?"

"Only if the exporters get their hands on it. We have it growing wild up here."

Anthea said she was the great-great-granddaughter of a Māori queen. She was raised as a full Māori and never was interested in her European heritage. She was eventually educated and even had two years of advanced education, although she didn't say what. Her husband worked in the mines and was gone overseas for months at a time. To pass the time and supplement their income, she began to take in foster children when her own kids grew up, married and flew the coop. She currently had seven, but three foster kids attended a daycare summer camp.

Three of the children were from the same family. They were found living in a hut with an old man. He was sick and was dying, and they were his grandchildren. Their parents abandoned them, and they were taken into foster care before their grandfather passed. They were not toilet trained and did not speak except in their own language. Anthea took responsibility for their care and taught them to communicate and the essential skills for life as adults.

Anthea showed me a report card for the oldest boy, who had demonstrated a tremendous improvement in his skills, and he was now reading at his age level. The other two were also improving. Anthea was strict but loving. They all had stories read to them each night. She was teaching them her Māori language.

I asked if there was any chance of the children going back to their parents. She admitted that was always the goal, but the older three were essentially orphans, and no parents could be found.

"Despite the goal, in this case, I aim for failure." She winked. "So, explain to me about this parasite. Can the children get it?"

Mac explained it is a parasite that resides in the horse's stomach. The parasite produces eggs that are then passed to the ground in feces. Fly maggots eat the habronema eggs. When the larvae develop into flies, they are attracted to certain areas of the horse. It is often the eyes, mouth, and exposed tissue. In the first pony, the wound that resulted from the initial surgery to remove the tumor was open and draining, which would have attracted flies. The flies deposited the larva, the larva set up housekeeping, and in that process caused irritation and reaction of tissue that resembles cancer.

"That's what fooled me. I thought it was old cancer. Dr. Kincaid is kind. She was the one who realized it was probably the parasite."

"And how do I know this? I know this because I have made that error before. In fact, more than once. And, for the record, I prefer to be called Maggie. If you'd like, we can send the tissue off to confirm the new diagnosis, but if you want to look at what we removed, you will see the yellow, small, rice-like beads that would suggest the parasite."

"No thanks, I'll leave that to you two."

We returned to three drunk ponies. We anesthetized the two ponies with lesions in the groin area. Mac had injectable ivermectin to kill the parasite. She removed most of the infected tissue. The remaining lesions were infiltrated with a mixture of ivermectin and a corticosteroid. We explained that Anthea needed to follow up with the regular worming paste. Mac was going to do that. We applied fly strike powder which is a product used on sheep in Australia and New Zealand.

We then headed back to the office. As we drove. Mac said, "I'm thinking of kidnapping you and never letting you go."

"It's been done before." There was no secret about my kidnapping in the States and Australia, but I guessed it never made the news here. I pretended to answer my phone. "Don't worry, our operators are standing by."

She looked at me and then shrugged. "Is there something you need to tell me?"

"How about I dazzle you with a story so bizarre you won't believe it. Let's wait for Kerry. I only tell th

Chapter 16

We did two more routine calls, and then we went to the shops to get dinner. I offered to take them out, but they thought Saturday night would be good to venture out among the ordinary people.

"Suit yourselves. I'm shouting." One nice thing was terms like 'shops,' which often meant the grocery store, or 'my shout,' which meant pay or treat, were familiar to Mac and Kerry. I had become so accustomed to the terms, I forgot and used them back in the States to blank stares of incomprehension.

We ate, and then Mac and Kerry had wine. I abstained and had a single glass of gin and tonic. They then sat, and Kerry tapped her finger on the table. "Okay, Maggie, spill your guts. Were you really kidnapped? When was this?"

"It's not as bad as it sounds." Who was I kidding? It was as bad as it sounded. They could Google this and get the facts. I wasn't going to lie to them, but I was selective in recounting the events.

"I was kidnapped and held for ransom by some men who were not playing nice. My neighbor owned a large corporation. He and I were seeing each other, so these men kidnapped me. My neighbor paid the money. However, I was able to free myself and walk out of the cave and woods where I'd been held."

Mac poured herself more wine, but Kerry put her hand over her glass. "Seeing a man? Details Maggie, we need details."

"His name was Charles McLeod, and he owned a big corporation called CLM Enterprises, Charles and Linda McLeod. Linda died several years ago, and Charlie and I became friends. It's kind of moot now. He was killed shortly after the kidnapping when his plane was returning from Texas. That's kind of why I'm here. My other neighbor knew I liked to fish, so he and his grandson brought me here to forget my troubles. Winter, snow, and lack of fishing may have contributed to my former blues. So here I am trying to educate my friends and escape the snow."

"What happened to your kidnappers?"

"There may be a bit more to the story, but if I told you, the FBI would kill us all. So far, they're awaiting trial. Enough about me. How did you two meet up again and get together?"

They told me about a chance meeting at the American Association of Equine Practitioners' annual conference in San Antonio. Neither one knew the other might be gay. They did connect, and then both said they had loved their time in Australia. They thought they might try to book a breeding season together.

Many vets who specialized in reproduction often headed to the Southern hemisphere to work on breeding farms. The work is seasonal, and many repro vets spend January to June in the Northern Hemisphere and July to December in the Southern Hemisphere. Sadly, Kerry got kicked and broke her palpating arm. Hence, they rerouted to New Zealand, and the rest is history. They were able to become citizens and planned to die here.

They showed me where the coffee was as they knew I would be up early. They went to bed, and I was alone. I checked for messages and emails. There was none of any consequence. I thought about the vet meeting where Mac and Kerry met up. I'd planned to go, but it is usually the first week of December, and I was still in the fetal position and grieving.

I thought about Colin standing by all those weeks and allowing me to grieve and waiting for me to wake up and see what I had and not what I lost. I already missed his acerbic wit and quiet way. I wanted him to put his arms around me and help me guide a fly right into the mouth of a waiting trout. We might have ten years together if we were lucky, and we might see one or the other out. One year was all I asked. I only ask for one year of watching him cast his line, playing catch with Luke, and one year of him lying beside me at night, praying another breath would come.

We were off to another one of Mac's complex cases the following morning. A horse had been castrated by a veterinarian on the North Island. He thought he had removed both testicles, but the gelding was anything but a gelding. He was as stallion-like as ever and mounted mares regularly. He'd been kicked twice for his efforts and had a nasty laceration on his forearm that wasn't healing. We arrived at the property, which bordered a river that looked fishy. "Hello, mister trout."

"Maggot, do you ever think of anything besides trout?"

"Uh," I paused, pretending to consider this question. "Nope. Not anymore. So, I'm assuming if we need to debride the wound, we might as well do the whole thing?"

"What whole thing? Do you mean a crypt castration? Nope. He'll need to go up to the university for that."

"Mac, I taught you how to do that surgery. Surely you can do it?"

She gazed away and smiled. "We could do it together."

"Damn, straight sister. He'll need to go off feed. Will the owners go for it?"

"We'll find out soon enough. I did a testosterone test. He's definitely a crypt."

I'd learned to remove intra-abdominal testicles over the years. Cryptorchidism was a frequent presentation in my practice, and I did five or six surgeries a year. Usually, one testicle was down, and the second might be hanging around in the abdomen. It required an aseptic technique, and there were many different approaches to the internal structures of the abdomen.

There were several complications to this procedure, and death was one. I was lucky, and over the years, I only had one horse die from the surgery. I thought long and hard, but maybe they would want to take the horse to the veterinary school or even to Canterbury, which would be much closer.

We arrived, and the owners were keen to meet me. Mac had told them about me and my recent retirement. They'd even read a few of my books. They had a scenic riding facility, and this horse was purchased to slot in and give the older horses some relief. Horses went out on trails with guests seven days a week. The herd had decreased due to age and attrition, resulting in pressure on the remaining horses to fulfill the guests' needs. Dakota, as I was told, was perfect, except for his "need to breed," as the owners described.

The owners were unable to leave during the peak season. They would prefer to have the surgery done here at their property, if at all possible. We advised them to take Dakota off all food until tomorrow, and we would be back to do the deed the following day.

"Yippee, skippy. A chance to cut is a chance to cure." Mac told me of another version. In her vet school, a student lived at the vet school and worked to pay his tuition. His job entailed removing dead horses from the surgical rooms with a tractor if euthanasia was decided during surgery. His mantra was "a chance to cut is a chance to drive the tractor."

"No tractors tomorrow, thank you very much." I searched around. "Just in case, do they have one?"

"Shut up. I have the best person in the world doing this. Nothing's going to go wrong."

"Big news, little sister. You're doing it. I'm only here to advise."

Kerry looked back and smiled. "Pull me closer, John Deere," she said, which was the answer to the children's riddle. What did the farmer say to the tractor?

"We'll need Kerry too. I wonder if we can find someone else?"

"What about your kennel man?"

"Not a chance. He would pass out."

"I may know someone. I'm moving in with an old friend who has a B&B. He might like to come. Do you know Ned Schaeffer?"

"What? Don't you like our company?"

I explained Ned's situation, and I wanted to help him. I hoped to finagle him into a fishing adventure. He's a nice guy, and he's big and strong. I opened my phone and saw a missed call from Colin. My heart sank. I knew he was long gone from the reception area on the mountain. I sent a reply by text asking him to call again when he is up on the hill. I didn't want to say anything too revealing. I finished by saying I hope he and the boys were well, and I was having a blast.

I felt like a schoolgirl with a crush. I admonished myself for such a ridiculous notion, but the surge of pleasure was ever-present. Mac glanced over at me, staring intently at my phone. "Everything okay?"

"I missed a call from my friend. It's probably nothing. He isn't a techno. He rarely texts me."

"Yeah, it's tough dating those old geezers."

"I'm not dating. We're friends, and that's all. Now, with more pressing issues. Have you got enough ketamine to keep this sucker down for thirty minutes?"

"Thirty minutes? I'll need that to get him prepped."

"This is a timed event. Kerry plays anesthesiologist, you get gloved and ready, and I'll prep. If we get lucky and choose the correct side, we'll have it done sooner. It's a fifty-fifty deal. Most crypts are on the left, but who knows." I observed her swallow hard. "Woman up. Failure is not an option."

I called Ned, and he had tomorrow off. He would love to come and help. Mac asked him to meet us at the clinic, and we'd all drive to the property from there. I'd bring my car and gear to the clinic, and after the surgery, I'd head to Ned's to settle in for the rest of my hiatus from the lodge. Mac had more cases, but she said I could have half a day off now and then.

I was happy with the arrangement. I had no real responsibilities and none of the pressures of practice ownership. I could get used to this.

Chapter 17

We stopped to get takeaway food and coffee the following morning, and then we headed up to the riding stable. Rain threatened, and we all knew we needed to work fast. I wasn't sure if I had instilled my motto on surgery when Mac worked for me so many years ago. "A good surgeon's a quick surgeon."

"Yeah, yeah, yeah. So, how long did it take for you to do your first cryptorchid surgery, Maggie?"

Everyone turned to hear my response. I grinned. "Oh, about two hours. It turned out to be a teratoma. It was the size of a cantaloupe." I turned to our helpers and observers. "I think you say rock melon here."

The owners asked what a teratoma was. I explained it is usually a benign tumor and has unusual tissue such as bone and hair, and sometimes teeth.

"I had to be rescued by an experienced surgeon who scolded me for not getting the testicle. When he scrubbed in to rescue me, he realized it would not be removed without a much larger incision away from the groin. That put me off doing it again for years. Thankfully, I got back on the horse, pun intended and started to do them again. Ain't gonna happen, Mac. I've got your back." *Oh, please, God, let this go well.*

It did. Dakota was a dream to anesthetize. He took only a few top-ups of a mixture of ketamine and another drug to maintain his plain of anesthesia. Ned whistled and shook his head. He'd been a paramedic in the army and hoped he would not get sick. His job would be to hold the anesthetized horse's front legs as the horse was rolled onto his back and balanced in a position technically called dorsal recumbency. Ned was a master at keeping the horse in place and taking all the tension off the business end of our surgical field.

"Okay, make your incision pre-scrotal as you do for all castrations." Mac followed my directions of a quick search for a remnant of the testicle and found none. I'd chosen the more common side of retained abdominal testicles to start with. I then directed Mac to go in front of the inguinal ring and shove her hand down with the tips of her finger and try to enter the abdominal cavity.

It took some work on her part, but she finally broke through the musculotendinous tissue and entered the abdominal cavity. I then explained how to feel around and described that it could take forever to find the testicle. "Are you holding your tongue to the right?" Mac stuck her tongue toward her right cheek but rolled her eyes.

Kerry gave doses of the anesthesia as needed to keep Dakota happy, but Mac struggled. I hated to come into the surgery, but I quickly scrubbed and went in and, like Mac, found no testicle. She promptly closed the incision with sutures and then, without my guidance, went into the other side and immediately located the testicle. There were claps and whistles all around. Dakota moved a tiny bit, so we didn't make any more noise until the testicle was removed and the incision was closed.

We still had to remove the sequestrum on his forearm. We left Dakota in dorsal recumbency, so his leg was off the ground and easy to access. Mac took over the anesthesia, and Kerry scrubbed in, made a small incision to open the draining tract, and extracted the sliver of dead bone. It was attached and difficult to remove, but finally, the job was done. We still had to recover Dakota from anesthesia.

Still, as Kerry told the owners, they usually get up as they go down, and Dakota was no exception. He sat up and began to eat the grass he lay on after twenty minutes. He was up and steady ten minutes later and looking for food. Mac instructed the owners on the aftercare. He should not eat for another hour due to the dryness in his esophagus and the potential of a resulting food bolus becoming lodged, causing a choke. They were all aware of that condition when the stable hand had fed some dry pellets to another horse. The pellets had lodged in the esophagus, which had to be treated by Mac to relieve the obstruction.

Dakota was given antibiotics and pain medication. He was up to date on his tetanus vaccine. We all climbed into the clinic truck, and we were off to lunch. When we were out of sight, we all high-fived one another. "Looks like you guys have a new part-time horse wrangler." I grinned and punched Ned in the arm.

"Oh, that's my cash register arm. Now I'm going to have to go out on a disability."

"As long as it isn't your casting arm, you'll be fine."

This was what I'd lived for, for over thirty-six years—these moments of triumph—a small victory. I was constantly reminded that all I did was not perfect. I certainly had some spectacular failures over the years, but this was a sweet moment for us all.

I reminded Kerry and Mac, "You two remember this moment. There will be plenty of times when you're facing disaster. When your darkest moments are staring you down, remember you got that testicle out."

Ned turned to me. "This is so true. I remember when I was teaching, and I would have a breakthrough with a student. So sweet. Maggie, how do you stay so humble."

"Ned, I do laundry or go fishing. That will keep you humble."

"You're right about the fishing."

We pulled into a small café and ordered lunch. We discussed the surgery and life on the South Island. There'd been a minor earthquake last week, but I hadn't felt it. Everyone looked at their watches, laughed, and stated they were due for another one any time now. It was two in the afternoon.

I wondered why my phone hadn't rung. When I opened it, I realized it was on 'silent.' I'd missed three calls from Colin and two from Luke. I excused myself from the table and went outside. There was one voice message from Colin. He said, "I'll explain later." Explain what? There was also a text message from Luke asking me to call him. I tried to call but received no answer. I texted him back, asking if everything was okay and could he call back this afternoon. He was using an app that required Wi-Fi. Where was he? Had he left?

I was confident that if it was an emergency, they would have left a message. Then I realized it must be me that Colin and Charlie were worried about. I texted Luke back and said everything was good and not to worry. I'd be back in a few days.

Ned and I went to his B&B and dropped off my clothes. I decided to go to the beach and swim. It was an hour away, and I was free until tomorrow. While lying on the beach, I watched an older couple arrive and set up chairs next to me. They said hello and asked if I minded watching their possessions while they swam. Their accents suggested they were fellow Americans.

When they returned, I mentioned I had saved their possessions from numerous incursions. They laughed, thanked me, and offered to do the same. I accepted, waded out in the cold water, and attempted to let my body adjust to the temperatures. I finally took the plunge and gasped at the cold water that enveloped my upper body. I swore quietly to myself, dove down into the icy water one more time, and swam breaststroke across the inlet toward a monolith that jutted out of the water.

It had been the target of many young people swimming in this cove. No one was currently on the rock and, knowing how out of shape I was, decided to swim to it and back if it killed me. It nearly did. I was about to reach the rock when I felt the beginning of a lower leg muscle cramp. It began to ascend up my leg, and my usual way to resolve it was to stand on it and walk. Still, I couldn't reach the bottom, and when I touched the rock, I found it impossible to climb.

I tried to relax, but I will say that my calm, unflappable self was melting into a basket case. I could feel my other leg start to cramp as well. I allowed myself to float in the water, and I bent down and massaged my foot and then moved up my leg. How I stopped the cramping is a mystery. The cramping in both legs seemed to decrease in intensity and then finally ceased.

I swam to shore using a freestyle without kicking. I walked up to my towel, and my kind, elderly couple was gone, as was my phone. I left everything and ran up to the parking lot. They were gone. I ran back to my towel and found my keys buried in the sand, where I'd left them. Fortunately, I'd left my credit cards in my purse in the locked car.

I had no way to contact anyone now. I was beyond furious. I couldn't believe anyone would do such a thing, let alone two geriatrics. They had to be in their eighties. I was sick at the thought of my family or Colin trying to call me. I may have used the F word—maybe several times. I returned to Ned's and explained the situation. He had an old phone. He said he would charge it if I wanted to buy a sim card. Even if I did, I would still have to retrieve my data and phone numbers individually. I prayed that Colin, Charlie, and Luke were all right.

I decided to wait until tomorrow to buy a card. The rooms at the B&B had Wi-Fi, and I did have my computer. I got takeaway and returned to my room. I would spend the day with Mac, and then Ned and I were going fishing the following day, and I would return to my lodge a few days earlier than I had expected. I decided the best plan was to leave when Colin and Luke left. Charlie spent most of his days in his studio and had become reclusive. I realized I really didn't know this man at all.

I sat out on the porch, and two men were on the adjoining patio. We saluted each other by tipping our beers to one another. I could hear their conversation, and while it was innocuous, it took away my concentration. I emailed my sister and all three kids explaining my dilemma and what happened. My son told me to get on Skype, and we could chat that way. He asked me when I had last backed up my phone.

"Uh, not sure, but when I got the new phone, it had all my numbers, and everything was on it, so I must have it on here somewhere."

"Mum, don't tell me you never backed up your phone onto your laptop?"

"Maybe," I said tentatively.

"Mum!" There was exasperation in his voice. He then explained where my data would be on the laptop. I followed his instructions and realized that I hadn't backed up the new phone.

"And they let you into that country? You're clueless, Mum."

"Maybe?"

"So, how did you get all your data onto the new phone when you lost your other one after you were kidnapped?"

"I'm not sure." I think I was sure. In fact, I was damn sure. My phone supposedly was never found, but the one Charlie gave me had all my emails, phone calls, and data. It had to have been transferred from the lost phone to the new one. The FBI said a tracker was placed on my new phone, which they said they removed. If they were using Charlie to get the cartel individuals, why would they even tell me this? Things were adding up, and it did not seem to add in the direction of Charlie's innocence.

Chapter 18

The two men next door entered the dining room when I did. They mentioned they saw a man outside my cabin last night. They said he was looking in the windows of my vehicle, and when they made their presence known, the man left after saying he was looking for his wife, who he was sure was having an affair.

"How old was the man?"

"Mid-twenties."

I laughed and commented, "I wished." Was there a tracker on my vehicle?

Ned took their orders first and then turned to me. "Hey Maggie, thanks for yesterday. I had a blast. Did you sleep, okay? Ham and eggs?"

"Oh, be still my beating heart."

"Good news. Kerry called this morning, and the couple that took your phone dropped it off at the clinic this morning. Apparently, you had the clinic business card in your phone case. They saw it, dropped it off, and apologized profusely. They have the same phone and didn't realize it wasn't theirs until it rang several times last night. They said someone named Colin had tried to contact you. They said he was worried about you, and he asked them to have you call him.

"Oh, thank goodness." I was really thinking, thank Christ, but there were kids in the dining room. "Yes, ham and eggs it is."

I drove up to the clinic, crowded with small animal clients. Mac had to see a few dogs and cats before we took off for the next client. I texted Colin, telling him all was good, one phone abduction aside, and I would return a few days earlier than I'd planned.

Mac finally finished her consults, and we took off for the hills. She'd returned to check on the new gelding. By all reports, Dakota was doing well and already showing less interest in the girls. Her final comment was, "Too bad we can't give a few guys the snip."

"I suppose. So, what's on the agenda today?"

"Saving the best for last."

"Uh-huh?"

"I have no idea what's going on with this horse."

"Tell me about it." I now thought retirement was a lot better than I had expected. I liked my old profession, but the dramas of complex cases made me anxious.

"She's thirty. Her teeth are in remarkable shape. She eats and drinks and is losing weight. Her Cushing's test result was within normal limits. I even did a stimulation test, and her ACTH is always low normal. Her labs are also within normal limits, and I even did the tests for malabsorption, and still, everything is perfect. The owner is a wonderful old man. His wife died, and the mare was hers. She's the last link to his wife."

"Mackenzie, I could strangle you. Are you trying to torture me? Tell me that she's at least gentle, and I don't have to work across a fence?"

"Oh, no. The mare's a kind soul. Sadly, so is the owner."

"No other signs of colic? Anything?"

"I wish. Mr. Harmer refuses to let her go. I'm sorry, but it's almost a neglect case, except it isn't. He sits out with her all day, tempting her with a range of hay and concentrates."

"Kill me now."

"This may just do the job." Mac steered the car with a death grip. "It's so frustrating. I don't know why this horse needs to die, but she needs to die."

We arrived at an old farmhouse up in the base of the mountains. I'd passed the property on my way to town. It was a well-kept hobby farm. Mac stopped the car near the barn, and I was introduced to Geoff Harmer, a retired engineer. He'd helped design and construct many of the dams and bridges that crossed the rivers on the South Island. His wife had passed over ten years ago, and he still pined for her.

The mare was a thoroughbred and had been Patsy Harmer's last riding horse. In her youth, Patsy had competed in three-day eventing. Toward the end of her life, she rode this striking chestnut mare around the property.

"What's her name, Mr. Harmer?"

"Duchess, doctor."

"She's beautiful. I can see why you'd want to save her." Duchess was a tall and regal chestnut with three white stockings and a perfect blaze. Her face and eye told me she was in pain. The indicators of pain in a horse's face were now a quantifiable observation. Those who knew the signs had probably unconsciously recognized it for years.

"She means the world to me."

"So, Mr. Harmer, when did this first start?"

He scratched his head. "Don't know for sure, but over a year ago." I went through the common causes of weight loss in horses and especially older horses. Many horses lived much longer, and Cushing's disease, a condition common in older horses, is a logical consideration. Horses with Cushing's often have a long hair coat, and their weight loss is more of a perceived loss of the epaxial or back muscles. The syndrome results in the weakening of all muscles. The weight often appears to shift to the abdomen, giving these horses a potbellied appearance. She'd been thoroughly tested, and her weight loss was all over her body. Duchess was gaunt, and her abdomen was tucked up, unlike horses with Cushing's disease.

"You've done a rectal, haven't you?" I turned to Mac, who was standing by the gate.

"Many, but it would be good if you would have a go, just to make sure there wasn't something that I missed." I loved Mac's humility. She was there for the animal and to learn, not her ego.

"It's been a while, but let me have a feel. My arm is a bit longer than yours." I turned to Mr. Harmer. "You know, we can only feel a small part of the abdomen due to the poor engineering design, but sometimes we get lucky."

Mr. Harmer had been quite serious until I mentioned engineering and design. That made him laugh, and he laughed so hard he bent over.

"Call me Geoff. You just earned it."

I performed a rectal examination, and like Mac, found no reason for the weight loss. "I'm at a loss to explain it. Do you have a picture of her when she was maybe a few years younger?"

While he was gone, I asked Mac about sand. She said she had done multiple fecal sand tests and never had any sand. I doubted it was the issue, but Mac's radiograph equipment was strong enough to shoot through this thin horse, and I thought it might be enough to help this man make a decision. He returned with his picture, and I discussed the indicators of pain in horses. I pointed out the relaxed head and jaw muscles and especially the eyes in the picture he showed me. We compared his image from before she began to lose weight and now.

"Dr. Williams and I think that the only other thing we can suggest is to do a sand radiograph. We can help many horses with sand accumulation, but if it's not sand, then I'm afraid we won't be able to help you. So, would you like to rule that out?"

He turned to Mac. "How come you didn't do that before?"

"It's a very new technique, Geoff. I did a few before I retired, and I think it will give you peace of mind. So, shall we go get the machine? I think we can do it today if that would be good for you?" He nodded. "Geoff, would you mind if I stayed here so I can observe her while Dr. Williams gets the machine?"

Mac left, and I sat down on a log and observed the mare. Nobody knew my real reason for staying. The ham and eggs didn't settle well with me.

If Duchess had a good appetite, why was Geoff sitting with her and coaxing her to eat? I watched her graze. She ate a few mouthfuls and then raised her head and then would look through the offering and maybe eat a bit more. It hit me like a hammer. "Geoff, I'm an idiot. You don't have cell phone coverage here, do you." He shook his head. "May I borrow your phone?" He took me into the kitchen. I was given a phone that was actually attached by a cord. I hadn't seen one for several years. I called the clinic. I knew Mac's truck would not be in range yet. A strange voice answered. "May I speak to Dr. Penfield, please?"

"Who may I say is requesting to speak to her?"

"A voice from heaven," but then I explained the situation. Kerry was on the line immediately.

"Hey, Kerry. You know how 'godlike' you all thought I was yesterday?"

"No, but go on." She was trying not to laugh.

"I saw your ultrasound machine, and I'm wondering if you have a probe that's around three megahertz?" *Oh, please, please, please say yes.*

"Yep, why?"

"Mac's coming into the clinic to get the x-ray machine. Can you have her bring the ultrasound and some sugar-free cola as well?"

"Sure, Maggie. Where are you?"

"I decided to stay up here with Mr. Harmer."

"You stayed with that old geezer? Are you safe?"

"Hey, I am among my people. I'm one too, you know."

"Whatever. Thanks for all the help. It's hard here. Especially when we're on our own."

"Try moving to a new country before the internet and only a handful of vets who shared the love."

"I forgot how old you are. I think Mr. Harmer's available. If you're looking."

"You never know my luck. See ya, sister."

Geoff made a bowl of stew from his dinner last night and offered me some tea. We talked about his wife and her accomplishments. They had a son killed in a drunk driving accident when he was eighteen. Geoff had a younger brother, but he was back in the UK.

I was concerned with his lack of interaction with people. He didn't belong to any clubs, and he rarely went to other people's houses for social occasions. Their friends were her friends. He was too busy building bridges. I had a knack for getting into people's inner thoughts. I simply asked. Older people loved to talk. Crap, I'm one of them now.

"Do you have any vices?"

"I'm not sure what you mean? I might have one drink now and then, and I don't smoke."

"No, I mean serious vices. Do you fly fish?"

Geoff's eyes lit up. "Well, I used to, but I haven't been forever. We used to fish when we were constructing the dams and bridges."

"Want to go fishing with me tomorrow?"

He pursed his lips. "I don't know if I can leave the Duchess."

"I'm going fishing with an old friend who also lost his wife. He's a bit despondent. I was wondering if maybe you could help him and get some tuition on fishing again? I'm going to tell you straight out, I think Duchess will either be okay tomorrow or not. You won't be able to help her. I hate to be blunt, but hopefully, I can eliminate the things you can fix when Dr. Williams gets back."

"All right. This sounds good to me."

"Is that a creek over there?" I pointed to the edge of his large paddock.

"Yes, it has a proper name, but I call it Steven's creek. As a boy, my son played in it all the time."

"Do you mind if I go over and have a look?"

"Those fences have a hell of a—Oh, I'm sorry, I shouldn't have sworn."

I laughed. "After thirty-six years as a horse vet, hell doesn't even qualify anymore. Can we turn off the fence charger? The cattle are on the other side of the paddock."

We went over to the paddock's edge to the tree line and saw several deep pools. The water was dark, and the shade made it difficult to see, but a fish rose. "Geoff, mate, you've been holding back on me. You have gold in this crick."

We studied the creek for several minutes. We returned to Duchess. I lay down on the grass and did the usual. I woke up when I heard a car coming up the road.

I gazed around and realized I may have slept longer than my usual power nap allotted time of five minutes. Geoff patted my shoulder and said my partner was back. It took me a minute to shake off the groggy feeling that usually happened when I slept for a long time. Geoff went into the house and returned with water. Mac stared at me and shook her head. "So, what's the plan?"

"SCC, but let's rule out the sand first." Mac knew SCC stood for squamous cell carcinoma. She also knew it would most likely be in the stomach. It was an insidious disease that often started well before any symptoms were noted. One of the first signs was a decrease in appetite. "Geoff says the mare eats well, but I watched her eating, and I would say her appetite was not even close to normal."

I helped Mac set up the portable x-ray machine and set the computerized program for the abdomen. I cranked up the generator to the limit. I showed Mac how to hold the plate to record and transmit the image to the computer. I explained that we had to have some of the receiving plate exposed without any interference so the computer could process the image. Kind of like you have to have a reference base.

We all donned our protective gowns. Geoff held Duchess's head, and Mac had the plate. I aimed the beam at the lower abdomen, near the junction of the ribs and xiphoid cartilage. "Ready, Mac?"

"I won't be if you don't get going. This plate is heavy in this position." I'd advised her to hold it at arm's length. There was a lot of radiation used to produce this image.

We took one shot and walked over to the computer, inside a shed and out of the bright sun. We missed, but I was ecstatic. We weren't lined up, but clearly, this would work. This time Geoff lined us up from his view. "Geoff, make sure Dr. Williams is holding the plate parallel to the spinal column."

"I am Maggot. It must be you who is off beam."

Geoff was enjoying this. It was engineering at its best. "She's good to go, Maggie."

"Well, we know it is never the radiographer who is to blame, so let's get that on the table. Everyone ready?" Apparently, Duchess wasn't. She moved just as I pushed the trigger on the generator. "Don't even bother, guys. Let's try one more time. And go."

Bing, again. I came around the other side of the horse, and there was the perfect image of the lower abdomen and the large colon. I showed both Mac and Geoff the image of the ribs, which were white streaks that ran diagonally across the picture. I explained that the sand was the same density in appearance as the ribs. I had old images of "sand rads," as we called them from my old clinic, still on my phone. Duchess did not have sand. *How would I have those images on my phone unless they had been transferred from the old one I had before my abduction to the new one?*

This left three other possible diagnoses. One was the squamous cell carcinoma of the stomach or another form of cancer in the front area of the abdomen. The second cause might be a slight decrease in the lumen of the gastrointestinal system, which is often in the small intestine and commonly referred to as ileal hypertrophy. I'd seen several cases of both over the years. Still, ileal hypertrophy usually caused intermittent discomfort and resulted in colic symptoms. Finally, a gastric impaction where food was stuck in the stomach had to be considered.

"Let's crank up the ultrasound Dr. Williams." We moved into a shaded area, and Geoff took us under his carport. The stomach lining could only be examined by endoscopy, which required a long endoscope. Kerry and Mac didn't have one and relied on horses to travel six or more hours to a referral clinic near Christchurch. The other less reliable diagnosis was with ultrasonography of the stomach.

We cleaned and prepped the mare's chest, and I watched as Mac guided the probe to the area adjacent to the stomach. The stomach lining was usually curved and had a smooth appearance. Duchess stood perfectly still. The application of cold alcohol made her react, and she turned her head in our direction. I took several images from the examination. I don't think I'd ever seen such a large mass as this mare had. Mac elbowed me, and we both gazed over at Geoff and shook our heads.

Geoff's shoulders slumped, and he walked away. He turned sharply. "Is there anything we can do?"

Mac turned to me and quietly asked if I'd heard of any new treatments. "Well, the coke was for gastric impaction, so I think we can toss that out of the window."

Mac smirked and gave me the evil eye. "I'll drink to that."

"You didn't just say that did you?" We both knew there were coping mechanisms that veterinarians used to relieve our personal anxiety. This was a form of that.

My former funeral director, or the man who picked up the dead horses from my veterinary practice, was a great tension reliever. That man could find humor in any situation. What no one knew was that we both put on a stoic face in front of the clients, and then when they were out of earshot, he would make me howl with laughter. It was years after his passing that I found out that he often cried if a small child or an elderly person was involved. I suspected he knew that I wept too.

"I did have a horse respond to a drug that I used to treat external cancers of this type. I suppose we could offer it. I saw the mass in the stomach of a chronically painful horse. We suspected gastric ulcers, but when I scoped the horse, I found a mass. It wasn't as big as this one."

I explained to Mac what the drug was and how easy it was to administer. I thought Geoff would know in a week or two if it would be of any benefit. I left it to Mac to propose it. At least he couldn't say we didn't try. He was going to consider it. He would decide tomorrow and let me know what his decision was.

He'd agreed to go fishing with me tomorrow. I said I would pick him up around ten in the morning after my fishing partner fed his guests. "Do you have waders? It's pretty hot. We might not need them. I'll make sure we bring enough gear, so don't worry about getting out your own."

We left. "Just tell me that there are no more complicated cases that involve sweet old lonely men and gorgeous horses. That just about killed me, Mac."

"He's about your age. Have you looked at your driver's license lately?"

Chapter 19

Mac, Kerry, and I hit the town that evening. We had dinner in a downtown café on a closed street, as an African street band entertained us. Mac and Kerry danced, but I only watched, claiming I was too old.

I kept thinking about Geoff and his mare. I suspected she wouldn't last for more than a year, and that was in the rare chance she responded to this unusual drug. The good news was that it was a human anti-inflammatory medication and reasonably inexpensive. However, I hadn't checked the cost of it here in New Zealand. My friends' enthusiasm didn't last, and we returned to their house, where I hugged them both and reminded them I was always available by phone. I returned to Ned's B&B and noticed the two men were still next door.

The younger man waved. "Did you enjoy the festival?"

"I did. Were you there too? You should have come over and joined my friends and me."

"They looked like they were pretty happy on their own."

"Yes, I guess so. So, what brings you here? Are you fishing, hiking, or seeing the sights?"

"Seeing the sights." The older one whispered to the younger man as they stood and went into the cabin. They were strange. They were Americans and somehow didn't look the part of tourists.

I slept fitfully that evening and needed coffee to get me functioning. "Eggs benedict, my dear?"

"No thanks, Ned. I'll have cereal this morning. I have a hot date with a couple of fishing partners. I need to get ready."

I ate, checked my messages and emails, and returned to my room while waiting for Ned. I explained to him about Geoff Harmer and his horse as we drove to the hobby farm to pick Geoff up. Ned said he would avoid talking about anything too serious with Geoff, but maybe they could help each other in grief.

"Ned, what's the story with the two Americans staying next door to me?"

"Yeah, what is the story? Strange men. I told them I didn't have any rooms, and they insisted that if there was a cancellation, they would like to be called. Damned if there wasn't one, and so they booked for the week. Their credit card is strange, but it goes through all right."

"Did they say why there were here or where in the States they were from?"

"I did ask, but they kind of blew me off. The men claimed they were on a working holiday, and this town was a stopover. Seems kind of strange for a week's booking for a stopover."

"Yeah. To be on the safe side. Don't tell those guys I'm leaving tomorrow?"

"Do you think they're following you or something? Maggie, you can stay with me tonight if you're worried."

"No thanks. I'm sure it's only a coincidence. So where are we going?"

"I thought we could go up to a private lake. We don't need licenses, and I'm guessing Mr. Harmer probably doesn't have one. My friend owns a boat, and we can go fish out on the boat."

We were wrong. Geoff had purchased a three-day pass yesterday, so Ned decided to go to a river that had been hot lately. As we crossed the river, Geoff mentioned he had designed this bridge. Geoff might be a little older than me. Ned was at least ten years younger. Despite our age differences, we had a great time. Geoff was modest in his assessment of his skill. He was an expert in fishing, and the two men outfished me, hands down. Knowing I was going back to Charlie's lodge, where the fish were under no pressure and were easy game, I let the men fish most of the time. It was all catch and release, and there were lots of both. I enjoyed watching both men forget their troubles, and I netted several fish. They insisted that I have a go several times. I did catch two, but they clearly spanked me in the fishing department. Geoff was even laughing along with Ned. I think I might be better at matchmaking than my other skills.

At the end of the day, we went to a burger joint and had a quick meal. Geoff told me he would try the new drug, but unless he saw an improvement in a week or so, he was ready to let go. The men decided to meet next Sunday and exchanged phone numbers. Geoff and I hugged, and he thanked me for coming and especially for staying with him after Mac left to retrieve the x-ray equipment.

"You need to know that when I practiced, I never would have done that, as I wouldn't have time, and I hope you understand how hard Dr. Williams worked to save Duchess."

He agreed and lamented that he wished he could have mentored some of the young engineers that worked under him. "I would love to help some of those guys. I hate the idea that I am going to die and know things that would help them and never pass on what I know."

I nodded. "I hear ya, brother. I hear ya."

When we returned to Ned's, my friendly neighbors were there on the porch with their beers. Once again, we saluted each other with a tip of our beer bottles.

The younger one asked, "Work or pleasure today?"

"It's all pleasure these days. I don't do anything I don't want to do. And you? Or do I need to ask?"

I stood up, and before they could answer, I walked back into my room. I rose early the following morning with a mission. I systematically changed every password I could remember on my computer, including social media apps, and went to breakfast earlier than usual. Oh, surprise, so did my neighbors. By prearrangement, I mentioned that I was off to the clinic for another day with Mac and Kerry. I got in my car and drove away. I waited for a few minutes and then returned to find my neighbor's car was gone.

I packed my gear and left, and I drove toward the ocean and then sat in a parking lot and waited. True to form, my 'friends' were there at the other end of the parking lot. My car was bugged. I got back into my car, knowing I would not lose them. At least, I would acknowledge their presence. I drove up behind their car and stopped my vehicle behind theirs, so they couldn't move away.

"We meet again. This is looking less like a coincidence. Wouldn't you think?" I got my phone out, took a picture of them, their car, and their number plate. I then sent it to my sister, Mac, and Colin in separate emails, asking them to save these images. They looked at one another and then held their hands up in an arrested mode and said, "Caught."

I was scared shitless, but I was taking my life back. "Who hired you?"

"A man, and we don't know his name, but he's paying us to keep you safe."

"Okay, well, if that's your purpose, let's hope you do."

"Do what?" The older man stared at me.

"Keep me safe." I suspected this was Charlie. How was he doing this? Where was this money coming from, and was Colin in on this too? Did these men think I was incapable of taking care of myself? How condescending. I guessed the most crucial question was, were they really doing this to keep me safe or keep me quiet? Were these guys the good guys or the bad guys?

Recalculating route. I was headed to Ned's B&B to pick up my clothes and the rest of my fishing gear, and I was getting the heck out of New Zealand. I hoped Colin and Luke would come as well, and for sure, they better not be involved in this. I had my limits.

Chapter 20

I was furious. Who did these men think they were dealing with? I was honest and loyal, but I wasn't going to commit a crime for them or anyone. I checked my speedometer and slowed down. Okay, maybe I committed minor crimes. I thought of an expression my mother often used. "I'm so mad I could spit."

I passed a tiny shop in a small town on the way to the lodge. I was thirsty. I walked out of the shop, sipping on a shake carrying a packet of chips. No one who observed me would realize I also had two new sim cards. Two could play this game. I was going on the offensive, and I was taking back my life. I would pretend to be the same innocent person who'd left a few days ago, and then I would be ready for battle. I hoped Colin and Luke wanted to come away with me if it came to that.

If Charlie was still wanted by the mob, was he worried I would be a target? Did they think the FBI would interfere, knowing it was in their interest to protect their star witness? Did either Charlie or Colin even know that the car was tagged, tracked, and followed? Who was housing Charlie in such luxurious accommodations if he'd sacrificed all his wealth and companies? Things didn't add up. What jurisdiction would the FBI have in New Zealand anyway? Having met several agents when I was abducted, those two guys from Ned's B&B didn't act or look the part.

I wasn't due back for two more days, but my guess was that Charlie knew I was on my way to the lodge. I entered the property and parked the car near the gate, well down and away from the compound's driveway.

I then placed the new New Zealand sim card in my phone and walked back toward the road where the car was parked. I left the original sim card and the other new one in a section of the fence down from the gate. *Was I paranoid? Yep, in spades.*

As I drove up to the lodge, no one was there to greet me. I searched the river and the hills around the compound. The place was empty, so I went to my cabin, showered, and then went up to the lodge. Everything was the same, including the Christmas decorations and the tree. I wanted to pretend that nothing was amiss until I could ascertain what was going on.

I realized I'd failed to bring any food when I arrived. The presence of the two men following me had upset me. I opened the refrigerator and found it stocked with milk, garden vegetables, cheeses, and beer. We weren't going to starve. I guessed Colin and Luke were fishing, and Charlie must be up in his studio. I wondered what painting he was creating now. He had a gift. His work was so reminiscent of someone's, I simply couldn't think of whose style it might be.

I sat down on the sofa and opened the book on art that I'd given him. It appeared that he'd been reading it and had marked some pages. I fell asleep for only a few minutes when Charlie came in and quietly tried to get some crackers and cheese without waking me. "I hear you. I'm awake."

"I see. What happened? You're back early."

"I missed you all too much. Well, I missed the fish. And I missed my bed. Or I got sick of my two security patrolmen and decided they could have a day off. So, what was that about?"

"Yeah, I heard. I can explain." This was interesting. How did he know?

"An explanation might be in order. Does Collie know?

"No. Just me. Can we talk about it later? They should be back soon. So, really, why are you back?"

"I finished quicker than I thought. It was so much fun, and I had a great time, but I was no longer needed. To be honest, the two guys kind of creeped me out." I didn't mention I sent photos to Colin and my family, but I guessed Charlie knew that.

"It won't happen again."

"Damn straight, it won't. You have my loyalty. I thought you would know that by now." I forgot to mention as long as he was legitimate and doing what he said he was doing.

"Can I get you something to drink?"

It was too early for beer. I'd had a New Zealand Boag's beer with Mac and Kerry—a girl could get used to that. "Maybe just some water. I'll get it. How about you?"

He didn't answer. He stood and walked to the door. "I'll be back in a minute."

He went to his room and returned with a new miniature portrait of Luke. "What do you think?"

"Nice, Charlie." It was of Luke standing with a hoe. In the background was my house. "How do you think of these things? That's a good likeness of my house as well. Do you have any others you've done recently? Has Luke seen this?"

"I try and do at least one new one every few days. I'll bring some down later."

"Do you have any of The Sanctuary? It must kill you not to visit the site and Linda's resting spot. You know we had a memorial for you there." I hadn't been to the magnificent property since the memorial, and I was surprised there weren't pictures of Charlie's former home.

He cringed. "Yeah, I can't tell you how much I regret putting you through all that."

"Roberta was devastated. We all were, as I think you can guess. She took me into your bedroom. How long did Roberta work for you?"

"Oh, maybe fifteen years. We hired Roberta to clean once a week, but when Linda became ill, she became full-time. Roberta had her own room and stayed with me five days a week until her brother became incapacitated. Do you know if he's still alive?"

"No, I'm sorry. Collie might. I kind of went to the ground after I thought you died. I think that's harder to accept than even the kidnapping."

"Will you ever forgive me?"

I stared him straight in the eye. "I don't know." There it was—the truth. It wasn't the whole truth, but it was probably enough for right now. I guessed Colin hadn't told Charlie about his and my developing relationship.

"That was quite a tribute to Linda in your bedroom. Do you have any photographs of Linda with you?"

"No, I wasn't able to take any. I only paint Linda from memory."

"Oh, so you did some paintings of Linda? I'd love to see them."

"They aren't finished." My guess was he didn't want to share them. It was probably too painful. "Maggie, when was the last time you saw Roberta?"

"At your memorial service. Collie gave a great tribute to you. Did he tell you?"

"Not in so many words. Collie did mention that he wouldn't do it again."

Was that the moment for Colin when his loyalty to Charlie was broken, and Colin decided he was free to pursue me. I know I no longer had any commitment to Charlie, especially when he had men follow me. I sat facing him as he stared at the picture of Luke. I felt like a line had snapped, and a fish got away. I had no desire to pursue this fish.

I heard Colin and Luke approach their cabins. "Hey, Grandpa. I think she's back. I'm going up to see her."

I heard Colin's reply, "I'm getting in the shower. I'll be up in a while." I listened to a cabin door shut.

Hearing his voice made my heart race. I stood up as Luke entered. I looked at Charlie. "Do you want to show him your painting?"

"I'll give it to him at dinner tonight." He picked it up and said he would be back in an hour to start dinner.

"Charlie, I'll do dinner. What were you planning?"

He told me he planned to cook steaks, potatoes, and vegetables from the garden. He stared at me, and I could see he was considering his options.

I smiled and shrugged. "Let me do it. You can have the evening off."

As Charlie stepped out of the lodge, he turned to me. "Can I trust you not to poison us?"

"Sadly, no. But it won't be on purpose." Charlie walked up to his studio. It was strange, but without ever saying, we all knew this was his private retreat. No one ever suggested that we go up uninvited.

Luke entered and came over, hugged me, and told me he was glad I was back. He smelled. "When did you last shower?" I waved my hand in front of my nose.

"The day before you left. Grandpa said it was okay to wait."

"You all are probably losing your sense of smell. Get your sorry ass into the shower now."

"But?" Luke lifted his arm and smelled himself.

"I can't smell anything." He smelled himself again as I shook my hand and pretended to shoo him out of the lodge's great room.

I went to the garden. The plants needed watering, and the weeds were beginning to take over. I smiled to myself. My life was almost perfect, a few creepy men aside. I had girl time, vet time, fishing with an old friend, and brought two lost souls together. I was going to see Colin in a few minutes. *Oh, please, Lord, let things be like we left them in my room the other night.*

Oblivious to the world, I watered one end of the garden and weeded the other. I sang as I worked until I finally heard a cough and straightened up. There was Colin. He had on the clothes he wore on the plane. He held out some wildflowers.

"If I call you Helen, you have my permission to slap me." I grinned. We turned and gazed over toward the cabin, and seeing no one, he came over and took me in his arms and kissed me. "I've missed you, Margaret, Maggie...."

I put my fingers on his lips. "I missed you too." We heard the cabin door open and shut, and we stepped away from one another. As Luke approached, I asked how the fishing was while I was gone. They replied simultaneously. Luke said "boring," and Colin said "lonely."

"Well, sorry gentlemen, I had a wonderful time. Luke, can you cut me some asparagus and a head of lettuce. My hands are too dirty."

"Yes, ma'am, and you got some dirt on Grandpa's behind too." Colin craned his neck, but I walked behind and whistled.

"You're a marked man Collie. I rinsed the mud off my hands and attempted to dust the dirt off his pants.

"Don't stop, Maggie."

"Grandpa, you're too old for that."

"Never, my innocent grandson, never too old."

I walked away and headed to the kitchen. I was afraid Luke might see more than I was ready to admit. "I'm not too old either, Lukey Boy."

Luke snorted and told us he would be sick if he heard anything more like that.

I was blushing and kept walking, so neither saw me. "Lukey, remember this moment when you're as old as us. We won't be around, but I'm going to savor the moment now, in anticipation."

Colin stood next to his grandson. "Listen to her, Luke. I only hope you have someone as nice as our Maggie. Despite our ages, we aren't dead yet."

Charlie came down from his studio and brought three more paintings. One was Colin on Digger. I would kill to have that painting. Colin appeared to be a few years younger, and he seemed so happy on his horse. He was moving cattle. One was of me fishing by myself. Colin came straight out and said if Charlie didn't give it to him, he was packing up and taking Luke and me with him. The last was of my house back home with Digger grazing near the house and Luke with my dog Baxter.

"Seriously, Charlie. You're unbelievable. I'm so impressed." I loved his artwork. I wondered whose work had inspired this style.

Colin nodded. "I don't know why you bothered to waste your time on wealth accumulation when you could paint such masterpieces." Both men laughed.

"Painting wasn't going to help Linda to save the world or Maggie for that matter."

"Don't blame me. I'm doing my own saving these days, two men at a time." I then went on to explain about Ned and Geoff. As we ate, I described my week. I was careful not to mention the two guys who followed me. I wondered how Charlie communicated with them and the outside world. He talked to someone. That was obvious.

I had a single beer, so I didn't get too drunk, unlike Charlie and Colin. It didn't matter, as they could still be perfectly reasonable, despite their alcohol consumption. Luke went to bed, leaving Colin, Charlie, and me. I glanced around the room and, remembering the Australian tradition, exclaimed, "Gentlemen, we're in danger of a serious threat.

Do you realize that if we don't get these Christmas decorations down in the next few days, we could have bad luck all year? It's a known Australian fact."

Colin stretched out on the sofa and closed his eyes. "I'll get onto that in just a minute." He smiled and pushed me with his feet. Charlie got up and poured himself another drink. I could see where this was headed.

"I'm going to bed. I want to get up early and call my sister. You guys are a bunch of entitled, spoiled old men. I'll do it in the morning. Sweet dreams." Charlie replied, but Colin was in a coma. I prayed he would wake up and come to say goodnight in my cabin, but he didn't. Or did he?

Chapter 21

When I woke up, my clothes were neatly folded, and a second blanket covered me. I smiled, thinking of this act of kindness. The barriers to the inner sanctum were falling down. I made coffee and took a mug to my room. I quickly drank it and then went up to the hilltop to contact my sister. It was too early to call my children.

Before I called, I checked my emails. There was one from my brother-in-law asking me to call him. I think that may have been the second email I'd received from him in the last ten years. Alarm bells rang. I immediately rang him and found him crying. "Miles, what's going on?"

"Christy's sick. Can you come home? She needs a bone marrow transplant. Bill's already been tested, and he isn't a match." My heart sank, and I was in shock. I began to cry. Of course, I would return. The family was gathering. I would catch the first flight I could get and be in San Francisco as soon as possible. After a brief conversation where Miles gave me more details of my sister's illness, I hung up and called the airlines. There was a law about traveling the same day as a booking, so I would have to wait until the next day. No flights would get me to San Francisco for several days.

I returned to my cabin and began to pack. I couldn't stop crying. Someone was in the kitchen. I went up and watched as Luke was pouring milk into a cereal bowl. He saw my face and immediately came over. "I have to leave Lukey. My sister's very sick, and she needs a bone marrow transplant. I need to go and see her, and maybe I can give her some of my marrow. I'm going to have to leave tomorrow. Can you tell your grandfather and Charlie when they get up?"

"No need, darlin'." Colin was in the doorway. He came over and immediately enveloped me in his arms. "You shouldn't wait. Let's get you a ticket today."

"I can't. I can't even leave for Auckland until the following day." I explained the situation with the travel laws. He took me to my cabin and told me to pack. He kissed my forehead and left. I sat down on my bed as Charlie knocked and entered.

"There will be a helicopter here within the hour. I've arranged for a private jet to take you to Hawaii, and then you'll have a commercial flight to San Francisco. I'm so sorry, Maggie. I wish I could go with you. Collie's going to go with you to Christchurch and see you off. Please don't worry. We'll do everything we can to keep you safe and get you there quickly." He stood up and went to the bathroom, wet a hand towel, and wiped my face. He kissed me on the top of my head and left.

An hour later, we heard the whirring of the approaching helicopter. Luke was crying and hugged me several times. Charlie draped his arm around Luke as the copter lifted off the helipad. Colin and I waved. As we gained altitude, Colin reached back and held my hand. He smiled and mouthed, "I love you," I smiled weakly, nodded, and pointed to my heart and then his.

We arrived in Christchurch. I was suffering from severe motion sickness. The flight had been rough, and I'd closed my eyes most of the way. Visibility was lacking for much of the trip. I had to be helped to descend from the helicopter. I turned to the pilot, and I realized he was the pilot who flew us to the lodge last month. He smiled and nodded in recognition. I mouthed a thank you, but all I wanted to do was vomit. I had two hours before Charlie's plane would arrive. Colin ushered me into a building away from the main terminal. I immediately went to a bathroom and relieved myself of my stomach contents. I cleaned myself as best as I could and emerged to find Colin coming from another bathroom. I stared at him and realized he may have done the same.

"It must have been something I ate." This did make me laugh, and I hugged him.

"Yeah, me too. The worst part is you have to fly back."

"No, the worst part is I'm going back without you. We need to talk." He headed me over to a private area away from the workers. It was apparent he was recognized. A woman came over and asked if she could get us something, but he thanked her and declined.

We sat on a sofa, and he put his arm around my shoulder. I leaned into him and waited. "There is no way any of this could have happened if Charlie is under the watch of the FBI."

"There's more," I explained the photo I sent of the two men who followed me while I was visiting Mac and Kerry. "You need to protect Luke. Collie, Charlie is no fool. He must realize we are suspicious of his behavior and about his circumstances. He might be getting desperate. Please get Luke and go home. I'm worried sick about you two."

All this time, Colin was holding my hand, which made me feel protected. We talked about my sister and the limited information I had. She had some form of acute leukemia. The prognosis was poor, and a bone marrow transplant was the primary treatment. She was receiving chemo, but it was a stopgap measure and failing to get a donor, she was doomed. I rested my head on Colin's shoulder. He put his arm around mine, and we sat while he tried to calm me.

"You realize this is not me. I'm not a crier."

"Yeah, I've only seen you cry four or five times. Nope, not a crier at all."

"When?" I was a rock. I was the person who managed all the crises and held everyone else up.

"It's been quite a year for you. I don't blame you." He rubbed my back. "There's been some good too, though, hasn't there?"

I smiled. "Lots of good things. Meeting Luke, fishing, Digger, fishing, heli fishing, Digger. Then there have been some not-so-nice things. I remember getting a scolding for fishing illegally on this crabby old geezer's land."

"Hey, I needed to protect my property. I remember meeting this woman who swore at my grandson about getting a gate attached to a post. The poor boy's been traumatized ever since."

We began to laugh. "Happier times."

"Anyway, you cast a line like a girl."

"I am a girl."

Colin stared ahead. "Oh really, I hadn't noticed."

"Uh-huh." I pointed to a window. "Would that be the plane?" A very new sleek modern jet pulled up outside the building.

Colin whistled. "Your chariot awaits." We stood, and I ran to the bathroom once again. I washed my face and checked my bag. Inside were my passport and the small box with my beautiful ring, which was supposed to be from Charlie. I pulled it out and, when I emerged from the bathroom, handed it to Colin. "I guess I need to return this."

He knew what it was. I loved it. If it was from Colin, I would have kept it for sure. He pulled out a similar box from his pocket. "Can we make a trade?" He handed me the box. I opened it, and it was almost an exact replica of the first ring, including the fish carved into the inside of the ring.

"Goddammit."

Colin stared at me in surprise. "What?"

"I'm trying to get a hold of my emotions, and when you do this..."

"It's not a proposal, Maggie. It's security. The proposal will come when I'm divorced and free."

I smiled, and we kissed. There were too many people, and they probably all worked for Charlie. The kiss was brief and sweet. The ring exchange was not apparent to the staff, and I doubted even Charlie would see the difference. "Okay, Mr. Chandler, you better walk like a man back to your helicopter while I go to my jet. Until we meet again. Please thank Charlie for me, and please get the heck out of there. I have a feeling he's going to implode. I don't want you and Luke caught in the crossfire."

I turned as I walked through the door to my waiting jet. Colin was standing watching me. He was still handsome and distinguished. *Please, God, just one year.* We waved to one another, each determined to get through what would be a difficult time for the other. *Please, God, one more request, let me be a compatible bone marrow donor for my sister.*

I didn't envy Colin's task either. He needed to leave and safely return stateside with Luke. Charlie had been more than gracious. Indeed, this trip would cost him a fortune. I was convinced he realized he'd lost my love, and yet here he was helping me to get to my critically ill sister. This made up for all the hell he put me through. Now he only needed to let Colin and Luke return home, and all his transgressions would be forgiven.

Charlie hoped I would go back and forth from summer to summer or hemisphere to hemisphere. Now he needed to make good on his promise. I think Charlie hated the lodge, yet it was purchased in a failed attempt to win me back. I wondered if he would sell it. What would Colin do? We were sadly confident that Charlie was on the wrong side of the law. Once it was determined that I could donate bone marrow, I would join with Colin, and we would do what was necessary. I prepared for any bumps in the road as we lifted off the tarmac.

Chapter 22

Wow, life at the top has its perks. You name it, and they had it on the plane. I could even make phone calls. Miles was so excited that I would be in San Francisco two days earlier than either he or I'd expected. Christy was holding her own, but she was sleeping most of the time. The kids had come home and were doting on her. The grandchildren weren't allowed to visit, as they might have bugs that could sicken Christy.

"I'm flying as fast as I can. See you soon, big guy."

"Can't thank you enough, Maggie. You know how much she loves you."

"Yes, I get it."

I then made a call I should have made a month ago. When I appeared to be back into cell phone coverage for my regular phone, I called the last FBI agent who'd taken over the kidnapping case. It was pretty simple. If Charlie was in protective company, I'm safe, and all is good. If he isn't, I have information vital to them. I can use that to protect Colin and Luke.

Two could play this game. If worse came to worst, I could say that Charlie was essentially holding me hostage. It was the middle of the night, and the number I rang had been changed, and there was a new number. I tried it, and it was a call center. This was strange. I wondered if my calls were monitored by someone on board the plane. I had an email address, and I sent an email asking for urgent contact.

I'd been given a small cubicle to myself. Two men, besides the pilots and a flight engineer, were on the jet, but they allowed me privacy. I was careful not to say anything that would arouse their suspicions. As we prepared to land in Honolulu International Airport, I returned to the main seating area and strapped in for a landing.

The attendant who sat next to me asked me where I was going. I explained I was catching a second flight to San Francisco. He asked me if I needed anything, and since I only had a small carrying case, I declined. He gave me directions to quickly clear customs to avoid missing my second flight.

"I don't know who you are, but you must be well-connected to get on board. We usually only have cargo." He adjusted his seat and signaled to another attendant to strap in as well.

"I'm a friend of a friend. This is a mercy trip. My sister is gravely ill, and I may be able to help her."

"Oh, I'm so sorry. If there's anything else we can do, please let us know."

"No, unless you want to donate some bone marrow."

"Uh, sorry. We're only moving cargo, and we'll be turning around in short order as soon as we change pilots."

"Wow, you work a lot of hours then."

"We get plenty of sleep. It's rare we actually have guests onboard since the old boss died."

"Oh, I didn't know. So, who owns it now?"

"Another company bought it, and we only know that it is then leased to some men who transport medical equipment and drugs to remote islands in the Pacific. It's been like this for years. We do the same work, but just for a different company."

"Nice. You must feel good about your work?"

"We do."

The plane landed before dawn, and after a long wait, we finally were able to disembark. Since it was near a freight terminal, mobile steps were brought up to the plane, and we all exited the plane together. The pilots and crew would stay in Hawaii, and a new group would take the plane back. The cargo was already being transported to an open bay.

I thanked everyone, and as we entered the building, we were all told to place our bags on a trolley, and we were escorted to a room off the entrance. Everyone appeared anxious, and I saw a significant change in the demeanor of the crew.

I was escorted through a small, designated area for inspection to clear customs. I was nervous and suspicious that what was on the plane might be contraband, but I sailed through. I was taken by a cart to the domestic terminal, and I was on a flight to San Francisco within an hour.

This flight was not packed, and I was separated from the next passenger by an empty seat. The petite woman in jeans smiled and returned to her magazine while I tried to sleep, but that was impossible. I was allowed to use my phone again, and I called Miles and assured him I was on my way. "Thanks, Maggie. We pray you're a match. She would kill me for saying it, but she's counting on you." *Pressure.*

"See you soon. Do you want me to catch a cab to the hospital?"

"No, Alex is going to pick you up."

"Alex, my nephew? I haven't seen him in five years."

"He'll recognize you. See you soon."

I had nothing better to do. I thought I would check on things. I called Carol, my real estate agent who sold me my cabin. She recognized my number and answered, "Haunted mansions are us. How may I direct your call?"

It did make me laugh. "Oh, darn. I thought I was calling the dodgy real estate grievance department. I have a complaint. Hey, well, since it's you. How are you?"

"Missing you. Hal has a new job, and he's gone more than before. How was New Zealand? Are you both back? How's Collie? We sure missed you guys."

"Collie's still there, and so's Luke. Helen sent him over." I fingered my ring and rolled it with my thumb. The feel of that ring gave me unending pleasure. "I'm flying from Hawaii to San Francisco to hopefully donate bone marrow to my sister. She has some form of leukemia and is in desperate need."

"Oh, Maggie. I'm so sorry. Is there anything I can do?"

"I think I'll do what I can and come home for a few days. I'm guessing my sister will be in isolation after the treatment. How's the snow?"

"Not bad. It snowed like heck when you left, and it's cold as the proverbial witch's, you know, but there's no snow predicted for the rest of the week. I can go and warm up the house if you know when you're coming for sure."

"Thanks, Carol. I'll let you know. Say 'hi' to everyone for me, please." After I hung up, I wished I'd asked about any news on Charlie. I wondered what the general public was hearing. I quickly searched the net and found only a short article on the demise of Charlie's philanthropic empire. It was titled, "How the mighty fall." This time my friend Sandy's nonprofit was mentioned. We were offered drinks and snacks. This allowed my fellow passenger a chance to talk.

"Hi. Are you heading home?" She turned to me when she passed me a tray of airline food.

"Yes. How about you?" Deflect and make it about them.

"I'm heading home to Iowa. I've been at a veterinary conference."

"Oh really, what was it about?"

"Ophthalmology."

"Interesting. Who was the lecturer?"

She said the name, but I was unfamiliar with her name.

"I'm Maggie Kincaid. I was a vet, but I retired last year."

"I know. You're kinda famous now, you know."

"More like infamous."

I extended my hand. We shook, and the woman replied, "Chelsea Drummond, pleased to meet you. I'm sorry, I couldn't help overhearing. Does your sister need a bone marrow transplant?"

"Yes. I was on a fishing vacation in New Zealand. My sister apparently began to show symptoms of what everyone thought was a nasty virus. Sadly, it appears to be far worse. I'm headed to see if I'm a match for the transplant. So do you know me for my books?"

"Yes and no."

"I'm not famous for much more than that." I'd been front-page news when I was abducted, but that kind of fame comes and goes quickly.

"I recognize you from your little adventure with some kidnappers. You're a vet, and that's why I remember you."

"Oh, yeah. I thought I was last week's news. So, what kind of veterinary practice do you work in?"

"Mixed. I see a lot of horses, but I see the whole barnyard. I know you only do horses. My boss is John Mitchell. I think he was in your class in vet school."

"You know John? How is he? Will you say 'hi' for me? Gosh, I haven't seen him for at least twenty years. It's such a small world."

"It is, for sure. I did like the book where your vet solves the mystery of the zookeeper who kills the animals for insurance."

"Kind of cringeworthy, actually. I got flak from that book. No one is ever going to kill animals for insurance again."

My phone vibrated. I checked, and it was an unlisted number. It might be my nephew, so I answered. "Hello?"

"Margaret, Maggie, Magster, Maggot, and I'm throwing in a new one, Magpie, and let's not forget darlin'. Where are you?"

"Over the Pacific Ocean and an hour to go. Miss you." Should I have said that? *Has he already moved on?* I rolled my ring with my thumb once again. *Waiting for a response—oh, please say you miss me too.*

"And beyond, darlin'." *Phew.*

"How are things, Collie? How's Luke? Have you been fishing? Are you packing?"

"I miss you too. We all miss you."

There was crackling in the connection. "Can you hear me?"

"I said I miss you too."

Which was so loud that Chelsea laughed and said, "He said he misses you." We both chuckled then.

"So, are you coming home any time soon?"

"We're having a blast. Luke caught a whopper yesterday, and we're going hunting tomorrow."

Chelsea shook her head, and I nodded. "He can't hear me." *Or could he?*

"Take care, Collie. Be careful with the gun." I closed my eyes. "Oh, God. Men and their weapons."

"My husband is the same." Chelsea asked if I wanted anything. I shook my head as she got up to use the bathroom.

I quickly checked the charge on my phone and noticed a message from Miles telling me that there was a change of plans and now he would come and get me. He asked me to wait outside the baggage claim area, and he would collect me.

Chelsea phoned her husband and told him she was sitting next to a celebrity. I rolled my eyes and shook my head. We talked about her children, who were approaching their teens.

"My commiserations. You're going to find the need to go to many out-of-town continuing educational junkets in the next few years. They're your only salvation. What does your husband do?"

"He's an orthodontist. I married him so I could get the kids' teeth fixed cheaply."

"So, he isn't their father?"

"No. My husband is definitely their father. We met when we both had braces. Those little bastards had no hope."

The announcement of our landing came over the speaker. I was relieved to finally be landing, and I would soon see my sister. "Thanks for the conversation. You were great fun. You should consider coming to visit us. I'd be glad to have you come for some fly-fishing tuition. Please give my best to your boss."

"By the direction that these kids are going, in two years, I'll be banging on your door."

We left each other as we entered the airport. Chelsea was catching another flight, and I was headed to the baggage claim. As I emerged from the building, Miles pulled up to the curb, and I got into his car, hugged him, and we took off. It was clear he'd been crying. I offered to drive, but he declined. "Maggie, it's bad. Real bad. Even if you're a match, it's fifty-fifty, and her doctor says it will be brutal."

"I'm so sorry for you all. I'm surprised the doctors aren't doing Christy's own stem cells."

"They are, but they want a backup. If you're a match, the oncologists will harvest your marrow stem cells and have them ready if hers aren't regenerating. She's already receiving chemo that will obliterate her own cancer cells. You're going to have to wear a gown and mask. She wants to see you as soon as possible."

We arrived at the hospital, and I was immediately swabbed, and blood was taken for matching. Miles then took me up to Christy's floor, where I was given a gown and mask, and he then ushered me into her room. Her daughter, Mandy, was by her side. Mandy stood up and hugged me. The last time I saw her was at her wedding. She now had two children. Christy was sleeping. Her face was bloated and pale, but she appeared to be pain-free. I whispered, "My turn. Go get something to eat and some sleep." She smiled, and we hugged again. She and Miles left the room.

I sat down and took Christy's hand. She squeezed it and whispered. "I effing had to try and die to finally get you to visit me, Maggot."

"Hey, big sis. Yep, you finally tricked me. Now get out of this damn bed and let's go have a glass of wine."

"Maybe tomorrow. I'm not feeling too good right now."

"What the hell Christy, you promised me we were going to Disneyland when I moved back. I left my kids and life in Australia to relive our youth, then you up and get sick. Well, I'm not buying it."

Bill and Lonnie entered. Our family has reunited once again. We hugged, and the tears began. We all had masks, gowns, and gloves. Totally off the wall, Bill, who has zero sense of humor, suggested we do a family Christmas picture. To my horror, Christy agreed, and we propped her up and took several photographs.

"What about Miles?"

Bill had a ready answer. "I'll photoshop him in."

I switched sides and resumed sitting next to my sister to hold hands. Christy jerked and looked at me. "What do I feel under that glove, Maggot?"

I smiled, and everyone could see my crow's feet. "It's a ring—a simple ring."

"Maggot, if I die and don't know what's going on, you can be sure I will haunt you down until you die."

"Haunt or hunt?"

"Haunt. Now I need details." However, Christy fell asleep before I even began.

We all retreated to a lounge for patients' families. Miles returned and explained that they would use Christy's own stem cells. Still, they wanted a backup, and if the family was willing to pay for it, we could use mine and bank it. They planned to take the bone marrow if I agreed. I would receive drugs to increase my marrow's quality, and the procedure would be done in a few days. If I wasn't a match, my marrow would be stored for someone else.

"Sure. What do I need to do?"

Miles took me to the nurse's station, and a nurse took me down to an office where Christy's doctor sat and was eating her lunch. We were introduced, and she asked me to sit down. She explained that Christy had acute myelogenous leukemia. Dr. Laura Hansen was a no-nonsense doctor. "Do you want the truth or the hard truth?"

"I'll take the hard truth."

"Do you have a medical background? I think Christy said you were a nurse?"

"Worse, horse vet, but I'm retired."

"Are you kidding me? Where are you from? Which practice were you in? I have a horse in Menlo Park."

"I practiced in Australia for over twenty-five years. Who's your vet?"

"Sarah Milligan. She's awesome. The problem is, she's due to foal, herself, in a few days, and my mare has a skin thing going on."

"Do you have any pictures?"

"Yep." Dr. Hansen opened her phone and showed me several pictures of her gray mare. "I don't have time to get away to meet the relief vet, and she won't come out unless I'm there with my credit card."

"Yeah, I wouldn't either. Doctors are the worst payers. It looks fungal. What have you used on it?"

"Well, funny, you should ask. It's from Australia, and it's a tea tree oil extract."

"That may be the problem. Half of my client's horses were allergic to tea tree oil. So, if it's no better, I would stop using that now. I can go look at it, but I am not licensed and can only offer you advice that would be only slightly better than your barn friends."

"I knock off at five. I can drive you there and back. I would be so appreciative."

We agreed to meet in the hospital parking lot, and then she gave me the talk about what I would expect if my bone marrow was to be taken and stored. I would be given some drugs to bolster my marrow. I agreed and filled out numerous consent forms.

"I guess the big question is the payment. How do I pay for this?"

"Oh, yes, that's a biggie. Let me take you down to the accounting department." She ate her sandwich while we went down to the second floor, and she took me into a room where several people were sitting behind a glass plate. I was asked to wait while Christy's account was pulled up. Dr. Hansen explained to the accounting department personnel that I was to have a bone marrow extraction procedure in a few days, and I wanted to pay upfront.

The woman who was behind the plate brought up Christy's account. "No need. She has an open credit card. It's all being paid for, and there are no other costs."

"I want to pay for this part. Can you give me an amount?"

"I'm under strict instructions that, since yesterday, an anonymous donor said no money is to be charged to the family. I'm not at liberty to say where it's coming from."

Dr. Hansen whistled. "You guys must have some wealthy friends."

"I guess. I'll have to ask my brother-in-law. How much would this cost?"

The woman peered onto her screen, "A couple hundred thousand. That's without insurance or Medicare. You're set up to three hundred thousand."

I wondered if Miles knew about this and where this was coming from. "Well, thank you."

Dr. Hansen left and said she had a gray Prius, and she would pick me up next to the park-n-pay bay on the first floor. I returned to the oncology floor. Everyone was outside Christy's door. The nurses were changing her, and they asked Miles and Bill to step out. Lonnie was still in the room.

"Miles, did you rob a bank?"

"No, why?" He stared down the hall to a room where someone had died and was being removed. He shook his head.

"I went to put some money toward my surgery, and there's a paid balance of up to three hundred thousand."

He didn't bat an eye. "It's a mistake. A nice mistake, but a mistake for sure. Nobody loves me that much."

I instantly knew who paid for it. "Okay. It's probably an error. Anyway, I'm scheduled for half-past eight in three days, and I'm going out to see Dr. Hansen's horse in Menlo Park this evening." We returned to Christy's room, and she asked me again about the ring. I couldn't talk about Charlie, but Colin was fair game.

"It's complicated."

"I don't have time for complicated. Where did it come from?"

"Colin Chandler."

"What about his wife? Hell, what about his ex-wife? What about his age?"

"All factors to consider. The current wife is asking for a divorce. Ex-wife sent Luke to me and asked me to consider Colin as a potential suitor, as she is not divorcing her current. As far as age, I advise you to try and keep up with him. Then there's Luke, who is coming back to live with Colin and wants to live with me too."

Lonnie propped Christy's head with a pillow. "Then there are those sticky, obnoxious questions, such as does he love you, do you love him, and is he trying to live off your inheritance?"

"Yes, yes, and who knows. Colin did fly me first class to New Zealand, and then we took a private plane to the South Island and then a helicopter to a private lodge where we were the only guests. I made it clear that if we joined forces, I wouldn't be paying for first class."

"Let's see it." I took off the glove for a minute while everyone gazed at the ring, and I showed them the inner carvings. Christy examined it and then said, "Is he for real?"

"I think so. That's not an engagement ring. It's an 'until he is a free man' ring. This necklace goes with it." I pulled out the necklace hanging under my sweater.

"I must say, he has good taste."

"I'm pretty sure Helen helped him."

Christy replaced the ring on my finger and promptly fell asleep. I could feel my phone vibrate. Again, it was an unlisted number.

"Maggie? Hi, it's Helen. Collie called me and told me about your sister. Am I interrupting? How's your sister? He said it's a little awkward at the lodge. He asked me to call and see if you need anything. I can't thank you enough for everything. I love that man, but not like I love Roberto."

"Helen, it doesn't look good, but they are doing a stem cell transplant, and they are harvesting my cells for a backup, as well. I'll have a quick anesthetic in a few days, and then my marrow will be processed for freezing. I'll hang around for a few days after the procedure, but then they say she will have to be in isolation. I'll head back to my place. Where's Baxter? Are you in LA?"

"Baxter is back at my place. I have the staff caring for him. I fly back to my place tomorrow, and I will be there for a week, but then we are heading down to our other ranch and getting out of the winter. These winters aren't easy when you hit the big eight-o."

"Helen, are you sure this is what you want? I know Collie loves you, and it would only take a phone call, and he'd be on a plane."

"Maggie, I am only going to say this one more time. I don't love Collie like that and haven't for years. He doesn't love me that way either and hasn't since he met you. If I hear any more, I swear I'm coming over and kicking your ass, and don't think I can't."

"Uh, yes, ma'am."

"And don't call me 'ma'am.' You aren't that much younger than me."

"Helen?"

"Yeah?"

"Thanks. I'm a bit thick. I'm slow off the mark and somewhat cautious, but I do love Collie, and despite my lack of maturity, I'll try and keep up with him and make him happy."

"Other way around, Maggie. Let him make you happy. He's had a great life. It's your turn now—no more catch and release. One of you needs to reel the other into the net. Let Collie and Luke try to spoil you. Thanks for Luke too. I know you'll give him the guidance he needs. I'm so happy he found you. Don't make me call you again. Am I clear?"

"Loud and clear." I knew better than to say, ma'am. *Sheesh, these old people...*

I looked at my watch. It was time to meet Dr. Hansen and see her horse. I said goodbye to Christy, who was eating yogurt, and hugged the rest of my family. The Prius arrived twenty minutes late. "Sorry, I should have taken your number and told you I would call you when I was finally ready."

"No prob, I charge by the minute."

"Would you like some healthy takeaway?"

"Do tacos qualify?" *Please say yes.*

"No. Well, only if you are donating marrow. Name your poison, Doc."

I pointed to my usual fast-food preference and mentioned we don't have it in Australia. "And thanks, but I'm not really a vet anymore, and even if I was, Maggie is my name."

"Oh, phew. I didn't want to offend you. I go by Laura to my friends and fellow taco consumers. So glad you chose this."

Laura told me about her life and passion. She described growing up in rural Northern California to become the town doctor. "I had an oncology rotation in my last year of medical school, and any dreams of an easy life went down the drain. I 'womaned up' and did all the training to cure cancer. I was never going into clinical practice, but the damned people are so nice. Here I am trying my best and losing half the time."

"Well, I'm glad you're here. Win or lose, my sister will go down fighting, and she's happy you're on her team. Me too."

"Your sister says you were engaged to some billionaire who was killed in a plane accident. Is that his ring?"

"Uh, no." I gazed down at the ring and smiled. "It's from a close friend. It's complicated. Nice complicated, but complicated, nonetheless. How about you? Have you got someone to share the load?"

"I'm gay. And yes, my partner shares the load. She's a good person, but you know. We have our ups and downs."

"My only marriage was like that. I hope yours turns out better than mine. My ex had problems sharing me with my other marriage, my work. Would that be something we share in common?" I glanced over and saw her wince. "It seems to me you have a higher calling than many, and you have to decide what is the best way to use your time on this earth. My kids would say I was a failure at motherhood. Here's the thing. Only you can decide what makes you happy. I was married to my work, and for better or for worse, I was happy.

"My ex wasn't around after the divorce. He and his partner moved away. The funny thing is the kids don't resent him, but they resent me as I occasionally didn't make it for school events. You can't always win, so if I may give you a small amount of motherly advice. Go on a vacation with her and see if the extra time together makes her happier. It never worked for me."

Laura turned into the driveway of her boarding stable. "Yeah, I kinda think it won't work for me either."

"There is one more suggestion. Are you listening?"

"Yes, ma'am." She turned off the engine.

"If you go on a holiday before Christy is stable and recovering, I will not be impressed. I'm always looking for names of villains for my books. Laura Hansen is an excellent name for a character who murders nurses out of vengeance." Laura quickly went to the back of the barn and brought out her Arabian mare.

The mare looked older than the photo in Laura's office. Either she was rapidly graying, or her winter coat was much lighter. "Did you say she's eight? How long did you say you had her?"

"Yes, and then add three years. Tilly only began to show symptoms this last month. So far, no one was able to diagnose this."

"Does she go out with other horses during the day?" I had a funny feeling this would not be fun—nothing like a contagious condition to raise the anxiety in a boarding stable.

"She did until she got this, then she was banned."

"My eyes are old, and even with glasses, I can't see close-up things. Can I borrow your phone?" I zeroed in on her mane and forelock and took two pictures, and then with the lens zoomed in, I shot a video. I smiled and then cringed, knowing this horse and her owner would be boarding stable pariahs.

"Laura, your mare has lice." I laughed, but true to boarding stable etiquette, Laura was horrified and turned to two other boarders lurking.

"You need to worm her with an ivermectin-based wormer, and I don't know what you have that will treat lice, but I'm sure you can get some from your vet or a feed store. You all need to check your horses. If they were all out at the same time, there's a reasonable chance more horses are infected."

"Oh, my God. I'm so embarrassed," whispered Laura as she turned to the two women standing away from us. "Will you tell them?"

I walked over to the two women. "Good news. It's only lice." The women then brought their horses over and asked me to examine them. I explained I am not a practicing vet, and I am only advising Laura as a friend. I showed them all how to look for the eggs called nits and how to treat them. I explained there was a cycle, and unless they treated them again in ten days with a product that would kill the nits, they were doomed to have a resurgence.

They had nothing to treat them in the barn. So, one of the women would go to the feed store in the morning. She would treat the two infected horses, and Laura could pay her later. They offered to pay me, but I declined. It was beginning to rain as we drove back to the city. Laura asked where I was sleeping, and I instructed her to take me to a motel near the hospital.

Laura offered me a bed at her house for the night. Usually, I would politely decline, and then there would be some back and forth until I agreed to accept the offer, but I was jet-lagged. "I would appreciate it. I would kill for sleep."

It was almost nine o'clock, and so I quickly called Miles. Christy was resting comfortably, and Bill and Lonnie had gone to Miles and Christy's house for the evening. They had moved out of the city, and the commute was now forty-five minutes. I explained I was staying with Christy's doctor tonight but would stay with them tomorrow.

Laura's apartment was across town but in a safe area. We entered the house and found her roommate was gone but left a note saying she was visiting her parents in Sacramento and would be back on the weekend. Laura shook her head. "If you can believe that."

"I take it that you don't?"

"She's seeing someone else."

"I'm so sorry." I could have said to move on or many other things, but this was a process, and she wasn't ready for options. She sadly had to go through the hurt and pain. When I was young and dating, I remembered the rejections. There was no reasoning with me when a relationship ended. It was the end of the world. It made me think about Colin. I would love to hear from him. Was it him or Charlie who had made the financial arrangement for me to donate my marrow? I sent him a message explaining I would be having my bone marrow extracted in a few days, and I would leave a message when I was finished. I asked if he had left or was planning to leave soon.

Chapter 23

I visited Christy and my family over the next few days and took the medication to booster my marrow. The evening before my procedure, Laura asked me to examine her mare and ensure no more active lice. In the end, I reviewed eighteen horses at the boarding stables.

The owners had been told I would be there and had wine and cheese for the event. It was fun. Most of the owners were women, but two gay guys had two miniature horses. We discussed the glory days when everyone wanted a mini. Now they couldn't give them away. They didn't care—they loved their horses. I teased the gathered crowd. "You guys are hard-pressed for entertainment if nitpicking is a wine and cheese event." The pun was acknowledged.

I stayed at Laura's once again, and sadly her roommate had not returned. Laura dropped me at the hospital and left me to go get breakfast. She promised to buy a bear claw to have after my procedure. My marrow extraction was first on the docket. I'd been asked to check in early. My family was already in Christy's room when I arrived at six in the morning. They were drinking coffee and eating cinnamon rolls.

"This is cruel. You all ought to be shot."

Bill came over and hugged me. "I'll treat you to dinner tonight. It's the best I can do." I hugged Christy, told her to stand by for launch, and left them.

The nurses were professional and kind. They explained what would happen and introduced me to the anesthesia team, who took me to change into a gown and robe, catheterized me, and left me in a small room. I checked my phone for any messages. There was only one from my vet friend, Mac, saying that Duchess, the mare with gastric cancer, had passed last night, and Geoff wanted me to know he was grateful for my help. He was joining the local fly-fishing club.

I quickly wrote back. *Oh, no. I've created an addict. Crack would be cheaper and so much more satisfying.* I was then summoned to begin the final prep for my short procedure. I was placed on a gurney and taken into a room with overhead lights and anesthetic machines. It was cold and not inspiring at all. The hospital needed an upgrade. The room reminded me of something you would see in the last century. They even had old radiograph viewers still mounted on the walls next to the digital screens.

I saw a syringe of a milky white substance sitting on a tray next to me. I turned to the anesthetist and asked. "Propofol?"

"Yep, nothing but the best for a donor." She smiled as she injected me and asked me to count to ten.

I began to say, "Yeah, right." But when I tried to form the words, I realized I was in the recovery room, and a man was sitting next to me. He was in a long gown, mask, and hat. I was so grateful that Bill had come and sat with me. I took his hand and went back to sleep.

A very rude nurse woke me up once more and said I'd taken up all the time I was allotted in her life, and I was instructed to wake up and get the heck out of her ward. She smiled as she said this. Bill squeezed my hand and bent over to kiss me. I realized it wasn't Bill. It was Colin. Wow, that woke me up. We kissed through his mask, and two of the nurses clapped.

"Oh, to wake up from a kiss from Colin Chandler," called one of the nurses from the other side of the room.

"I only have kisses for one woman these days, sorry, ladies."

A male nurse shouted, "Does that mean I'm out of luck too?"

Colin was quick to answer. "You never know your luck."

"Okay, she seems awake enough to go back to her room." The nurse and Colin helped me off the gurney and onto a wheelchair. As the three of us left the room, the nurse turned back to the other people in the recovery room and said, "I may never be back. I think this woman might need round-the-clock care."

We left to hoots, and one of the nurses commented. "The real hero today is our bone marrow donor." Everyone stopped and clapped.

I was taken to a small room with a bed and chair. Colin was allowed to remove his mask, and he kissed me one more time while he held my hand. I dozed and then opened my eyes and realized that I'd been joined by Luke and my family.

I was told Christy was going into isolation, and only Miles would be with her. He would call us daily but suggested we go home. They were going to fight like hell. With my potential bone marrow in the bank, they always had plan B if she didn't respond to her own transplant. I was allowed one more visit. I was hellaciously sore from my procedure, so Colin wheeled me down to Christy's room. He stayed outside when I saw her for what might be our last visit.

As I entered, she smiled and waved to Colin, standing outside the room observing us through the glass windowpane. She motioned for him to come in. He shook his head. "Maggot, he's almost family. Tell him to get his sorry ass in here."

I went out into the corridor. "Christy says, and I quote, get your sorry ass in here."

He came in and stood by the door. I took Christy's hand, and she felt my hand and said, "Is the engagement off?"

"I had to remove all my jewelry when I went into the operating room. I think it's in a security vault."

Colin reached into his pocket and showed Christy my necklace and ring. "She's not getting away that easily—no catch and release in this family. Christy, you can count on me to keep her safe. In these modern times, I suppose I should ask both you and Bill for permission to marry her, but I can't yet, so when I can, will you give me permission?"

"I don't know, Colin. What makes you think she'll agree. She's fairly independent, and she can be tough. What do you have to offer?"

"Well, it won't be a lifetime, but I have a nice new fishing rod, eternal permission to fish on my"—he paused—"on our property and of course Luke and Digger."

I turned to Christy and reached back and took Colin's hand with my free hand. I whispered, "Christy, if you don't say yes, I'm going to jump on top of you and drool in your face."

The poignancy of this moment was not lost on me. Christy appeared to consider his offer. "Uh, okay, I guess. I should probably conference with Bill first."

Colin smiled, although we could only see his eyes. "Well, I may have already discussed the subject with him, and he said it was up to you."

I turned from Christy, who I could see was smiling under her mask. "Do I have any say in this?" I was happy that Colin had asked them both. It was old-fashioned but still such a respectful and kind gesture.

"Not at this stage. You haven't been formally asked." Colin squeezed my hand as he said it. "We may have to get Luke's permission too."

Christy was asleep when we turned back to her. I knew I wasn't supposed to kiss her, so I got up, returned to my wheelchair, and we left, knowing it might be the last time I talked to her. Colin wheeled me out of the room and bent over, and wrapped his arms around me. He didn't usually carry a handkerchief, so he reached for a tissue at the nurse's station. "Am I going to have to carry a damned snot rag for you the rest of my life?"

"It might be handy when you get to the drooling stage." Colin pinched my shoulder. "Ouch, I'm calling the elder abuse hotline."

"I can see I'm going to need to get that number on speed dial too."

We turned to the family waiting room. Luke was sitting with Lonnie and Bill. He stood up and asked how Christy was. "Grandpa and I missed you, Maggie."

Christy's children were also banned, and they asked about their mother.

"If I said she was a cantankerous bitch, would that make you all happy?"

Miles came over and hugged me. "That's my wife, for sure. Maggie, I'm going into isolation in a few minutes so let me hug you and thank you. Colin, all the best. These two women are hell on wheels, and I must sit down and give you the owner's manual for marrying a Kincaid." He turned to Lonnie. "On second thought, which might kill the deal. I'll send it to you after the cooling-off period. I want rights for river access as well." Colin and Miles hugged. "Thanks for your contribution. I'll let you know how that goes."

Colin took me back to my hospital room. We would get my clothes and walking papers, come back for Luke, and head to a motel to wait for a flight back to the ranch tomorrow. "Want to tell me about your contribution?"

"It's between Miles and me, darlin'. Some things in our relationship aren't up for discussion. You're going to have to get used to that. I'm a modern man, but I have my limits."

"I suppose we both have our limits, but I'm willing to consider options if you are too."

Colin smiled. "Certainly, let me help you out of your gown and into your street clothes."

"Not gonna happen, Collie. Seeing an old lady naked would make you run for the hills. That's going to have to wait."

"Aren't all things up for negotiation?" He pretended to be crestfallen.

"Oh my God, that's right, I'm marrying an actor. Many have tried to break my resolve, but few have succeeded." I waved him out the door.

"Surely, you understand who you're marrying? We could live in sin. I could be happy with that."

That made me grin. "I love sin. No prob with me, either. What about Luke? He seems to have some ancient concept of marriage being important in the relationship of two people?"

"We better stick to plan A then. I'll be back in a few minutes. I need to see someone. I only hope you don't continue to drain my funds. Maybe you could write another book?"

Chapter 24

"**M**aggie, you're free to go. We got a great sample, and so far, your testing shows you're a potential donor. But we won't know for sure for a while yet. The excellent news is we found patient zero, and it's not my horse. I'm off the hook for the stable gossip crowd. Measures are now being undertaken, and everyone is sending me text messages thanking me for inviting you to come to the stable."

"Yes, lice can be insidious. They carry diseases, and I'm sure this is worth waving all the fees for my sister and round-the-clock vigils in trying to save her." I hugged my new friend, Laura, and reminded her I was always available for a call and wished her good luck with her quest to find true love. "It only took me thirty years. The day is young."

"Thanks. Good luck with your relationship too. Your fiancé is quite a catch, you know. Even at his age, the nurses are all swooning."

"It will be a miracle if I can keep him when there are so many babes out there willing to steal him away. I'll have to stay on my toes to run interference."

Colin had entered, overheard the conversation, replied, "I wish. Sadly, Maggie's the only one who will have me and can hold a fishing rod and think at the same time."

Remembering the comment I made at the lodge, I burst out laughing. "Laura, have you met the famous, at least in his own mind, Colin Chandler?"

Laura asked for a photograph. I brought out my phone, and Colin moved behind her. "Uh, no. I want one with Maggie."

I shook my head. "Hysterical. Darling, I guess you're going to have to get used to this."

Colin chuckled and took my phone. "I can hardly wait." He took two snaps of Laura and me and then a selfie with the three of us. I knew she wanted one of him and her, so I took one as well, and we did a transfer of the pictures, including the photos of the lice.

We picked up Luke and said goodbye to everyone. "Bill, please stay safe. Let's call at least once a year."

Lonnie said she would be in charge from now on, and we would talk as needed. Luke hugged Lonnie and Bill and fist-bumped his soon-to-be cousins. Christy's adult children were in saying goodbye to their mom.

Colin had secured a two-bedroom small suite at the Fairmont. Neither of us was dressed for dining out, so we had room service. We ordered pizza, but when I went to shower, Colin changed the order to crab and sourdough bread. I was happily surprised. I was still slightly sleepy from my anesthesia and the drugs for my postoperative pain from the needle punctures.

"Hey, you two, I hate to eat and run, but I need to sleep for a while. I'm sorry to leave this social, but I'm exhausted. We have an early start, so I would suggest, and it's only a suggestion, that you two get some sleep. Sweet dreams." I kissed them both and went to my room. I took a heavy pain pill that Laura ordered for me and was zonked for hours.

I woke up and felt Luke next to me. I batted him away, but he put his hand on my waist. "Luke, piss off."

"Okay, I'll leave." But it wasn't Luke's voice, and when I felt it, it wasn't a boy's hand.

I smiled, knowing who my guest was. "Ah, sorry. Room service. Excellent. You can stay. Be careful, though. There may be a jealous man in the other room." I attempted to turn over, but lying on the other leg was painful, so I reached back, put my hand on his hand, and shifted back so we could spoon.

"I'll only stay for a few minutes. I missed you."

He kissed the back of my neck, which sent chills through me. "If the good-looking guy in the other room comes in, I don't want to get in a fight. I hear he can be very jealous."

Colin rubbed my shoulder. "You seem pretty tough too."

I ached, and touching my skin was almost painful. "Maybe you could come around on the other side, and I could rub your back."

"Darlin'. There would be no going back from a back rub. Can I get you anything? We need to get up in thirty minutes."

"Bugger. So disappointing."

"That's an Australian expression?"

"Yes. An expression of extreme frustration—so close, and yet so far. Some Tylenol would be good, though."

Colin brought me some coffee and Tylenol. "Is there something I can do to make it better?" I almost felt feverish, and my throat was still sore from the intubation when I was under anesthesia.

"Oh, yes, but not with a young boy next door and a twenty-minute time frame. No, piss off. If you get caught in my room, I'm going to say—"

Colin bent over and kissed me and said, "You're safe for now, but don't expect me to be a gentleman again."

"Here's hoping." I smiled as he went to wake up Luke. *God, I love that man.*

There was the elephant in the room, and we both knew we needed to acknowledge it. Colin hadn't mentioned Charlie. Why had Charlie let us all go? Did Colin have any more details about Charlie's story that he was in witness protection? Luke came into the room as Colin was leaving. He got into bed and under the covers.

Colin observed us. "Luke, she's my girl. Think twice about treading on my woman. You need to get up and into the shower. We're leaving in fifteen minutes."

Fifteen minutes! "Me too. Both of you get out while I get dressed."

A limousine was waiting for us as we walked through the foyer. "There's a first time for everything." I was impressed.

"Not for me, Maggie. I've been in one before. Haven't I, Grandpa?"

"Several, Luke. Let Maggie decide where she wants to sit."

I had not considered Colin's wealth. I guessed in comparison to Charlie's, it was minuscule. I knew that I could afford to carry us both until our death on my savings. I could probably get Luke through college, and if things imploded, I could count on my book income to get us through the next few years. We could go on a few trips each year and even visit the kids in Australia once a year. I didn't ask Colin about his financial status. Hopefully, Colin was not living on his last earnings.

Several people said hello to him as we walked through and entered our ride to the airport. A woman who appeared in her forties and had several bags came out to the pickup zone and became distressed when she realized the taxi she'd called was delayed. Colin looked at me a nodded. He knew what I was thinking. "Excuse me. We're headed to the airport, and if you don't mind, we'd be happy to take you."

"Luke, move over here, next to me, so our guest can sit on her own. Hi, I'm Maggie. This is Luke and Colin."

Colin tipped the hat he'd worn and then removed it. He asked her where she was headed and what terminal she needed. It was raining heavily, and the dampness made us all chilled. My hips were sore, and I was trying to make myself comfortable. My sore throat was getting worse, and I began to doubt this was from an endotracheal tube. I was glad I didn't kiss Christy. I was convinced I was getting sick.

The woman was thankful, and clearly, she had no idea who Colin was. She said she was headed to Chicago to see her ill father, who was not expected to live more than a few days. The woman worked for an advertising agency and was schmoozing a client in California. Her mother had died last year, and the woman said she was her father's only living relative.

I extended my hand. "I am so sorry. Is there anything we can do to help you?" I watched Luke and Colin shake their heads. I knew they were both thinking, *here she goes again.* I ignored their stares and told the woman that we could leave her off first if she would be late for her flight. Quietly Colin took my hand.

"This is why I'm in love with this woman, Luke." I squeezed his hand back. Luke rolled his eyes. The woman looked up at us, and then she realized who Colin was.

"Oh my God. It's you, isn't it? I can't believe it." She was suddenly shy and embarrassed. "I'm so sorry to interfere in your private life."

My phone rang. It was Miles giving me an update on Christy's condition. She was now getting her own stem cells, and she wanted to talk to me. "If I'm not the matron of honor, I will take you down, Maggot, and you know I can do it."

"He has to ask me first."

Colin could hear the conversation, and he took the phone from me. "Done deal, Christy, but you better get healthy. As soon as I'm free, I'll be whisking her off to the county courthouse."

"Not gonna happen, Collie. I want a wedding in the garden."

Luke took the phone. "Hi Christy, it's Luke. Grandpa says we have to do whatever Maggie wants, so I hope you're better soon."

Christy replied, "Luke, thanks. I'm sorry I couldn't see you yesterday."

"Christy, if you're the bridesmaid, I'm going to be the best man." Luke was already planning a wedding and his role. This time I rolled my eyes.

Our guest looked at us and realized she must be overhearing gossip many people would want to hear. "Your privacy is safe with me. I'll need to plan, so have you set a date? What color are the bridesmaid dresses? I look good in teal." This made us all laugh.

Colin shook his head again. "I haven't asked her yet."

"So, you're planning a wedding, and the bride hasn't been—"

"I haven't said yes yet, either."

The woman looked confused. "Well, your secret is safe with me. Have you been visiting a sick friend?"

"My sister," but I paused, and then the tears started.

Colin had tissues in his pocket. He put his arm around me, and Luke took my other hand. My loss of control was only momentary. I asked the woman about her father to get my mind off my sister.

"He was a biochemist and worked at Northwestern University and oversaw a laboratory studying the suppression of stem cells in blood disorders. Her sister died of leukemia when they were young. I'm guessing that's what your sister has?"

We nodded. "Your sister is so lucky. When my sister got it, there wasn't much that could be done." She went on to say her sister died at nine years of age. We exchanged emails when we arrived at her terminal and wished her well.

As we approached our drop-off, Colin asked Luke and me to go through the check-in, and we proceeded to the VIP lounge. He would come in after. "I'll explain later." I could see he was nervous about asking us to do this. I began to feel feverish, and my surgical sites were increasingly painful.

Luke seemed to take it in stride. "I'll keep her safe."

"Thanks, Luke." Colin patted him on his shoulder as we left the limo to enter the airport. He squeezed my hand as I emerged from the vehicle and waved goodbye.

We went to the counter and were taken directly to the VIP lounge. Colin joined us a few minutes later. "I hated doing that, but if my soon-to-be ex knows there is another woman in my life, it could be expensive." I still had no idea about Colin's financial status. I'd heard about many faded movie stars who had burned through their money and lived in poverty. I would be happy to support him.

"Don't worry, Collie. I'll take care of you."

He could see I was genuinely concerned, and he laughed. "We need to have a serious talk, Maggie. Thanks, your offer is truly appreciated. Hopefully, I won't take you up on that. Let's get home. I hope we don't have to dip into your funds, but who knows how life turns out sometimes."

"We won't starve. I can always catch some trout for dinner. Now that I've been first class, I'm going to struggle to go back into the cattle cars, though."

We did go back into the economy seating on that flight. Colin saw three returned servicemen and asked the ground crew to exchange our seats for the servicemen so they could sit in our first-class seats. No one knew who had sacrificed their seats, and of course, Colin was recognized by many of the passengers. Luke sat between us, and no one knew we were together.

We arrived in the state capital and were met by our helicopter pilot, Doug. By the time we arrived back at Colin's ranch, it was clear that I was sick. I had a fever and was seconds away from vomiting, and my throat felt like a five-alarm fire. My hips were aching, and all I wanted to do was get to my house, vomit, and sleep. Two out of three ain't bad. There was no way that Colin and Luke would let me go and be by myself.

"Like hell, Maggot. Get into bed now. I'm calling Eric. You need his doctoring services."

"I would prefer his trout guiding services, but I agree."

Colin spun me around and propelled me into a large bedroom with a fireplace and a bathroom the size of my bedroom. I barely made it to the toilet to relieve myself. Colin held back my hair, and I vomited several times. He left me to dress. I was in bed and almost asleep when he returned. "Eric will be here soon. If I get you some Tylenol, will you keep it down?"

"I think I'm done with the vomitorium. I'm so sorry for all of this." I reached out and then thought about Colin catching whatever I had. "Collie, it's probably too late, but I don't want to pass it on. How about I." I wasn't allowed to finish. Colin put his finger on my lips.

"We're in this together, darlin'—in sickness and in health. Besides, with you as sick as you are, I may get to see you naked."

My eyes were closed. "Collie, picture me rolling my eyes under my lids."

"Oh, I'm picturing you, but it isn't your eyes I'm picturing." It did make me smile.

Eric arrived and woke me up. "As the town doctor, I would say you have the flu, and I would not be too concerned, but as your fishing partner, I'm going to take some blood, and I want to see your surgical sites to make sure they aren't infected. I can't afford to lose you, Maggie."

Eric said the puncture sites on my hips were not the source of the infection, and my throat screamed a strep infection. He advised us not to share glassware and not to kiss. He peered at us both and shook his head. "I'm too late, aren't I? You damn kids. Colin, let me have a look at your throat. You both are too old for this nonsense. I'm going to send over some antibiotics for you both. In the meantime, Maggie, you're getting an injection."

"Shit, that hurt, Eric. Don't expect me to go fishing with you anytime soon."

Colin held my hand. "Eric, take her whenever you want. We're forever grateful that you came. She's become a precious commodity."

Eric left, and Luke came in but was stopped at the door. "She's contagious, son, and off-limits for forty-eight hours. Let's see if Doug or Gabe has time to take you to your grandmother's and get your things and Baxter. If not, you and I'll drive there tomorrow."

Gabe was the military-trained ranch hand who worked for Colin. As a side job, he protected Luke from his previous encounter as a witness to his mother's drug dealings and murder.

"I should be right by tomorrow. Lukey and I can go there and get his gear." I was already feeling better.

"Not on your life, Maggot. You need to get some sleep. Give me your phone too."

"You better be careful too, Collie. If you start to feel bad, let me know straight away."

"Grandpa, did Maggie get a shot?"

"Yes, right in her backside. I saw it."

"Did not." I was sure he hadn't.

"It's a nice backside for such an old woman, though." He ducked as I threw a pillow in his direction.

Chapter 25

Colin had a sore throat the following morning. I was much better, so we reversed roles. I cared for him as he took to the bed. For a man, and an old one at that, he wasn't too bad. He only mentioned how he thought he might die once an hour. I got a lot of eye-roll practice that day. I crashed again in the afternoon. Luke had gone to Helen's to retrieve his clothes, books, and Baxter. Mrs. Gillard, Colin's cook, was sent home to protect her from this mildly contagious form of what Colin called people strangles—insert another eye-roll from me.

"Collie, you're close. They are both streptococci, but we don't get abscesses as horses do."

We both had fevers and could hardly eat or swallow. Due to our age, Eric came back. Colin was in bed under the sheets, and I lay on top of the bed under a heavy blanket. Eric had a few things to say about this, but he could not dissuade either of us from moving. Luke will not be back until tomorrow. Colin groaned. "I get you all alone and the whole house to ourselves, and this is the best we can do. Kill me now."

"Certainly not, Collie. Not until you're divorced, and we are married."

"If I died today, you'd be set for life. That's already been sorted, darlin'."

"Just for the record, I don't want you to die ever, but if you don't stop talking and let me sleep, I may have to kill you." I turned away and buried myself inside the fleece blanket. "Consider yourself kissed, Mr. Chandler."

"You too, Dr. Kincaid."

The following day we were both better. Last night there was a massive snowstorm, and Luke and Gabe couldn't return to the ranch. Colin showed signs of cabin fever, and despite his mild illness, he was like a caged bear. I wanted to walk over to my house, but Colin said it was crazy. He knew me well enough to only suggest I might die if I tried it. I did heed his warning. "Do you want to talk about Charlie?" I sat sipping hot lemon and water. Colin had some as well but added whiskey to his drink.

"I've been dreading this conversation. I'm afraid of what it might do to me and you."

"Why?"

"Maggie, it's all true. Everything he said was true. He's in witness protection. He's a good guy, and he's under threat from the cartel again. The cartel people know he's alive, and the agents came the day before we left and took him without notice. The two guys you met were from the cartel, not FBI agents, and they weren't working for Charlie. Knowing all of this, will you stay with me?"

"Well, are your intentions to make a better fisherwoman out of me? I'm not settling for marriage when it's the casting skills I'm after. You must understand that don't you? You're a smart, talented, good-looking man, but it's your casting lessons that make you the obvious choice, Collie."

Colin roared. "Charlie said you were a mercenary. He said you would wear me down. He also mentioned he still loved you and would do anything to change this last year."

"Too late. I'm putting love aside for right now. I'm looking for fishing lessons and lust." I patted his arm. "And a beautiful, adopted grandson probably tipped the odds in your favor."

We weren't kissing lip to lip until we had the all-clear from Eric. Colin did take me in his arms, spun me around, and took my arm in the position for casting a fly rod. With his left hand, he may have adopted a placement that would not enhance my fishing skills at all. I didn't mind.

My brother-in-law called, disrupting our lesson. "They're done with the infusion, and they said it would now take some time to see if it is going to work, or failing that, they are going to use your donated bone marrow. She wants to talk to you."

There was some shuffling, and a weak voice came in the line. "Maggot, how are things?"

"I'm doing better. I contracted strep throat somewhere. How's your throat? How are you feeling?" I prayed I didn't pass it onto her or anyone in California.

"Oh, no. We're fine. Did Colin get it too?"

"Sadly, yes. We've been nursing one another depending on who's the sickest. I'm staying at Colin's house for another day. We had a massive snowstorm. Poor Luke went to get his clothes and Baxter for me, and he's stuck at Helen's. They'll be able to come back tomorrow."

"Are you and Colin stuck in his house alone? I hope he's taking advantage of you, Maggot."

"He's trying, in between his fever or mine. We aren't a lot of fun right now, one fishing lesson aside." As I said that, Colin pulled me down onto his lap and took the phone. I was close and could hear the entire conversation.

"Christy, don't believe a word she says. I'm too old not to be the perfect gentleman."

Christy replied, "Colin, don't waste too much time on civility. Life's short and precious. She's worked her butt off, as you can see. She needs to have some fun and joy in her life now. She's earned it."

"Christy, I'll get right onto that project. A couple more days, and we should be back to normal. Take care and rest. Let Miles do the hard yards for you."

We hung up, and there I was, sitting in Colin Chandler's lap. He kissed me on the forehead and mentioned he was now under orders to spoil me.

"I would kill for some hot chocolate and a back rub." Colin got up while I lay down under a blanket in front of the fire. When he returned, apparently, I was asleep. I did wake for a second while Colin placed the blanket up around my neck. I heard him mention that he still owed me a back rub as he left the room.

Later we discussed Charlie once again. "Collie, did you tell him about us?"

"I didn't need to, darlin'. Charlie knew."

Colin got up from the sofa that was moved closer to the fire and placed two more logs on the iron grill. "I don't need to tell you, but he's gone. The FBI was on their way when Luke and I left. Charlie was going to be moved, and this time we won't know where."

"God, it's got to be lonely. I do feel sorry for him. What about his lodge?"

"Sometimes, it amazes me how thick you are." He sat down next to me again, and I put my legs over his.

I was hurt. "What do you mean by that?"

Colin could immediately see the sting of that phrase. "Darlin', the lodge is yours. He gave you that lodge. He would never take it back. I know Charlie, and he has a long game plan. He'll wait for me to die, and then he'll woo you back to his side."

"I'm going to stop you right there. First, I will not let you die anytime soon. Second, I'm not chattel, and I will not be handed down from one man to the next. Am I clear?"

I started to get up, but he pulled me into his arms and kissed the back of my neck. He laughed. "I win that bet. Too bad it may be a year before I'm able to collect."

"I should kick both of your—" Colin put his hand over my mouth.

"Let's have a little decorum here."

"Donkeys, kick both your donkeys. Oh, you didn't think I was going to say A double S, did you?"

Luke arrived two days later and brought Baxter into the house. The reunion was as expected. Poor Baxter ran between Luke and me and couldn't decide where to sit. I went up to the barn and saw Digger for the first time. He appeared to be recovered from his illness and was happy for any attention. Gabe said they took him out and lunged him daily.

I decided to have a quick ride. My hips had been almost pain-free since my bone marrow procedure. My saddle was still at my house, so Gabe found one that would fit me. It was comfortable and was much nicer than my own. I laughed to myself, thinking this was another reason to marry this man.

Gabe peered at me and cocked his head. "What's so funny?"

"I stole his horse, and now I may have to steal this saddle." There would be no mention of the growing relationship between Colin and me until his divorce was all but a done deal.

"Apparently, it was Luke's mother's saddle. I think the boss would be glad it's getting some use. I'll oil it for you if you think you would like to use it."

"We better ask him first. He may want to save it for Luke."

I climbed on Digger, and that familiar feel of a well-trained horse under my legs reminded me of how much I loved this gelding. I patted his neck and then circled him and gradually trotted and loped around the indoor arena. *God, I love this horse.*

Colin came up and stood outside the arena and watched me riding. "You look great in that saddle. I think it's yours to use. How about you let an old man have a go?"

I returned Digger to the wash bay, and we changed saddles, and using the same mounting block, that I used, Colin mounted Digger. Colin walked around, then gradually put Digger through his paces. He performed a stock horse routine with sliding stops and spins.

"I am impressed, Mr. Chandler. You're not just a movie cowboy, are you?" That brought a smile, and Gabe tipped his hat.

"The boss is our top hand. We all take a back seat when he decides to ride."

I took Digger back to the wash bay after Colin dismounted. "I see riding lessons in my future as well." Colin got the joke, and fortunately, Gabe didn't.

"So much to teach you and so little time, darlin'."

Mrs. Gillard was back on duty. She rang a bell to indicate lunch was ready. I decided to have lunch and then go over to my place and spend a day or two—nothing like a separation to keep the romance going. I loved my house, but Colin's bedroom with the fireplace and enormous space was clearly becoming my favorite place to hang out. He'd set up a small table for me to use for my laptop.

I announced my plans, and both Luke and Colin protested. I promised to be a regular guest, but I didn't want tongues wagging, and Baxter could come and go. I knew he would choose to stay with Luke. Colin was concerned about me being alone. Both he and Luke insisted I take Baxter, and we would leave the gate open from now on. Colin was going to call his lawyers tomorrow and find out what was happening with the divorce proceedings. Colin poured me more juice. "At least we have your family on our side."

"Collie, that was only the first barrier. You haven't met the real obstacle. Wait until you meet my kids. They play for blood and take no prisoners. My sister and brother are amateurs compared to my kids."

Colin shook his head. "I'm beginning to think you may not be worth it. What do you say, Luke?"

"Can't you two just live in sin? Everyone else does it."

I spewed peas out of my mouth, and Colin pretended to cuff him.

"Lukey Boy, you may be onto something." I winked at Colin. "On second thought, I might not get the tuition on casting, and now riding, I need to improve my skills."

Colin stared at me without a smile. "I have certain standards, and living in sin is not one of them. Are we clear?"

I glanced up at him and noticed the edges of his mouth twitch as he suppressed a smile. "Yes, sir, crystal." I got up, took my valise, and headed to the door. "Later, dudes. Dinner at my place tomorrow."

Chapter 26

 oth Luke and Colin stayed away the rest of the day. Colin called me and told me he had to tie Luke to a stake. "I kinda had to stake myself out too."

"Collie, I miss you and Luke too. I do love my home, but without you here, it's kind of lonely. And don't ask me to elaborate on what kind of lonely. I'm still too sick for that kind of lonely." I coughed to emphasize that I was still sick.

"And that's why they call it the weaker sex." Colin snorted.

"We'll review that in ten years, mister." Now I laughed.

"Maggie, should we be planning a trip to Australia to meet your children?"

"Do you have a death wish?"

"No, but I have an"—he paused—"I think you call it an inner sanctum wish."

"Visiting my kids will not get you into the inner sanctum. It might get you killed, but as soon as I am healthy, you will receive the gold pass."

"Maggie, I don't deserve you. How did I get so lucky?"

"Clean living and the truth. Oh, Digger the wonder horse and access to your river doesn't hurt either. The truth is, I'm madly in love with you. I'd take a bullet for you if I had to."

"That only happens in the movies. Any chance we can have an old-fashioned date this week?"

I could hear coughing in the background. "Is that Luke or your secret lover, I hear."

"The terrible news is I think it's either Luke or Mrs. Gillard. I hope they aren't coming down with this."

"If it's Luke, we need to get him on antibiotics quickly. Will you go check? I'll wait on the line." I waited for what seemed like an hour.

"Luke has a fever and a sore throat."

"Biosecurity fail—how did we let that happen? I'll come over."

"It kills me to say no, but I don't want you out again. It's snowing something fierce. I'll give Luke some Tylenol and one of my tablets. If he needs to go to the doctor, I'll call you in the morning."

"Oh, already telling me what I can and can't do. I'm going to have to begin the cowboy retraining program earlier than I'd planned."

"Good luck with that venture, darlin'. Many have tried."

"Sweet dreams, beautiful boy."

"You too, darlin' girl."

I couldn't wait for a phone call. The snow was impressive, and it took me great effort to get over to the ranch the following day. I was soaked through, and Colin and Luke were asleep in Colin's bed. I quietly entered and felt Luke's forehead. He was burning up but smiled at me when he opened his eyes. I put my finger over my lips, so Luke wouldn't wake his grandfather. I went to the bathroom and found some Tylenol, Colin's antibiotic tablets, a glass of water and returned to Luke. Colin turned over and shot up when he saw me.

"Maggie, what the hell?"

"Call me Flo." Colin got the reference to Florence Nightingale. "You know I'm an early riser. I couldn't rest until I knew Luke was okay. Which I may add, he is not."

"Should we call Eric now or wait until his office is open?"

"I just gave him some of your antibiotics. Let's see how that goes, and we'll wait until the office opens."

Colin hadn't opened the curtains. "How much did it snow last night? I see your legs are wet."

"Not as much as the other night. I'm sure we can go to his office, but he may just prescribe more antibiotics, and I can go get some."

"I don't want you driving in the snow until I give you some instructions. Make a list of what you need, and one of the men or I can drive to town to get supplies."

"You must know I bristle at receiving instructions like that, but it's true. I don't have a clue about driving in snow. I'm soaking wet, and I'm going home to get some dry clothes. I'll see you in an hour or two."

"Happy to help you with those wet clothes, Maggie." Colin smiled mischievously.

"Grandpa!" Luke looked at his grandfather.

I was secretly pleased. "Luke, your grandfather is only trying to help."

I leaned over the bed, high-fived Colin, and left. "Another day."

When I left Colin's house, the snow was falling once again. It was exciting for me after never living in the snow. I was glad I didn't work in it, but as a tourist, I enjoyed the novelty. I knew it wouldn't be long before it would be more of a burden than a blessing.

It was apparent I required waterproof clothes if I was going to slog around in the snow. I saw a trip to the big smoke with retail therapy in the next week or so. I called Carol Carter to thank her for heating my house while I was gone and to report in.

"Maggie Kincaid back on duty." I tried to sound casual.

"Maggie Kincaid? Do I know you? I used to know someone with that name, but then they flew off to who knows where, and we haven't seen or heard from her. Or are you the Maggie Kincaid who is reportedly shacking up with one of our county's most famous citizens?"

"This is the one who flew off and disappeared and now is back with the living. No shacking up here, but the day is young, and all systems are set to go." I coughed to emphasize my lingering illness.

"Would you care to elaborate?"

"Over a glass of wine and dinner. I need my hair done, and I think I still owe you for the last job. The bad news is, I'm sick and contagious, and that may be where the shacking up story came from. Colin, Luke, and I have been in New Zealand. Then there's my sister, and now I'm home, and the fog has lifted. Amazing how fishing can take a bedridden zombie and put new life into a body."

"Or pending nuptials with an old film star? Would you care to elaborate?"

"It's a bit early on that front, but I won't deny the subject is being discussed. How is Hal's new job?"

"Fine, and don't think you can change the subject that easily."

"Okay, how about I come over next week when I'm not contagious, and then we plan a dinner with you guys and the Wests later in the week?"

"Not sure if I can wait."

"Collie and I have a very catchy strep throat. Luke came down with it late last night. If you want to come over, I would love to get my hair done."

"Uh, no thanks. The local gossipers can wait. Do you think you'll be safe next Wednesday, and then we can have dinner at my place on Friday? Will you be bringing anyone?"

"I hope so, but we shall see. Colin and I would love to host you all."

I told her about Christy and mentioned I fished with Colin and later Luke in New Zealand and briefly mentioned my work at the veterinary clinic. I didn't discuss anything about the fishing lodge or Charlie.

Carol said she'd call Sylvia and Trent. They didn't know that Charlie orchestrated my abduction in a faux money laundering scheme or that he was alive and not killed in a plane crash, as reported. Charlie would give evidence to put many people in jail from all government levels in the US and abroad. I suspected Carol knew about the drug running stories and CLM Enterprises. I didn't broach the topic.

I then Zoomed my kids and told them about their Aunt Christy and explained that I had to cut my fishing trip short to come back and donate bone marrow. They forgave me for not visiting them and promised we would all get together for Christmas next year. "If I could come next month, could I entice you all to meet somewhere?"

The hands-down vote was for Hamilton Island. Oh, surprise, they couldn't see me for Christmas, but they could all get away from work and school. "And can the kids come too?"

"Mum, is there someone you want to tell us about?" They'd all talked to their uncles. "We heard there was a new man in your life. Uncle Miles and Uncle Bill said they were sworn to secrecy. Is it serious? Can you afford to pay for us all to meet there?"

"Well, that's what this trip would be about. I'm free any time, so can you all agree on a date that would be good for you? I know the kids go back to school in February, so when are the next holidays?" The kids said they weren't sure, and they would get back to me.

Colin called me and said that Luke was already feeling better. Betty Lou, who was on maternity leave, was going into town to get the antibiotics and paracetamol. Betty Lou was getting close to giving birth, and she had an appointment with Eric anyway. She'd pick up the prescription and run by the pharmacy for Luke's antibiotics. Betty Lou only had a few days to go, so she was steering clear of anyone who was ill.

"Collie, should I come over? The snow's piling up. I'd hate for you two to need me, and I'm stuck over here."

"Maggie, stay where you are. As much as I want to be with you, Luke and I can get through this." I could hear Luke coughing in the background.

Luke's voice was weak and interspersed with paroxysmal coughing. "Maggie, I want you here. Please come back. Grandpa doesn't know how to care for sick kids, and Mrs. Gillard's been sent home."

"Okay, your call, mister."

"I'm outnumbered. Damn, I guess you win. Bring some extra clothes. I'll meet you at the gate."

"Collie, I don't want to risk you getting any sicker. I'll be over in an hour."

"Thanks, darlin'. I think Luke should get an Academy Award for that performance. I'll overlook it all, though. I'd rather have you here, anyway."

"Hmm, runs in the family? See you soon, beautiful boy."

I entered the house an hour later. I changed into sweats in the laundry. I quietly walked up to Colin's bedroom. Luke was sleeping on the sofa in front of the fireplace. I felt his forehead, and it was much cooler. I sat down, and he put his head on my lap. I looked up at Colin, who smiled and left the room. I began to tickle Luke's back as my mother had done to us all, even when we were older and in college.

Luke was in heaven. "Please don't stop. Where have you been all my life? I love you Maggie, please don't go away again." This poor kid was starved for attention and maternal care.

"Luke, back tickling is one of the great pleasures of life. While no one can tickle your back like me, anyone can do it. I'll show your grandpa how. He can do it."

Colin stood in the doorway holding three cups of boiling water and the mixes for either lemonade or chocolate. "I'm not sure I like this method of healing the unwell."

"Grandpa, it's so nice you should let Maggie tickle your back someday." Colin almost dropped the tray while I stifled a laugh.

"Okay, Lukey Boy, sit up and scoot down so I can have some hot chocolate." Colin sat on the sofa next to me. We drank in silence and stared at the fire.

"I talked to my kids this morning. They're up for a trip to Hamilton Island in March. Would that work for you?"

Luke glanced at me. "Where's Hamilton Island?"

Both Colin and I answered, "Australia."

"Can't they go sooner? I sure wouldn't mind escaping the snow again." Colin pulled a blanket over us all, quietly took his free hand, and rubbed my thigh under the blanket. I looked at him with an expression of caution and pleasure. He ignored the cautionary look, and his hand strayed higher up my leg. I took my free hand and pushed his hand down to a more respectable area.

Luke was totally unaware of this and asked if he could go with us to Australia. Colin took the cue. "If you leave the room now and don't come back until morning, I'll consider it."

"Colin Chandler, you need a good thrashing." I now took his hand and pulled it out from under the blanket. "Lukey, want me to tickle your back again?"

Colin interjected. "Luke, I would strongly advise you to say no, if you ever want to see Australia."

I got up and said we were all having an early night, and I was headed to the kitchen to find us all some dinner. Luke only wanted soup, and Colin said Mrs. Gillard had prepared some pork and potatoes that only needed microwaving. "Does Mrs. Gillard come with the package?"

"Darlin', I'm not into threesomes." Which made me spew my potatoes while Luke gasped in horror. *Lesson learned—this kid knows more than I did at his age.* Colin got the look from me, and he nodded.

We watched an old movie and then sent Luke to bed. I bent over and kissed him goodnight. Luke snuggled down into his blankets. "Maggie, promise me you'll be here in the morning."

"Scouts honor, Lukey Boy." I tucked him in and stood up. Colin was at the door observing this ritual which I had performed a million times with my children. He smiled, and we both went into the great room.

"You know I heard you promise him. I would never break a promise to a child like that."

"No, that could be devastating to such a vulnerable young boy. I'll be here in the morning." He took me in his arms and kissed me.

"Finally, we are alone and almost healthy. With this snow, there's no escape. Any chance I could get my back tickled too?"

"I'm considering it. You know back tickles aren't free. It's a reciprocal action. I tickle your back, and you tickle mine."

"I'm willing to learn." Colin motioned me to sit down and the leather couch. "Shall we discuss a trip to Australia first?"

"Seriously, you want to discuss trips right now?"

"I received a call from my lawyers in the UK. She's finally ready to make a deal. I may be able to make an honest woman out of you."

"Excellent news, sire. I'm pretty sure I am still an honest woman. I may not be able to say that in the morning, though."

"Hopefully." But his phone rang, and it was not good news.

Chapter 27

"God damn it. And she doesn't think she can get here? How long has she been in labor? Okay. We'll be up in a minute."

I didn't hear the other side of the conversation. It sounded like Betty Lou was in labor, and she couldn't get to the hospital. I was panicked. "Colin, I've never delivered a—"

"You've never delivered a foal?"

"A foal? I thought it was Betty Lou."

"Tell me you've delivered a foal. Please."

"Hundreds. I'll head up to the barn. You can stay with Luke."

"Not on your life, darlin'. Let's get some warmer clothes on and go."

"No time. I need thin clothes on if I'm going to get a feel around inside. I'll wear my jacket up to the barn. Let's ride, cowboy."

We walk-ran to the barn. While neither of us was fit due to our recent infections, Colin quickly surpassed me. "I want to look at your birth certificate when we get back to the house," I gasped.

"I want to look at much more interesting things, myself."

We entered the barn, and Gabe and two other ranch hands attempted to restrain the mare as she lay rolling on the ground. They'd already wrapped her tail, and there was a box of gloves leftover from when Digger was ill. The men had also prepared a bucket of warm water with a disinfectant. They had calving chains in a separate bucket.

As I removed my ring and watch, I quietly mumbled to myself a phrase I often used when I arrived on a property to perform a difficult task. "Showtime." The mare was in a fair amount of pain, and when I took her tail in my left hand, she stood up. As I entered her vagina with my gloved arm, she began to go down, but the men kept her standing by pushing against her shoulders and flanks.

I felt around and tried to get my bearings. The initial examination was often tricky. I wanted to feel two legs and a head. It usually took me a minute or two to figure out what was really presented. If it was a single leg, was it a front or a hind leg? If it was three legs, where was the head, and which was the odd leg? Was it two hind legs and one front leg or the reverse, with two front and one hind?

There were presentations that I knew were doomed without a cesarean section. If I feel a back with no head or extremities, I usually suggest euthanasia or surgery. I frequently preface this with my favorite phrase, "never say never." Still, in my thirty-five years of working as a horse vet, I don't remember extracting a foal from a mare with that presentation.

I finally felt I had this orientation as a head and front limb coming through the vaginal vault and one leg back at the shoulder. I could reach into the uterus and feel the forelimb of the mispositioned leg. However, as I pushed past the pelvic brim, the mare would contract and crush my arm against the bony pelvis, causing extreme pain.

I felt no movement from the foal and assumed it was probably dead. I'd learned that lesson years ago. So, when one of the men asked if it was alive, I replied with a shrug. I needed to get my hand in and guide a chain around the forelimb of the flexed leg. I suggested we let her go down on the ground. I would have killed for an anesthetic. I was going to be down on the stall floor, and even if she rolled, I would not usually be in danger of getting kicked, but again, never say never.

The mare was becoming exhausted, and she lay on her side without rolling. I lubricated my gloved arm and attempted to slip a chain over the foal's flexed limb. I hoped it would drop underneath the limb as I fed more and more chain around the leg. Then I could catch the enlarged end of the chain link from the other side with my finger and pull it through. The mare allowed me to do this for a few minutes. I couldn't get the chain to drop through from underneath the malpositioned leg, and the mare eventually rolled.

The men attempted to keep the mare's hooves from hitting me, and even Colin grabbed my legs and pulled me away. In the new position, I had a better chance of placing the chain and threading it through to the other side. I paused for a second for her to settle, replaced my glove, and added more lubricant. I reached into the vagina and advanced into the mare's uterus. Using my fingers, I pushed the chain between the amnion portion of the placenta and the limb itself.

This time I was successful and could get my finger into the last ring on the chain from the opposite side of the foal's flexed limb. With all the strength I could muster, I pulled the end of the chain out of the mare. I secured it by threading the external end of the chain through the large loop on the opposite end. I now had a chokehold on the malpositioned leg.

We then attached hooks to the chain, and I asked the men to gently pull on the chain as I once again reached in and attempted to guide the leg out past the pelvic brim. This time the mare reacted and kicked back and caught me in the chest. It wasn't a hard kick, but it knocked the wind out of me, and I gasped for a second. Colin pulled me away, but as I regained my breath, I gasped. "I've almost got it. We can let her stand, and I think we can get it out." Colin was propping me, but he reluctantly let me go.

The mare wouldn't stand, so Gabe put a rope around her back pastern and held it so she couldn't kick. I was too sore from the kick, but I did reach in, and as the men pulled on the chain, I was able to grab the fetlock and guide it over the pelvic brim. I placed a chain on the other leg, and I scooted back while the men quickly pulled the foal out of the mare.

The foal was alive, and it blinked and gasped as I removed the amnion that still miraculously covered its head. I was exhausted, and my sternum was killing me. It was painful to breathe. Colin put his hands under my armpits and pulled me to a standing position. I stepped out of the stall. "Jesus, I'm way too old for this. I sure as hell hope Luke decides to go to vet school."

I went over to a chair and sat down while Colin and the men attended the mare and foal.

"Colt or filly?" I asked.

"Colt. He's gigantic," responded one of the men.

It took everything I had to talk. My chest was so sore. "I can't believe this foal's alive. How long were we at this?"

"An hour at least." I could see Gabe placing disinfectant on the umbilicus as it broke when the mare stood up.

"Collie, who is this mare? Are there others that are due to foal?" I realized I didn't know how many horses Colin owned.

"I bought her before our fishing trip. Digger isn't going to last forever, and I knew I needed to have a good riding horse to keep you coming over here."

"You could have planted a redwood tree too. That would have kept me coming."

I stood up and kissed Colin full on the lips in front of everyone. This brought a few whistles. I went to the barn door and noticed the colt did look like Digger and had similar markings. I could feel my emotions getting the better of me, and I turned to go back to the house.

Chapter 28

Another night of unrequited love. We walked into the warm house. I was wet with placental fluids and snow from our walk back.

"I hate to ask this, but let me see your chest."

"Nice try. I need a shower. My hands were swollen, and my arms were red and would be bruised tomorrow from having them crushed so hard between the foal and mare's bony pelvis.

"Let's compromise. You jump in the shower, and I'll draw a bath for you with Epsom salts, and you can soak after you get the dirt and smell off you. Deal?"

"Promise not to watch?"

"No. I certainly don't promise. I'm eighty years old, and you are ten years younger than me. I want to look at you every chance I get. You need to get over yourself. You are the most beautiful woman on earth in my eyes, and I don't see you as old. Now go get in the shower. I'm going to get some pain meds and a brandy. Prepare to be spoiled."

I grinned. "Could you put that in writing?"

I received the no-prisoners-taken look and turned sharply toward the shower. I stripped down and left my bloody and wet clothes in a heap. I went to turn on the shower, but it was electric. Colin came up behind me and, leaning over me, reached in and touched the control panel. "This is the start button, and these buttons here control the temperature. Hurry up before I take advantage of your position." I emerged from the shower five minutes later and climbed into the bath. Colin had turned down the lights and lit two candles. He began to sponge me until he saw my chest, where a large bruise formed between my breasts. I took a hand towel and covered the area.

"On a scale—" Colin started to ask, but I interrupted his question. I knew he was going to ask how much pain I was in.

"Eleven."

"I think you need an x-ray." He felt the area without touching my breasts. "Have you ever had anything like that happen before?"

"Not from a foaling."

Colin started the water jets on the tub and left. "I'll take you into the hospital in the morning."

An hour later, I lay in bed next to the man I was growing to love more by the hour. I was drugged to the hilt and felt no pain as long as I lay flat on my back. "So, what shall we call the colt?" Gabe had called and said he was standing, nursing, and even cantered around his mother.

Colin squeezed my hand. "Special Delivery?"

"Uh, no. Nope. Shall we let Luke name him? Luke's going to be furious that we didn't call him to come and watch."

Colin groaned. "Yeah, I'll let you tell him. Maggie, when can we go to Australia? I want to meet your children. I know I can win them over. They can't be any tougher than you. Can they?"

"I'm a walk in the park, in comparison. The grandkids have school, but I'm sure they could come if we set a date during the school holidays, and I tell them it's my shout. I mean, we pay for the accommodations. I need to meet your other son as well. Have you told Jake yet? How is all of this going to go down with your boys?"

"Jake keeps asking me when am I going to get the courage to tell you how I feel. He's fine, and Kyle will love you. You can meet him when we go through LA to Australia. I mean to talk to you about finances. I keep forgetting."

"Collie, don't worry. We may not be wealthy like Charlie was or is, but I can always go back to work in an advisory capacity. We won't starve."

He laughed and said he would "open the books" tomorrow after I saw Eric. "You're seeing far too much of that man for my liking."

"And he is seeing far too much of me for my liking as well." I pulled up the top of my gown and peered at my swollen sternum. "I think I'm growing a third boob."

Colin leaned over and stared down at my chest. "I wish."

I was sore and battered the following day. It hurt to move and even sit on the toilet, and my arms were now obviously bruised. I took ibuprofen and slowly attempted to dress. Colin was keen to help, and he held out my bra. "Let me help you."

"They will be free today, Collie. There is no way I can have pressure around there. If you see them hanging below my shirt, let me know."

"I'll keep an eye out. I called Eric's clinic, and he wants you to go get an x-ray before he sees you. The boys are clearing the road so we can get out of here. Luke's going to have to come with us as I don't want him to stay alone, and I don't want anyone else getting strep throat."

I put on a shirt and pants. Bending to put on my socks was an effort. If the pain from the dystocia was unbearable, it paled in comparison to Luke's disappointment in missing the ordeal. We got into Colin's SUV and drove up to the barn. I slowly got out and entered the barn. The mare and foal had been moved to a larger stall, where the foal was sleeping. I wanted to perform a colostrum test on the colt. I needed blood from the foal, and I would take it into Eric's sister's veterinary clinic. Patty Tilmouth could run the test to ensure the colt had enough colostrum to give it adequate immunity.

"Luke, foals get all their immunity from the mother's first milk, which is called colostrum. The milk is rich in antibodies or immunoglobulins. The antibodies have about six to twelve hours to pass through the intestinal wall after a foal is born. If there isn't good colostrum, or if the foal doesn't drink in time, it is immunocompromised. So, we can test that in the foal's blood. You can hold the mare, and Gabe can hang onto the foal, and I will get the blood.

"The foal looks healthy, but you can't tell from the outside. Until the foal is infected with a bacteria or virus, it can look healthy. That's why we will run the test. If the foal has low or no immunoglobulins, the condition is called FPT or failure of passive transfer. Are you paying attention, Luke? There will be a test tonight. No more back tickling until you can show me you understand."

Colin nodded. "You know what she means, son. She's tough, and I wouldn't want to cross her."

It was painful to take the blood, and I didn't spend too much time observing the foal. I did see the colt was mildly knocked kneed, but we could deal with this later. We drove to the vet clinic, and Colin took the blood inside. He returned with Patty, who came out to say how sorry she was to miss the event. I told her about the presentation and said it was a fluke that I got hit by the mare's hock. We agreed to have lunch next week when I felt better.

"We need to talk. We've missed you. Glad to see Colin has you getting out in the world again."

"Me too, but I'm seeing way too much of your brother, considering it isn't even fishing season."

Colin drove us to the hospital in the neighboring town. I was radiographed and sent to Eric's clinic back in our rural community. I saw the radiographs and knew there were no fractures. I'd been kicked in the head once. While my hands protected my skull, the blow caused me to separate my ribs from my sternum. This wasn't as bad. I suspected it might only be a few ribs. While coughing and laughing was painful with a capital P and was annoying on many levels, it would not take long to heal. The implication for Colin's entry to the inner sanctum being delayed once again was obvious. I suspected he understood.

Eric looked at the radiograph, which had been sent to his computer. He gently pulled up my shirt and looked at my bruised chest. "Do you realize how lucky you are?" We both knew what he was thinking, and I had to try not to laugh. "Three more months until the fishing season, Maggie. What if this had been the opening day of the season? I guess you know the drill, rest, rest, and then rest." Eric followed me out to the car where Colin and Luke were waiting due to their strep throats.

"Colin, the less she does in the next two weeks, the faster she'll heal. I need her ready for fishing in April. I'm counting on you to make sure she doesn't lift a finger until she feels good enough to hold a rod." Of course, this made me laugh, which caused me to go into a spasm of pain in an attempt to stifle my reaction.

Colin whispered into Eric's ear, and Eric nodded. "Yes, that's a great idea."

They both laughed, and we drove back to the pharmacy to get more supplies. Patty messaged me to say the colostrum test showed suitable antibodies. All that was left was to go home and rest. I was a willing participant in that aspect of my recovery. It had been hard to sleep last night with breathing so painful. It's incredible how much a normal finding on a radiograph reduces the pain. I went back to Colin's ranch and fell asleep in seconds.

I slept through lunch and didn't wake until the late afternoon. Colin was gone, and Mrs. Gillard was back and wearing a mask. She brought me some fruit salad and coffee. I struggled to get out of bed and wandered around the house. I walked into Colin's office and was reminded that several months ago, I had been summoned to this room to discuss hiding Luke by taking him to Australia. I remembered his vast library. I picked up a book I had read many years ago. I decided to reread the book.

I sat on the sofa in Colin's bedroom. Baxter was sitting on the floor next to me. I dozed off and on. The medication for pain made me sleepy. I woke to both Luke and Colin holding flowers and standing in front of me. "Oh, you shouldn't have." I was so pleased to see Colin educating Luke in the finer art of making a woman happy.

"We want you to feel at home and welcome, darlin'. Unless you don't want to be here, this is your home now too."

"Please say yes." Luke appeared worried. "We need you."

"We love you." Colin bent down and kissed my forehead. "Eric thought this would be a good idea too. He reached into a bag and pulled out some medicinal ointment. "It's to be applied frequently to the affected area."

"Don't make me laugh. If you guys make me laugh, I'll go back to my place, quick smart."

"Luke, go up and tell Gabe the foal is fine. Take my phone and get some pictures for me. I need to talk to Maggie alone."

"Yes, sir. Is this about Australia? Can I come too?"

"Not if you aren't out of here by the time I count to ten—seven, eight, nine."

"How are you really, darlin'? Do you feel like a serious discussion?" Colin picked up the book I had taken from his library. "*40 Years' Gatherin's*, one of my favorite books. You'll love it. I met the author."

"I have the same book at home. I loved it too. Maybe we could read some to Luke. Okay, shoot. What did you want to discuss? You know I've done many difficult foalings, and I can be fairly sore the next day. It's just my chest and ribs. I'm predicting I'll be back in the saddle in a week or less. Are you planning on breeding any more mares?"

"After last night, I doubt it. It was so hard to watch you struggling with that mare floundering around in pain and you dodging her legs. I know I'm too old for that. How about you?"

"I know it looked bad, and we did get lucky, but one hock to the chest aside, I have to say it was one of the most satisfying moments in my retirement. I wanted to save that mare and foal for you, Collie."

"I've meant to talk to you about all the essential things. It's time you know the facts, so you can stop worrying. I know you're in the dark about many aspects of my life, but there is one thing you need to know. The richer and poorer thing—darlin', there ain't no poorer. I'm not poor, and you won't ever have to pay for anything by working. I've been lucky, and I've accumulated assets—lots of assets. If I was doing a movie that I knew was good, I deferred payment for a piece of the profit. If it was a stinker, I would take a salary upfront. I still get royalties from all the television work and many movies. The Comstock royalties are particularly rewarding. We won't starve.

"I've already changed my will. My children get the beach house, Luke gets this ranch, and you'll have income from the royalties until you die, and then this will be split as a percentage, and one-third will go to your children. You keep all your assets, and you get all the royalties from your books. I don't do movies anymore, but Charlie taught me well. I oversee my, I mean our, investments daily. I know how to manage them, and I want to show you if you'd care to learn. You don't have to worry anymore, darlin'. I have this covered. Oh, and the lodge is really yours. I paid off Charlie for the property. I hope we can use it in the January and February months, although we will have to work something out with Luke and his schooling.

"So, what I'm saying is, I am informally asking you to marry me. My divorce should be completed in two months, and then we are free to marry. That's if your children agree to let me marry you."

I sat without any comment until he was finished. He was now down on his knee while I sat on the sofa. I was shocked beyond anything I could ever imagine. It would not have changed my feelings if he had said that he was in debt to the mob. This was no time to make a joke, or tease, or do anything but say, "Yes. A million times, yes."

"Several million, darlin'. Several."

"Colin Chandler, I don't care about your money. I love the current Colin Chandler, not the dashing sexiest-man-alive guy. It isn't your money or Luke or anything else. It's you."

Colin joined me on the sofa. "You know I could fall off the perch without notice. I won't be around for very long, and who knows if my brain will function toward the end, anyway."

"The same could be said for me too. If we can enjoy a few years together, and help Luke get launched, then it will all be worth it. But sometimes, life isn't fair. If I go first, I'd want you to be free to seek out anyone else that might make your aching bones more comfortable. I don't know what you were like in your zenith, but you are humble, caring, and funny. The feel of you standing behind me, helping me cast a line, was the best moment, last night aside, I've had in years. Give it all to your children. I'd like to keep my house next door. When you die, I'll go back and live out my days there, and maybe I might keep the lodge in New Zealand as well. I won't be marrying anyone else. Remember, that's if we survive telling my children."

Colin stood up, bent over, and kissed me. "I love you, Margaret, Maggie, Magster, Maggot, darlin'. I'm a bit old-fashioned. Any chance you could become a Chandler?"

"Is that the name you were born with?"

"No, it was Smith, but it is who I am."

"Luke isn't a Chandler. I'll take the name if we make sure he is given the same opportunity."

"Oh my God. Let the negotiations begin. Do I have a say in anything?" Colin shook his head and pretended to hit his forehead with the palm of his hand.

"I'll give you a list. My ex and my kids would say I take no prisoners. I like to think I'm open to change."

Colin stared away for a moment, and I could see he was considering his following words. "Can we switch sides on the sleeping arrangement? I'm an old man, and I need to be close to the bathroom."

"Oh, nothing like asking for the big stuff upfront. What do I get in return?"

"I'll learn to tickle your back."

"Deal. Hmm, so many contentious issues to negotiate. I would prefer to stay in the background. Is that all right with you? I'd like to see this beach house, though. And remember, if Ryan Reynolds or Bob shows up, you need to—"

"Make me a list, darlin'. I want to call my kids and tell Luke the good news. Luke knew what I was up to, and he promised to stay away until the negotiations were done."

"The negotiations won't ever be done, Collie. You do know who you are marrying, don't you?"

"For better or for worse."

I coughed twice, and I started to get up and get more pain medication, but Colin saw my pain and brought me a tablet and a glass of water. "I love you, darlin' girl."

"You too, beautiful boy."

Chapter 29

Two days later, I had tickets to Australia and was comfortable enough to have Carol do my hair. She came to the ranch, and we set up shop in the basement bathroom. Colin was gone for the day, and Luke was enrolled in the local school. He had advanced enough that he was moved up a grade. Despite being a year younger, he was tall enough to fit in. Carol and I rescheduled the dinner for Saturday night here at Colin's ranch. Eric, his sister, Patty, and her husband, and Sylvia and Trent West were now invited.

"Details Kincaid, I need details." I knew she was referring to my new relationship with Colin, but I feigned ignorance.

"Well, he is a cute little sorrel colt, and his markings are a—ouch." Carol hit me on my arm with her hairbrush.

"You know what I want to know. Don't mess with me. I'm making up the color. I'm really into purple."

"Don't you dare! Okay, I was under the influence of a lot of medicine from getting my ribs separated from my sternum. I was not thinking correctly, and he took advantage, and he proposed. Well, kind of. He still wants to formally propose when he is officially divorced. I said yes. Is that enough?"

"Not hardly. Any major plans or concessions? Any romantic details?"

"I really was under the influence. Have you ever had a rib and sternal separation? Do you know how hard it is to cough or laugh? He got down on his knee. We had a crane come in to help him back up."

Carol shook her head. "That man is fitter than you and me together."

"We discussed some of the more contentious issues, such as who sleeps on what side of the bed and how I want nothing to do with his Hollywood social life. You know, no red-carpet stuff. I did agree to a picture of us fly-fishing together."

"Oh, how romantic. Probably something that should be made into a movie." I could hear the droll tone in her affirmation.

"Sandra Bullock can play me. Oh, and I told him all plans are off if Ryan Reynolds comes calling."

Carol ran her fingers through my hair. "Still not ready to admit you are old and gray? I picture you more of an aging Melissa McCarthy kind of character."

"Hold that thought. Melissa's wit and comedic timing would be good. How about Diane Keaton for me?"

"Not you, me. I've always thought Diane Keaton could play me." Carol attempted to comb out the knots in my hair.

"Of course." I rolled my eyes, and Carol whacked me with her hairbrush again.

"Seriously, in a million years, who could've conceived of how things would evolve since you arrived?"

"You're not kidding there, are you? Who'd a thunk it?" I was sad that I couldn't tell Carol that Charlie was still alive. I wondered what she knew about his clandestine activities. She had to know more than she let on. "To think my greatest worry was the former owners of my house and their murder-suicide."

"Yeah, I hated hearing those rumors about Charlie and the Calhouns. Thankfully, he was out of town when the incident occurred. I knew he was getting art lessons from Mr. Calhoun, but that was only to help him paint some pictures of Linda. Mrs. Calhoun was doing some clerical work for him to help with the medication costs, slowing down Mr. Calhoun's mental deterioration. It didn't help anyway."

I didn't know any of this and wondered if Colin was aware. I pretended that I did. I needed to learn more. "Did you tell me why anyone suspected it was a murder and not a double suicide?"

"The pistol was missing three bullets, and one was found in each of them, but a third was unaccounted for. You know they did examine the scene, but it was a long time after they'd died. We aren't like these big city investigation places."

"So, Mr. Calhoun was mentally incapable of doing this, and they think it was her. Their son has an airtight alibi? He was in Florida?" There were so many questions.

"Yep, but they thought it could be a hit job. The Calhoun's son may have hired someone to kill them. That way, he could get his inheritance before his parents spent it."

"Why would Charlie be involved?" If the son could have hired someone, then so could someone else.

"Charlie was buying and paying for Mr. Calhoun's medicine. I think it was like what Linda was getting. I don't think it did either one of them any good in the end. Mrs. Calhoun may have been angry, and while she didn't pay for anything, she let Charlie know she thought he should stop importing the medicine. She told me she thought it was doing Linda and her husband more harm than good."

"But you said he was cleared and out of the state at the time?"

"Yes, we all know it wasn't him. Poor Charlie was beside himself with grief. Linda died a short time later."

There was a knock at the door coming from upstairs. "Are you two done yet? I'm going to the school to pick up Luke. Do you need anything?" Colin was doing all the shopping until I was better. Mrs. Gillard was off for the day.

"Collie, I think we're getting low on dog food if you don't mind."

He left, and Carol turned to me. "You never ask, but I can do waxing." She pointed to my pubic area.

"No way, I'll take a bullet for that man, but not that. Uh. Ouch with a capital O."

"And here I thought you were such a modern woman. You know most men want a smooth landing strip. Just sayin'."

I would never mention that despite our best efforts, the landing strip had not been approached. Colin had seen me when I took a bath after the foal extraction. He hadn't mentioned it. I guess it wouldn't hurt to ask. *Oh God, what if he wants it smooth?*

"Can't say I didn't offer." Carol began to collect her equipment.

"Nope, I sure can't. How many women do you know that—"

"Clear the landing strip? Most, but not all."

"I am so behind the times." And hopefully, I would stay there—the pilot's choice?

"See you Saturday. Let me know if you want to follow up on my offer."

"Uh, don't sit by the phone."

After Luke was in bed, I sat down on the sofa. Colin and I had begun reading books to Luke. We started with *40 Years' Gatherin's*, but one story was so sad that we skipped it and then read a more modern book. Luke took the older book to bed and said he would read it by himself. "I hate to think he's in there on his own when that story ends."

"He'll be okay, darlin'. He's a Chandler, or he soon will be." Colin had made a formal application to change Luke's last name. "And you? Will you change your name?"

"That depends." I was going to ask Colin a question that I dreaded.

"On what?"

"I'm kind of embarrassed to ask this." I stared away, avoiding his gaze. "How do you feel about pubic hair?"

"Huh? What do you mean?"

"Carol does waxing. To be honest, I've never done it."

"You know that topic has never come up for me. Pun intended. I take it you aren't a fan. To be honest, if this is a deal-breaker, then I guess I can live with the au natural look and feel."

I inhaled deeply, and I knew my face was red. "I'm willing to try it, but at my age, there isn't much left anyway."

"Darlin', I know what you look like. I'll love you no matter what's down there." Colin pointed to the area of topic. "Maybe I should inspect it and make a decision after a good observation."

"Yeah, maybe."

Colin woke the following morning and told me he liked me just as I am. I brought him coffee in bed. He pulled me down into his arms and said, "I've only been with a few women, and none of them waxed. I was interested in the concept, but I like you just as you are."

We could hear Luke in the kitchen, and we both rose from the bed. "Darlin', we need a day to ourselves. This parenthood thing is rather annoying."

"At our age, we should schedule a night and day alone once a year."
"Speak for yourself."
"I don't want to kill you before we get married."
"I don't know about your God, but mine is high fiving me today."
"My God is a woman, and she's pretty happy too."
"So, how much does Carol charge to smooth the landing strip?"

Chapter 30

"We leave on the first of March. We arrive in New Zealand on the third and go to the lodge for a week. Then on the tenth, we fly to Brisbane and onto Hamilton Island on the eleventh. My kids arrive on the twelfth, and we are there for four days. I then go to my old clinic and do a locum, and you and Luke fly home. The good news is I'll never have to work again. I'll be a free woman."

"May twentieth is the wedding date. Have you got your guest list planned?"

"You, me, and the kids. Too bad Christy can't come. Bill could, but I'd rather not torture him. Is there anyone you want to come to the wedding?"

"My kids and Helen. If she's up here, I know she'll want to come."

"Collie, invite anyone you want. I'd feel bad if I didn't invite our friends. I was kind of thinking if neither Bill nor Miles came, Eric might walk me down the aisle."

"Who walked you down the aisle when you were married before?" Colin was shaving, and I was dressing just outside the bathroom, imagining how I would put my clothes in the closet.

"I didn't have a wedding. It was a celebrant, and we did it in a park. A forgettable moment, I might add. How about you?"

"I had a big wedding with Helen and the second was a lot like your wedding. I want you to be happy, so if you want to have a big party, then I'm up for it. It's your day, Maggie."

"Collie, it's our day. You get a say too. Just not on the music, theme, food, or guests. Everything else is up for grabs."

He shook his head. "Do you have any friends from high school or vet school that you might like to invite? You never talk about old friends."

"My best friend from vet school was killed less than a week after graduation. She went to Lake Tahoe to interview for a vet job and was killed in a rockslide. They never found her body. She had a three-year-old daughter, but when I moved to Australia, I lost contact with her husband. He was one of my instructors in vet school, and he taught me about dystocias. He was much older than us, and I guess he's dead. You can thank him for saving your foal the other night."

Colin pulled me into his lap as Luke walked in. Luke covered his eyes. "Are you two at it again?"

"Wait, say that again." I distinctly heard a crack in his voice.

"What?" he rolled his eyes.

"Somebody's getting hormonal."

Colin smiled and squeezed my backside. "Luke, Maggie's going to be painful for the next few months. It's a bridal thing. We need to play along."

"Luke, don't listen to him. What song should I walk down the aisle to?" I grabbed Colin's hand so he could not inflict any more pain.

Luke considered the options. "I'd say *Walk Like a Man*. How about she's up at the front, and you walk down the aisle?"

"Do you hear it? He's losing his voice. Lukey Boy's becoming Lukey Man. My beautiful little boy is going away."

Mrs. Gillard came into the dining room and asked us what we wanted for dinner this evening. Colin considered his options. "I haven't had a roast for a while. Can we have roast beef?"

Since the dinner party venue was changed to Colin's ranch, Mrs. Gillard and I discussed the menu for tomorrow evening. We planned to have salmon, asparagus, and wild rice. I would kill for artichokes, but the locals wondered what it was and how to eat it. Asparagus was exotic enough for this crowd. There would be some beef skewers as well. I hadn't seen Sylvia and Trent since Charlie's funeral, and I was keen to show them our new colt.

I had slipped last night when I went up to the barn. The snow was persisting and getting icy. I was afraid Colin might fall and be seriously hurt. I couldn't say anything for fear it would hurt his feelings. I sat and considered how I might broach the subject.

"Maggie, I don't want you to be offended, but you need to hear this. I'm concerned about you."

"Huh? Why?"

"Osteoporosis. Darlin', you're the right age to fall and fracture your hip. It's slick as snot out there. I want you to be careful."

"Thanks. I guess we're both vulnerable. I appreciate you reminding me. Mrs. Gillard, we both need to be reminded. I thought I'd try and ride Digger today. What are your plans?" Luke left to brush his teeth, and Mrs. Gillard retreated to the kitchen.

"I'm going to talk to the minister about our wedding. Don't you want to come too?"

"I forgot. I can ride after lunch then. I'd like to go home and get some clothes and maybe bring a few things over. Would that be all right with you? We don't have to make it permanent yet."

Colin appeared to be alarmed. He glanced at me. "I thought it was permanent. I want it to be permanent. Don't you?"

"Yes, I do, but I want to give you space and let you ease into a life together. I don't want to overwhelm you."

"Darlin', how many years do we have to be together—ten, twenty, God forbid. I want them to be with you. If you don't feel the same—" I stopped him.

"No, I do too. I promise that won't be discussed again. I'll get ready to go."

The minister was a riot. "So, Colin, we meet again. This is becoming a habit."

"Sam, it's been how many years? The good news is this is the last time. I swear on a stack of bibles."

"That can be arranged." Sam Hampstead turned to his bookshelf. I was introduced and quietly sat there as the minister jokingly admonished Colin for his past and present sins.

He flat-out asked if we were living in sin at the moment. When Colin sheepishly nodded in the affirmative, he smiled and said he was sure that God would say it was okay since we were so old. As long as we took precautions, God would look the other way.

He asked if we wanted a traditional service or a theme-based service. He did pagan, Disney-based, and even once did a matrimonial service at a nudist colony. He quickly pointed out he was a "man of the cloth" and officiated in his traditional robes. *Oh, boy, I like this guy.*

"So, Maggie, tell me about yourself. You must have an interesting story to catch Colin's attention."

"No, sir. I'm boring as bat—" Whoops, I didn't finish the expression, to which he then responded.

"Bat stuff? I'm guessing that is an Australian expression?"

"Sorry." I could feel my face redden. I wondered why, at my age, how could I blush so often?

Colin smiled and told him about how we met and how I helped his grandson, and yes, I occasionally swore. Still, with my veterinary background, he was willing to put up with it.

"I think God probably swears some too, especially when he looks down on the earth and humanity."

"Sam, Maggie and I want a traditional marriage. We'll have it out at the ranch, and you can wear whatever you want."

Sam stared at me. "Maggie, are you letting Colin decide about the wedding? I would hate to think we aren't considering your feelings."

"Sam, you are the only choice that I'm allowing Collie to make. The rest is being planned by Luke and me. We may have a *Four Seasons* theme, but we haven't decided for sure."

"Ah, a bit of spring, summer, fall?"

I held up my hand, "No, *Walk Like a Man, Big Girls Don't Cry*—that kind of wedding."

Both he and Colin rolled their eyes. "I haven't decided for sure." I smiled sweetly. "I think it will be a surprise on the day. You two simply need to show up and do your part. It's not like I do this every day, and I need to keep this beautiful boy on his toes."

Sam gazed at Colin and quietly smiled. "I seeeee. Okay, now we need to make sure you two can legally marry. Do you have your divorce papers?"

"Je—" Again, I stopped before I said Jesus out loud. *I hoped they thought I meant gee.* "I don't even know if I still have them. It was twenty years ago."

"Sam, I'll have mine in a few weeks, and we are headed over to Australia, and we can get a copy of hers then. Don't worry, we'll be legal, and I'll make sure she's on her best behavior that day."

Sam insisted we pray. "Dear Lord, we thank you for bringing these two people together, and we pray that you help them find the joy and love in matrimony under your guidance. We pray for a beautiful day for their wedding and that by *Working My Way Back to You,* Lord, that the day makes *An Angel Cried,* and there is no *Bye Bye Baby.*"

I laughed and said, "Amen to that." Colin agreed. I was pleased with Colin's single input into the wedding. We walked out of church, and Colin squeezed my arm, as he opened the car door. "Okay, we have permission to keep on keeping on. Let's not squander this opportunity. I don't want to make the man upstairs regret giving us permission to sin."

"No, I sure don't want to rock that boat."

"Collie, do you mind stopping for a second? I need to run a personal errand. Would you wait in the car?"

"Okay?" he was curious, but he didn't ask why.

I ran into the second-hand shop and checked in the women's clothing area for wedding gowns. I knew that would not go down well, but this was my call. There weren't any, and I returned to the car.

"Mind telling me what you're looking for?" I hoped he thought it was something old or borrowed or blue.

"Wedding registry."

He shook his head. "Old fishing rods?"

"Don't spoil it. I want to give you a surprise on our wedding day."

"I have everything I want sitting right next to me."

"Me you too, beautiful boy, me you too."

"Will you ever dress the part of a film star's wife?" He smiled as he asked it.

"Probably not."

Chapter 31

T he following evening, we had a great time with our guests. Mrs. Gillard put on a spread that would please everyone. She left instructions on how to heat and bring out the food. No one was fooled. I was only the server. We formally announced our engagement, and we were congratulated.

Trent kissed me and shook Colin's hand. "Took you long enough. We thought you'd have her all stitched up by Christmas, Collie."

"It took some work, but in the end, she finally saw my inner qualities."

Both Carol and Sylvia simultaneously said, "Luke."

I nodded but admitted Digger played a significant role in the breakthrough. We all went up to the barn, and the little colt put on a show for us. He ran around his mother and reared and leaped in the air. The left leg was still considerably knock-kneed, and I mentioned if it didn't respond to trimming, I would need to hire Patty to sort out the growth plate. Carol and Hal had no idea about the growth disparity and how releasing the periosteum by transecting it would allow the slow-growing side to catch up, and the leg would straighten. Colin put his arm around me and said, "And it's this kind of bedroom talk that attracted me."

Patty Tilmouth arrived late with her brother, Eric. Patty's husband was in the National Guard and was on duty. Eric's kids were babysitting the Tilmouth kids. Gabe called to say that he and Betty Lou were heading to the hospital and asked me to prepare the calving chains. "Standing by with my OB gloves. Good luck to you both." Eric had suggested that due to the baby's size, as measured by ultrasound, this might end up on the cutting board. They had a thirty-minute drive and decided to go in before things got to the chain stage.

Sylvia, Patty, Carol, and I described our pregnancies and births. They all had cesareans, while my births were all-natural. "Born to breed, baby." I slapped my hips.

Colin gave me a stern look. "I certainly hope not."

I retreated to the kitchen, and Carol and Sylvia came to help me. "Where's Luke?"

"In his room. He said, and I quote, 'Are you going to talk about boring stuff?' His voice is cracking, and I am preparing for rough waters. Hey Sylvia, do you need some help on the ranch? Luke's a great worker, and he's always asking what he can do to earn money." I pulled the salmon out of the oven and took it into the dining room.

The women brought the other food trays. "Trent's always looking for a hand. This might be a match made in heaven."

"Dinner is served." Carol and Sylvia placed their food on the table. Patty and Eric were extolling my virtues to Colin. I was so proud to be his future wife. How close I had come to traveling down a different path.

Colin stood at the head of the table and asked us all to stand. He had his wine glass in hand. "To my beautiful future wife. What this woman can't get out of a tight squeeze is nobody's business." Everyone cheered, and then as we thought it was over, he went on. "Not only did she save me a considerable veterinary bill last week, but she's trying to save money on the wedding by looking in the second-hand shop for wedding dresses."

I muttered, "Is nothing sacred in this town?"

"Darlin', Lilian from the shop asked me to tell you she received three dresses with her last shipment."

Sylvia looked at me and said, "You can borrow mine. It might fit."

Trent put his arm around Sylvia. "Prettiest wedding dress I've ever seen."

Luke came out of his room, and I served him some dinner. I asked him to join us, but he declined. "Are you feeling okay, Luke?" I felt his forehead, and he tried to dodge me.

"I'm fine." He retreated back to his room.

Eric astutely diagnosed puberty blues. "Don't worry, it shouldn't last more than ten years."

I'd forgotten about Luke's first girlfriend, Tiffany. Were they talking?

Trent commented as he helped himself to the salad. "There's always military boarding school."

"Maggie and I have raised four boys between us. We'll get through this one too."

Hal stood up and raised his glass. "We're forgetting someone. I'd like to propose a toast to Charlie McLeod. I don't care what anyone is saying. He was a prince of a man."

Colin nodded. "He was my best friend. He's probably got heaven organized, and the angel wing procurement is well underway."

I raised my glass and stared at Colin. *What an actor*. I felt I should make a toast too. "I'd like to toast my future husband, who brought me out of a coma, and through fishing, made me see that life was worth living. I love you to the moon and back." I could see Colin was pleased. He nodded, smiled, and wiped his eye. I remember my father became teary in his last years. I was beginning to lose my filter as well.

As we prepared for bed, Colin kissed me and thanked me for dinner and especially the toast. "I don't ever remember even Helen announcing her love for me in a public forum."

"I don't think any of us did much of that when we were young. I'll bet Helen would now. Have you heard from her? Will she be back for the wedding?"

"Not a word. What are your plans for tomorrow?"

"Ride Digger."

"I don't suppose you want to go to church?"

I dreaded that but suspected it might come up. "Collie, I don't mind right now, but don't expect me to go to church when the fishing season starts. By the way, a nice tribute to Charlie. Now that I know you are so convincing when you lie, is there anything you care to tell me?"

"Not that I'm ready to tell you yet. I'll wait until I have you in a legal stronghold." I sat up and stared at him. He could see I was worried. "Darlin, if I told you I'm so nervous that you'll change your mind and losing you would do me in, would you think less of me?"

"If I told you I feel the same way, would you run for the hills?"

"To the sun and back, darlin'."

"Sweet dreams, beautiful boy. Are there really three dresses?"

"Nope, I lied." I kicked him. "Ouch, that hurt."

"I hope so. Let me at those bridal magazines. Didn't you ask when I would dress like the wife of a movie star? Oh, I'll need the credit card. Ouch, that hurt too. Excuse me while I call the elder abuse hotline."

Chapter 32

"Eight pounds three ounces by cesarean section at three in the morning. Mother and daughter are doing well." Colin reported the call from Gabe.

"Excellent news. We'll need to get Gabe and Betty Lou a present for the baby." I stirred the eggs and turned the bacon. "What time is the church?"

"One Shetland pony coming up. Ten o'clock and you don't have to dress up."

"Maybe a stuffed one to begin with? I'm assuming, as a man of the cloth, clothes are mandatory?"

"Killjoy." Colin came up behind me and kissed the back of my neck.

"On which account, the pony or clothes?" I scooped out the eggs while Colin buttered the toast.

"You have to ask?" Colin carried a tray of food to the dining area. "Luke?" he shouted.

"I heard him on his phone last night when we were going to bed. He's probably still sleeping. Collie, you don't think he has a girlfriend?"

"He's my grandson, isn't he?"

"Maybe you should have a man-to-man with him? He's awfully young."

"I kissed my first girl when I was—" He stopped and smiled. "Nope, not going there. I kissed my only girl this morning."

"I was a tomboy. I was a very late bloomer. I first kissed the man I will love until my dying day in a remote lodge in New Zealand. I kissed him again this morning." I reached over and took his hand. "The past is the past. You are my present and future, beautiful boy."

"Are you two at it again?" Luke staggered into the dining room.

"Always, son. Remind me to teach you the finer art of keeping a woman satisfied and maintaining your independence and money in the bank. We're heading to church this morning, and then we may go to the Community hospital to see Gabe and Betty Lou's new daughter. I'd ask if you want to go too, but since there's no one here at the house, it's probably best that you come with us. We'll be home by noon."

"I can stay by myself. I'm old enough." Luke helped himself to the food.

Oh, here we go, the first signs of independence. "Luke, we get that. You need to meet the minister. He's a cool dude, and he knows the *Four Season's* songs. He won me over, and I'm a total heathen."

Colin appeared concerned. "You are?"

"Card-carrying member, Collie. But I'm open to persuasion."

The snow wasn't too bad this morning. "I'm going to run over to my house and get a skirt. I can't imagine going to church in jeans."

"I don't think I've seen you in a skirt. I'd be up for that."

Luke rolled his eyes. "Do I have to?"

"Yes," Collie and I replied simultaneously. We turned and high-fived each other across the table. Colin started to hum the tune to *United We Stand.*

"Have I heard you sing before? You sound like a pro."

"I'm hurt. You don't have my history memorized?"

"Did you do a musical?"

"Several." Colin put his hand on his heart and bowed his head. "Wounded to the heart."

"Collie, what are the names of my children, and what are their birth dates? Just because you're a public figure, don't expect me to worship at the altar of your body of work."

"Fair enough. I'm sorry. I'm glad you're here to keep my ego in check."

Luke peered from Colin to me and appeared concerned. I knew he thought this was a significant dispute. "Hey, just for the record, I still love you, beautiful boy." I rose, poured Colin more coffee, and took the plates to the kitchen. As I walked out of the room, I listed, "*West Side Story* in college, *The Fantasticks* in the sixties, and *Best Little Whorehouse in Texas*. Is that the lot?" Then I hummed the tune to *Sneakin' Around*, and he hummed the tune to *I Will Always Love You.*

"Luke, you can load the dishwasher. I'm headed to my house. I'll be back in thirty minutes. Baxter, come on. You need some exercise."

I took my jacket and ran across the lawn before the boys had a chance to protest. I reached my house and noticed both animal and human tracks leading up to the house. Baxter's hackles rose, and he stopped and stared at the cabin. There were deer, antelope, and possibly a large dog or a coyote's prints in the snow. I didn't think it was big enough for a mountain lion. The human tracks were from a large man and were not fresh. Did Colin or one of the ranch hands come over to check on the house?

Baxter continued to show his concern. He stayed by my side, and his hackles stayed at attention. He either whined or growled. I went up to the door, and as I inserted the key, but before I turned it, the door opened. Baxter stood at the entry and would not advance. I couldn't decide whether to go into the house or retreat. "Hello?" I said several times, becoming louder each time.

I suspected Colin had sent men over to check on the property, and most likely, they had not shut the door properly. I began to relax. I searched around, and Baxter finally followed me as I went upstairs. He began to calm down as well. I entered my bedroom and saw nothing amiss. I walked out onto the balcony, and in the snow, which was still present in the shade, were more human foot tracks. Someone had been there for sure. I rarely locked the door from the balcony to my bedroom, which may be how someone had entered the house. I searched my room and, again, I saw nothing unusual or missing.

I went to my closet and quickly took the skirt and a few other items that I wanted to take back over to the ranch. I hurried back downstairs and did a quick check of the security video. It was turned off. I checked all the doors to make sure they were locked, turned the security system and camera recording device back on, and left. I ran back to the gate between our properties, shut the gate, and hurried to the house.

Colin could see I was upset. I hugged him without saying anything. "What's going on, Maggie?"

"Collie, when was the last time anyone was over to check my cabin?"

"I don't know. Maybe last week before the last snow. What's going on?"

I described what I saw when I went over and mentioned Baxter's reaction when we approached the cabin. I explained the security video system was turned off. He said it may have been the ranch hands, but when I said there were footsteps on the balcony outside my bedroom, he called the sheriff's office immediately.

"Maggie, I may be old-fashioned, but I could throttle you for even going into that house. I know it's modern times, and you modern women want to be independent, but don't you think a little caution would have been wise?"

"Yeah, I know you're right, and I know it was verging on stupid." I felt guilty for putting myself at risk and guilty that I let this man lecture me without standing up for myself.

"Verging?" I could see his anger rise.

"Do you want to go to church, and I'll wait for the sheriff?" I could see Colin was trying to contain his anger or disbelief. I was pushing his limit of patience. "Or not."

"I am gobsmacked that you would even think I wouldn't stay with you. Luke." Colin yelled down the hall. "Maggie and I can't go. We need to run next door. We'll be a while, then we can come back and get you before we go see the baby. Are you all right?"

"Is something wrong?" Luke came out of his room with only his boxers on, further angering Colin. "What are you doing? Get some clothes on." He turned to me and tried to block my view. This made me laugh, which I tried to hide, but sadly couldn't. "Collie, I raised two boys by myself. I know what young boys look like, with or without knickers." This possibly was not the right thing to say. Colin flapped his hands in exasperation, and then both Luke and I laughed even more.

"This is my house, and in my house, there will be no one parading around in underwear outside of their designated bedrooms. Am I clear?"

I then turned and walked away without replying. Luke swore under his breath, taking Colin's anger up another notch. I was now what I called in Australia "American pissed." Australian pissed would be drunk, but American pissed was flat-out angry. "I'll talk to you both later. I'm going up to the barn." Without looking back, I left the house and went up to the barn. I saddled Digger. Colin's reaction was reminiscent of how my ex had tried to control me. If this is the sign of things to come, I had significant plans to reconsider.

I was aware that my anger could spill over and affect my beautiful, kind horse, so I went out of my way to slowly brush and saddle him. I heard Colin's car start and head down to the road. I assumed he was going over to meet the sheriff. I knew I should be there, but I couldn't face Colin at this moment. This disagreement wasn't a deal-breaker for me, but it might be for him. It would kill me if he asked me to leave and decided not to marry me.

Who knew what an entitled, wealthy man would expect in a wife? Maybe this is why Helen left? Was I seeing the real Colin Chandler for the first time? Was this the point where I realized I've made yet again another poor choice in a partner? I was sick. As bad as I felt, Digger didn't let me down. I love this horse. I rode in the arena for an hour or more. Digger had grown a long wintery coat despite our attempts to prevent it with lights and blankets. It took a long time to get him cooled and dry before blanketing him and returning my beautiful gelding to his stall. "No grass for you, old man. A couple of months, and you'll be grazing in tall clover." *Would that be with me and my cabin?*

As I left the barn, Colin pulled up and motioned for me to join him in his car. Snow was falling, and I was sweaty from riding and grooming Digger. I looked inside and tried to gauge Colin's mood. I hesitated, and he motioned for me to hurry. He had the present we had purchased for Gabe and Betty Lou's baby. I entered the car and tried to maintain my calm demeanor while he backed and turned the car.

Without even glancing sideways, he began to tell me that he met Tom Sutton, who heads the county sheriff's department. "Tom thinks it was a break-in, and he is suggesting that it might be some local kids. He indicated that the house should be monitored every other day since no one lives there. Tom feels you should not go there on your own until things settle down. He plans to run by every few days for the next week or so."

"Thank you for your advice. I'll take it under advisement." I stared straight ahead. "Where's Luke?"

"He said he didn't feel well and asked not to go. He is to call me every thirty minutes and check in." I wondered if they had spoken since I left. I sat without comment as we drove to the hospital and entered Betty Lou's room. The small hospital room was crowded with two other ranch hands and their wives. I held the baby while Colin took a picture with his phone. We said our goodbyes, returned to the car and drove home in silence.

I was considering returning to my house. I went to Colin's bedroom and sat on the couch which faced the fireplace. The fire was not burning, and I stared into the ashes. Luke came in and, without a word, sat down and laid his head on my lap, and pulled up his shirt. I began to tickle his back. He lay with his head on my thigh, and then his body convulsed, and I knew he was crying.

I leaned down and kissed the top of his head. His crying finally ceased, and he regained his composure. "Maggie, please promise me you won't leave."

I didn't reply. Luke sat up and realized I was contemplating just that. I heard Colin's cell phone ring while charging on his nightstand. "Lukey Boy, will you take your grandfather's phone to him, please."

Luke got up, turned to me, and pleaded one more time. "Please, Maggie." I couldn't promise him. The whole episode was so ridiculous and blown out of proportion. What if we disagreed on something important? I understood he was "old-school," but I wasn't. I'd lived on my own as an adult for thirty out of forty years. It wasn't his attempt to protect me that was obnoxious. It was his reaction to my aversion to being told what to do.

I could hear Luke and Colin arguing, and then I heard Luke come down the hall and slam the door to his room. I glanced around the room. I would begin to pack and leave. As I began to rise, my phone rang. It was my brother-in-law, Miles's number. "Maggot, it's your favorite sister here."

"Hey Christy, you sound chipper. How's it going?" Her voice was strong, and she sounded happy.

"I want to book your place for the summer. I hope you two aren't planning on selling it?"

"Oh, no. We'll definitely keep it." I didn't want to burden my critically ill sister with the details of the pending dissolution of my engagement. "So, are things looking up?"

"Early days, Maggot, but they aren't looking down. By the way, you are a good match, so stay healthy. We haven't used your marrow yet, but it's sitting in a vault waiting for me to use. When are you two leaving for Australia?"

"In a few weeks." I hated thinking about how this was all going to change. I was reminded of the fishing lodge that was in my name. Colin had paid for it, and I would sign it back over to him. I was no gold digger. I might move away from this area anyway. There was too much drama associated with it all. I suspected Charlie would return after giving evidence at his drug trials. While I would love to see Carol and Hal's reaction when they became aware of Charlie's resurrection, I still wasn't convinced that Charlie told us the truth.

I could hear Colin coming toward the bedroom. "Hey Christy, can I call you back tomorrow?"

"Well, if we don't answer, we may be under the sheets. I'm feeling pretty perky this week."

"Gross, I don't even want to think about you two going at it. That's about as gross as Mom and Dad doing it." I hung up as Colin entered the room. He saw my small suitcase open on the bed.

"Can we talk?" He sounded almost apologetic—almost.

"Sure."

"Not here. Can we go somewhere—maybe to your house?"

"I'm heading there now. Let me collect a few things."

"No!" He almost shouted. "I mean, please no. If when we are done, and you want to move back, I won't stop you."

He thought he could stop me? What an entitled, spoiled man. "Okay, let me tell Luke we'll be gone for a few minutes."

"He knows." Colin took my hand and directed me to his car. We drove down the drive to his electric gate, and he realized he didn't have the gate opener. He began to get out, but I stopped him. "I'll do it." The snow was coming down, covering the ground once again. I went to the locking mechanism and turned it off, and then pushed the gate open. Colin drove through, and I hopped in. We would have to call Luke to open the gate when we returned. Colin would never leave the gate open.

We drove next door to my driveway, and we stopped at the entrance while I got out and opened the gate. I was going to leave it open. We wouldn't be there long. The point was Colin was going to tell me it was all a mistake. He was calling off the wedding and trip. He brought me here to leave me. No-fuss and no arguing in front of Luke. Short and sweet—dismissed. *So long, it's been good to know you.*

We parked close to the house, and Colin took several logs from the pile under the balcony, and we walked up the stairs to the locked door of the great room. The house temperature was kept low when I wasn't there, so I dialed up the heater. At the same time, Colin went to the fireplace, placed logs on the rack, and started the gas burner. "Maggie, would you mind if we open a bottle of wine? This may take a while."

"I'll get it, Collie. I'm not going to object, so if you simply want to say it, I won't argue the point, and you don't need to stay. I get it."

He shook his head. "No, I need to explain." He went into the cupboard and looked at several bottles. He laughed, "Ah, this one's on Charlie. He returned with the highly regarded and expensive Penfolds that Charlie had given me last year. He poured us each a glass. *With a bit of alcohol to ease the pain, Colin thought of everything.*

A blanket draped over the sofa's back, which Colin pulled over and placed over both our laps. There was an enormous distance between us. It may have appeared to be six inches, but to me, it was six miles. I waited.

"I could say I'm sorry, but that would not be enough, and I need to make sure that you understand where I'm coming from. I'd like to explain, and then you can respond." He glanced at me, and I nodded.

"I know you know the shock of losing a loved one when you, well really, we both thought Charlie died. Then add on the grief of your child dying, and to that, add on your guilt that you didn't do something to prevent it." He looked into the fire, and I could see tears forming in his eyes. He reached into his jacket and brought out a handkerchief. I took his other hand. Even if he was leaving me, I still felt compassion for his grief.

"I guess the first thing I need to tell you is, it wasn't a break-in. But the explanation won't amuse you, so I'll understand if you want to call everything off." I sat up. *This was almost hopeful.* Then I remembered his overreaction, the yelling when Luke was seen in his jocks in front of us both. *No, I would never put up with that kind of abuse.*

"When we went to New Zealand, I asked the men on the ranch to come over and check on your property once a week or so while we were overseas. Gabe asked me if I wanted him to continue once we returned since you stayed over with me. I thought it was a good idea. Two days ago, he went over but forgot the key. He looked through the window, noticed a faucet that was dripping, and he decided, since he was a fit young man, he would scale the pole and enter through your bedroom. He knew you didn't lock that door. When he finished fixing the dripping faucet, he decided to reset the tape on the security camera. Then Betty Lou called to say she was getting contractions. He forgot to close and lock the door upstairs, and he raced out of the house. He called me a while ago to tell me that he wasn't able to check the garage and the upstairs and turn the tape back on."

All this time, I said nothing. I only held Colin's hand. "Collie, I've been on my own for more years than you. I even had to survive a kidnapping and three teenagers, who, by the way, walked all over the house in various stages of undress daily. I understand where you're coming from, and I hope you can see that, despite your desire to keep me safe, I am capable of taking care of myself. I think your reaction was over the top and the subject matter was trivial. If it was something important, such as who fishes upstream and who fishes downstream or fly selection, then I could understand."

I tipped my empty glass, indicating I needed more wine. The bottle was closer to Colin, and he poured more into my glass. "There's more. My ex is in my past, and I don't want to go into it, but his need to control me was what did us in. You're going to have to let go a bit. Oh, hell, you're going to have to step back a country mile from your need to control me. Other than that, I don't mind attending church, but it's not my thing and a visit once a year or special events is plenty for me. Finally, I love you to pieces, beautiful boy, but no man is worth the kind of drama we had today. If you feel the need to change me or direct me out of harm's way, I want a fair warning, and then you need to run for the hills. I'm buying a cattle prod, and I know how to use one."

My relief was immense. I turned away, so Colin didn't see my tears, but he brought my head around and kissed me. He pulled me closer. "I need to call Luke. He said he was going to move in with you if you left. I need to tell him to stop packing, then why don't we stay here for a while. I could give you some more casting lessons."

"I'm always ready to learn more." I smiled, and more tears came. "Jesus, my filter is gone—the bloody wine."

"Maybe if we have a warning word that one of us is going past the other's limits?"

"What would yours be?" *Stop you effing idiot, castration. The list was endless.* "I'll take that under advisement." I could see the wheels turning. What would his word be?

"Collie?"

"Yes, darlin'?"

"Were you close to calling it quits? I need to know for future reference."

"I was furious with you for ignoring how dangerous it might be. I was more furious at myself for upsetting you and Luke. As I said, I'm old-school. I never once considered letting you go, but I sure as hell wanted to make you realize how foolish you had been to go into your house with the signs you saw."

"Even though you were a right twit, I still loved you. My heart was about broken, but whether it's old-school or stubbornness, I am proud and won't give an inch. Buyer beware."

Colin finally smiled. "Duly noted. Neither of us is perfect. I'm willing to bend if you are too. Oh, you're correct about my knowledge of you and your life. Brandon's birthday is November twenty-third. He's thirty-one. He and his wife, Cathy, live in Tasmania, and they have three children. He teaches high school. Trevor is twenty-nine, and his birthday is April fifth. He's married to Simone, and they have two children. He lives in Adelaide, and he's a chef. His wife is a nurse. The bane of your existence is Colleen, who is married to Nigel. She manages a sporting goods shop in Newcastle, and her husband is in the Air Force. They have a daughter. Colleen is twenty-eight, and her birthday is August tenth."

I nodded and smiled. We postponed any "lessons," and I retrieved some photo albums. I showed Colin pictures of the children, our house, and my veterinary practice. I showed him photos of the grandchildren and a few of my friends and clinic staff. He took it all in and asked questions that made me realize he was paying attention.

The release of tension made me exhausted. As we went through the albums, I realized that we both had dozed off. I let Colin sleep for a few minutes, and he woke with a start and apologized profusely. "Collie, we both fell asleep. We probably ought to get back to your house and to Luke. He is going to worry if we aren't back soon."

"Let's bring some albums back so Luke and I can see and hear more about your life in Australia."

"I thought we should do a movie night and watch one of your films."

"Absolutely not. I never watch my films."

"Phew, so glad to hear that. I was trying to think how I would stay awake—ouch. Mr. Chandler, corporal punishment is only acceptable on Tuesdays. Fetish night is Tuesdays."

"Is there such a thing?" Colin's eyebrows raised.

"Anything is possible, Mr. Chandler." *I hoped he knew I was kidding—maybe I needed to up my game.* "Oh, by the way, my word of caution will be gelding—the verb, not the noun."

Chapter 33

I brought some old photo albums over, and Colin started the fire in our bedroom. Luke, Colin, and I sat by the fire going through their family albums and a few albums of mine. Luke had never seen most of the pictures of his mother and uncles when they were young. Observing the photos, you would never know these kids grew up in such a privileged childhood.

Colin found one album from his youth. "Hot, hot hot, Mr. Chandler." His hair was dark and thick. He was good-looking even as a child. I could see he resembled his father. I could sense a strain when he traced over the pages. "He was a spare the rod kind of father. My mother was kind and doting, while my father wanted me to experience all the opportunities of life he never could afford."

"Was that good or bad?"

"Some of both. Dad made me do things that I really didn't like. I was expected to play every available sport. I would have preferred to play one or two, but he made me play them all. He would take me away most weekends to go hunting and fishing. I enjoyed that, but my poor mother hardly ever saw me. My grandfather went with us, and he taught me how to fish. Dad used bait and lures, and Grandpa Joe gave me a fly rod. We weren't rich. My rod was bamboo, and one day I broke the end of the rod off. My father beat the holy hell out of me, and he and my grandfather almost came to blows over it."

Luke was taking it all in. "Maggie, were you spanked when you were little?"

"It was different times, Luke. Most kids were spanked then. It kept me in line, and I don't think I was irreparably damaged from my experience. Christy was always in trouble. She taught me to protect myself. The phrase that struck terror in us kids was 'go to your room and wait until your father gets home.' Well, my clever sister would put on several pairs of knickers or underpants, and then it wouldn't hurt as much."

Colin and Luke roared. "The bad part was I wasn't as clever, and I overdid it. Dad felt the difference, and in short order, I got it bare-bottomed. Lesson learned I can assure you."

I glanced at Colin, who shook his head and asked if that was on Tuesdays? Colin got the look from me and refrained from any more questions. Luke wanted to know more. What was a "spankable" offense, and did I spank my kids?

"Swearing, destruction of property, stealing, cheating, and sassing my mother. Yes, I spanked my kids, but only when they were little. I used a wooden spoon. If they were exceptionally naughty or were going to hurt themselves or each other, I would simply reach in the drawer and mention that the spoon was coming out of the drawer. That usually sorted any variance in decorum. Oh, and staying up too late and not letting elderly people get their sleep. That's definitely a wooden spoon offense."

Luke jumped up. "Maggie, will you come and tickle my back when I'm in bed?"

"I'd be happy to, Lukey."

"Did you tickle your kids' backs when they were as old as me?"

"Way older Lukey Boy. You can ask them when you meet them. Hurry up, and I'll be there in a minute."

When I returned to our room, Colin was in bed and had pulled his nightshirt up. "How old do I have to be before you stop doing my back?"

I eased into the bed and rolled onto my side. "One hundred. Collie, what made you do your *Comstock* television series?"

"You know that's kind of a funny thing. I knew my associate producer Alex Conrad from a few guest appearances here and there. He approached me and said he had been up vacationing in Tahoe. He and his wife were antique junkies. One day she found an old trunk and bought it. Inside were some journals that a local rancher had hidden in a false bottom. He began to read the journals and discovered a family called Buchanans who lived in the 1800s in the area. He never showed me the books, but it made him investigate the area and its history. He would disappear for weeks at a time, learning about the history of the Eastern Sierras. He told me about this family and suggested we use their names for a television series."

"Was it a family of a widow and three boys?" I'd never known this was based on a real family.

"Well, it was initially, but according to Alex, the patriarch eventually married, and they had more children. After so many seasons, we knew the series had run out of steam. People were turning off the westerns and moving to comedy more and more. You have to know when to exit. The fact that the network was canceling the series may have played a role." Colin turned to me and smiled sheepishly. "Alex and I kept the rights and control over distribution, and eventually, we became popular again. And that's why you don't have to worry, darlin'. I can't spend all the money I make."

"Have I talked to you about my friend Sandy down in Georgia?"

"No, but Charlie warned me. Your turn." I knew he would never stay awake long enough to do more than a few strokes on my back, but it was kind of him to offer.

I declined and mentioned we had a wedding to plan in the morning. "That's if you still want me. Ouch, hand me the phone. I need the elder abuse hotline again."

As I returned from the bathroom, Colin was on the phone. Someone he knew had died. Colin was discussing the memorial service. I knew he would attend the funeral, and it sounded like he would give the eulogy. Colin hung up and sighed. He turned onto his back. "Eulogies are my new vocation, darlin'. Sadly, I'm frequently in demand these days."

"Who died, Collie?"

"My stunt double. The man who kept me safe and took the knocks for me. It was a stroke, according to his son. Damn, I'd talked to him only last month, and we were planning a fishing trip next summer. You would have loved him. He was anxious to meet you. I'd love for you to go with me, but maybe we should wait until the ex signs on the dotted line."

"Collie, remember, even when we're legal, I'm not keen on becoming a public figure. I'll hold down the fort and stay with Luke. Were you close with—what is his name?"

"Dan O'Keefe. Yes, but it's been years. I would never turn his family down."

"This reminds me. What are your plans when you die?"

"I don't have any. I'll be dead, darlin'."

I kicked him. "What am I supposed to do with your body?"

"Do you have that number for the elder abuse hotline?"

"Yes, 1-800- you deserved it."

"Cremation and toss me up on the hill overlooking the ranch. And you?"

"You'll be dead. Ouch. Hand me the phone and hit redial. That hotline is getting a workout tonight."

"I used to want a few ashes on different rivers, but let my kids decide. I don't care. I think a better question is, how do you want to die?" Colin gazed over at me and gave me a devilish grin. We both knew what he meant. "As long as you've completed your obligations, I could follow you."

"Did I ever tell you I have a pilot's license?"

I knew he was referring to Carol's euphemism about the landing pad. "When's the funeral?"

"Wednesday, I'll have to leave tomorrow."

"Oh, darn. You'll miss Tuesday." I smiled and turned away, preparing to sleep.

"Is that really a thing on Tuesdays?" He pulled me into him.

"Let me make this perfectly clear. Gelding."

"I love you, darlin' girl."

"You, too, beautiful boy. I'll be here, waiting for your return."

But I wasn't.

Chapter 34

Colin left after lunch. Doug Cameron came to take him to the airport. They still didn't trust me to drive in the snow. I would have brought the car back from the airport, and that was inconceivable for my chauvinistic fiancé—insert eye-role. "You have me a wee bit too high on a pedestal to suit me, guys."

"It's my favorite car, darlin'. It's a limited edition."

"Grandpa, she still has to drive me to school and back." Luke was used to his grandfather coming and going. He enjoyed his independence. He and Mrs. Gillard were close, and she always stayed at the ranch when Colin was gone. These days, Luke required more and more privacy. I forgot to ask Colin if he had spoken to Luke about the facts of life and especially with the access to porn on the internet.

I might have to grandmother up and make sure the subject had been broached. I was lucky that my boys only had access to the single computer we owned when they were young. I could easily see search history. Don't think they didn't try... Boys will be boys.

Gabe and Betty Lou returned home, and I got another cuddle with the new baby, who was named Charlotte Anne after their mothers. She was the kind of baby that made you foolishly want more. She ate and slept and was perfect in every way. Gabe was taking another paid week off from my soon-to-be betrothed. The ranch house they lived in had been remodeled to accommodate a baby. Colin had the room decorated in a neutral color but with horse wallpaper.

Gabe apologized to me for how he left my house the other day. He didn't know how much it scared me and almost led to me breaking my engagement. I told him I would take over the duties, and I wanted to spend some time there during the day since Colin was gone for a few days. I planned to resurrect my writing career. He asked if I would report any concerns. "Yes, sir. Gabe, thanks for all that you do for Colin and me. We need to have a riding adventure again, but for now, go home and hug that beautiful daughter for me."

"I know the boss is gone for a few days, and Whit Williams is on patrol, but if anything is wrong, please call me. Remember how talking about Luke was a fireable offense last year?" I nodded and laughed. "Well, allowing you to get hurt has made that edict obsolete. We have all been warned. The boss thinks you hung the moon, Doc."

"Hardly, my value is so overrated."

"Not after watching you get that foal out of that mare and especially at your age."

"At my age? Any discussion of that descriptor is another fireable offense. So much to teach you and so little time. Get on your horse and get home. Betty Lou probably needs some sleep."

"I'm going into town in an hour, and I'll get Luke for you. If that's not pushing the limit of you or Betty Lou? She's cute and sweet, but that little rabbit is going through diapers like nobody's business."

I suspected that was a ruse, but I let it pass without comment. After how many years of doing it all myself, it was nice to have people to help me do the day-to-day things, such as negotiate a vehicle in snow. "Thanks again, Gabe." *Oh man, he still had his Marlboro Man good looks—a girl can dream.*

The snow stopped the following morning. As I let Luke out of the car at school, one of his teachers saw me and asked to speak to me. I'd almost driven Luke to school in my pajamas, as I had many times when my kids were young. Fortunately, I was appropriately attired except for my slippers. I parked the car and entered the school office in the main building at the high school.

How many times had I been summoned to the office to sort out one or another of my child's transgressions? The teacher took me into a small room off the primary office. She left me for a minute and returned with the principal. "Mrs. Chandler, this is our principal, Mr. Hansen."

"Hi, I'm not Mrs. Chandler. My name is Maggie Kincaid. Mr. Chandler is away. Is everything okay?" I was now alarmed. They both had their arms folded and stood over me. This would be a power play at my kid's school in Australia.

"Luke is somewhat distracted at the moment. Are you aware he is communicating with one of our senior girls, and he is texting with her day and night?"

The look on my face said it all. "A senior?" That's what we called "punching above his weight" in Australia.

"The girl's parents are concerned. While she is of legal age in our state, he is not. We feel it would be wise for a united effort to end this without exacerbating the problem. You know, there's nothing more enticing than forbidden love." The principal continued. "Luke's probably one of the most advanced students we have ever had at this school. His test scores are always near 100 percent. We have no concerns with his academic endeavors. If the girl's parents hadn't brought it up, we would never have known."

"Let me speak to Mr. Chandler about this, and we'll talk to Luke. Thank you for bringing it to my attention. Is there anything else?"

"No. As we said, we're happy to have Luke here, and we want him to succeed. He says his goal is to be a veterinarian like you. We always are appreciative of positive role models."

That evening Luke and I sat in the great room in front of the fireplace. He was reticent as he read a book from his assigned freshman reading list. I had my laptop open, but I reviewed my last novel, which was a series. It had been so long that I didn't remember some characters in the previous manuscript. Luke's phone was on silent, but we both heard the buzz from the vibration. Luke jumped up, and after glancing at the phone, announced he was going to bed.

The funeral would be over, and unless Colin was having a drink with the boys, he should be free to talk. I rang, but I could only leave a message. It was late, and I went to bed. I was woken early the following day. It was an undisclosed number. "Maggie? This is Jodie from your old clinic. Can you hear me?" I laughed, thinking how many people believe they need to shout when calling overseas.

"I can hear you fine, Jodie. What's going on?"

"Derek's mother in the UK died. He wants to go home and help his dad, and he's wondering, since you were going to do three weeks of work starting next month, if you would mind starting it sooner?"

Derek Taggart and his wife, Lucy, had bought my equine veterinary practice in Australia. They were the perfect solution to my retirement needs. Both were equine vets. My practice was expanding due to the attrition of large animal veterinarians wanting to take on the commitment required to run a twenty-four-hour per day, seven days per week practice. I was accustomed to the lifestyle, but the young veterinarians did not want to do the hard yards. So, I was one of the few equine vets left in our area. My practice should have been a two or three vet practice, but since I knew I was retiring, I stuck it out. The Taggarts had a second vet employed, and I would work with him.

"How soon?" This was not the worst idea. Until Colin had asked me to marry him, I had no plan. Now, spending time apart was going to be torture. I might as well get it over sooner than later. I could work, then go meet the kids with Colin and Luke, and happily, we could return home together and never part again.

Colin finally returned my phone call. The funeral went well, but he needed to stay for a few days and see his son and meet with his accountants. I explained that I had been called into the principal's office and the nature of their concerns about Luke's relationship with a senior.

"That's my boy," was his response.

"Gelding, Collie. Not the response I was looking for. Do you want me to talk to him, or do you want to do it yourself?"

"Darlin', this is a man-to-man job. Chasing a woman three years older? He's going to exceed me before he's done."

"He's only twelve. Should we put him back into middle school again? They said he's doing well academically."

We had already discussed our first crushes and, to some extent, our first experiences. I knew Colin was a late bloomer. Like me, he was slow off the mark in dating. Despite his good looks, Colin was a shy teenager. He boasted that he was a high school heartthrob, but the truth was he only dated once or twice in high school.

"I'll be home on Saturday. I'll talk to him then."

"Collie, I don't want to be a great-grandparent anytime soon."

"I do, but not this way. I miss you. When do you think you'll head across the pond?"

I explained the plan change and how my last obligation to spell the Taggarts would be completed earlier than expected. I knew not to discuss Charlie on the phone, so I asked about our mutual friend's news.

"Not a word. Are we going to be two ships that pass in the night? Darlin', is there any way you could stop in LA for one night on your way, and then I could introduce you to Kyle? He's dying to meet you. I talked with Helen, and she'll be back for the wedding. She wants to walk you down the aisle."

"Well, that would be interesting. Tell Helen she'll need to get in a long line of potential father substitutes. Hey, I've got to get Romeo to school. To the moon and back, beautiful boy."

"You too. God, I miss you."

When Luke and Mrs. Gillard were in the kitchen, I explained that I would leave for Australia tomorrow, and Colin wouldn't be back until Saturday. Mrs. Gillard was happy to stay at the house and assume the kid wrangling duties again.

"Okay, Luke, break out the gin rummy cards, old man. Prepare to have your—" but she paused while glancing at me.

"Oh, so there will be a bit of donkey beating while I'm gone? Have you two been holding out on me? I'm marking all the liquor bottles, so be sure to buy your own."

"Mrs. G, I'm pretty busy with school, you know, but I'm sure I can spare a few minutes to teach you the finer art of gin rummy."

Mrs. Gillard shook her head. "Maggie, I liked him better when he didn't talk."

"Oh, that reminds me, Lukey Boy. Trent and Sylvia would like to have you come out next week. They're doing some cattle work."

"Cool, will some of the work be vet stuff?"

"They didn't say. Let's rock and roll, cowboy. I've got to organize my new travel plans. I don't want you to be late. I don't have time to bail you out of school detention."

I called Carol and asked for a quick hair appointment. "All I need is a trim," I explained my change of travel plans. She asked me to meet her at the house after I dropped Luke at school. She was showing a property to prospective buyers later in the morning.

"Let's hope this hair appointment doesn't end in an abduction this time. I can't be late for my showing. It's The Sanctuary."

"You're kidding. How exciting. That would be a commission and a half, wouldn't it?"

"I could almost retire. See you in thirty. Don't be late. Did you decide on the runway for sure?"

"Thankfully, my future husband is happy with his role as a bush pilot."

"Pun intended?"

"Totally."

When I arrived, Carol yelled to come in and head to the living room. Carol hung a few pictures that she and Hal had inherited from Charlie and Linda's personal estate. The property had been confiscated by the government as reparations for Charlie's criminal activities. No one knew the extent, and Carol was none the wiser. She thought the property was going into a trust to be handled by a corporation that would give out the proceeds to McLeod's charities. Still, as the only living relative, Carol received all the personal effects. Linda's old truck was parked by the barn.

"Can you hold this while I get a hook?"

"Will you deduct this from my account?"

"Yeah, sure. That will be thirty dollars minus ten cents. Now get your sorry butt into the kitchen."

I realized where I'd seen the paintings that reminded me of the ones Charlie painted in New Zealand. Charlie must have been painting before he "died." "Hey Carol, this is one of Charlie's, isn't it? Why didn't he sign it?"

"Nope. That's from Leonard Calhoun. The man could paint. It's a shame he died."

Carol pointed to the other side of the room. "That's one Charlie did. He took lessons from Calhoun and was one of the star pupils. Sadly, it ended so soon. Charlie had a real flare, didn't he?"

"So, Charlie knew them both pretty well?"

"Some say too well. There was innuendo that Charlie may have been a little too friendly with Mrs. Calhoun. It wasn't true, and they had some disagreement. Charlie ended up firing her for abusing her position as his secretary. That was one reason Charlie was examined as a potential suspect in the Calhouns' deaths. Of course, none of it was true."

"But why did Mrs. Calhoun kill her husband and then herself?"

"She'd recently lost her job with Charlie, and her husband was spiraling down with sudden onset dementia. There are other theories, but no one knows for sure. It wasn't clear who shot who anyway. The gun wasn't in a position that made it obvious who really did it. It seemed like it was her, but Tom said there were other circumstances which were never divulged to the public."

"Tom Sutton? Your cousin? Like what?"

"Well, we all know there was a missing bullet, but what we aren't supposed to know is their dog was left in the house, and he may have disturbed the evidence." Carol stared at the painting she'd just hung and walked across the room and straightened it.

"Don't tell me the dog was in the house alone and didn't have food and water?"

"Yeah, maybe. Tom didn't say for sure, but that's what he kind of alluded to."

"Jesus. I'm surprised she didn't kill the dog as well. No telling who did what, though?"

"No telling. Let's get you trimmed, and I see a few gray hairs. Shall I do the regrowth?"

Chapter 35

I emerged from the LA airport where Colin and another man were standing. Colin was talking to a woman who was seeking an autograph. He was signing something for her, and I could see the adoration in her manner. The younger man must be his son, Kyle, who appeared amused. They didn't see me, and I watched as another person walked up to them. This time I did join them.

Colin bent down and used his knee to write on the paper the first woman had given him. He was gracious, gave the woman his full attention, and thanked her for stopping to chat. Colin then glanced toward the second woman. I wasn't sure if he realized it was me next in line. The woman requested an autograph for her husband, who was picking her up. She continually scanned the oncoming cars, turned to Colin, and directed him to add "thank you for your service" on the paper. Her husband must be in the military.

Colin asked the woman if she needed a ride. She declined, saying her husband would be here soon, but we could see the worried expression. "He's never late. I can't imagine what could take him so long."

Colin turned from me, took the woman by her arm, and walked to the curb as cars pulled in and out, picking up passengers. Kyle gazed at me and shrugged. "I'm sorry. Do you have something for my father to sign, or do you want a selfie?" He stopped, and I could tell he had only just realized who I was. He turned to the curb and yelled, "Dad. The goddess is here." He turned to me and then laughed. "You don't look like you can walk on water. Have you got special shoes that allow you to?"

I extended my hand. "Hi. I'm Maggie, and you must be Kyle?"

"Sure am." Kyle turned to his father, who helped the woman place her suitcase in the trunk of a vehicle. Colin opened the passenger door and bent over to shake the man's hand, picking up the relieved woman. He then leaned into the passenger's side of the car and began to chat with the man. He finally emerged when a policeman told the driver he needed to move on. Colin held the door for the woman and then shut it and bid them goodbye.

He turned to me and hugged and kissed me. He glanced at Kyle and began to introduce me, but Kyle cut him off. "Dad, we've been talking for an hour while you schmoozed old fans. Maggie and I have exchanged life stories and discussed philosophy and religion. We were about to get to our favorite sports teams when you finished."

"That man is a congressional medal of honor recipient. We're going to meet for lunch tomorrow after we drop Maggie at the airport."

Kyle rolled his eyes. "Here we go again. Dad, we're going to be late."

"Maggie, this rude son of mine actually thinks he can keep me on a schedule."

Kyle took my bag, and we headed to the car parked in a VIP area of a parking lot. We emerged onto the highway, and Colin explained that we would make a quick stop at a facility to introduce me to a few of his friends.

We first stopped at Colin's family law offices, where he signed his divorce papers. They were still waiting on his soon-to-be ex-wife to sign hers. I didn't go into the room until Colin called me in with him and Kyle. There was another set of papers to be signed. He had drawn up a prenup that protected my assets and still had generous provisions for all my children and me upon Colin's death or my death. Colin's lawyers suggested I have my lawyer look them over before I signed.

"I don't have a lawyer." So, one of the lawyers took me into a separate room and read through the contract with me, and then asked if I had any questions. "Yes, I do. This seems a little one-sided. If I die or want a divorce, I get all my assets, and Colin gets none of mine. If he dies, I get a fourth of his assets. If I want a divorce, he gives me a tenth of his assets. That's too much."

"We thought so too, but that was the way it reads. We cautioned him. Even Kyle seemed happy. Upon his death, the ranch goes to his grandson when he turns thirty, and you are the caretaker until Luke is of age to take over. That's payment for your care for Luke. The beach house goes to Kyle, and you will have access to it for one month every year. Jake gets a house in Arizona and an apartment in New York. You own the horse Digger, and you have fishing rights until you die."

"Okay, do I sign today or just before the wedding?"

Colin entered the room. "What's taking so long? We need to get going."

"Collie, I think we need to talk about it. Do you mind if we have a word in private?" I glanced at the lawyer, and she stood and walked out.

"This is too much. How about you keep your stuff, and I keep mine, and we leave it at that? Either one of us could die tomorrow, and that wouldn't be fair to you or your family."

"There are times you test my limits, Maggot. Sign the damn paper, or you will not like the consequences. Am I clear? Marriage is a give and take. I'm giving, and you are taking whether you like it or not."

"I wish I had more to give to you." I was grateful but annoyed I could not match his generosity.

"You gave me my grandson. You've already earned your share. Now I need to earn mine. It is effective as soon as you sign. I've already signed mine. I still haven't come up with a word or phrase that says stop like your 'gelding,' but I'm thinking wooden spoon."

"That's only to be considered on Tuesdays. Hand me the damn pen."

He did, and Colin had the lawyer come back in and witness my signature. We stepped out, and Colin asked Kyle for a twenty-dollar note. "Fought like a banshee, as I predicted. Learn from me son, I know women. She was never going down easy, but it's done."

So, Colin bet I would not accept the terms, and Kyle thought I would be so happy I'd sign immediately. "You both are officially in the doghouse." I leaned up and kissed Colin and gave a stern stare at Kyle, who held up his hands. "Take no prisoners."

Kyle sheepishly smiled. "Lesson learned."

"I hope so." I shook my head. "I can be bought, but it ain't money. It was the fishing rights and Digger that clinched the deal. Your father knows my weak spots."

Colin laughed. "I wish."

We left and headed for the beach house in Malibu, but we only went a few miles when we pulled into a retirement village. The sign said Studio Retirement Village. There was nothing to indicate it was a retirement home for former employees of the film and television industry. There were thirty or so residents, and most of the residents worked with Colin at one time or another. Colin had been here earlier in the day, and they were expecting us.

An older gentleman in a wheelchair introduced himself. He told me he had been elected the head of the welcoming committee. "On behalf of the men here at the lodge, we welcome you. The women are not happy, but they said they would give you a chance to explain why you stole their sweetheart."

I wasn't sure what to say. Colin held my arm and urged me to talk. "Thanks to the menfolk, and as for the women, I'm happy to share." Two women whooped, and the others told me they had alternatives and it was all right to keep him.

We spent an hour talking to former technicians and actors who chose to live out their last few years with former colleagues. Two men went fishing on a charter with Colin when he was in town, and they invited me to join them. "I'll come but only if the sea is calm. You won't want to be with me if there is any swell above one foot."

The residents had coffee and a small cake. I was impressed with their cheerfulness and the overall ambiance. "Collie, could I live here when I get old?"

"I'll book you in. There's a waiting list. Would next year be okay, Maggie?"

"Might be a little soon, but we could live out our last few years here."

We left after a kiss from at least fifteen men and one woman who mentioned I was just her type. I suspected mild dementia.

As we headed to the car, Colin asked for us to wait, and he returned to the residence. I heard a loud whoop from the group gathered. I turned to Kyle. "What would that be?"

"Dad told them he would buy them all a beer if they treated you well."

"I see."

"Dad wanted them to like you, and he came here earlier to ask them to give you a chance."

"Where was the management?"

"Not sure. You do know that dad owns the facility, and he visits them every time he comes to LA?"

"Uh, no. Obviously, there's a lot I don't know about your father. Care to enlighten me?"

"I think the drip-feed method might be best. If Dad wants you to know something, he'll tell you."

"As long as it's legal, I don't care."

"He went to jail once." Kyle peered over his shoulder and saw Colin emerging from the building. "I better let him tell you that story."

Colin opened the door next to me. He leaned into the car and kissed me. "It's unanimous. You can stay." Colin went back to get their permission for him to marry me. "You're going to have to go fishing with Mick and Roger, but the rest only ask that you come and visit once or twice a year and tell them about Australia. The only thing left is to get my current wife to sign the divorce papers. Pedal to the metal, Kyle. I want to show Magster the beach house and open a bottle of red."

"Wow" was all I could say. The Spanish-style house was the most luxurious house I had ever been in. It was above the beach, protected from the heavy seas, and had a swimming pool deck that went out over the sand. The views from the master bedroom and living room were spectacular.

Colin went upstairs to the bedroom we would use and sat down on the bed. He patted the bed and indicated he wanted me to join him. As romantic as it was, he and I both fell asleep. I woke quickly and left Colin to join Kyle in preparations for dinner.

I made a salad and cut string beans. Kyle was preparing potatoes and steak. He was quite a culinary savant, and I could see we would have a wonderful meal. It was still winter, and the pool did not call to me. I sat and watched the oncoming sunset. Despite winter, it wasn't too cold. I walked out onto the deck, and as I leaned over the railing, Colin came up behind me and put his hands around my waist. He kissed the back of my neck and ran a finger down my back which gave me a chill.

"Is it safe to come out?" Kyle brought out some crackers and cheese. The three of us stood on the deck and watched the sun go down. We returned to the living room, and Colin and Kyle set the table and placed food on the table. I was not allowed to help. We ate, and I switched from my gin to a lovely Australian red. "Dad has a new love in his life. You seemed to have turned him onto Australian wine."

"Funny, I never was much of a wine lover until I moved to Australia." We then discussed my life in Australia and my children. I was allowed to help with the cleanup, and then Kyle took me into his studio, where he showed me what he was preparing for his next show, which was in a month. "I think I'll be in Oz then. I'd love to come. How long will it be open?"

"Only a few weeks. I'll send you some photographs. My last show did well, and I sold out in three days. Having my dad there didn't hurt."

"Collie, did you wear a tux? I don't think I've ever seen you in a suit."

"And with any luck—" But I didn't let him finish his sentence.

"The wedding, beautiful boy, if you don't wear a plaid shirt and a bolo, I ain't sayin' yes, sir." I tried to appear to lay down the law.

"See what I have to put up with, Kyle? She's a total ballbuster."

"Yeah, Dad. I don't see what the attraction is." Kyle smiled, and Colin reached for me.

"That's because you haven't seen her cast a line. She can fish."

"Oh, you sure know how to flatter me. Not. And here I was spending a fortune on dolling myself up every day."

"It's late for me, time-wise. I hope you two will excuse me."

Both men stood, and Kyle kissed me on the cheek. "Pleasant dreams, Mom, or should I say, Mum?"

"You have a beautiful mother, Kyle. I'm not even in her league. See you in the morning."

I left the room and went upstairs to the bedroom that overlooked the ocean. I changed into a nightgown and opened my laptop. Several messages arrived from my old clinic with instructions on my arrival and transportation to the clinic. Luke left a note saying he was off to bed and missed his grandfather and me. He wanted me to know he soundly beat Mrs. Gillard in gin rummy. He was going to a school dance this coming Friday. I needed to remind Colin to talk to Luke about women and all that dating entails.

As I was dozing off, Colin joined me in bed. He spooned me and rubbed my back. At our age, the flame should be dead and out, but the newness of this relationship awakened long-dead desires in us both. We weren't going to see each other for several weeks after tonight, making our needs more urgent.

Chapter 36

I stood in line to check-in for my flight to Sydney. I enviously remembered my flight to New Zealand when I went first class. I was guided all the way by helpful staff. I stood in a long line and thought about my last twenty-four hours. Colin had deep-reaching investments and layers that I did not realize when we were at his ranch or New Zealand. Talk about punching above my weight.

Kyle quietly told me that the retirement home residents paid for their rent, but it hardly met the actual cost of running the retirement home. Colin made up the difference. Not one resident knew they were being subsidized by Colin. According to Kyle, the home would continue until the last resident's death. Then it might be converted to house aging military retirees.

There was an income stream from investments that Colin set up over fifteen years ago. It continued until Colin's death, and then the property could be sold when all the current residents passed. Kyle and Jake had no plans to discontinue the everyday use of the property. They thought the idea of using it for retired military personnel was a logical next step. I had suggested aging horse vets, but one look from Kyle and that idea was abandoned.

As I stepped up to the counter, the agent smiled and said I had been upgraded and didn't need to stand in the economy line. "After all the years flying with your airline, I'm finally rewarded. Thank you."

"Or someone paid the difference from economy to first class. Anyway, you have an entrance to our VIP lounge, and welcome aboard. An attendant will come and get you when we are ready to board. Do you have any dietary requests?"

Colin had changed my ticket for sure. As I walked to the VIP lounge, I texted him and said thanks. He responded, "Maggot, you deserve the best—to the moon and back, darlin'."

I reminded him he needed to talk to Luke regarding his lofty goal of dating a senior. Luke would need help to prepare for the upcoming dance. He responded that he'd raised two boys, and they had turned out all right, and he would deal with Luke and be home until the two of them flew out to join me for a family meet and greet in a month.

My only response was, "You, too, beautiful boy. You too."

Jodie Vanderpool was my former office manager. She was sold to the Taggarts along with the business. Well, that's what I told the Taggarts. I didn't mention it to Jodie, who ran the company as if it was her own. I emerged from the local airport after a dream flight from Los Angeles to Sydney and then a rough ride to the closest airport near the clinic. I'd always driven and had never flown to this remote airport, but the clinic paid for that part of the trip.

"You're going to love our new vet. He's run off his feet currently, and he takes the pressure in stride. His name is Rich Hamilton. He's been practicing in South Australia for the last few years. He's a yank like you, and he has a story you wouldn't believe. Do you remember the vet in South Australia who was accused of murder?"

"Vaguely. Wasn't the vet acquitted?"

"Something like that. Someone else was charged, and the charges against the vet were dropped. She took over another clinic, and he worked for her until a few months ago. He didn't say why, but he left and came out here. I'm totally in love."

"Is he in love with you? How does your husband feel about this?" I shook my head and laughed—*home sweet home.*

"A minor detail, Maggie. The problem is he is still in love with his ex-boss, and he's licking his wounds."

We arrived at the clinic, and the new vet was out with my former best nurse, Lexie. "Isn't that a dangerous combination? Has Lexie settled down? What happened to the last guy? Is he history?" Lexie could only be described as hot. Long blond hair, a nice figure, oozing sarcasm. She wasn't bad in the horse wrangling department either.

"No, all good. Lexie's sworn off men and spends all her time with her show horse these days. Mojo is cleaning up in the show ring. He's the high point gelding at the Hills Equestrian Centre."

That reminded me. Not only did I have to drive on the wrong side of the road, but I also had to spell words like center with a "re" instead of an "er." Thankfully, the driving was a breeze. Despite writing books, I was a pathetic speller. Nothing had changed.

I walked up to the house, and there was my old dog, Cosmo, and my cat, Blacky the Fourth. I loved black cats, and as one would die, I would replace him with another and continue the name. Snakes were the primary cause of death for both my dogs and cats. The current two had become wary, and while both had survived snake bites, unlike the others, they had learned their lesson and steered clear of the creatures.

Over the years, I'd found that cats could survive without antivenom, but the dogs required it urgently to survive. Horses died despite the antivenom. The intense activity of veterinary practice and farming had reduced the number of snakes on my old property. Mouse plagues happened once every six or seven years, and then there would be a rise in the snake numbers, but I welcomed snakes when mice were at plague levels. Having a mouse run up your pant leg is not an experience that needs to be repeated often or ever.

At least it wasn't a snake that went up into my pants. I did know two clients that were snake bit. Both survived, and one didn't receive antivenom and never had symptoms despite a local reaction at the bite site. *Welcome home, Maggie, give me a bear or a kidnapping any day.*

"Get some sleep. We have a full day for you starting tomorrow. Do you mind taking the emergency calls tonight? Rich has done some long hours in the last few days." Jodie had stocked the house with my favorite foods and my brand of coffee. I'd left all my electrical appliances, including my coffee maker. The voltage in Australia was different than in the US, and there was no point in bringing them over the pond. I like my Australian coffee maker more than my fancy American model.

"Are there any hospitalized cases or anything urgent? I can take over. I had plenty of sleep on the way here."

"I don't know how you can sleep sitting up. It killed me when I went to the States. I don't think I slept for a minute."

I considered telling Jodie about my new circumstances. I'd taken off my engagement ring for my trip over here. I didn't want to damage it wrangling a horse or, worse, have it catch on a halter and tear my finger off. This story would require alcohol and would be best saved for later. "I had a good rest on the plane. I'm still on US time. I'll start tonight. Have the new vet stop in when he knocks off if I need to follow up on anything. One thing I do need is a shower."

"Rich lives in the cottage behind your house. He's only temporary. You'll like him." Jodie left to go back to the office.

Man, oh man, that shower was heaven. I thought I heard knocking, but it may have been the dog wagging his tail next to the door. I threw on shorts and my old clinic shirt and listened to the knock again. This time there was an accompanying, "Hello."

"Be right there." I combed out my wet hair, entered the foyer, and saw the young vet through the screen door. "Hi, I'm guessing you're the new vet? I'm Maggie. Come on in."

He entered and apologized for coming at an inconvenient time. "I want to welcome you and thank you. I'm getting a wee bit backed up on calls. So glad you could come and help out."

"Think nothing of it. I haven't even looked in the fridge, but would you like a beer or something?"

"Can I take a raincheck on that? I need to get to the store before it closes."

I laughed. "Have you ever noticed the locals don't say store? They say 'shop.' I didn't know it until I'd been here for over fifteen years."

"Really, are you sure?"

"My old staff took the piss out of me over it. Until then, I'd never noticed."

"Lesson learned. If you don't mind me saying, you look much younger than I was expecting."

"Retirement will do that to you. So hopefully, this little stint won't age me too much. Have you got any cases I need to know about tonight?"

"Thankfully, breeding season is over. There's a little Shetland pony with colic in the barn. The owners don't want to invest too much, but they left it for observation. The pony has been colicky off and on all day. She's twenty-one, and their son will outgrow this pony soon. Hence, no surgery or exorbitant measures tonight. He's in the first stall in the barn. There's a cryptorchid castration in a box stall, and he's getting starved for surgery tomorrow. Then there is a post-op enucleation I did today. The only one that needs attention is the pony with colic. He received pain meds an hour ago."

"Nothing like a slow start to my last stint as a horse vet. How do you like the staff? I was surprised to see that everyone hung in and stayed with the Taggarts. Isn't Lexie a riot?"

"Total smart-ass, but so competent. The nurses are all fun to work with. Jodie runs a tight ship. I'm enjoying working here. What's with the Australians, though? The place is full of us foreigners."

"The vet students all go overseas to get experience after graduation, and if they are any good, they are scooped up by the clinics where they work and never return. So, it's left to us ex-pats to run the place. You need to get to the store. Oops, I mean shop. How about I cook you dinner on the weekend and I can hear about your Australian adventures. A crypt? Really? Nothing like jumping into the frying pan."

I unpacked and strolled down to the office. The staff was leaving, and I was given the after-hours phone and keys to the clinic. The smell of the office was just the same, bringing back such good memories. Lexie and Jodie were planning the schedule for tomorrow. Lexie came over and high-fived me. "Lexie, are you ready to assume the most important part of your work?"

"Watch me roll my eyes, Maggie. Yes, with everything else I do, I'm adding 'keeping you safe' to the list. They don't pay me enough. So, are you ready to come back full-time? I'll bet it isn't nearly as interesting as living here."

"No, it's boring as bat stuff, but that suits me just fine. I have an old lady broke to death horse and a nice river to fish in, and one abduction aside, life is pretty boring."

Jodie reached for her purse, which was the size of a feed bag, and turned off the light. "Yeah, we heard about that. Why don't we have a staff dinner this weekend, and we can all catch up."

"Sounds good. How about others? I invited the newbie. How do you like him, Lexie?"

"Good vet, but he's totally on the rebound from a vet in South Australia. He can tell you. He's too old for me anyway. Got to go and get a ride in on Mojo before it gets dark."

One of the things I liked about my old practice was that the schedule was only a rough guide to what might happen. This practice had a combination of routine and emergency medicine. I never knew how the day would go. With extra vets on board, at least one vet could expect to have a routine schedule go to plan, but that was rare for me. That was why I loved my job right to the end. Nothing was boring about my job. "Who owns the pony?"

"Kate McMillen. It's their son's pony. They already have another larger pony he's riding. Bobby is one of a kind. He's a bit of a terrorist, but he's packed this kid around the ring for two years."

"Which nurse is on call if I need help?"

"None. The vets do it all at night, now."

Oh, great. I'm going to be killed on my first night.

"Rich will be around, and he'll still be available if you need help."

"He seems nice." I was really thinking *hot*.

"He's way too young for you. Anyway, he's still in love with a vet in South Australia."

"Yeah, that would be robbing the cradle. I'm taken anyway."

Both heads jerked in my direction. "Mag Wheels, what's that about?"

I'd forgotten Lexie's moniker for me.

"Well, come out to the barn and show me around, and maybe I'll tell you."

"Um, naw. I can wait. Barbecue on Saturday? I have a show on Sunday."

Jodie stared at me and cocked her head. "Not sure I can wait that long. If you need help tonight, call me."

I went down to the barn. My ex and I built it when we first bought the property and set up the clinic. I occasionally saw a goat or sheep, but most of what I practiced was equine veterinary medicine. Our area had three small animal clinics, but no one locally did horses. It wasn't long after we finished setting it up that my ex and I split the sheets.

I had small children, a growing veterinary practice, and no family to help. Those were the happiest and most stressful times in my practice career. Over the years, my staff did double duty with babysitting and childcare until along appeared Mrs. Donovan, who came to live with us. Can you spell military boarding school? She was a gift from above. My children thought the opposite, however. She was ex-military, and that is how she ran our house for ten years.

When her tour of duty with us ended, the children were teenagers, and she abruptly said, "I'm out of here. You don't pay me enough to put up with this phase of their lives." The truth was she was dying of uterine cancer, and she wanted to spare the children the agony of watching her die. She moved to Melbourne to be with her sister, and within six months, she passed away.

To this date, she still runs our lives. My kids still refer to her and admonish each other how Mrs. Donovan would never accept unruly behavior or an untidy room. Mrs. Donovan lives on through my children. One secret she kept to her dying day was where Mr. Donovan was. We went to her memorial service, and that is when I learned the truth. There was no Mr. Donovan. Our Mrs. Donovan was gay, and her lover had left her for another. She never found love again.

Mrs. Donovan had amassed a small fortune, and she bequeathed each of my children enough money to finance the first two years of their university. She left me enough to pay the down payment on my cabin, which tided me over until the practice sold. I was able to buy my American log cabin outright. I could not look at this place and not think about the blessing she extended to our family with her presence. On the rare occasions we said grace in our house, it always ended with, "And please keep Mrs. Donovan safe in heaven." To which the kids would look up, and one or the other would say, "And don't let her look down in my room today."

As I entered the barn, I knew the pony was in trouble and in pain. I could hear the pony pawing the ground. I took a stethoscope from the stockroom and entered the stall. "Oh, little boy, you don't look so good. Let me see what's going on."

I auscultated the abdomen and heard faint noises. Still, the heart rate was challenging to auscultate due to the pony's morbid obesity. I went out and checked the treatment and observation sheet. The pony's heart rate had been forty-four when he was last examined, but he'd been given drugs that would slow down the pony's heart rate and confuse the accurate level of pain. In most, but not all horses, the heart rate was a good indication of pain. In the last few years before I retired, I began incorporating ketamine into my armament of pain control for horses. I could see the ketamine was slowing the heart rate but still not sufficiently controlling the pain.

Thankfully, there was an intravenous catheter in the jugular vein. I decided to give the pony more intravenous fluids. After two liters, I took the slightly groggy pony out and walked him around the property. Not much had changed. The fences were still in good shape, and the summer hadn't been too hot. There was water in the small dam that often would turn dry in the summer. The dam water was used to irrigate one paddock to provide green grass year-round for hospitalized horses for one reason or another. I returned Bobby to the stall and listened for gut sounds. They were rare and 'tinny' sounding, indicating a gas-filled large colon. All ponies with colic have small colon impactions until proven otherwise. My guess was nothing heroic would happen, and it was still early. He may resolve this without the need for surgery. In any case, surgery wasn't an option.

The pony was old, and I don't judge owners. We all have different priorities. Maybe the owners were going through financial difficulties. There could be other behavior problems with this pony that made him a poor candidate for expensive life-saving procedures. I returned the pony to his stall and walked down the aisleway. There was a paint horse with half of his head bandaged. This must be the enucleation case. He was eating and had passed several motions. Next down the aisle was the potential cryptorchid surgical case for tomorrow. He was a typical nut job. He was constantly walking and neighing to anyone who would listen. He was slightly underweight, and I suspected this was due to his constant agitation. Some horses should not breed. He was one. He was ewe-necked and was offset in his knees where his cannon bones were not aligned with his forearm. I could see he also had a little parrot mouth. Removing both testicles would solve some, but not all, of the issues. Bring it on.

As I walked back to the house, the phone rang. It was Jodie. "Hey, Maggie. I forgot to turn the phone over to you, and someone named

Colin is trying to get a hold of you. I wasn't sure if I should pass on the number, so I said I would pass on the message. He seemed keen to talk to you. Do you need his number?"

"No, all good. I'll go into the office and change the phone over. Were there any other calls?"

"I already changed it remotely. Nope. So, who is this guy?"

"Just a deadbeat who I met over in the States. I might be marrying him in a few months."

"You're kidding, aren't you? You would have told me straight away, wouldn't you? If this is true and I am in the dark, you have a lot of explaining to do, sister."

"I have a lot of explaining to do then." I then heard screaming.

"I didn't see a rock. You aren't settling for some jerk-face who doesn't even give you a rock, are you?"

"I have a rock. Better than a rock, I have his horse and access to a river with lots of trout. I'll tell you more tomorrow. I better check in." I hung up and immediately texted Colin and asked if he wanted to talk now or wait until morning. He immediately called me.

"Hi, Collie. How are you? I miss you. How's Luke? Did you sort out his love life?"

"Darlin' one question at a time. We're fine, and I'm back at our home." My heart skipped a beat when he said, "our home." "Let's see. I miss you too, and yes, Luke is sorted. You are so off base on that one. Sadly, it wasn't a crush. He's tutoring her. He was incensed that we thought he would even date at his age. She was paying him. She went from a D to a low B average, and now he has two other seniors he's tutoring."

"Oh, that's hysterical." What a relief.

"According to Luke, the girl was too embarrassed to tell anyone that she was getting help from a freshman, so she asked him to keep it quiet. Seems he's a bit like me and a slow starter on the girl front."

"But you're a great finisher, and that's all that matters. Has Luke earned enough for a car yet?" I found this so hysterical and yet satisfying.

"Why a car?"

"I made my kids earn their first car. I'm hoping to do the same with Luke, with your permission, of course."

"Darlin', I may be old, but I know the finer art of a successful marriage. I think the phrase is, 'whatever you say, dear.'"

"Pretty much. Yet another reason I miss you. How're Digger and Baxter?"

"I'm fine, in case you have forgotten me. Are you starting tomorrow? How does the place look? Are you seeing your old friends?" On went the interrogation. I explained that I was already into it and mentioned a cute young vet who needed a night off and the colicky pony who possibly needed Jesus. The owners didn't want to go the distance money-wise.

"If you want to do more, I'd be happy to cover the costs." *Boy, I love this man.*

"If this was my clinic, you know I'd cover it myself, but I'm only an employee. Let me see how the little bugger goes tomorrow. We have surgery in the morning anyway."

I described the lunatic crypt colt and discussed other jobs I might do tomorrow. Colin asked me to be careful and let the young vet do the dangerous stuff. "Maggie, I have my limits. If you get your head kicked in and didn't recognize me, I'll still marry you, but I'm putting you straight into the rest home."

"Duly noted. You can expect the same. Especially since I met this cute young vet. I need to ask him if he is into grandmother types."

"Oh, boy. I think I better head over there and protect my newest acquisition."

"Jodie said he's on the rebound and is still in love with someone. You're safe, beautiful boy."

"Phew. Is this going to be a problem in the future?"

"Nope. I might kid you once in a while, but you are my main and only man. You're stuck. I think it's nice to look, and unless you're dead, you're free to look as well. As you know, it's not your looks I'm after."

"Do you have any idea how painful it is for me to come in second to a horse and river access?"

"Well, there's casting lessons too. I've been gone two days, and I miss your instructions."

"I miss instructing you. I better sign off. Hope you get some sleep and remember, I'll cover the bill. Love you, darlin'."

"You, too, beautiful boy."

Chapter 37

P hew. When I was in practice, my goal was to keep colicky horses alive until sunrise. I don't want to kill them in the middle of the night and have people think I'm doing it because I was tired, which was the easy way out. The pony had not passed any feces and was starting to bloat. I saw Dr. Hamilton come out of his cabin and place his hand palms up and cock his head. I gave the thumbs-down gesture and pointed to the barn.

I'd called the owners about nine o'clock and gave them an overview of Bobby. They were adamant that they would not go any further. The pony was old, and their son was growing and had already begun riding a replacement. I knew Bobby was savable. When Lexie and Marty, the new vet nurse, showed up, I had them hold the pony to perform a rectal examination.

"Holy heck, Heloise. I can feel the impaction! It's at the tip of my fingers." I smiled and asked Lexie to get Rich. I asked him to see if he could reach it and grab it since his arm was longer than mine. Rich arrived a few minutes later. With lots of lubrication, he inserted his gloved arm into the rectum. He nodded and smiled.

"It's moved for sure. I couldn't feel this yesterday. Marty, will you get some buscopan, and let's give a light sedation." Marty was new, so Rich explained that giving buscopan and sedation would cause the intestines to relax, which allowed Rich Hamilton to grasp and massage the fecalith, and then the mass might pass without the need for surgery.

I drew up what I thought would be a reasonable dose for this pony and had Marty give it through the intravenous catheter. She chased the medication with some intravenous fluids to clear the catheter. Within seconds the pony was sedated and relaxed, and Rich could safely reach the mass. Many men would struggle to get inside a pony with a tight anus, but Rich's arms were not overly muscular.

He spent some time massaging the mass. After several minutes, he felt he had reduced the obstruction. He removed his gloved arm from the rectum and inspected it for blood which would indicate a rectal tear. "Fingers crossed."

"Fingers crossed there's only one. Time will tell. We'll have to wait for the drugs to wear off. The bad news about the buscopan was it slowed motility. The pony's intestinal motility won't kick back in for quite a while. Shall we tackle the crypt?"

I walked to the office, and Lexie came to retrieve the surgical packs for the cryptorchid castration. "Maggie, you may have fooled them, but my guess is that you could have done that yourself. I'll bet you could easily have reached that impaction."

"Maybe, but Rich has at least another twenty years, and I'm done in three weeks. I get more pleasure from teaching others to do the things I learned the hard way. Have you got the anesthesia ready?"

I walked into the office, and there was a beautiful bouquet of roses. Jodie placed them on the counter so the clients and staff would see them. "Oh, who got lucky?"

"As if you didn't know."

My face reddened. "For me?"

"The card says they're for Maggie Kincaid. We need to talk. I am not putting up with this extra work when I don't have the details."

"Extra work?"

"I had to carry the damn things from one counter to another."

I went over and took the card. Inside was a simple message. "We miss you, Luke and Collie." What is it about flowers that make a woman go weak at the knees? You could not wipe the smile off my face. I pulled out the necklace, and hanging inside my shirt was my engagement ring.

I showed it to Jodie, who screamed. This brought Lexie out of the kitchen, and she shrieked as well.

"Mag Wheel, if you can sucker someone in at your age, then so can I, so thanks for the inspiration. Who's Luke? Curious minds want to know."

"After we save the world two testicles at a time. I'll give you the outline at morning tea." That was one Australian tradition that I had accepted. I'd fought it for the first ten years. I finally acknowledged that the staff expected a break with food mid-morning and mid-afternoon. My favorite was fresh scones with butter. The team thought that was horrible and had the traditional whipped cream and jam or jelly, as they called it.

The surgery was as routine and easy as I did with Mac and Kerry. Marty allowed the horse to lie on his side for the recovery and gave the tetanus booster. While they cleaned up and reassessed the pony, I stayed with the sleeping gelding. I chuckled to myself, thinking of the noun, a neutered male horse, or the verb, the act of castration. I laughed when I thought about telling Colin that was my safe word.

The gelding recovered and was back in a small enclosure. The complication that would be fatal was an evisceration of the horse's intestines out of the inguinal incision. Keeping the gelding in a small area for twenty-four hours would help to ensure this wouldn't happen. I had horses begin to eviscerate following routine castrations. It was rare, and I was always lucky to catch it and fix it before it became a critical situation. I always put the horse on a thirty-minute watch following a crypt castration. Fingers crossed, this would be my last one.

We headed into the office where the staff had gathered. The other staff members, including the second receptionist and the gardener-stable hand, were in the kitchen. They were glad to see me. They'd read the books that were out and had heard about my kidnapping, which made news over here. Still, the exciting news was associated with the arrival of the roses. I was asked to give an account of my adventures.

"Not enough time, but the short version is I'm engaged to a wonderful man who has a grandson. He is my next-door neighbor, and the prenup includes the permanent use of his horse and access to his property which has a river that has trout in it." I showed them a picture of Luke, Colin, and me from our helicopter fishing adventure.

"What's his name?" Jodie showed a hint of recognition. She was old enough to possibly know him. Although Colin had aged, he was still movie-star good-looking, at least in my eyes.

"Colin Chandler." I tried to sound casual.

"The old geezer, movie star, one foot in the grave, Colin Chandler?"

"None other." Again, I didn't react like it was any big deal.

"You're marrying a famous movie star?" Lexie seemed to know about him as well.

"Unless either of us dies of old age first. In case you've all forgotten, I retired because I was getting old."

"Yeah, but you aren't really old. We couldn't keep up with you when you worked."

"You wouldn't keep up with Colin either."

"Ooowee, I can't imagine two old people going at it."

"Me either. Do you remember Magic and Mustard, the Harvey's two old ponies that used to do it? There are exceptions to all the rules, and that is where that topic ends. Am I clear?"

Rich shook his head. "Well, I'm inspired. Maybe there's still hope for me." He got a stern smirk from me.

The phone rang. Jodie answered it. We listened as she took information about a colicky horse. The caller was put on hold. Jodie glanced at me from the computer screen. "Colic season has started early. Maggie, it's Mrs. Blanchard, do you want to go see her?"

I rolled my eyes. "I don't think you pay me enough."

Jodie returned to the call. "Good news Mrs. Blanchard. Maggie's back for a few weeks, and she said she would love to see you and Rumple."

Chapter 38

One pooping pony aside, that is how my first week went at my old clinic. We got lucky on the pony with the impaction. Bobby started passing diarrhea within an hour of the rectal maceration of the fecalith. Rich was none the wiser on me asking him to do the procedure. In truth, the impaction may have rectified itself without our help, but we took full credit, and the owners were happy. I never told anyone about Colin's offer to pay for the surgery.

We saw many colicky horses due to the extreme heat. Horses don't drink when it's scorching, and despite our warnings, owners still leave their horses with water that grows hot during the day. We didn't see many horses with injuries as most competitions are canceled when the temperatures go above the mid-nineties. We had some allergies and horses with hives and a couple of horses with choke. In this poorly named condition, a food bolus gets stuck in the esophagus. It often occurs when horses eat dry pellets or, in the case here in my former practice, eat export quality hay. That hay is compacted and very dry, so it can be shipped overseas.

The worst one belonged to Mr. Henry Silva, a nicer, kinder man you could ever imagine (not). His horse was of similar disposition. "He won't let you needle him."

"How is he about a twitch?" Marty was with me, and she thought she could twitch him, and then I could slip some sedation in his vein.

"Nope," was all the man replied. Marty went up to the horse, and as she patted his nose, he struck out and barely missed her.

"Maggie, you don't pay me enough."

"Yep, me either. Let's put the horse across a fence, and we can work from the opposite side. Sometimes when we aren't in a horse's space, a frightened horse will calm down. Maybe they sense we are calmer too." We took him to his yard, and thankfully the fence was solid and sturdy. It was amazing how much he calmed down, and I could get a needle in him. I then was able to get a twitch on him and pass a stomach tube down to the area where the blockage was evident, midway down his neck. It didn't budge.

Mr. Silva had many questions. "If you want him to behave, why do you put that awful painful nose clamp on? Why are you giving him some more drugs? Do you charge extra for all those drugs? Why don't you run a water hose down his throat?"

My calm composure was being tested. "Mr. Silva, some drugs are to relax the esophageal muscles to release the spasm around the food bolus. One drug is to push the bolus through, and yes, I know it sounds counterproductive. Still, one area of the esophagus has normal muscle, and one has smooth muscle and acts differently. Then we need to decrease the inflammation. The twitch does exert a small amount of pain. Still, more importantly, it causes a release of endorphins, which calms the horse down so we can pass the tube and attempt to gently push the bolus down. We don't try a pressure hose as the water will backflush and go into the trachea and drown him or rupture his esophagus.

"He's not choking then? Why do they call it a choke?"

"I don't know. Probably because it looks like the horse can't breathe." Just then, the horse exploded once again. Fortunately, he was on the other side of the fence, but he caught me with his hoof, and he almost came over the fence rail.

Marty knocked me down as she tried to get away. My hand was bleeding, but it was only a tiny nick. "I'm so sorry, Maggie. Are you all right?"

"I'm not sure." I looked up from the ground, and the twitch was still on the bastard. I got up and reloaded the syringe with more and heavier sedation. I noticed a significant reduction in the saliva he was producing. Horses produce a large amount of saliva, and since they can't swallow the saliva, it comes out the nose. "Let's have one more try on the tube."

We made sure the horse was sedated. I was able to pass the tube up the nasal passage and all the way into the stomach, indicating the choke or the esophageal obstruction was gone. Marty and I high-fived each other. Even Mr. Silva was impressed. "Good thing I didn't bet on this. I would have lost." *One thing you can be sure of is a bet that I won't come out again for this creature.*

When we returned, my beloved former mailman, or postie, as they are called over here, was leaving the office. He smiled, and we hugged. Stavros was the heart of this community. He knew everyone's business and never gossiped. He was incredibly kind to the seniors who lived alone. His presence reminded me of what I had left behind when I moved back to the States.

"Maggie, you have a package. I hear you're engaged. Congrats to you both."

"Thanks, Stav. How are you? Anyone getting the benefit of your attention?"

"No, not really. Well, there's someone whom I met, but early days Maggie."

"Details, Stav?"

"The only thing I'll say is she is beautiful, and I'm not sure she knows I exist."

"Anything I can do to help things along? Do I know her?"

He glanced back at the hospital, and I instantly knew it was Lexie. "You can't go wrong there. Let me put in a good word for you."

He peered around the corner of the office and gazed longingly at the barn. "That would be good, but I don't have my hopes up."

I entered the office, and there was a small package for me. It was from Luke, and it contained a necklace with a dark blue sapphire gem. There was a note telling me that this was his mother's and he wanted me to wear it at the wedding because he heard I should wear something blue. It brought tears to my eyes. I was officially homesick. Very homesick.

We had a barbecue this evening with the staff. I was on call, but I usually had a sixth sense when I was going to have emergencies and when I wasn't. I wasn't too worried, but as usual, I had one drink, and that was it. The swimming pool wasn't heated, but it was warm from the searing heat. We all had a swim and then a great meal. I gave a short description of my new home, horse and displayed pictures of my fishing and a few of Luke and Colin.

Lexie was impressed. "Not bad on the eyes for an old guy, Maggie. You could do worse." *I almost did.*

When everyone had departed, Rich and I sat down and had a second drink. I waited for him to start. Rich sat and stared out of the window. Then he finally began to tell me his story. He graduated from vet school and met an Australian woman working in the States on a visa. They became engaged, but her visa ran out. She returned to Australia, and he followed her, but within three months, she broke off the engagement.

Rich mentioned he was devastated, but for several reasons, he decided to stay here while his visa was valid. He then traveled to South Australia to help with a veterinary practice with an associate accused of murder. That was interesting. I had read a short news article about it. I was under the impression that his boss was exonerated. Rich said she was fully cleared of the murder, and the two of them then went to an equine veterinary practice north of Adelaide, and they worked together for three years.

The vet had four children and had been abandoned by her former husband. She and Rich became close, and he fell in love with her, but she pushed him away. She was a few years older than him, and she felt he would get tired of her and her four small children. He adored the children, but the vet had been blindsided by her ex, and she was wary of becoming involved with anyone else.

"I wanted to buy into the practice, but she was worried that if things didn't go well, she would be unable to buy me out, and the practice would have to be sold. I was willing to sign any kind of an agreement that would protect her assets, but she was still reeling from the way her first marriage ended."

"Boy, four kids? You must be a glutton for punishment."

"Her oldest is nine, and she goes on calls with me all the time. No question that she's going to be a vet."

"Lucky her. None of my kids wanted to be a vet. So, no chance of a reconciliation?"

"I don't know. I hated leaving, but we had an argument, and I felt it was time to leave."

"Well, all I can say is it was the parting of fools. Your boss for not realizing what she was turning down, and you for wanting to take on a family. Don't you want kids of your own? I'll bet she is over that aspect of her life. Do you want me to speak to her mother?"

He laughed, but it was a halfhearted laugh, and I could see his pain. "Her mother died last year. So that's out."

"Isn't love an interesting human emotion. Love defies all logic. What a ride when you first become attracted to someone and hope it's reciprocated. It took me to Australia as well. I feel your pain, and I wish I could help, but when the burden of life and the drama of raising a family gets in the way, sometimes people can't see what's in front of them. Is she hoping her husband comes back to the fold?"

"No, he's remarried with two more of his own. He even moved away last year. Carly has a nanny and a med student who helps her. Otherwise, her staff does double duties with work and babysitting."

"Rich, who's helping her in the vet department since you left?"

"She has another vet who is working for her on an internship for the year. I decided it was best for us both if I left."

"Do you still communicate with her?"

"I do, but I talk to her daughter almost daily."

"I don't know if that's such a good idea." I sure wouldn't want my old boyfriend talking to my kids.

"She asked me to. It's hard for me, but Casey has been through the wringer with her father, and I seem to be a father figure to her."

"Man, this is one messed-up relationship."

Rich winced. "I guess you're right."

"I'm always on the side of the woman, and so for my two cents, I would only consider you if you didn't want kids of your own."

He finished his glass and stood up. "Maybe I should head back to the States."

"Rich, I am really sorry. I truly am. I wish I could solve the issue, but..." I didn't finish. He knew the "but."

Three days later, Rich received a phone call from the South Australian vet, Carly. Her intern abandoned her, and her three-year-old son had been diagnosed with a brain tumor. "She didn't ask me to return, but she was grateful that I agreed to come back when I finish up here in two weeks."

"Rich, don't be an idiot. Go now. I may be old, but I ran this practice for years on my own, and with the staff here, I can do it again. That woman needs you far more than this clinic needs you. You're a good man and a good vet. Now, get the hell out of here, and I wish you well."

Chapter 39

Jodie called the Taggarts and explained the situation with Rich Hamilton and his friend in South Australia. They were sad to see him go but understood the reason and supported his decision to return to his former practice. The locum agency said there was a husband and wife team from America traveling in Australia for a few months. The agency said they were available for five to six weeks, but they planned to return to the States in late May at the latest.

The couple arrived a few days before I was due to finish up. The Taggarts would be back in another week and try to find a permanent replacement for their growing practice. I was out on calls and wasn't there to greet them. When I returned from the farm calls, they were up in the cabin that Rich had stayed in.

I walked up and knocked on the door. "Hello? Anybody in there?" A tall man with light brown hair and a receding hairline came out.

"Hi. Are you Maggie? I'm Jim Kennedy. My wife's in the shower. She'll be out in a minute."

"Maggie Kincaid." I held out my hand. "Where're you from, Jim?" Man, he looks so much like the Hank character on *Comstock*. Too bad Colin can't meet him.

"That depends on which month you ask. My wife and I move around quite a bit. We're both from the States. It seems like there's an American invasion over here. Come on in."

I sat down, and Jim offered me a drink of water. "It's probably too early for a beer," I explained the dilemma, and Jim said that while they were both vets, he was a small animal vet, and his wife, Lauren, was the horse vet. Jim was happy to step in and help. He admitted that helping vets in need was what floated his boat.

After a minute, his wife emerged from the shower. She was tall and had curly long brown hair. We shook hands and chatted about what was expected over the next month. We talked about where they went to veterinary school and where she had grown up. They were escaping the North American winter. I asked her how she decided to become a horse vet, and she said both of her parents had been vets.

"Oh really. So, I guess your parents influenced you. Where did they practice?"

"My mom died shortly after graduating, and my father went into research for a private company in Kentucky."

I was stunned. "Your maiden's name was Harper, wasn't it?" This was the daughter of my best friend in vet school.

"Yes." A perplexed look came over both of their faces.

"I babysat you when you were little. I was in your mother's vet class, and we were besties. Your father is Jeff, and your mom is Becky?"

Lauren was shocked and was lost for words. "You knew my mom?"

"We lived together before she was married. I was a bridesmaid at their wedding. It was such a shock to lose her right out of vet school." I could see Lauren was lost for words.

"Do you have any pictures from vet school?"

"Yes, back in the States. How long are you staying here?"

"We're practicing in Nevada and need to get back in another month."

Jim watched Lauren and put his arm around her. I could see he was concerned. "We heard this was your practice, and you came out to relieve the Taggarts while they are in the UK. Your last week is next week, and you return to the States? Maybe we can catch up back then?"

"I would love to. I lost track of my classmates when I moved here over twenty years ago, and I lost track of you and your father. Is he still alive?"

"Yes. Dad and my mom live in Kentucky. He finally retired, and he and my mom travel around the country and fly fish and hike in the mountains."

"That's wonderful to hear. Will you please say hi to your father for me? He taught me so much about reproduction in vet school. I am so pleased to find you. It's almost like finding a lost daughter."

"Do you have children?"

"I have two boys and a girl. They still live over here. I haven't seen them in almost a year. We're catching up when I finish here before I return to the States."

"They must miss you."

"Uh, well, they had all moved interstate and have children of their own. I like to fly fish as well, and so I decided to move back, and I have a place where I can fish in the summer, and now I even have a fishing lodge in New Zealand where I can escape in the winter."

"Which lodge? My dad used to go down to fish in New Zealand every few years."

"It doesn't have a name. It was given to my fiancé and me as a wedding gift." A small lie, but this would explain some uncomfortable details.

"You're engaged?" Lauren appeared to be surprised.

"I know what you're thinking. You're like my kids. Yes, even in old age, you can sometimes find love. It's a long story. How about you get settled in, and tomorrow night we have dinner? I want to hear more about your family."

Jim relaxed and said that would be great. They would look forward to catching up. I was pleased to see Becky's daughter. Becky's death right out of vet school was a tragedy. I had never heard if they found her body or not. I wondered if I should ask for any details or wait and see.

"Okay, well, I'll see you in the morning. I think that Jodie has the house stocked with food, so you should be fine tonight. I'll leave you so you can settle in. I'm in my old house behind the clinic, so let me know if you need anything. Oh, by the way. The fishing is crap around here. That's why I returned to the States."

Chapter 40

I met Lauren in the barn the following morning. I had two horses on drips for colic. She asked about the treatment and was surprised how many horses get colic in this practice area. I explained that while many management practices were good for Australian horses, I felt that Australian horse owners relied too much on chaff and wheat, which they called wheaten hay.

"This summer is hot as hell. So, we're seeing many more colic cases than we normally expect. The hot weather heats up the water, and then, well, you know the rest. We see lots more than most practices do in the States."

"Weird."

"Weird, but profitable. A vet's gotta eat." I wryly smiled.

"I guess. So have you figured out what kind of colic these two horses have?"

"The bay has a large colon impaction, and the buckskin may have a nephrosplenic ligament entrapment. They both came in last night. We drench them, hydrate, and with the nephro, we run them in the paddock, and we can undo most of them."

"I don't think I've ever seen one." Lauren auscultated the bay. "The gut sounds aren't too bad. Have you rectalled him this morning?" She moved to the other side to listen for more signs of intestinal movement.

"No, I thought I would leave that to you. I'm going out to see a horse with a nail in his foot. I'll leave Lexie here with you, and you two can work on these. The nail horse is quite a distance. If you want to ultrasound the nephro case, be my guest. He isn't massive, so I could feel it rectally last night. It's light out now, so when those fluids finish, you and Lexie can run the nephro case. Are you finding everything you need? I'll make the dinner tonight. Bring your swimming suit and plan to use the pool too. What's your husband up to today?"

"He's going to help me, but right now, he's doing some business stuff with our clinic back home. He's a geek."

"Oh, really. Lucky you."

"I think so." Lauren smiled broadly. I suspected she was still in the infatuation stage of their relationship. Join the club. One week and Colin would be here. I missed him terribly. The work made the days go by quickly. I desperately wanted to be reunited with both my children and lover. I left the barn and headed up to the office.

The nail in the foot was far more than what I expected. They left the nail in the hoof for a radiograph. That would determine if it went into vital structures in the foot and make the return to soundness unlikely.

There was another reason they left the nail in the hoof. It was a hind leg, and this horse was a kicker. Not just a kicker, but a line you up and try to knock you into the next century kind of kicker. "And we're trying to save this horse because?"

"Maggie, he was my uncle's horse, and my uncle could do anything with him. He's a one-man horse."

"George, maybe it's time the horse joined your uncle?"

"Uncle Ted's in heaven, Maggie."

I stared at him without replying. It took longer than I expected.

"Oh, you mean to shoot him? No, I couldn't do that."

"Okay, we need to get a radiograph of the foot. I'll have you hold the plate."

"Uh, isn't that dangerous?

"No, if I stand on the opposite side and you hold the foot off the ground, I should be okay."

George looked at me and then got the joke. "Maybe you're right. Maybe Smokey should be with my uncle."

"How old is he? Does he do anything? Is he happy grazing in the paddock?"

"Old, no, and yes."

"Final question, how much do you love him?"

George Jackson scratched his head. "That ain't the question. The question is, how will the misses feel if we don't try?"

"I think you've answered the question. Now, usually, I suggest that my clients go rob a bank. In your case, I'm going to say go get a shovel."

George Jackson had been to jail many times for various illegal activities. He was known to keep money from illicit activities buried on his property. At my suggestion to get a shovel, he pretended to be offended, and then he roared with laughter.

"I'll need the backhoe for you today."

"At least." I chuckled. "You know me well."

We anesthetized the horse, took a radiograph. Fortunately, the nail was close to but not into the navicular bursa and bone. That would have been a disaster. I removed the nail and injected a disinfectant into the hole, and then poulticed the entire hoof. I gave him a tetanus booster and an antitoxin to cover both immediate and long-term protection against tetanus. I gave him antibiotics and pain meds. I wrote up the bill and handed it to George.

"Jesus, I'm going to need more than a backhoe, Maggie." George smiled and reached into his pocket and pulled out a large roll of money. He peeled off the amount that would cover today's work and asked if I would return in two days to reassess the hoof. He offered to pay me upfront today. I declined. Either this horse would be fine and need no more treatment, or it was going to be a nightmare. Time would tell. All I could think about was how much I wanted to be back at my property riding Digger and worrying about where my next trout would be caught. This was not a game I wanted to play anymore.

I returned to the clinic. The owners of the nephrosplenic ligament entrapment horse had arrived and were out in the barn. I strolled out and listened to Lauren Kennedy explaining the problem to June Sullivan and her daughter, Nicole.

"A loop of the intestine has displaced itself over a ligament that runs from the kidney to the spleen. The weight of the ingesta in the intestines pulls down on the ligament, causing mild abdominal pain. We need to lift the loop of the bowel off the ligament. Right now, we are giving him oral and intravenous fluids to soften and move the ingesta, and hopefully, when we run him, it will bounce off, and then he should be fine."

"What if it doesn't come off?" June was a nurse, and she understood most of what Lauren was telling her.

"We can try rolling him, and there is a drug that might help, and there is always surgery. This works most of the time, so let's not worry yet."

I was impressed with how confident Lauren sounded. Her mother would have been so proud. I considered inviting Lauren and Jim to my wedding—we would talk later today. I walked back into the clinic and described my call to Jodie. She appeared kind of unsettled. "Is something wrong?"

"Have you got any milk in the house? We need some for coffee."

"Here's the money from George. It's surprisingly clean. I'll head up as soon as I do the medical record."

"Maggie, I have needs, get your sorry ass up to the house and bring me some milk. Life is not all about you and your needs."

I was surprised. If I thought Jodie was kidding, her tone canceled any suggestion of that. Without a word, I turned and said I would be right back. Boy, a kicking horse, and a crabby office manager, what's next? I was ready to hit the trail today. I entered the house and heard the shower running. I yelled, "Uh, who's in the shower?" I received no answer. "Hello?" I listened to the shower water being turned off, and I stood in front of the bathroom door and, as it opened, out stepped Colin.

"Hello, darlin', I couldn't wait any longer. Luke's in the pool." Colin only had a towel wrapped around him, and it slipped when I hugged him. He smelled fresh and wet. He bent down and picked up the towel as Luke entered the house.

Luke observed the scene, and without a single word of hello, he went into one of the bedrooms and finally yelled, "Let me know when it's safe to come out. You both know I'm too young to see this."

I kissed Colin and went to Luke, and we hugged. "Missed you, Lukey Boy."

"Missed you too, Grandma." For this, he got a smack.

"Get some clothes on and come on out. Are you hungry?"

I returned to the living room. Colin already had on pants and a shirt. I kissed him again and said I had to run some milk up to the office. "I'll be back in a sec."

I took my milk up to the office. When I entered, Jodie was drinking coffee with milk and calmly said, "Give me the basics of your call with George, and I'll do the medical record. I'd offer to keep Luke up here, but we all know you're too old for any hanky panky, and you certainly do not have the Lord's permission until you're married."

"Did you know he was coming?" I wagged my finger at her.

"Only for a week. No one saw your lover boy. I picked them up at the airport while you and George Jackson were having a moment. Don't worry, I covered for you. I took him straight to the house, so no one knows he's here. At least have some lunch, and I've booked the rest of the day out for you. You've earned it. Oh, by the way, I'm sure you're feeling terrible about the names you were calling me on the way to the house, and I forgive you. You can keep the milk."

"Consider yourself kicked, sister. I was going to give you the milk and pack my bags."

"One more week, and then a lifetime of servitude has ended. Hang in there, Maggie."

"With the junior over in the barn, you really don't need me."

"She's good. I'm impressed. Maybe the Taggarts can talk them into staying."

"Did she tell you I knew her mother?"

"No, really?"

"We were classmates, but her mother was killed right after vet school. I was even a bridesmaid at her mother's wedding. It was a tragedy. Isn't it so remote that we would meet here in Australia?"

"Piss off Maggot. I have work to do."

I headed off to the house. Colin made sandwiches and drank a beer while Luke was flipping through the television channels. They had on the air conditioner, and the place was almost bearable. "Welcome to my world, gentlemen."

Colin glanced up and grinned. "Were you surprised?"

"Oh yeah. Not a clue, beautiful boy, not a clue in the world. By the way, we have company tonight. You would not believe this, but do you remember me telling you that my classmate died, and I lost contact with her daughter?"

"Yes. Did you find the daughter?" Colin glanced up.

"Yep. Lauren's a vet. Not only is she a vet, but Lauren's also a horse vet! She and her husband, Jim, are working here for a few weeks until the Taggarts get back. They're coming for dinner. Oh, maybe I should cancel. I'll bet you two are jet-lagged."

"No, we'll be fine. This is important to you, darlin'. I wouldn't stop this for anything." He came over, put his arm around me, and handed me a plate. "Maggie, we didn't come to interfere. We came to support you."

"How about I take you for a tour after lunch?"

"I want to see too, Maggie." Luke seemed eager.

"For sure, Luke. I think you might get a good idea about what a vet's life is like from this."

When we headed down to the barn, Jim changed the intravenous bags on the horse with the impaction and had just run the horse with the nephrosplenic ligament. The owners were still there. Their daughter, Nicole, was about Luke's age. I watched as Luke slicked his hair when the girl hugged her horse. I introduced Jim to Colin. They each did a double-take as they stared at one another. I've seen a few people look at Colin with admiration or awe, but this was different. Jim and Colin shook hands, and then every few seconds, he would look over at Colin and stare until Colin would notice, and then Jim would look away.

"Hi, Jim, anyone ever tell you that you look like Hank Buchanan on my old *Comstock* series?" Colin was just as curious.

"Yes, many times, but we can't all be movie stars. Some of us have to actually work for a living."

This made Colin roar. "I guess."

Jim grinned. "Oh boy, is my wife going to love to meet you."

I was slightly alarmed by Jim's reaction to the sight of Colin. He finally shook his head, "I'm sorry for staring, but you remind me so much of a family friend."

"Don't tell Maggie, or she might want to trade me in."

I rolled my eyes and walked on. Both horses appeared more relaxed, and as we walked past the impaction horse, he raised his tail, passed some gas, and produced a watery motion. "Yeah, boy. One down and one to go. Good job, Jim. We can make a horse vet out of you yet."

"Uh, I don't think so. The hours are not conducive to my beauty sleep."

"There is that, but I think sleep is overrated." I walked on and observed Luke watching Nicole, who was holding her horse. "Luke, this is Nicole. She owns Seeker. Nicole, this is my soon-to-be adopted grandson, Luke."

They both said a shy "hi" to one another. "Why don't you two walk Seeker down to the road and back and let him have a bite of grass. Not too much, but enough to stimulate him to get his guts moving." Both Luke and Nicole left the barn.

Colin observed this and smiled. "So, Jim, where did you say you live?"

"Nevada, sir. Near Tahoe."

"Oh, I know it well. I worked in the area for many years."

"So, you're the person I think you are?"

"Yes, I'm Maggie's fiancé. Guilty. Oh, and in my distant past, I used to be an actor."

"My wife is going to fall down dead."

I couldn't help myself. "Not until I'm long gone, please. We'll see you at the house tonight. Make dinner at six-thirty. I have it covered."

We went to the office, and Jodie was on the phone and giving me the thumbs-up. She hung up and stood up. "Welcome to the clinic, Mr. Chandler. Is our staff treating you well? We pride ourselves in meeting your every expectation."

"It's Colin, and the day is early, but so far, she's keeping up."

I smirked and replied, "He's demanding, Jodie. I may have to have the rest of the day off to meet all his needs."

"Uh, nope. Lauren is still out, and we have a stitch job coming in soon."

I groaned. "Who?"

"A new client. Don't worry. It's a small laceration above the eye. It won't take long."

Jodie ran a tight ship, and she wasn't going to let me off the hook for the day when there was an emergency. "Okay, I'll be at the house. Text me when they get here."

We returned to the house and left Luke mooning over the young horse owner. Colin appeared exhausted. I put him in my bed and told him to rest. We had the young vets coming for dinner. I would have put the dinner off, but I was so keen to learn more about this young daughter of my classmate. She was older than my kids by about four years.

Colin asked me to tickle his back, and he pulled up his shirt. "The young vet sure did stare at you down in the barn. Didn't he?"

"I get that every now and then. I try and ignore it. Once people are around me and see I am an average person, the adulation goes away. Well, except for you." I pinched him, and he reached around and pulled me into his arms.

"Remember, I've seen you naked, and I've heard you fart, beautiful boy."

"Ditto, old girl. I'll always idolize you." We heard a knock on the front door. It was the new nurse, Marty.

"Maggie, the stitch job is here."

"Be right there. Can you get the horse into the crush and get a suture kit and some lidocaine ready, and I'll join you in two seconds?"

"Righto, boss." We could hear her yelling to the client to unload the horse.

"Get some sleep if you can. I may not let you sleep much tonight, lover boy."

Colin smiled. "With any luck."

I went to the barn, and Luke was with Jim, and they had just moved the "nephro" horse out of the crush. The horse with the laceration took its place. He was a small quarter horse, and he appeared to be compliant.

Jim commented that he liked the idea of some of the descriptors for things like crush for stocks and drenching for nasogastric tubing. "But why do you say snitch for a twitch?"

"Oh, that's just us. No one else calls it a snitch. One of our clients didn't know the difference and called it that, and we thought it was so funny that we all called the twitch a snitch ever since. Our other personal term we adopted was 'the crunchers.'"

"Let me guess. Are they the emasculators?" We all nodded.

The laceration was just under the forelock, and he didn't want it touched. I gave the horse my usual sedation and then gently pulled up on the forelock, and up came a V-flap of skin that ran from midway between the eyes to each ear. The owners were shocked and appalled, and even I was surprised.

Jim whistled. "That's one thing I don't get to do much with small animals."

"You can have a go if you want."

"Really? I'd love to."

I turned to the owners and explained that Jim was a board-certified specialist surgeon and that he was here with his wife filling in for the regular vets. "Do you mind if Dr. Kennedy does the honors?"

They were happy, so while Jim got set up, I did some minimal cleaning and placed the local anesthesia into the skin. I stepped back while Jim assessed the wound and asked for appropriate suture material. He quickly and expertly sutured the skin. Luke observed the whole procedure. Jim had Luke cut sutures as he finished each knot. Luke was chuffed. He would occasionally glance over at the young girl who was now watching as well. Oh, boy, did I like this guy.

It went well, and in no time, Jim said. "Done and dusted." I was impressed. He turned to me and said, "A good surgeon's a quick surgeon."

"Or vice versa." We smiled at each other while Marty gave the tetanus vaccine booster and instructions on wound care and antibiotics.

The owner asked how long Jim would be here, and he said long enough to remove the sutures, which were due out in two weeks. The horse had stood quietly and allowed Jim to easily place the sutures, but he was coming out of the sedation, and he'd had enough. The owners followed me up to the office, paid their bill, and thanked us for doing such an excellent job. They left the office, and Jodie and I high-fived each other.

"Maggie, you always say anyone can suture a facial laceration, but those people were impressed. You can be replaced."

"I have been replaced, and I am happy to never do one again. Give me a laptop, a fishing rod, and a good horse any day." As I said that, Colin came into the office.

"So easily pleased, you may be the least expensive investment I'll ever make." Colin put his arm around me and kissed my cheek.

Jodie waved her arm. "Hey, public displays of affection are not allowed in the workplace."

"Funny, I don't remember you saying that to Lauren and Jim."

"They're married. You're not."

"Who died and made you the love police?"

"Jesus Christ. That's who died." I could see Colin thought we were serious.

"Let's not break with the practice decorum, darlin'. She's the boss."

Jodie glanced over to Colin. "Well, according to Maggie, you're going to outlive her. She probably only has a few years left, so I'm going to allow a little hanky panky, but try to keep it to a minimum."

I shook my head. If Colin wasn't there, I might have continued with negotiations. Still, knowing his limits, I thanked Jodie and said I was heading to the shops to get steaks for the new arrivals. I yelled to Luke, who never would leave the barn or Jim and his latest interest in the opposite sex. Colin and I headed into town. My town was smaller than our tiny American town. "Don't worry, it has all the essentials: a bottle shop for grog, a small grocery shop, and a thrift shop for used clothes. By the way, I've secured a wedding dress."

"Promise me you're kidding." He paused, and I didn't reply for quite some time.

"According to the ladies in the shop, it's the same dress as Diana wore in her wedding to Prince Charles. You know they drove through here on their wedding tour."

"Did you see her?" Colin had mentioned he had met her.

"I'd just graduated from vet school. You don't think the ladies in the thrift shop would lie, do you? I had to pay ten dollars more. Any chance you'd reimburse me? It was thirty-five altogether."

"And here I am bragging to everyone that you're a bargain." Colin looked up at the sky and shook his head. "God, are you sure I'm not making a big mistake here?"

"Did you hear that?" I cupped my ear with my hand.

"Yes, that was God telling me that you are a bargain at twice the price." He reached over and kissed me. "Let's get this dinner over with. I may have plans for you this evening."

Chapter 41

Luke was finally back at the main house. Colin watched Luke without comment. I could see he was studying the boy. I wasn't holding back. "Still want to be a vet, Lukey?"

"I do. But now I want to live in Australia."

Colin put his hand on Luke's shoulder. "Might that have to do with a certain young woman?"

"Lukey Boy, the day is young. There are going to be many ports of call that are going to draw you." He was going to be a heartbreaker, and the agony of love was just beginning. How lucky he was.

"Maggie, maybe not call me that when we're outside the house. I like it, but maybe just with us." Luke left to get on his swimsuit in preparation for the arrival of the Kennedys. Colin and I glanced at each other and smiled that knowing smile. I remembered my first infatuations. Colin began to hum the tune to the song "Young Love" by Sonny James.

The salad was done, the beans were steaming, and the potatoes and sweet potatoes were in the oven. The barbecue was fired up. I had a gin and tonic, and Colin had a beer. But where were the guests?

I thought I heard the clinic car pull up an hour ago. I finally peered out the window and saw the pair walking from the barn up to the house. I went out on the porch and greeted them. Jim held Lauren's hand as they walked into the house. Colin had gone into the bedroom and emerged after the drinks were ordered. When he appeared, Lauren opened her mouth and gasped.

Jim held her hand and said, "I told you that you were in for a surprise."

"Lauren, this is my fiancé, Colin. Colin, Lauren's the girl that I told you about. Her mother and I were classmates in vet school." I didn't need to state the obvious. Lauren's mother was killed right after graduation when she was only three years old.

Colin walked over and took her hand. "So good to meet you. My beautiful, soon-to-be betrothed thinks you are the greatest. How are you finding Australia?"

In her sweet, strong, Southern accent, Lauren could barely answer with a short "Fine, sir."

Colin persisted and was obviously trying to make her comfortable. "Are you going to swim? The water is a perfect temperature."

Luke emerged from his room. He had on his swimsuit, and he smiled when he saw Jim. "Thank you for letting me help you today, Dr. Kennedy."

"Luke, I go by Jim to my friends and work associates. You haven't met my beautiful wife. Luke, this is Lauren."

Luke was smiling ear to ear. "Hi." That was all he could say.

Lauren stared at us and was obviously confused as to who was who.

"Lauren, Luke is Colin's grandson. Luke lives with us. Actually, come to think of it, I'm the recent addition." Colin came up and put his arm around me.

"Well, she's on trial—try before you buy."

I smirked. "It goes both ways, darling, so try and be on your best behavior."

Colin laughed and squeezed my shoulder. "Oh, for Tuesdays," he said, which made me spew my drink. Both Jim and Lauren realized it was an inside joke.

Lauren looked perplexed. "Maggie, maybe we can discuss this Tuesday thing sometime?"

"Oh, yeah. That is definitely a discussion we need to have. Head on out to the pool, and I'll bring out some nibbles in a second."

The Kennedys and Luke went out, and it was seconds before I heard splashing. I turned to Colin. "Did you see her reaction to you? Do you have any young girls in your past? She was mesmerized."

"Never saw her, and I was never attracted to young girls, FYI. I like women who fish."

I went out with the food tray, stripped to my swimming suit, and jumped in. The cool water was heaven-sent. I swam a few laps, then got out and returned to the kitchen. Even Colin was in the pool when I returned. They had been chatting, and Colin smiled when I returned. "Maggie, I'm rethinking that last statement. Turns out Lauren fly fishes."

"Did you tell her about the gelding you gave me?" I emphasized the word gelding, which made Colin laugh.

"No, I'll get right to that, darlin'."

After a brief swim, I put the steaks onto the barbecue, and Colin and Jim took over the cooking while Lauren put on clothes over her suit and joined me in the kitchen.

"How's the nephro?"

"I think he's exhausted from having two young teens drag him all over the property."

"Tomorrow morning, if you don't think he's any better, then we should knock him out and roll him. Has he passed any manure today?"

"Yes, and he's fairly empty now, so maybe we should run him one more time, and then if it doesn't flip, we could knock him out before it gets too hot. I don't know how you practiced in this heat. It's worse than Kentucky."

"Lauren, do you mind if I ask you a few things?"

"Oh, no, not at all. If you were worried about talking about my mother, please don't be."

"It was more about your dad and grandfather. Becky and I went up to Montana twice, and I met your grandfather. I'm assuming he's passed?"

"A few years ago. When I was old enough to visit Grandpa, my mom and dad sent me up every summer to stay with him. For many years we rode around the area where my mother was killed. My grandfather was sure she was still alive. You know they never found anything. He finally found peace and died as well."

"You mention your mom? I guess your dad remarried?"

"Yes, Dad ended up marrying my aunt, Becky's sister, so she's who raised me. I know it's a bit confusing. I'm happy with my life, and look how it turned out. I'm married to the most wonderful man in the world, and we love what we do and the path we've taken. I hope you're lucky too. He seems so nice. He reminds me of a dear friend. You must be so happy."

"I'm the luckiest woman in the world, for sure. Well, I guess maybe next to you. I wish Collie and I had met earlier, but we'll take advantage of the time we have left. We both love to fish, and we both love Luke."

"Yeah, he's going to be a heartbreaker someday, isn't he?" Lauren looked out of the sliding glass door at Luke diving into the pool.

"I think he may already be breaking one heart and vice versa. That young nephro owner seems to be quite enthralled with him."

"Can I take that out to the table?" I handed her the beans.

"Do you mind checking how the steaks are coming? I'm not into cremations."

We all sat down at the table, and Colin toasted our guests. We ate and talked. I watched Lauren, who could not take her eyes off Colin. Colin was aware of my concern. Colin told the Kennedys how we met and how I could swear a blue streak, mentioning the gate-hanging episode, the trespassing, and my inability to cast a fishing line. Despite all that, he fell in love with me and had to fight Luke for my attention.

Luke grinned, and Jim tousled Luke's hair. "Sorry, mate, but it seems like you've found a nice replacement. That young Sheila's easy on the eyes for sure. Ouch, what was that for." Lauren had socked him.

"For general purposes, Jim Bob." She turned back to Colin. "My dad and I've been fishing since I was little. He goes to New Zealand with my mom at least every other year. They used to go to a remote lodge on the South Island, but it closed down a few years ago. I taught Jim to fish too." Lauren glanced over to Jim and mentioned how much they enjoyed fishing together.

This was not lost on Colin and me. "Maggie and I like to fish too. I'm instructing her on casting, and she's getting better all the time."

This made both Lauren and Jim laugh, and he almost choked on his meat. "Lauren's been teaching me the finer art of fishing as well."

I had a feeling they might also be using the term fishing lessons like Colin and I did. Colin immediately invited them to the ranch this summer for some fishing. He even suggested that she bring her mother and father. Lauren said they would try to come, but she mentioned her father was getting pretty old.

I put my hand on Colin's forearm and suggested that we could accommodate old geezers. To which Colin replied, "Well, that's not really been tested, but I'm sure we could get your dad down to a spot on the river. Maggie and I bought an old fishing lodge in New Zealand, and we're hoping to get it back up and running soon. After I attempt to win over Maggie's kids, we're headed over there to have a quick fish and meet some guys who may manage it for us."

I rolled my eyes. "Collie, dreams. He thinks he's going to survive meeting my kids. As if."

We talked more about Jim's background and how they met. I was surprised that Lauren went up to the area where her mother went missing. Still, she had fond memories of riding in the mountains with her grandfather for weeks every summer, searching for any signs of her mother.

Of course, Colin had been in the area for years when he produced, directed, and acted in his television series. He mentioned he'd been long gone from the site, but many of his crew still lived in the area. They helped search, and Colin had donated some money to pay for some of the excavation work.

"Did you ever find anything? It was so strange. I followed it for a year or two, and then I moved over here and had my own dramas, and I never checked to see if there was any resolution."

Lauren reached into her blouse and pulled out a locket. "This was found in the water many years later."

I stared at the locket on the gold chain and nodded. "I remember when your father gave it to her." I turned away, and we all were silent.

"I guess that's it." Lauren placed it back inside her shirt.

"Your mother—I mean, your real mother would be so proud of you. I'm sure your dad is."

"He comes out every now and then and rides with me on calls. We have a favorite place we like to camp and fish. It's called Miner's Meadow, and we try and go when no one else is there. Dad and I stayed in a cabin once, and a gigantic tree was hit by lightning and fell when we were there.

Colin nodded. "I know where you're talking about. We filmed up there once a year—beautiful."

Jim stood. "We have another full day tomorrow. We better get some shut-eye, Lauren. After we roll the colic, and if we roll the colic, how about I take the boys and head to the beach? Is it about an hour from here? I think they have charter boats, and maybe we can go out on the ocean and go fishing. Are either of you up for it?" Colin and Luke nodded.

"I'd like to come unless I'm needed to walk the horse."

Jim smiled and turned to us. "If Luke's needed, then we can wait until he's done. Work comes first."

As Colin and I lay in bed after the Kennedys left and Luke was asleep, Colin reached out, lifted my T-shirt, and began to tickle my back. "Your turn, old girl. Thanks for tonight. I really like Jim and Lauren. He's a good role model for Luke."

"Sure is. Over to the left a bit." I shifted so Colin could reach more of my back. This didn't happen often, and I was taking full advantage. "Lauren looks at you like she's seen a ghost. Are you sure you don't have any possible daughters? Ouch."

"Serves you right. I may have been tempted, but, darlin', I never did, and I never will. You can take it to the bank."

"I won't bring it up again, but she sure thinks you're someone she knows. It was far more than adoration."

"Turn over, darlin'. Can I hold you? I'm not long for this world."

"Sweet dreams, beautiful boy." Colin did not reply, and I heard his rhythmic breathing.

I woke in the middle of the night and walked down to the barn to check the gelding, which was not improving. I administered more pain meds and restarted his intravenous fluids. I stayed with him until they were finished, and around four in the morning, I returned. Colin had slept through the entire night. It was cold in the house, so I turned down the air conditioner and replaced a sheet over Colin. He reached back and pulled me up to him.

"Any joy, darlin'?"

"No. I'm freezing. Will you spoon me so I can get some sleep?"

He turned, and I pushed my back into him as he kissed the back of my shoulder and pulled a sheet over me. I woke several hours later to an empty bed. Colin described what transpired while I was asleep. He'd woken early the following day and had gone down to the barn where he, Jim, and Lauren had decided it was time to anesthetize and roll the horse. Luke and I were still sleeping. By the medical record, they realized I had spent three hours with the horse, so they decided to let me sleep. Colin returned and woke Luke.

The four of them and Lexie anesthetized the horse and then rolled him on his back, and while Lauren lay on the ground with her arm in the rectum, they rolled the horse side to side. They repeated this procedure, hoping the loop of the intestine would move and be released.

Luke was ecstatic when they finally returned to the house and described the procedure. "Maggie, it was so cool. I got to help roll him, and Jim even drew a picture to show me what was happening. Seeker stood up and then did the biggest fart you could imagine. Lauren and Jim seemed happy, and they thanked Grandpa and me for our help. We're going to the ocean after breakfast. Grandpa's making breakfast now."

The house was hot once again. Instead of showering, I put on my suit and jumped into the pool, and swam a few laps.

When Luke was in the bathroom, Colin asked me if I ever swam in the pool without my suit.

"Never. Don't get any ideas. I heard you all may have fixed the colic."

Colin's rendition was like Luke's, and he remarked how impressed he was with Lauren. Too bad they won't move and work with Patty Tilmouth. After we ate, Jim came and picked them up. When I knew they had gone, I texted Colin. "About the swimsuit, I lied. Meet you after Luke's asleep." He replied with a smiley face and a quick message to prepare the landing pad.

Chapter 42

Lauren and I did the hard yards while the guys hopefully went fishing. Our nephro horse appeared to have responded to the rolling technique. He drank a whole bucket of water, ate a small amount of food, and passed oily feces. I was happy that Lauren had been taught to use a small amount of oil. The use of mineral oil or paraffin oil, as they called it over here, was considered old-school. Owners would watch for the oil to pass, making them feel more confident that their horse would recover.

"There are many ways to skin the cat, but I like water, mild exercise, and pain control, except for nephrosplenic ligament entrapments. I think running works well with those." We sat in the barn, drank ice water, and went over the schedule away from the staff. "Do you guys need some time off?"

"No, I'm so glad to meet you and see how you do things. My guess is you and my bio-mom would have done things similarly. Do you mind me asking about your and Colin's reference to Tuesdays? Are those special days?"

I choked on my water and had a coughing fit. When I regained my voice, I could not say what I wanted without laughing. It was one of those rare times when I would try to say something and then laugh so hard, I couldn't complete the sentence. Finally, I was able to control myself. I explained that I had introduced "fetish Tuesdays" when any-thing goes. I explained that it was only in jest, but Colin thought it was a good idea. "Lauren, word the to the wise. Don't offer anything to Jim unless you plan to follow up on the offer."

I didn't talk about our safe words. I was sure Lauren would have been shocked enough for people our age to even think about these kinds of things. She sat quietly, and I could see she was preparing to talk about something. "You two seem to really love one another. Was it love at first sight, or was it gradual?"

"Ha. I was almost engaged to someone else last year. I'm the number one worst judge of a person who would be a good partner. I suppose I chose the other guy over Colin because Colin was married, and I'd heard he took his vows seriously. I'd also heard he married his second wife on the rebound, and he still loved his first wife. Then there was the age thing. I'm as guilty of ageism as the next person."

"So, what made you switch? What happened to the other guy?"

"Some of it is too complicated, but I will say I am a loyal person. I don't switch from one person to the other easily. The other guy died, but it was more than that. He began to display qualities that I didn't think I wanted to live with. Then Colin and I had such a good time together, and we had similar interests. Then there was Luke. Do you know about Luke's story?"

"Yes, as much as you can from reading the newspapers."

"When I met him, he hadn't spoken in years. He came to help me with odd jobs around my new property, which was next door to Colin, and eventually, he began to speak and come out of his tough shell. That is what got Colin's attention. The bigger question is, why did Colin Chandler become interested in an old vet? Do you know he has never seen me in a dress? I'm no beauty, and I'm not into glamour or the life of a celebrity. I like to ride my horse, fish, and write my books. I don't have expensive tastes. When he finally knew he could get a divorce from his current wife, I thought we might have to live off my retirement savings. I booked a flight in the economy seats, and he changed it to first class. There's so much more. What attracted you to Jim?"

"Funny you should mention that. I was engaged to someone else for three years during vet school. He cheated on me, and you only get one shot with me. Jim wasn't my first choice, and that guy died too, but I know it wouldn't have worked in the long run. Jim came to the practice when my boss died, and while he wasn't dead set good-looking, I noticed his kind manner and skills. He couldn't fish for crap, and so we began fishing lessons."

I smiled and remembered when Colin came up and showed me how to improve my cast. I was reminded of the time he continued to hold my hand when we finished crossing a river. The thought made my heart swell. "I see what you see. He is a unique man. You are fortunate to realize that you've found gold."

She shot up when I said that and turned to me. "You have no idea. Do you believe in anything weird like the occult or time travel or reincarnation?"

"Never say never, but no. I'm a basic, 'just the facts, ma'am,' kind of girl. Lauren, I noticed you keep staring at Colin. I've seen a few women look at him, and they are mesmerized by his fame. With you, it's different. Do you mind me asking what it is?"

"Oh, it's not what you think. You know how often we think we all have a doppelgänger in our lives? I've met Colin's. He's dead now, but the similarity is uncanny. He was someone very dear to me."

Lexie came into the barn and announced morning tea was served. We stood, and Lauren turned to me. "So, I suspect that you'll want us to have Luke come and spend the night next Tuesday."

Chapter 43

A week later, Colin, Luke, and I left for Hamilton Island. The last week was still viciously hot. The colics continued, and we lost two horses due to various factors. I was not sorry to see the end of the summer here in Oz. I loved my life here, but at times it was brutal. Now it was Colin's turn to carry the load. I wished him luck with my kids and took a back seat—way back.

"Darlin' girl, I didn't get where I am by not understanding human motivation and managing competing interests. This will be great. Luke gets to meet more of his relatives, and I will have them eating out of my hand by the end of the first day. You have no worries."

"I can hardly wait, Collie. I could say that better men have tried, but in your case, that isn't true. Oh, did my eye just roll? By the way, have you noticed your grandson? He's missing Jim and Lauren already."

It was true. Jim and Luke formed a bond, and the two of them did everything together during the day. Even I had become passé. Luke was tired from all the work he and Jim did during the day and then swimming at night. Jim even helped Luke with homework since Luke had missed classes.

Lauren mentioned that Jim said Luke was a very clever boy and could just get into any college he wanted. Jim and Lauren invited him to come and visit when school was out, and we did the same to them. I loved working with Lauren. Not so much that I would want to work again, but I did learn some newer techniques, and I was able to teach her tricks of the trade that would make life easier.

We caught a plane to Brisbane and then to Hamilton Island, where a van met us and escorted us to our hotel. Wow, that was all I could say. "You know, Collie, I've never been here. Many of my friends have, but I never took time off from work."

"You've led such a sheltered life. I'm surprised you can write about things. I'm just grateful for the cool breeze. Shall we get in the pool now? It looks like rain."

"According to my research, it won't be much. Do you mind if I have a nap first? That last horse did me in."

"I need to make some reservations and get a few things ready, so knock yourself out, darlin'. Pun intended."

The rooms were air-conditioned. Our suite had a shared space that had a kitchenette and bar. Luke's room was off the main room. He was already in his suit and was impatiently waiting for his grandfather. After they left, I headed to the bed and instantly was asleep. It didn't take long to revive myself. I put on my suit and headed down to the pool. Colin was sitting with three women who were chatting with him. They were older and apparently recognized him. I waved to Luke, who was already talking to a young girl.

Luke was in the water, and I joined him. The temperature was perfect. The clouds were gathering, and we all heard thunder in the distance. We swam for another thirty minutes until the staff suggested we retreat. Then, a wind arose and knocked over two umbrellas and the table below them. I was nervous. Was the weekend going to be like this? Would our idyllic vacation be spent indoors?

"Don't worry, darlin', I ordered better weather for tomorrow." Both Luke and Colin showered, sat down in the living room, and watched television. Colin cringed at the commercials, which were amateurish at best. Then the cricket came on, and try as I might, I could not explain the rules so they could understand what was going on.

After dinner, and when the storm was finally over, we all went for a walk on the beach. I broke all my rules of personal etiquette and put on a floral skirt and blouse. It was not fancy or new, but I was comfortable in it. Colin smiled broadly. "Not quite as sexy as you are in your waders, but nice."

Luke whistled. I admonished him. "Luke, whistling is not acceptable anymore in society. But you can whistle around me anytime. Just so you know."

Colin rolled his eyes and asked what was becoming of the world. "I filled out the dating consent form in triplicate. Damn, I didn't include the consent to whistle when you wear something sexy."

"Well, mister. You better hire a lawyer next time. My daughter will bring you up short without the whistling addition to your contract."

Luke stayed behind us as we walked arm in arm and examined fauna and a few shells that had surfaced from the wind and waves. You would never have guessed that such a ferocious storm had recently passed through. As we turned to return to our hotel, Colin took my arm and stopped. He reached into his pocket and dropped to his knee. "Margaret, Magster, Maggot, Maggie, darlin' girl, will you give me the supreme honor of becoming the woman who will marry me and live out our lives forever and eternity? I love you more than life, and I will do anything to make you happy. I'm officially a free man, and I will love you to my dying day. I know I asked before, but now I'm really free."

I was shocked beyond belief. Tears came to my eyes, and I took his hand and helped him stand. He placed the new ring on my finger as I cried. I was surprised that yet another ring had been made. This one complemented the one he gave me at the airport in Christchurch. It was smaller but fit against the larger one. I had removed the other ring from my necklace. It was back on my finger when we left my old veterinary clinic earlier this morning.

Luke was standing in the palms and was filming the proposal. I turned to him and wagged my finger. "You knew, and you didn't prepare me. So much trouble, mister, so much trouble."

"I had to choose between you and Grandpa. He swore me to secrecy. Us men need to stand together."

"Darlin', you haven't said yes yet. These contractual obligations must be confirmed."

I looked into his eyes and, on tiptoe, reached up to kiss him and quietly said, "Yes."

He turned to Luke. "Luke, are you still filming. Did you get her response?"

"Yeah, but it's on my phone, and you'll have to see my lawyer about the film rights. I know you're family, Grandpa, but the *National Enquirer* might want to outbid you for this exclusive."

The move was quick and entirely unexpected. Colin had Luke in a headlock before anyone could say, paparazzi. "Okay, you can have the video. I give up."

My entire family was on a flight the following day. I was nervous as we waited for the plane to arrive. Colin held my hand, and I could feel the tension in his grip. "Collie, they can't shoot you. Only the crims have guns in Oz. It may get ugly, but there won't be any physical violence."

"Small comfort, darlin'."

For the umpteenth time, Luke asked when they would get here. The plane had been delayed, and the arrival time had been pushed back twice. Finally, we saw the plane landing, and then anxiety kicked in. I hadn't seen my family in almost a year. It took forever to see people coming down the steps from the plane walking toward the terminal. As they emerged into the main building, the grandchildren all ran and hugged me.

"Hey, you guys. How was the plane? Boy, have you all grown? You're all so big now."

I was enveloped by the grandchildren, and it was impossible to reach their parents. Brandon whistled, and all the kids stopped and looked up. Brandon then walked over and hugged me. "Hi, Mum, welcome home."

This was followed by Trevor and Colleen, who were obviously not as welcoming. "About time, Mum." I introduced Colin and Luke, who were warmly greeted by everyone. Nothing like star power to warm a hostile crowd. Luke was older than the grandkids, but he immediately joined the pack as we made our way to the bus to take them to our hotel.

Colin had arranged everything. My children had a room like ours with flowers, champagne, wine, and a well-stocked refrigerator with drinks and fruit. There were small packages for each of the children and an envelope that contained tickets for a fishing trip, a snorkeling adventure, and dinner for the next two nights. There was a picture of the proposal taken from the video that Luke made last night, a list of activities, dinner times, and a voucher for adults to spend in the hotel shops.

"Mum, this is too much. You shouldn't have." Brandon bent over and kissed me.

"Brandy, don't thank me. Colin did this on his own."

Colleen came out of her room and asked me to go inside. "Mum, if you think you can buy me with this crap—" But she didn't finish, and she stared at me and shook her head. "Well, it's a good start. I'll say that for him."

"Make him earn it, Colleen. It will only be to my benefit." I walked away, and she asked me to stay.

"Do you mind if we have a talk?"

We walked out to the beach, and she turned to me and said she had been in contact with her dad. "Mum, he's changed. He realizes he's made a stuff-up of his life, and he wants to get back with us all. He's even sent me some money to help with the school fees. He'd like to talk to you. Will you talk to him?"

"Colleen, there is no way in hell I would go back to all that. Talk to Colin, and I think you'll see the difference."

"But Mum, he's so old."

"Colleen, try and keep up with him. I thought the same thing. It's hard for you to understand, but maybe give it a day or two and see if you feel the same way. I guess the other thing you have to realize is at our age, anyone could die unexpectedly. I tried dating, but with you three and the clinic, I felt I couldn't really juggle a man with it all. Now, I'm free, and to be honest, getting involved with someone was the last thing on my mind. He was only a friend, and he patiently waited when I was, shall we say, involved with someone else. He's a good man, and he has organized all of this while I worked at the clinic. He wants to win you over, and I hope you will give him a chance."

"But you will live over there, and you'll never come back. We all hoped you would return once you realized how crazy those Americans are and how much you missed us."

"Well, you're right on one account. I'll let you figure out which one that is."

She stared at me and then laughed. "Okay, I'll play nice. Besides, Nigel already thinks he's cool."

"Thanks. Don't slack up too much. I might be able to get more concessions if you play hardball. I'm counting on you to make Colin work for it."

Well, that didn't happen. As soon as my children sat at lunch and talked to Colin, it was apparent they were on his side. Colin knew about both sporting goods in Australia and the Australian Air Force. He had them eating out of the palm of his hands. In fact, toward the end of the first day, it was Colin and my kids against me in all aspects of wedding planning and living arrangements.

The women all expected me to wear a new wedding dress. They instructed me to sell my property and live full-time with Colin, and they insisted on a formal wedding to which they would all be invited. They planned it for the Australian school break so even the grandkids could come. I was outnumbered. Colin and I sat side by side at the pool later before dinner. He had two kids on his lap, while I had one. My family had been won over. He gazed over and quietly smirked and said, "I told you so."

Breakfast was quick as Colin, and the boys were headed out to go fishing on a charter. The rest of us went snorkeling, and we all met up again for dinner, where Colin had booked a room for our family. I was seated at one end of the table, and he was at the other. Luke and the children were all sitting at an adjoining table. Despite Luke's reluctance to sit with the younger children, he agreed to hold court over the grandkids. There may have been an exchange of money, but I was not informed.

Colin stood and proposed a toast. "Please raise your glasses to my beautiful soon-to-be bride. She has brought joy to Luke and me like I never expected. She is kind, spirited, and shares my love of fishing and horses, and Luke and I would be lost without her. To Maggie."

Everyone all cheered, and it appeared that Colin had won them over. Then he asked the question that I had dreaded. "One more thing. I'm a traditionalist in many ways. The wedding vows may vary, but one thing I would like to clear up right now. When Sam, our minister, asks if there is anyone who objects to the wedding, can I have your word that you won't be among the objectors?"

There was an awkward pause, and everyone gazed down at their plate. The silence was deafening. Finally, Brandon spoke, "Colin, uh, Cathy and I, well..."

Trevor responded, "Mum, Simone, and I, well, we don't think—"

But then he was interrupted by Nigel. "No, we've all been talking." I stared down the table at Colin, who was shaking. "Sure, we all think you're a great guy but, I guess here's the truth. In what, thirty-six hours or so, we've all got to know you, and we've somewhat come to understand things."

At this point, Luke jumped up and, sensing his grandfather's embarrassment and dismay, came over and took him by the arm. Nigel continued. "Well, Collie. It's okay to call you Collie, isn't it?" I was now beginning to weep. "Collie, we like you so much we feel you need to be protected. It isn't you. It's our mum. We feel you are getting in over your head. You are no match for our mother. She's going to make mince out of you. She's a total ballbuster, and we aren't sure you're strong enough to stand up to her."

Now I saw where this was going, and despite my tears, I was beginning to chuckle. Not knowing my kids, I thought Colin was not catching on to this game. It was my turn. "Brandon, Trevor, and Colleen, you better apologize for this. Where is a wooden spoon when you really need one?"

In unison, they all stood and high-fived and cheered themselves. "You aren't the only actor in the family. Keep it in mind. Mum thinks she ran the house, but she was never in charge. If you want to take her on, we will stand by you until hell freezes over, which could be soon from mum's weather reports."

Colin pointed to each of the adults and nodded in a slow, knowing way. They totally fooled us both. Colin came down and pretended to kiss me and quietly whispered in my ear. "You are so right about your children. Game on."

We had one more day to enjoy before we all would depart. We were going to dedicate the day to the grandkids. Colin, Luke, and I were going to take the grandkids for the morning and send them back to their parents after lunch. "Maggie, you know, with them having a free morning and a luxurious room, surely we can get another grandchild out of this."

"Colin Chandler, wash your mouth. Six is enough."

"Little Amy is going to be a heartbreaker, darlin'. I wish I could be around to see her as an adult." This made me feel guilty and kind of sad. It was apparent I would only be a distant memory with the older kids and no memory for the younger ones.

Colin's phone rang, which was odd. He was only using it to text messages back to his accountant. He stared at his phone and mouthed, "Helen."

I mouthed back, "Say 'hi' for me." He waved and stepped out onto the balcony. When he came in, he was shaken.

"It was Jake. Helen's had a stroke."

Chapter 44

C olin continued. "They don't expect her to live much longer. She's in LA and was attending Kyle's showing."

I was shocked. Colin was barely able to keep from crying. We hugged, and Colin began to tremble. I told him over and over how sad I was. I knew Luke was in the shower, and I waited until I heard him emerge. Colin went into his room and shut the door. In less than a minute, Luke appeared and ran to me, hugged me, and cried. I don't think I ever saw him as sad as he was then. He had cried once when he thought Colin and I had come to blows, but not like this. I held him until his crying slowed and finally ended. Colin sat on the end of the bed, and we all hugged.

"Collie, you and Luke need to leave immediately. Let me make some calls." I had been given a number to use when I flew over and was upgraded to first class. I called the number and requested immediate flights back to the States for Colin and Luke. I needed to stay here, and I knew my presence would not be expected by the immediate family. I loved Helen, and I knew we could have been close friends and allies if she had continued to live, but unless there was a miracle, it would never be.

While I packed, I said I would continue onto New Zealand, where we planned to meet Ned Schaeffer and Geoff Harmer. We had scheduled to meet them and go up to the lodge to discuss a potential reopening of the fishing lodge, which would cater to fishermen who wanted a unique New Zealand experience. We felt if we kept the guest numbers down, we could keep the trout levels high and wild enough to give clients a satisfying experience.

So, the plan was to meet Ned and Geoff, take them to the lodge, and learn if the two men were willing to live there for the fishing season. They would maintain the property and give the clients a unique experience. Colin planned to come as well, but he needed to go to be by Helen's side. I would meet the men, and we would go up to the lodge together and assess what needed to be done.

Colin and Luke were booked on flights back to LA, which left only this afternoon to get to Brisbane in time to meet their international flight. I called the concierge, who found a private charter pilot who would take the two of them within the hour. I packed Colin and Luke's bags and took them over to the main building. I saw Colleen and explained what had happened. She walked over to Colin, hugged him, and told him how sorry she was. She cried for a moment, hugged Luke, and asked him to come back over and stay with them next Christmas.

A wagon arrived and took the boys' suitcases, and we embraced and cried once again. "I love you, and I'm so sorry, Collie." I then hugged Luke and whispered, "Take care of your grandfather and maybe tell your grandmother that I love her and wish her peace on her next journey."

Colin enfolded me one more time and thanked me for arranging this. I could see he was at a loss to make any effective plans. "I love you, darlin'. Please stay safe and hurry back. I hate not being with you."

"Love you too, beautiful boy." I stood back, and Colleen put her arm around me as they drove away.

We spent the day on the beach. I told the rest of my family what happened and passed on Colin's regret that he had to leave a day early. I recounted meeting Helen and becoming partners in crime with our mutual love and concern for her grandson and her insistence that Colin loved me.

We had a fantastic time snorkeling in the shadows and building sandcastles. The older children said they missed Luke. They asked when they were going to see him again. As Colin predicted, we had become a family. Colin's attention to each member of my family and his knowledge of their work won them all over. He and Trevor exchanged recipes. Brandon and Colin discussed the politics of the Australian educational system and the pros and cons of the heavy private school presence in the country. Nigel and Colin discussed flying and planned an outback flying adventure next year, to which both Colleen and I said no. Colin had purchased some small fishing rods and taught the older grandchildren to fish.

Colin did precisely what he intended to do. He won them over. Colin began to heal the family rift regarding my departure from Australia and leaving my family for a new life. When we were all leaving the following day, I had not heard from Colin. I was feeling homesick, and my children could see I was upset. Trevor hugged me and promised that he and Simone and the children would be at the impromptu wedding and quietly warned me, "Mum, you're forgiven. We all love your fiancé, but you need to know we took a poll. If you two split for any reason, we're going with Colin."

"As crazy as that sounds, I would too. God, I love that man to the moon and back. If I can have only one good year, it will all be worth it. And I love you all too. You three were worth it too."

"I'll bet you weren't saying that when we were teenagers."

"No, I sure wasn't. That was when I had to put the wooden spoon away, and I discovered embarrassment as my only means to control you three."

Brandon laughed. "Colleen, do you remember when Mum came to school in her pajamas to pick us up in the afternoon after we had stayed out past curfew?"

"It worked, didn't it? I don't remember any more curfew breaks."

Colleen rolled her eyes. "Yes, but we are all scarred for life. We all had to leave the state to get away from the shame."

"As I said, the perfect solution. Do you know that Chad Little still lives with his mother? Terry is still trying to find a way to get him to leave." Chad was one of Colleen's boyfriends in high school.

"Mum, his mother has dementia. He has to take care of her."

"Colleen, if he told you that, he's lying. His mother is still teaching school. I guess I should count my blessings. It didn't take much to get you all launched."

"You can think it was you, but once Mrs. Donovan left, what was the point of staying?"

The bus pulled up, and I stayed behind while my family left. I was not going for another two hours, and I thought I would make use of my time by writing a chapter on my new book. As I walked back to the suite, I received two text messages. One was from Colin telling me they had arrived in LA, and he was headed to the hospital. The other message was from Brandon, saying, "Mum, best short holiday ever—hurry up and make it legal, with or without us."

Chapter 45

I arrived in Nelson on the South Island. I was to pick up the two men and drive up to the lodge. I rented a car and picked up enough food to feed us for a week, although I would only be there for two days. I called Ned and received no answer. I then called the vet clinic and explained I was back and heading to the lodge and needed Geoff Harmer's phone number. They offered to let me stay and mentioned I could be employed again. "No thanks, I have needs, and they are at the end of a fishing line or on the keyboard of a laptop."

I called Geoff, and he answered and reported that Ned had to attend a funeral for one of his relatives. He asked if they could drive up tomorrow and meet me at the lodge. I was happy with that. It would give me a chance to clean and prepare the place for their arrival.

It was remote, and the gate was locked. There was little chance anyone would come up there, but the homeless situation had increased in other parts of the world. Who knew if someone wouldn't go and squat on the place? I could wait, but I was anxious to get up and see what would need to be done to get the site ready once again. The fishing season was over, and it was becoming wintery. The lodge was high enough that I knew there would eventually be snow, but for now, it would be cold with rain.

I decided to drive to the lodge and begin a list in preparation for the fishing season. Colin told me where the key was. I tried to call him and tell Colin my plans, but there was no answer. I knew he was busy with Helen, and I hoped he could get there and communicate with her. I knew Luke would be upset. I would settle things in the lodge and then walk up to the hill to talk to Colin later. I also promised to call Trevor and let him know I was all right and give him an update on Colin and Luke. I continued to think about Helen. Granted, she was close to eighty, but she was so vibrant, and it was a reminder of how fragile life is. *Please, Lord, just one year.*

I arrived at three in the afternoon and quickly found the key. I noticed car tracks that appeared to be a day or two old. The caretaker, who Ned had employed for us, must have been up recently. I left the gate unlocked and drove up to the compound. Nothing had changed. The grass was mowed, and I saw nothing to say that unwanted visitors were trespassing.

I opened the back of the car I was driving and removed the two bags of groceries. I went to unlock the door, and it was already unlocked. That was careless. I'd have to sort that out with the maintenance people. I went to the refrigerator and found it stocked with milk, beer, and fresh vegetables. Colin must have organized the delivery. However, nothing else was out of place.

I decided to walk down to the river. It was flowing at a much higher level, but the clarity was still good. I went up to the knoll where I'd spotted the fish feeding on my first night here in December. There were two fish feeding. Legally I could fish since it was my property, but I chose to let the fish live and hopefully be caught and released by a guest in the spring.

It was late, and the sun was setting. I returned to the main building and made a salad and some bread. I'd been living too high on the hog for way too long. I would make a great meal tomorrow when the boys came. Tonight, I would semi-fast, except for alcohol, and I had a gin and tonic—heaven on a stick. I even forgot to call the boys until I ate and figured it was too dark to climb the hill. Colin thought we could put in a transmitting tower and receive phone calls at the compound.

I went to my cabin, and everything was the same, except the sheets were laundered, and new soap and towels were in the room. I needed to call Colin tomorrow and thank him for having the maintenance people prepare for our return. I slept well, but as usual, I rose well before sunrise. I could make coffee in my room. So, I had no need to leave my room. I used the time to finish another chapter in my new book. This book was going slow, and I was not making the progress I usually did. I vowed to kick up the pace. My literary agent didn't know I had resumed writing. She didn't communicate or send me encouraging small kicks in the behind, so I didn't feel the pressure internally or externally.

When it was light, I dressed and began to walk to the top of the hill, where I knew I would have phone reception. It began to drizzle. I kicked myself, realizing I'd forgotten to check the weather report. I remember one fishing trip several years ago when the rain gauge showed ten inches of rain overnight. There was no fishing that day or for over a week.

The rain became heavier with each minute until the deluge was too great to continue. I opened my phone, and even though I was close to the top of the hill, there was no reception. I said a few rather rude words to myself and began my descent back to the lodge. On my way down, I slipped, and my ankle twisted. It was not a big deal, and despite a very mild persistent pain, I barely limped, but I could have run if I really wanted to.

The rain pelted down, and I realized that at the rate it was coming down, the guys would not be able to get through to the lodge, nor would I be able to return either. I laughed to myself. *Oh darn, here I am, stuck in paradise.*

Then tragedy struck. The electricity went out. The lodge had a primarily solar system with a power bank. There was no reason to have used all the power stored in the battery. Charlie had shown me the diesel generator and where the diesel was kept. It was up in the shed where the tools were kept. This power outage would not magically resolve by some guy working on a downed line. Either the battery failed, or there was a break in the power line.

I put on a rain jacket left by someone and limped up to the shed where the generator and batteries were housed. It was a mystery to me how it worked. The rain was now deafening and showed no signs of abating. I looked at the equipment and cursed my lack of knowledge. I would never make a pioneer girl. I figured I probably wouldn't survive an apocalypse either.

I found the diesel and checked the generator. The generator was at capacity. All I had to do was start the engine. It started quickly, and I then turned to the line that came from the engine. It went up to a box with written directions to switch from the power bank to the generator. I performed the sequence of changes, and instantly I had power.

I returned to my room and set my phone and laptop on charge. I then went to the kitchen in the main building and checked the refrigerator. The food was still cold, and I realized I had not eaten. I cut a piece of cheese and had an apple. I watched out the large windows as the rain continued.

My emotions ranged from sadness for what Colin and Luke must be going through and the delight and satisfaction at having the freedom of being alone with electricity—def not a pioneer woman. I would never have survived on *Comstock*. That didn't last long. The electricity only stayed on for an hour and then it went off again.

I put on my rain jacket and limped to the shed again. When I entered the hut, the motor was running. I peered at the switch box, and it appeared that everything was in the correct position. I followed the cable out of the shed and into the second bank of terminals that went to various areas. Nothing was working, but one terminal split off to the two buildings where Charlie had made room for Colin and me to write and paint and his private shed where he painted. Both were locked.

I was sure there was a set of keys in the kitchen, and I went down and retrieved them. I was soaked and cold. I was beginning to get a chill. My plan was to see if the electricity was on in the annex rooms and if so, I would see if Charlie had a mini-fridge where I could put the meat and milk. I was practically wading as I traversed the driveway. The water ran so fast it was almost like a river in front of the cabins.

I found the key for the one side designated for Colin and me. I'd never bothered to go in there last time, and I opened the door and flicked on the light. It had power. The room had an easel and a table with two chairs. There were the art supplies I had given to Colin for Christmas. That was all there was. It was hard to tell, but I thought I heard a motor running in the other room. With the sound of the rain, I wasn't sure what I heard. Charlie rarely came out of the room, and I suspected he had a small refrigerator in there. I ran through the keys, but none of them fit. I thought about where he might hide a key. Did he take a key when he had to abruptly leave the lodge with the FBI agents?

I turned off the light and went back to the shed where the diesel generator was housed. I turned off the generator. I sat on a stool in the barn and thought about where Charlie's key might be. The obvious answer was in his personal cabin. So, I waded down to the row of guest cabins, and of course, his room was locked. I then remembered there were several keys along with the tractor key. Despite my sore ankle, exhaustion, and increasing chill, I trudged up to the barn. I was careful to look for old nails that had lacerated my leg on my last visit.

The keys were on a single ring, and the tractor key was in the ignition. The other keys didn't look promising. As I turned to head out of the barn and return to the lodge, I noticed a footprint that appeared to be recently made. I guessed it was from the maintenance man. I had to think about this. The only thing in the barn was the tractor. Why would the man come in here?

I thought I heard an engine start, and I turned quickly, but it was only a wind that rattled through the open barn door. I walked around searching the barn walls, and there was another shoe print. I gazed around, and suddenly I noticed a small metal container fastened to the four by four on the side of the barn. The keys did not work to open the locked box, but hell, Colin and I now owned the property. I decided to go for it. There was a sledgehammer near the tractor, and I took it and attempted to open the box by hitting it. Three whacks and I opened it. Inside was another set of keys. I knew one was going to get me into Charlie's inner sanctum.

Chapter 46

Bingo! I entered and was amazed and delighted to find several easels and paintings. The ones facing the front door were of scenes here at the lodge. They were beautiful, and I was excited to use them in the lodge for the guests. Many were of the rivers and mountains that surrounded us. A few paintings were in the valley next to the river, and one was of a scene where the old buck stood with water streaming from his mouth and steam coming from his nostrils.

I saw a small refrigerator in the corner which was purring. It would be large enough to hold what I needed. There was a small heater in the corner of the room. When I turned to head up to the house, I peered at four easels that had paintings that were covered. I pulled the cloth off one, which was obviously a portrait of Linda holding the reins of her old arthritic horse.

The second was a portrait of the girl I had encountered in Charlie's kitchen. She was nude and lay on a bed with all the signs of eroticism. I laughed, thinking that all this time, Charlie was probably not sleeping with her, but painting her. I have to say, if I was a guy, I would like the painting. Maybe I should give it to Colin. Then I remembered Luke was in the house and quashed that idea.

The next one I unveiled was Linda in a similar pose. I was shocked that Charlie would paint such a picture for the world to see. Then he did have the door locked. It was probably meant for his viewing only. I dreaded the final one and was relieved to see it was not me. Phew, that would be awkward. I had seen this woman, but I didn't know where I'd seen her. Well, I could see why this was off-limits to Colin and me. I would have died to let even my husband see my erotic intimate thoughts. Call me modest, but that is hot and way too hot for me. It isn't a game-changer. I still prefer men.

I returned to the main lodge, and yet again, the torrent of water increased. I don't think I have ever seen rain like this in my life. Leaks were starting from in the main lodge. It was becoming dark, but I got all the perishables into two plastic shop bags and carried the food back to Charlie's hideout. I closed the door and went back up to my cabin. The cabin was awash.

The cabins abutted against a rise where the water rushed onto the joins of the floor and walls. I waded back to the shed where the generator resided. I took a shovel up to the cabins. I attempted to dig a trench, thereby diverting the water from coming into the cabins.

It wasn't hard to do. As I would dig one shovel's worth of mud, the rest of the soil eroded with the water torrent. I soon had the cabins cleared. I checked all the cabins beside Charlie's, and then I remembered I had keys, and I decided to check that room for leaks. The door opened with a key that was unlike any others. Inside the room, there was an unmade bed. There were three handguns and a rifle. There were several pictures of Linda and two of me, and again there was a picture of the woman who was so familiar, yet I could not place her.

There was an accordion file folder that contained several pictures of Linda and the young woman who I had met at Charlie's. Some were pictures of the woman and a man sitting on my porch outside the bedroom of my log cabin back home. A bolt of lightning went through me. These were the Calhouns. The picture was taken from inside my bedroom. They both appeared happy to be photographed. They seemed to be healthy and normal. I didn't see the faraway look that was common in dementia sufferers. I had to assume Charlie had taken the picture. The photograph of the woman sitting in my log cabin was the same one Charlie had painted. It was Mrs. Calhoun. I think Carol was wrong about Charlie's interest in the woman. I saw more than a casual interest expressed in the painting.

I mopped up the floor where the water had crept through. I noticed a spot where the floorboards didn't match. I pushed on one end, and the board rose slightly. I pried it away, and under the floor was a cache of letters bound and sitting in sealed plastic bags. My hands were shaking as I opened them. I prayed they were love letters to or from Linda.

The first one was to Charlie. It was handwritten in a beautiful script. There was no date on some, but they seemed to be in some sort of sequence.

My Dear Charles,
Oh, how I have come to admire you. We both know it can never be, but we can never forget that night and the way we held one another in our mutual grief. Please understand that as much as we want the same thing, we are both married until our spouses depart the earth. Sadly, it will be soon, we must remain apart. I will be thinking of the day when our bodies and souls will be reunited.
With all my love,
Sherry

The second one was harsher.

Charlie,
You must stop. Len is getting suspicious. You know it's a matter of time. I am using your medicine, and it seems to be having the opposite effect on his mental condition. How sure are you that this will help him? I still want and desire you, but you must understand, I won't hasten his death so we can be together. Our son was here last week, and he is becoming suspicious. I grieve for what you and Linda are going through, and I pray it is a peaceful and merciful death.
Always,
Sherry

There were more, but the final one was telling.

Charlie,
Firing me was the final straw. You should rot in hell for what you're doing to Linda and to my Len. You are no better than a drug merchant. If you

don't stop calling, I will call the police. This is not an idle threat. I think I understand what you are up to, and I will turn you in if you don't go away. Len is getting better now that he's off your drugs. We want nothing to do with you.
Go away or else,
Sherry

I was physically sick. I walked out of the cabin, and I vomited. The rain persisted, and the torrent of water was endless. It was a sea of gray mud. I could see that the lodge and cabin could hardly withstand the deluge. I was scared and sick at heart. I wanted the protection of Colin. I never wanted to go anywhere without him again. I knew he was probably grieving, and hopefully, in a few days, we would be reunited. Still, tonight I was alone in a large fishing lodge and failing in an epic battle with the weather.

Chapter 47

I went into the kitchen and found enough to eat without using the food I had sent to the small refrigerator in Charlie's art studio. With no electricity, I was cold, and I was soaked. I attempted to start a fire in the fireplace, but the water was coming down the chimney, and smoke was going to the hearth. I gave up. I had dry clothes in my cabin. I also remembered there was a flashlight there.

I could not stop chattering. I had no warmth, no light, but no fear of being killed. There was no way anyone could come here tonight. There were no predators that could harm me. I wasn't going to drown. The buildings were leaking, but they weren't going to fall down. The rain could not continue like this for many more hours. Despite this, I only slept for an hour or two.

By daylight, the rain had let up for an hour. I took the time and limped up to the top of the hill. I opened my phone, which I had left charging in the art studio. The phone came on, and the screen said words that brought another shock to my system. "No sim card detected."

I began to cry. I looked around and saw no one. The sim card could have been displaced in the phone, or was it due to the moisture? I had a card in my old phone that would not make contact and would do this regularly, and I would hit the side of the phone, and the sim card would work. Occasionally, I would open the slot and reset the sim card, and then it would work. Despite my knocking, it would not connect.

My ankle was killing me now from walking in the water all yesterday. I would have to go back to the lodge and get a paper clip to open the slot to access the sim card. I headed back, and the rain started again. This time it was not as bad. The daylight was good enough to visualize the river below the lodge. It was a raging sea of debris and muddy water. It had to be halfway up the hill from the lodge. The river crossed the road several miles from the compound. No one would ever get up here for days. I gazed at it, and my resolve took a considerable blow. I found a paper clip, and I popped open the slot.

Unless I was sleepwalking, I was not alone. Someone had removed my sim card. I quickly peered out of the lodge. My heart was racing, and I remembered the guns in Charlie's room. I was paralyzed with fear. Who was this person, and what did they want? I wanted to go back and get a gun, but how did I do it and not get caught? Where was this person? I sat in one place for what seemed like an hour. I just sat and watched out of the lodge window. I began to silently pray. *Please let me survive this and get back to Colin.*

The rain had washed away all the evidence of any tracks. I sat for at least an hour. Finally, I had to get up and go to the bathroom. I took as much food as I could carry and then went to my cabin and locked the door, and put a wedge under the door. I quickly peed then returned to watch out of my window. The rain began again, and the intensity returned. I had no idea how I was going to get free. I was essentially trapped—but by who?

Several hours passed, and by late afternoon I was exhausted with fear and lack of sleep. Was my predator tired? Were they sleeping, knowing we were the only ones here and that they could afford to sleep? I knew I couldn't.

It was finally growing darker. I would at least have the advantage of the darkness to hide. The rain continued, but it had decreased in intensity. I was again soaked, but this time, I hardly noticed it. I considered just coming out on the porch and giving myself up. I was too afraid to try to get to Charlie's guns. If I took one, then there would still be many more. I was surprised he had so many, but then with his life of crime, I guess anything was on the table with that man. I would kill for him to be here with me. Then I thought about the letters and the Calhouns. Was this the missing link? Did Charlie kill the Calhouns to protect his secret? Where had the FBI taken him?

I wanted Colin, but that wasn't going to happen. The only way in or out was by car or helicopter. Neither was viable in the rain. So, I sat and watched and thought about all my options. I had no way to contact anyone, and even if I did, I was unreachable now. If I snuck out in the dark and made a run for it, I would still be trapped by the raging rivers. At least I might survive until the rivers settle. But that might be a week or more. Was my best option to stay and pray that whoever was up here wasn't going to kill me? What did they want?

I sat just inside the window for at least two hours, trying to see any movement or something to indicate where the person stalking me was hiding. In the rain, I saw nothing. The intensity waxed and waned. All I could do was sit and wait. I thought about my family, past, present, and future. How would they feel about me? I laughed to myself, thinking about Colin and me taking the kids for a few hours and wondering if any of my children would take advantage and reproduce. I knew my younger grandchildren would not remember me.

How would Colin and Luke carry on? Maybe Luke would begin to ride Digger. Baxter was already sleeping in Luke's bed despite Colin's objections to a dog in the house at all. Then there was my beautiful boy. He was going to lose both of the loves of his life in a single week. Would that do him in? Where would Luke go after that? Most likely, he would go to live with one of his uncles.

The rain abruptly stopped. It was almost like a cannon had been firing for days then ceased. I peered out of the window, and with total cloud cover and no moon, it was still black outside. I reconsidered my options. Could this person simply want me to stay and be a companion? Did they want to keep me as a prisoner? Did they want to kill me? Why hadn't they shown themselves to me? Was that why there were fresh provisions in the kitchen?

"Enough of this bullshit," I whispered to myself. I remembered the sim card I had hidden in the log near the gate. It was only a remote chance that it would work, but it was all I had. I began to consider how I could leave my cabin and run to the gate. Could I find my way in the dark? Would the towers be down and all cell phone communication disrupted in this area? It had to be the atmospheric event of the century. I could send text messages. Would anyone receive them?

I changed into my waders but left my regular boots on. I knew there was one small creek I crossed to get to the hill with phone coverage. I put on the rain jacket from the main lodge building, and I put my phone in the water-resistant pouch in my waders, along with my paper clip and a fishing knife.

When the rain started again, I opened the door to the cabin and went out behind the structure. I crept up the incline, ran to the vegetable garden, and felt along the garden beds until I was well clear of the buildings. I fell once. My ankle was definitely a limiting factor, but the adrenaline canceled out ninety percent of the pain. When I felt I was alone, I turned on the flashlight. I looked at my watch. It was a few minutes after two in the morning. I had four hours to get help or notify someone that I needed assistance.

The rain was slow and steady and made my torchlight less than perfect, but it did help me avoid big trees and boulders dotting the area. I never turned the light behind me, and I prayed that I wasn't followed. I continually glanced over my shoulder and watched for any signs that I was observed or followed. Thankfully, I saw none. In the dark and with the ground so slippery, it took me thirty minutes to reach the log where I had hidden the sim card.

It was still inside a log and wrapped in a baggy. I removed it, and with my cold hands, dropped it twice on the ground. I dried it on my shirt, protected by my waders, and finally inserted it into the slot on the side of my phone. I turned on my phone, and it started up. I had a 70 percent charge which should last me for at least six hours.

I sat down under a tree and texted "help" to as many people as I could remember and had phone numbers for, using both New Zealand and international numbers. I didn't waste time with my location and figured someone would know where I was. I sent one with more details to Colin. "I love you and want you to know that I am trying to get back to you."

I sent one to my sister to stay strong, at all costs. Finally, I sent one to my children, texting that I loved them and to carry on no matter what. I hit send on all of them, but I knew they would not go until I reached the top of the hill, where I was exposed to anyone following me. I put the phone on silent.

I then skirted the exposed hill and prayed I would get the messages sent and then come back and head down the road toward the bridge and wait for the water to recede. I finally reached the top of the hill and turned toward the cell tower. I reached into my waders to retrieve my phone.

"Maggie, don't even try it." My heart stopped. I couldn't see him in the dark, but it was Charlie's voice. "Let's go back to the lodge before it begins to rain."

"Charlie, what the hell is going on here? You scared me to death. Thank God it's you. I should shoot you for what you just put me through." But that was not what I was thinking, and I doubted he believed me. I was scared to death. Was this the man I knew, or had he gone over the edge? At least I knew who my enemy was now. I still couldn't see him.

"I would have let you go, but you crossed the line, Maggie. You knew the studio was forbidden, and yet you entered without my permission. I don't think I can let that pass."

"Charlie, all I saw was your beautiful art. What's the problem?"

"Then you went into my cabin."

"Again, I did see you had some guns, but considering your precarious situation, why would you be unarmed?

"Colin and I own the place now. All I was looking for was electricity. Is there something else you're hiding?" *Yes, there is—another affair and probably a double murder.* I needed to think. I'd hoped I would be able to talk sense into him. This was not the Charlie I knew. Charlie McLeod was a rational and kind man who I thought I had loved. In the dark, as we descended off the hill, I felt my chest vibrate twice. At least two of the messages had been sent. *Oh, please, Lord, let them be to someone who knows me.*

I walked down the muddy road, and we both tripped and slipped in the mud. I had on my boots which gave me an advantage over Charlie in his shoes. When we got to the lodge, it was still dark. Charlie directed me to go into my cabin. He told me he was tired, and I must lie down on the bed. He then zip-tied me to the bedpost and told me he would be back.

Charlie left me in the dark with one hand secured to the post. He returned two minutes later and asked for my phone. My heart sank. There was no other option for me. I reached into my waders and tried to unzip my waterproof compartment, but I could not. He came over, and a feeling of disgust came over me when he reached inside my waders and lifted out the pocket and, without even the slightest interest, unzipped the bag and removed my phone. He left the room, and I heard him walk away. I was paralyzed with fear and exhaustion. Despite my best effort, I fell asleep. When I woke up, it was dawn, and there was a hint of blue sky.

Chapter 48

I lay there for another hour. I needed to go, and I prayed Charlie would come, and I prayed he would never come. He did, though. He threw the phone on the bed and shook his head. "We're going to need to move. Apparently, I can't trust you."

He walked over and gently cut the ties. He asked if I needed to go and allowed me to use the bathroom by myself after removing a pair of scissors. He didn't see a scalpel blade that sat inside the top drawer. I used them to cut my cuticles. I still had my waders on, and I slipped the scalpel blade that was in a protected sheath inside my pant leg.

I could see my breath in the cold air as we walked up to the main building. The sun was out, and only a few threatening clouds remained. The fire was going in the fireplace, and the room was warm. Charlie had made bacon, eggs, and toast. He also had sandwiches prepared and wrapped. Charlie brought the food over to the sofa near the fire and told me to sit and eat. I ate in silence as he explained what was going to happen.

"We're leaving. You're going to be my hostage, but you are going to pretend that I am your savior. I rescued you from an unknown person. I'm Todd again." He held up a passport. "We'll be transported to one of my cargo planes, and then we will go to a new place. Then I am going to win you over. There will be no force. You will want to be with me, and you will willingly forsake all others."

Don't rock the boat, Maggot. Grin and nod, grin and nod. Don't ask any sticky questions. Remember, the goal is to survive. Live to fight again. "Okay, I'm in. When do we leave?"

"In two hours. There's a helicopter on its way from Christchurch. By the way, your messages didn't send. As far as anyone knows, you're stuck up here having the time of your life."

I groaned inwardly. "Sounds like a plan. What can I do until then? Do you want me to pack?"

"I'm going up to the studio. It's probably best if you return to your cabin." He took me by his arm and gently walked me over to the cabin. "Take off your waders. You won't need them where you're going. He stood and watched me and then zip-tied me once again. He turned to go, and as he glanced back at me, he saw a paper tucked under my pillow. He stood and stared at the bed and table but walked away and closed the door. I pushed the letter down under the mattress with my free hand. I reached down into the waders, found the scalpel blade, and put it inside my sock.

Charlie was gone for an hour. He returned and untied me again, and asked if I needed to use the bathroom. I didn't need to, but it would give me time to think. I walked into the bathroom and locked the door. "Leave it unlocked, Maggie." I did, and when I emerged, Charlie was sitting on the bed holding the letter implicating him in the deaths of the Calhouns.

He stared at me and didn't say a word. Neither did I. The concept of time seemed to slip away. Was it seconds, or was it an hour that we stared at one another? He tapped the envelope on his thigh. Finally, he rose. "I guess this changes things."

I swallowed hard. "Why? I don't think it necessarily has to change anything."

He pointed to the bed, and when I reluctantly sat down, he zip-tied me again. He was going to kill me. I was sure. "Charlie, it can stay between you and me. I don't care. I can see Sherry Calhoun was going to turn you in. You were doing such remarkable and noble deeds. Sometimes the outcome is more important than the method. Linda was probably so proud of what you were doing to help people, and I am too.

It doesn't need to end. I'll be by your side the whole way. Didn't I bring you Sandy and the students down in the South? Don't throw it away. How many women have you met that admired you for what you were doing?"

He walked down the way and returned with a gun. He cut me loose, but this time he was rough. He jerked me to my feet. He told me to walk up toward the hill. He picked up a gun on the small table outside my room. The driveway was still running with mud and water. We both slipped and stumbled as we walked away from the lodge. My heart was in my throat, and I was almost paralyzed with fear. I couldn't think.

"Charlie, it doesn't have to end like this. Remember, I'm a whore. I can be bought. I'm happy to do whatever you say. No one needs to know. If you kill me, you know Colin will hunt you down, but if I leave him to come back to you, he's an honorable man. He won't stop us. He loves you, Charlie, and he even said you were a good guy when I left for San Francisco."

Charlie didn't respond. His pace slackened as we came to the steeper rise on our ascent. At one point, he told me to stop while he caught his breath. If I could keep from getting shot, I thought I could probably outrun him. The problem was I would most likely be shot. At least, I was beginning to consider options. The mud made the climb more difficult. Even I slipped, and he came up and kicked me. I rose from my knees and continued to walk. I turned back. "Do you want to rest?"

Charlie gazed over to the mountains where his helicopter might be arriving any minute. "No, keep walking."

"Charlie, you're going to have a heart attack. Please, for your own sake, slow down." Instead of slowing down, I picked up the pace. His breathing was labored, and his face was red. Even I struggled to maintain my speed, but I was determined to give him a heart attack. *Oh, please, Lord, just a small one. Please.*

"Maggie," Charlie gasped and put his hand to his chest. Was it a ruse?

"Charlie, enough. Sit down. You're no good to me dead." *Oh, please die.* He did sit down, and I asked to feel his pulse. He wouldn't let me near him, but his face turned from red to gray. His hand was clenched, and he stopped even looking at me. He set the gun down, but as I approached, he picked it up again and pointed it at me, and I backed away. I continued to retreat, and finally, I made a run for the woods. A shot rang out, and mercifully it missed me. A second shot rang, but I felt it before I heard it. Again, merciful god. It went through my upper arm and felt like a sting, but no more.

I was running for my life. In my hysteria, I remembered the family in Colin's television series getting shot in the arm many times. The characters would say they were "creased." If I survived, I could tell Colin I was hit, but it was only a crease. I continued to run in a zigzag motion and never stopped to look back. I ran down the wooded side of the hill. I ran for as long as I could and finally stopped when I reached a tributary of the river. It was raging, and a waterfall had been created in the torrent.

I looked at the ground and saw no visible tracks due to the moss and ferns that grew along the waterway. There appeared to be a tunnel under the waterfall which would allow me to cross the raging creek. I ducked under the water and found a small cave. I had to decide whether I stayed there or kept running. I could not imagine that Charlie could follow me in his condition, but when his pilot and at least one other person might come to get him, he might send them on to try to find me. I was cold and wet, and I decided to continue past the waterfall. I ran until I could go no further. I rested for ten or more minutes and then went up a steep rise. There was no way he could follow me.

When I was at the peak, I could see a great distance from under a tree. I sat down and waited. I had good cover and a great vantage point to watch for an approaching helicopter. I was so scared, I could not stop searching near and far for the copter. Finally, I saw one approach over where I thought I had landed in front of the lodge. I watched and waited. I saw nothing nor heard anything for at least an hour. Then I heard a gun go off near where I left Charlie.

Did he kill himself? Did he signal where his men could retrieve him? I knew he was a great distance from me, so I was no longer worried about him. I was going to stay put. I was high enough, I would have had cell phone coverage, but I didn't have my phone. I sat and waited. Again, I had no concept of time, but as dusk approached, I saw the helicopter rise from near the lodge, and it left.

Did they take Charlie to a hospital? Did they leave someone? I couldn't take a risk. I stayed where I was and prayed that I could survive the night. I gathered as many plants and fauna as I could carry and attempted to cover myself with anything that would insulate me. There was no wind and no rain. I could see the river below. I was not thirsty, and my hunger didn't compare to my desire to survive. My gunshot stung, but that was all. I didn't try to look at it.

Just before dusk, the old buck strolled up to the river's edge. The stag kneeled down and ate some plants under the reeds by the ever-decreasing water flowing through the stream. His presence gave me an inner strength to survive the night and to carry on through tonight and for one more day. I knew I would survive.

I stayed awake for most of the night. I was freezing, and I felt signs of mild hypothermia. My skin was cold and verging on numb. I was exhausted. I stood up and walked around for half the night to increase blood flow to my extremities. I finally saw a hint of light in the east that kept me going. I was going to survive. I sang to myself. "Hitchin' a Ride" and other songs came to mind. Was I delirious? Of course.

Chapter 49

When the sun was up, I decided to return to the lodge or walk out of the property. I knew both Geoff and Ned would be worried sick, and they would have informed Colin, who would have notified my family. I slowly made my way down to the top of the hill where I left Charlie. I walked around the clearing and peered through the ferns and trees. There was no evidence that anyone was waiting for me. I walked on and kept myself hidden. I came to a thick stand of trees where I watched and waited for at least another hour. I saw no signs of Charlie's men.

I finally walked out of the trees, crossed over to the main building, and went straight to the kitchen. The power was still off, but all I needed was calories. I ate an apple and some bread and washed it down with warm juice. I then went out and watched for several minutes and ran up to my room. I took off my shirt and saw my bullet wound. A neat hole pierced my upper arm from the back and exited toward the front. Colin's television boys would never have shot someone running away. I laughed to myself as I hummed the introduction music to his television show. Clearly, I was verging on delusional.

I locked my door and lay down on my bed for a moment. I prided myself on my ability to power nap. I was asleep for only a few minutes when I heard the whirring of a helicopter. I jumped up to see what the copter looked like. The sky was different, and I saw a helicopter that said Rescue on its side. As connected and clever as Charlie was, I knew that was not him or his men. I ran to the heliport in front of the lodge. I waved to the pilot, who dropped like a shot put onto the landing pad. A man ducked under the whirring blades, put out his hands, and told me to wait until the helicopter blades stopped.

"Margaret Kincaid?" He shouted. I nodded. For once, I didn't cry. I was too exhausted. He bowed and lowered his outstretched arm. "Your chariot awaits." We both grinned.

"Just a second." I ran back to my cabin and retrieved my suitcase. I wasn't leaving my beautiful rod or my computer. The copilot shook his head but took the case and helped me into the cockpit. Off we went. I surveyed the area as we ascended. All the rivers were flooded, and trees were down along many riverbanks. The pilots signaled that they were returning with the stranded tourists. They had been informed not to mention my name if Charlie's men listened in. They turned to me and gave me the thumbs-up. I didn't have a headset, and I had no idea what they discussed. I saw them point to the rivers closer to Nelson. The area was awash. There was flooding all over the place.

We landed at the hospital heliport, and I was met with a stretcher. The pilot and copilot waved the men with stretchers away. The pilot hugged me as they helped me out of the cockpit and shook my hand. "You must be one well-connected lady. The whole fleet has been on your case. Sorry we couldn't get there sooner."

"No, I think your timing is perfect." I was taken into an emergency reception area and immediately ushered into a booth. A nurse helped me out of my clothes and into a hospital gown. She saw my scratches, bruises, and my swollen ankle. When she saw my upper arm, she whistled. "What's this?"

I laughed to myself and, in my best western voice, said, "Awe, it's nothin' but a little crease, ma'am."

"You were shot?"

"Yes." And that is when I had my first cry.

Hours later, I was in a bed and receiving intravenous antibiotics, fluids for my minor dehydration, and salves on my scratches and scrapes. There was a knock, and both Mac and Kerry came in. "Well, aren't you just a drama queen."

"Hey, can I borrow your phone? I need to call someone."

"Would that be your loverboy?"

"Yes, that and my kids."

"Did you know you have armed guards outside your room? What the hell, Maggot?"

"Yes, hell just about describes it. Have you heard from Ned or Geoff? They were coming up the day after the rain started."

"They know you're safe. Ned and Geoff repeatedly tried to cross the river. Ned's now rescuing others from the backcountry, while Geoff's been commandeered to help bridge repairs. Apparently, his bridges have all held, and he's been asked to help with the bridges that collapsed. They said to say how sorry they were not to come up that night."

I pointed to the phone. "Pretty please?" Mac handed me her phone, and I logged onto my account and called Colin.

Cue more tears. "Hello?" The voice was far away, and it sounded old and tired.

"Hi, Collie. It's me. I'm all right, and I'm a little worse for wear, but I will be on the first flight I can get on. How are things at your end?"

"Darlin', Helen passed, but Luke and I got to see her before she went, and we said our goodbyes. How about you? I know you can't talk. Tell me you are all right, really."

"It was just a crease, cowboy. I'll be back in the saddle again." I waited for his response.

"A crease? Were you shot?"

"It's hardly worth mentioning. It's no worse than any of your television family received, and how many times were you shot, anyway? Well, speaking of friends. I guess you know another one of ours passed yesterday."

"No, I didn't. I haven't talked to anyone except a nurse and a doctor." Colin sounded exhausted.

"I want to come home as soon as I can. If I can bust out of here, can you get me a bus ticket home? Have you heard from my kids? Can you call them for me? How's Luke? Have you heard from my sister?"

"Everyone knows your safe, darlin'. Your sister said thanks for nothing. You haven't heard, her own cells kicked in, and she is going home in a few days. She wants you to stop by on your way home."

"Collie, where are you?"

"Malibu, but I'm headed back to New Zealand tomorrow. There are a few things that are going to take a while. I'm not spending one more night away from you than I have to. I miss you terribly." Cue more tears. Mac and Kerry stepped out while I tried to compose myself.

"What about Luke?"

"He's headed back to the ranch. Doug's picking him up, and Mrs. Gillard has set out the playing cards. He knows your safe, but nothing else. I feel like there's much more that I need to know, but I'll wait until I get there. Until then, you need to get some sleep. Tuesday's coming up, darlin', and I'm not missing another one."

That made me laugh. "God, I love you, but you need to know something."

"Don't say it. I don't want to hear about anything like that. I barely survived hearing Santa Claus wasn't real."

Chapter 50

My reunion with Colin was bittersweet. Helen and Charlie were dead. Colin was in mourning and stressed. He was not aware of what I had been through. He thought I was stranded at the lodge and had to wait to be rescued. The authorities were unaware of Charlie's existence until I placed the call from Charlie's plane when I went back to help my sister several weeks ago.

No one knew how such a brazen move could be accomplished without Charlie's cartel knowing I had tipped off the FBI. I hadn't told anyone about the letters that implicated Charlie in the death of the Calhouns. I knew Charlie had burned all the letters, and it would have been my word against his. What no one knew was I had photographed three of the letters and put them on my computer, and then erased them from my phone.

Charlie lived for less than a day and died of a cardiac arrest in the Christchurch hospital. His lies and deceits went far beyond anything Colin or I could have imagined. We all felt so duped.

I was going to be discharged from the hospital the following morning. My "crease" was only mildly infected, but the bullet track lay next to the tendons that allowed me to raise my arm. The doctors took no chances, and I remained on intravenous antibiotics until the next day.

Colin had aged in the last week. He sat without speaking and held my hand. He usually controlled and directed traffic, but he simply sat and observed the doctors, nurses, and even the FBI agents who came to interrogate me. They interviewed us on our experience with Charlie, the lodge, and what we thought we knew. We were both embarrassed about how gullible we had been in believing Charlie's version of the events.

I hadn't been in contact with my friends back in our town. None of this was to come out until the drug smuggling court cases were heard. Of course, the star witness was no longer available, but they felt they had enough without his testimony. The FBI was aware he'd survived the initial plane crash.

Still, in a mix-up that could only happen in the movies, two separate branches of government each thought the other was keeping him in witness protection. They finally realized that they had lost him. They had audio evidence that Charlie would go back on his agreement to give evidence at the upcoming drug trials. Charlie was doomed either way. Both the cartel and the FBI were holding him hostage.

A week later, we were home. The plans for the fishing lodge were put on hold for the foreseeable future. Helen's ashes were brought to the ranch. With Colin and his two sons and grandson, her ashes were spread next to Luke's mother's ashes. The official ceremony had been conducted in LA to a large crowd of Helen's and her current husband's friends. I did attend, but I played no role in the ceremony, and no one from the press noticed my presence. Colin gave a beautiful eulogy, and he and Helen's husband seemed to make amends.

Roberto was devastated, and he returned to South America. He declined to come to the ranch. Helen's ranch would be sold, and the proceeds would be divided into three ways for Jake, Kyle, and Luke's further education. Luke grieved for his grandmother, and each night we would write some memory about her in a journal that Luke kept in his room. "Maggie, you know I loved her, don't you?"

"Yes, I sure do. Your grandmother loved you too."

"She never tickled my back. I'm glad you are going to take over being my grandmother."

"Well, I don't think taking over is really the way I would think about it. I'll never replace her, Luke. You and I will start our own traditions and find our own way. For instance, don't expect me to buy you a car, mate. You're going to have to earn money to get your first wheels."

"That's what Uncle Trevor said to me. I've already got a lot of money saved. I've got three more seniors I'm helping with their classes."

"Impressive. Just don't do the work for these kids. Make sure they do their own homework, Lukey Boy. Say, I forgot. Did you go help Sylvia and Trent while I was gone?"

"Yeah, I got to help with a round-up. I can come back anytime I want. The Wests said I did really good."

"Okay, Lukey Boy. Lights off and sweet dreams. Love you."

"You too, Grandma." This time I didn't correct him.

I finally told Colin about the letters I found regarding Charlie and the Calhouns.

"We'll go see Tom Sutton tomorrow." It was another blow to Colin. His faith in the world was eroding. We discussed how he and Charlie were together in LA when the Calhouns died. "He must have hired someone."

When Colin and I were in bed, I mentioned that maybe it was best to sell my cabin. "You know, Collie. Now that we know what happened and who killed the Calhouns, I kind of think it's lost its appeal for me."

Colin patted my thigh and said that it pleased him. "Don't you have an appointment with Carol tomorrow to get your hair done? Why don't you ask her to list it for you?"

"Yeah, I guess I can. Good idea, Collie. What have you got on tomorrow?"

"Business darlin'. I've got one of those damn Zoom meetings with the accountants. We are trying to sort out what I owe Helen's estate. You know we still owned property together. We may be broke when the kids demand their shares and payment for her part in the houses."

"I don't envy you. The good news is fishing season starts tomorrow. I'll get us all licenses in town. I think Luke's going to need one too."

"How's your casting arm?"

"I think I'll be able to cast a line just fine." I raised my arm out from under the blanket. I pretended to make a back and forth motion of the cast. "Yep, all good."

"So, is there anything that would keep you from performing your wifely duties?"

"That depends. What do you think my wifely duties entail? You know I'm not really a wife yet." I gently kicked him but turned to gaze at him resting his head on the pillow.

"We could start easy and build up. Maybe a back tickle?"

"Oh, yeah. I def could do that." I turned over onto my stomach. "Go on."

"Darlin', I thought you could tickle my back."

"Oh, gee. Hmm, you know I'm still under doctor's orders to rest."

"You know I played a doctor on television. I could play doctor now."

"Interesting concept. Roll over, big boy. I'll tickle your damn back, you big baby."

Later that night, I dreamed I was being chased by Charlie again. It had become a recurring dream, and once again, I was woken by Colin holding me and telling me I was home and with him. "Darlin' girl, you're safe, and no one's chasing you."

I was panting, sweating through my gown, and it took a moment to orient myself. "I'm so sorry, Collie. Go back to sleep." I rose from the bed, changed nightgowns, and returned to bed. Colin held me and told me he loved me, and nothing was ever going to happen to me again. This was a regular occurrence. In the morning, we talked about me seeing a therapist. I said I would consider it. I knew I wouldn't.

Chapter 51

Colin called Tom Sutton and asked to make an appointment with him. He was away for the rest of the week. Colin considered giving the evidence to a second deputy. He then decided it would probably be best to contact the FBI. Perhaps it was one of the cartel men in custody who had killed the Calhouns under Charlie's orders.

I left for Carol's office. She was doing double duty today. She had an appointment to show a small farm that had come up for sale, but she would do my hair first. The Sanctuary had sold, and Carol and Hal had paid off their home with her commission. She now knew Charlie had not been killed in the plane crash but had died on the mountain in New Zealand. I know Carol was mad that I hadn't told her. However, she understood that Charlie had asked us not to tell anyone. Carol was still loyal to him, despite all the evidence that he had imported narcotics for several years. What did she and Hal know? Did they know more than they let on? Colin was clueless, so it was reasonable to think they could be as well.

The story we were asked to report was that Charlie and I had been trapped together at the fishing lodge. When we tried to get help, Charlie had succumbed to a long-standing heart condition. Carol still told everyone how wonderful he was. I hated to burst her bubble, but I was sworn to secrecy until the FBI had all the evidence they needed.

"I'll go to my grave loving that man, Maggie. Did he say anything when he died?"

"Huh? Like what? You know I ran to try and get up to the area to obtain help. I wasn't with him in the end." I hoped she didn't know that he made it to the hospital in Christchurch before he died. He was in a coma, but I don't think anyone knew for sure, aside from his immediate crew.

"Hey Carol, not to change the subject, but I'm thinking of selling my property. It doesn't make sense to have two properties. Are you interested in selling it again? Did you sell it to the Calhouns when they bought the land and built their home?"

"Maggie, I've been wondering when you would sell it. I'd love to help you. I even have the original listing, and we can copy a lot of the original paperwork. Let's get your hair color in, and then I'll go look it up."

"Do you have time?" I hated to mess with her schedule.

"We can't go anywhere until you're done anyway. I have plenty of time." She applied the color and foils and then went to her files. She pulled out a large envelope containing copies of deeds and sales agreements of my property dating back to before the Calhouns first purchased the land. She thumbed through the titles and papers, looking for the last contract. The phone rang. She answered it and then returned to her filing cabinet in the adjacent room to gather some information for a prospective client.

I thumbed through the file and realized two proposals to sell the property existed. The original contract was dated several years before the contract I'd signed. I had an agreement with Calhoun's son, but there was a contract signed by Sherry and Lennard Calhoun.

They apparently put their property on the market and signed a contract with Carol's company on the first of May. That would be three days before they supposedly died on the fourth of May. I remembered the date they died. I was reluctant to even say killed. I didn't know for sure that Charlie had them killed. I hadn't known that they had planned to move. I examined the date, and the signatures, noting Carol was the realtor in both cases. I quickly photographed the original contract signed by the Calhouns.

When Carol returned, she apologized and found the two files sitting open on the counter. "Wow, I'm one lucky girl. I could never have afforded the cabin if the Calhouns hadn't died there. One hundred thousand dollars is far less than when the Calhouns made their original contract. That is a hell of a hit to the family."

"Yep, you're one fortunate girl, Maggie."

"I see you signed the contract a few days before one of them did the deed. What did they seem like?"

"Well, I didn't notice too much. I think the Calhouns were simply ready to move. Mr. Calhoun was deteriorating, and Sherry had lost her job and knew she would have to put her husband in a home. I think it became too much."

"So, were you the last person they talked to before they did it? What a shock. I bet you were sick."

"I don't know if I was the last, but I was one of the last. I know it sounds horrible, but I lost a lot of money when the house didn't sell. I sure would have wanted them to live."

"It does all appear to be so improbable that she would decide to sell the house and then kill herself three days later. Well, anyway, how about you finish me up, and then Colin and I can come over next week, and we can sign a contract to sell the property."

"Okay, let's get those foils out. I'm not going to have time for a runway job today, sadly."

We both laughed, and I hoped Carol wasn't too alarmed with our discussion. "Darn, I can always come back tomorrow."

"Nope, you know I never work on Thursdays."

"Never? I swear you showed me the house on a Thursday. Oh, well, Colin is going to have to take me as I am then." We finished up, and I paid her and left. I couldn't tell if she was nervous or not.

I went to the school and picked up Luke from school. He was talking to a guy who was much older than him. I saw an exchange of money. It better not be for drugs. He got into the car, and I turned and stared at him. "So, are you doing deals in front of the whole school?"

His face reddened. "Yep, but just tutoring deals. Carl wants to go to State next year, and he needs to improve his GPA. He needs to raise his math and English grade from a C to a B. We're going to Zoom tonight."

"Good work, Lukey Boy. Hey, do you know what day of the week you were born?"

"You're kidding, right?"

"No, not really."

"You can Google it."

"Okay. Thanks." I had a few dates to research.

When I was home, I went up to the barn to see Digger. I hadn't ridden since I left for Australia. Lifting the saddle with my arm was still painful. No one was around to help, but I eventually got the saddle on the horse and had a great ride. I even went out to the outside arena. As I was walking Digger so he would cool off, I pulled my phone out of my pocket. I had a one in seven chance of solving this mystery. I quietly took a picture of the contract when Carol was busy and checked the date. I entered the date and asked Siri what day of the week it was.

My heart dropped. The first of May was a Thursday. Carol was lying. I returned to the house and gave both the boys their seasonal fishing licenses. This was the first one that Luke was required to have. I laminated all three, and Luke said he was going fishing. Then he remembered he was going to tutor his newest client.

I was alone with Colin. My heart was racing. "Collie, how do you feel about Carol and Hal and their loyalty to Charlie?"

"I have no idea what you're talking about. They were very loyal. So what?"

"If Charlie murdered the Calhouns, or had them murdered, since the timeline doesn't fit, who could have come into town and done it?"

"Yeah? What are you getting at?"

"Who may have done a hit on the couple for Charlie?"

"Do you think Carol and Hal may know more than they're saying? Have you got any proof?"

"I think I do."

I showed him the photo I took of the contract. I pointed to the date and let Siri tell us that the first of May was a Thursday. I explained that Carol never works on Thursday. I showed him how easy it was to change the date and when I blew up the picture on the contract, I showed him the telltale signs of altered dates. "The thing is. The contract had at least ten places to sign and date, but one had been missed and was dated the 4th. Oh my God, I hope I'm wrong, but I think Carol or Hal killed the Calhouns."

Colin sat dumbfounded. It seemed like an hour as he stared at the photos and the dates. "Did Carol notice what you were doing?"

"I don't think so, but you've got to admit. It's hard to believe that Carol and Hal were unaware of what Charlie was doing."

"Well, I always was. That's for damn sure. Darlin', we need to call your friends." He was referring to the FBI. We were both sick at heart. The FBI agents agreed to meet with us here at the house in the morning. We all knew nothing could be discussed on the phone.

Chapter 52

G abe took Luke to school as we prepared for another interrogation. "Collie, are we suspects?"

"I don't think anyone's clear in this debacle. All we can do is tell the agents what we know. We present your evidence, your pictures and let the FBI take it from there. Darlin', you and I both know that we're both innocent. I can prove where I was, and you were in Australia. The fact that we called the FBI has got to help show them that we have nothing to do with this."

"But what if they don't believe us?" I was worried that we would be implicated in all of this. We had to admit that we had been up with him in New Zealand for several weeks, thinking that we were under the watchful eyes of the FBI when in truth, we probably weren't.

The agents called from a speaker at the gate out on the road. Colin opened the entrance gate from the house. Of course, they were totally new agents who didn't know us. We explained the situation, and they did have their notes, so it wasn't like we were starting fresh.

Colin could not fathom that Charlie ordered their deaths. "All along, I just couldn't believe that. But Carol? In a million years?"

To me, the evidence was clear that either Carol or her husband, Hal, had to have been the ones to murder the Calhouns. "Collie, do you remember if it was Hal who was in LA with you and Charlie?

The two agents looked at the pictures I'd taken and the dates to ensure that it really was a Thursday when the papers were supposedly signed. They conferred and called their bosses, who suggested that we quietly do a bit of background on Hal and Carol.

They left, and later in the day, they called and asked us to meet with them once again. The agents came back to the ranch the following day. They repeatedly asked us questions that suggested they were testing whether we were fibbing or not. I think we passed. They knew we would meet with Carol on Monday, and they asked us to wear a wire. Colin objected two any idea of me wearing a wire, but he said he would be happy to wear one. We agreed to let them come to the house on Monday morning to outfit Colin.

Luke was going over to help Trent at the Bar Double X on Saturday. They were going to drive some of the cattle up into the mountains. Luke would spend the night in a drover's camp and head back late Sunday afternoon. While Luke was excited to be doing a man's work, he also realized that he would be missing out on tuition for his new clients and their need to improve their grades.

Luke complained that not only was he not going to get to work with the students, but he was going to be paid far less for much more work. This did not sit well with my future husband. Colin took Luke out for a walk, and when they came back, Luke was ready to rock and roll.

"Lukey boy, I know you're disappointed, and I know you want to make a lot of money, and I know you want that first car, but remember the long game. To get into veterinary school, you don't just need good grades. You need experience. The worst thing you could possibly do was think that being a veterinarian and working on horses or cattle or even dogs and cats would be easy. You're getting an experience that very few pre-veterinary students would ever have. I sure hope you appreciate how lucky you are to be working with Trent and Sylvia. Now get your sorry ass into bed."

As Colin and I prepared for bed, I noticed Colin appeared tense. "Are you nervous? I know I am. At least we have tomorrow night to ourselves." I gave Colin the cue to turn over, and I would tickle his back.

Colin turned to me and said that he would take the lead in the conversation with Carol.

"Okay, but what are you going to say?" I didn't have a clue.

"I don't know, and for some damn reason, they haven't written me a script." Oh, that made me laugh. "Just kidding, darlin' girl. I won't say much, and maybe I'll ask about the potential for the sale and any other ideas about how we can quickly get rid of the place. Of course, I'll mention that one of my friends would like to come up on Thursday or Friday.

"Collie, don't you think we need to have a few questions along the line of, 'So why did you kill these poor people?'"

He laughed and said, "Great idea. I'll get right on that."

The next day after Colin dropped off Luke, Colin and I snuck out to the river. It was our first chance to fish since the season opened a few days ago. We were both rusty, and neither of us presented the perfect fly. After a few casts, Colin had his mojo, but I was struggling. Colin smiled, walked over, and came behind me. He put his hand on my forearm and gently raised and lowered my arm. I leaned back into him, and we cast the line together.

"One month to the big day. Are you ready to take the plunge, darlin' girl? How's your arm?"

He felt solid and warm. "Ready when you are, beautiful boy. Well, as you can see, my casting is not great, but I'll get there. Collie, excuse me." Colin had his lips on the back of my neck.

"Yes, darlin'."

"I have a fish on my line."

Colin persisted in kissing the back of my neck. "Oh really? A fish?"

I stepped forward and began to play the fish. He put up a good fight. I landed him and threw him back. That day we each caught two fish and threw them all back. Somehow, I felt holy when I returned a fish to the river. I knew we would take the odd fish now and then, but not today. We had bigger fish to fry—catch and release.

Chapter 53

"Wired and set to jet, darlin' girl." Another agent was taken to my log cabin and had set up a monitoring device in the basement, well ahead of Carol's arrival. We walked over from the ranch and began to warm up the house. I made coffee. Colin held my hand as we waited. When the designated appointment came and went, I called Carol and asked if she remembered our meeting. I mentioned Colin and I were sitting at the house waiting.

"Damn, I knew there was something I needed to do. I'll be right over." The sun was out, and the day was promising.

As Carol drew up to the house, I quietly whispered, "Showtime. Don't forget your lines, Collie."

"I pride myself on scene preparation. Stand by for the performance." Colin and I hugged, and as Carol walked up the stairs to the deck and front room, I went out and welcomed her.

"Hi, Maggie. I'm so sorry. I am totally perplexed these days. I don't know what's come over me. I think I'm still reeling from Charlie's death, not to mention his return to life. I don't know when I'm gonna forgive you for not telling me, but I'll get over it someday. Shall we get down to business?"

I wanted to ease into the conversation. I tried to act nonchalant. "I made some coffee. Do you take milk? I can never remember what you guys do with your coffee."

"White and one. The good news is I think you can raise the asking price."

Colin sat and watched for a minute and then finally began to ask questions that the FBI agent suggested. "Carol, what makes you think we could get anyone interested? It took how many years since the..."

"Collie, having Maggie in the house is a huge bonus. I think we can ask for the original amount."

He persisted. "Setting aside the murder-suicide, what's changed so much?"

"Well, for one thing, the house is decorated. The Calhouns had only recently completed the construction. They hadn't even begun to decorate. Maggie has this place looking like a million bucks."

"OK, well, that sounds like a good starting point. What do you think, Maggie?" Colin turned to me.

"A million? I'd be up for that. Shall we start it a million, Carol?"

"Oh great—sellers that need a reality check." Carol rolled her eyes.

Colin got up from his chair at the bar. "More coffee?"

Carol was quick. "Yes, please."

"Can I look at the original contract? Do you have any pictures from the original listing? You know how I like to save money."

From my perspective, Carol didn't appear to be concerned. "Collie, they're out in the car. I'll get them."

She returned and handed the original contract to Colin, who sat down and studied the document. "I must have the pictures back at the office." I watched Carol, and she kept staring at a place on the floor in the great room. "Shall we go out and get some pictures of the garden and stables? That's where you might get a boost. Everyone wants a horse these days."

I did a double-take. "Do you do your own pictures? I'd have thought you had a professional do it. When I was buying the property, it surely looked like professionals had taken these pictures."

"Did I ever mention that I took a course in photography? I'll save you at least a couple hundred dollars by doing the pictures myself."

"Do you have the old ones? I'd love to compare them." Carol and I went down toward the barn. I wasn't wired, so I had to remember what she said for future trial evidence.

"Maggie, I'm so impressed. If I can find the original pictures, I'll send them so you can see the difference."

We returned to the house, and Colin had read both the original contract and the one used in my purchase. "Carol, you leave nothing to speculation. Any chance you want to come and work for me? I could certainly use a detail person."

"Nope, I like things just the way they are. It used to be a struggle to make money in this industry, but these days, it's a walk in the park. Do you guys want to take the contract, look it over, and get back to me? I hate to admit it, but I've double-booked myself. Maggie, I'll see if I can chase up those pictures. I think you'll see what a difference you've made."

Colin wasn't going to let her go without more info. "Carol, I have some friends coming up from LA to visit later this week. Should I be showing them around, or should we wait for you? It'll either be Thursday or Friday."

"Suit yourself. It's a known fact that owners are completely unable to showcase a house for selling. I can come Friday, but you know Thursdays are my big day to myself. Let me know, Collie."

I was curious. "Carol, why do you always pick Thursday? I thought most realtors had Monday or Tuesday off?"

"I'm sure I told you, but my aunt lives in an aged care home in the big smoke. I haven't missed a Thursday in years and years. I pride myself on helping her to live out her days, and Thursdays are the best day of the week for her."

Colin smiled. "Well, I won't interfere then. I'll try to delay them till Friday. Carol, you're amazing."

Carol hugged us both and left. She didn't notice that Colin had quietly removed a sheet of paper from the original contract. He'd quickly run upstairs and scanned it and replaced it with the staple binding the document.

I walked Carol to her car, returned, and found both agents and Colin examining the single page that Colin had quickly scanned. "Carol says she's going to try to get me those pictures. They would have a digital date on them, wouldn't they? If she can digitally change the dates, can you assess that that's the correct date that the pictures were actually taken?"

One of the agents replied, "Probably. You guys did great. I wished you had worn a wire too, Dr. Kincaid."

Colin scoffed and stood to go. "You know I'm not really a detective, but I have played one on television. I wonder if the facility where her aunt lives has a registry of visitors?"

"Mr. Chandler, the FBI is always searching for a few good men. You could always apply to join us if retirement is boring you."

"I could use a few boring days, gentlemen, but you never know."

We all went back over to Colin's ranch. Mrs. Gillard made us lunch while we discussed the case. "We know Dr. Kincaid was in Australia, and we're eliminating her as a suspect, but Mr. Chandler, where were you when this murder occurred?"

"That's easy. I was in LA with Charlie. I was his alibi. There was an unusual snowstorm, as I remember, and we couldn't fly back. I feel ashamed to say this, but I didn't know them. I was having dramas of my own. My daughter had just been murdered. I was caring for her son and trying to sort out what we would do. My daughter's husband hadn't been arrested. He was the prime suspect in my daughter's death, and hence we had Luke with us. I remember Charlie was frantic because his wife was close to dying, and he wanted to be there."

The agents left. They said we had been a great help. I felt relieved that we had done what we could to get the truth out. It would be up to the FBI to handle this case. Knowing that Sheriff Thomas Sutton is Carol's cousin, there was no way that they were going to give this information to any of the local sheriffs.

Chapter 54

Colin was becoming anxious about the upcoming wedding. He had returned to his commanding persona. I think that's good, but I'm not one to worry about the small details. He wanted to go over our vows and what we would say. "Collie, my only requirement is a big 'no' to the obeying thing. Anything else is on the table."

"Dangerous darlin', which leaves many options." Colin smiled that mischievous smile that won me over. I don't know how many years we'll be together, but it's going to be fun.

"Back to the task at hand, old girl. So, my boys and Luke will be the groomsmen, but who will be your maid of honor and bridesmaids? Oh, and let's not forget the ring bearer and the flower girl."

"Christy wants to be the matron of honor. I thought I would invite Lauren Kennedy to be one of the bridesmaids, and Colleen said she would participate under protest."

"That's funny. Colleen has called at least twice to ask me to not break my promise to join the family."

"Ah, daughters. Here's a sad truth. I would have invited Carol to be one too. I suppose I could invite my former office manager, Jodie, to come over. She's done so much for me over the years."

"You need to get cracking, darlin'. This little party is less than a month away."

"Well, they can wear whatever they want, so let's not make it too formal. As I said, a plaid cowboy shirt and a bolo, and you're set. I've got my wedding dress from Australia. Jake's kids are a bit old to be the flower girl and ring bearer, so how about I use my grandchildren? Would you mind?"

Colin pulled me onto his lap and was about to kiss me when we both felt the buzz from the phone in my pocket, indicating that I had a message. I pulled out my phone, opened it up, and true to form, Carol had sent images. They were screenshots and only had today's date on them. Colin and I looked at them. Colin abruptly slapped me on my backside and said, "Bingo."

"What?" I only saw the images.

Colin pointed at the picture and pronounced, "Carol's going down."

"What tells you she's guilty?"

"Darlin', there's snow. If you look at the pictures from outside the house, there is no snow. If you look at images taken inside, it's snowing. The freak snow happened on the fourth. I'll never forget Charlie's distress when he couldn't return home to Linda. Helen would remember, she was there. We were all basket cases, with our daughter's death and Linda's pending death. I'll never forget that time." I could see this reminded him that Helen was gone. I hugged him and held him for a minute.

Colin was like many older men. He readily admitted his filter was gone. "I'm so sorry, beautiful boy."

We immediately called the number that the FBI agent had left. Colin explained that while the images were only screenshots of the original pictures. There was snow. "If you look at the weather reports for that year and those dates, I know you'll find that we had an unusual snowstorm in early May. We have to assume she took the pictures when she came to the house to sign the contract. There was no snow on the first of May. It was a few days after the snowstorm that she probably came to the house and murdered both of the Calhouns. My guess was it was the fourth, and for once, she probably didn't visit her aunt that day."

The agents asked us to sit on all of this, and they would take it from here on. They thanked us for our help. I went back and sat down on the sofa in our bedroom. Colin came over and joined me. It would be a few days before the FBI agents promised to contact us. They planned to visit Carol's aunt's nursing home. They were going to verify Hal's flight logs and weather reports for the area. The phone records might take a week or so, but they were confident that if the Calhouns were murdered, they would get to the truth of the matter.

"I'm sick. What was Carol's motive? What would she gain by killing them unless she was directed by Charlie to do this?"

"I really don't know, but I'm guessing that Hal and Carol were well aware of Charlie's activities. One thing's certain. It wasn't Hal. He was the one that called us and informed us that he couldn't fly out of LA and expect us to land within five hundred miles of our destination due to the snow."

"There's nothing to do but wait."

"You know that obey thing you're so stubborn about? I'm asking you to stay away from Carol unless either one of the men or I am with you. I'm only asking."

"Yes, and the same thing goes for you too." We agreed and returned to our wedding preparations.

Luke was still working part-time for Sylvia and Trent, and life was returning to normal. I secretly started to write Dr. Chandler on pieces of paper. I liked the way it looked. Colin was as active as ever, and he was experiencing all the emotions that a bride might have before a wedding. Of course, I was cool, calm, and collected, if you can believe that. Colin and I lay in bed a week before the wedding. He turned onto his front and, with his right hand, picked my arm up and swung it onto his back.

"I've created a monster. Maybe we should have one night a week devoted to tickling."

"I'm not changing Tuesdays, so take that off the table." In truth, there had been no fetish Tuesdays, but the relationship is young. My family will be here in two weeks. The rest of the crew would arrive a week later. I was excited to meet my old teacher, Dr. Harper, from my vet school days. Colin planned to take him fishing. In the end, Colin had a significant say in how this wedding was going to proceed. I was the luckiest woman in the world. *Please, just one year, but I wouldn't say no to ten.*

I continued to fish at least three days a week. Eric had come calling after work, and the three of us would go down to the river in the evening and fish until dark. We would come back to the house, and Luke would be on his computer trying to help students of all ages do homework or prepare for a test. Last week his name change came through. He was officially Luke Chandler.

Carol called five days before the wedding. She needed me to get more updated pictures of the house. She decided she didn't like the old ones. Colin was away and unreachable. I was reluctant to meet her alone at the cabin, but she knew I had security cameras. I was convinced Carol had no idea that she was now the prime suspect in the double murder of the Calhouns. I tried to put her off, but Carol said a professional photographer was coming as well.

I walked over from Colin's house and met her as she drove up to the house. I waved and smiled. I hoped I didn't show any signs of nervousness. "Hey, are you ready for the big day?" Carol was reaching into the back and brought out her camera bag.

"As ready as I can be. How about you? Where's the photographer?"

"He'll be here in a minute. I'm so excited about the wedding."

"I hope you've got a pair of new jeans for the event?" I was searching the rise in the hill and listening for the approach of a second vehicle.

"Oh, yeah. Let's start in the house. He'll be here. He's always late. Where's Collie?"

Was she planning something? "He'll be over in a few minutes. You know how he likes to be involved." I didn't want her to think I was over here without Colin knowing.

That's when Carol stopped and regarded me. "I don't really need pictures, Maggie. I need to talk to you."

"Oh? Look if it's about me getting a hairdresser for the big day, Carol, I—"

"Cut the crap. You and I both know what's happening. Linda knew what was going on. She knew about a few others too." Carol stopped and opened the lid of her camera case. She glanced up at me and then reached into her briefcase. Her hand stayed in the bag.

My heart was racing, and I was desperately trying to think of something to say. "Carol, they're all dead. It doesn't matter anymore. No one needs to worry about it. It's in the past. No matter what happened, they are all dead. I know you're trying to protect Charlie. I don't know how he did it, but he's dead, and there's no point in reopening the case."

Carol seemed to consider it, and then she smiled. "No, I suppose not. It isn't as if any of it matters. I was a good sister, and I played my role. Do you think you'll carry this secret to your grave?"

She saw my confusion. She immediately realized that I didn't get the whole picture. She laughed to herself and then pulled the pistol out of the case. My heart sank. It was surreal. I wasn't afraid for myself, but I immediately felt profoundly sorry for Colin and Luke. I knew Colin and I had ten years if we were lucky, but poor Luke. I had to do something. I had to try. I was going to be killed if I didn't at least try.

"Carol, tell me what happened. If you're trying to protect Charlie, it's not worth going to jail over a dead man. I know we can get through this. You know I was married to a philanderer. They aren't worth protecting. Was he holding Hal hostage?"

Carol's eyes brightened, and she seemed to consider this. She stared at the gun, and I had hope. "No, you really don't get it. It was Linda. My sister shot them both. You know how sometimes, in the last few days of life, some people get a burst of energy and do miraculous things. Linda asked me to drive her here. I didn't see it. I stayed in the car, but I heard it."

"Oh, my God, Carol, you poor thing. You've been carrying this burden all along. I'll vouch for you. Let's go see your cousin now, and you can tell him right away." I knew she was lying. I stood, but she lifted the gun in my direction, pointed it to the couch, and told me to sit.

"I don't think that's going to work this time. Tom won't be able to help. You got the damn FBI involved, didn't you?"

"Carol, kill me if you want, but I can assure you it will only make it worse. Collie knows, and the security cameras are recording as we speak. You won't get away with it, but now I know you don't have to. Linda pulled the trigger. Linda shot Sherry Calhoun. She didn't want Charlie to marry anyone after she was dead. Linda hated the woman. I'll support you."

Carol shook her head. "Hal and I can get away. I can walk out the door. We own his newest jet plane, and Hal is no fool. We will be across the border in two hours. Hal knows the whole story, and he knows what Charlie was up to all along. He was hired to protect Linda and Charlie. We aren't that stupid, you know, Maggie. Linda had some reservations about her medication, and she asked Hal to have it checked out. We were paid well to keep it all quiet. Oh, and if you go over to the security camera, you'll see it isn't on. Go ahead, look behind you."

I turned to observe the monitor, and my heart sank. It was off. I turned back toward Carol, and there peering through the window was Gabe. Gabe had his finger to his lips, and I immediately turned back to the camera to deflect any notion that I saw anything. I needed to draw her attention away from the window.

Carol picked up her phone and pushed a single button. "Hal? It's time. Are you ready?" I couldn't hear his reply. "I'm leaving now. I just have one small detail to take care of."

I was frightened, but I remembered how Carol had described the murder-suicide to me almost two years ago as a "small detail."

"Carol, you won't make it to the plane. Take me as a hostage. It's your only chance. Collie will be coming up the road any second. Don't be foolish. No one will even think about the two of us driving out of here. When you get to the airplane, you can fly away."

She did seem to consider this. Gabe had stepped away from view. I didn't see which direction, but I saw the barrel of a gun pointing from both sides of the windows now. As crazy and as dire as the situation was, I also remembered my children telling me that all Americans have guns and are crazy. Either way, they will get the last "I told you so," and either way, it was going to be ugly.

I thought I heard a siren in the distance. I never heard traffic in my cabin, but as the sound drew closer, even Carol heard it. She stood and motioned for me to stand. I prayed she was reconsidering, which was as ridiculous as it sounded.

"You're going to drive, Maggie. Now walk to the door. Open it nice and slow." Without a word, I opened the door and peered both ways. I saw no one. "Now, let's go down to the car. Carol stepped out of the house and also glanced around. There was no evidence that anyone was nearby. As we walked down the stairs, I heard Luke call from the woods that separated our properties.

"Hi, Maggie. Grandpa's not home. Can I come over for a while?"

I shouted. "Luke, no, not now. Carol and I are leaving, darling. I'll be back home in an hour. I know you have homework."

I glanced back and saw Luke watching us walk toward the car. "Maggie, are you going to town? I need some things. Please can I go too? Hi, Carol."

"Goddammit, Luke. Do as I say. Go home now." I hoped that was enough to deter him from persisting. I thought that would be the last thing he heard from me. I hated myself right then. I turned and yelled that I loved him, but I doubted he heard me from across the meadow. The path to the car was a flat stone walkway. In the melting snow, it was slippery, and there were crevasses. I had on boots, but Carol was wearing her standard heels.

Oh, God, please catch your heel for a second—just one second. God failed me, but as I went to the driver's side, and she went to the passenger side, Gabe and Betty Lou stepped out of the garage door, and each had a rifle pointed at Carol. I ducked as I heard a single shot. Gabe yelled at me to stay where I was. He slowly walked to the other side of the car and picked Carol up off the ground. No one had been hit. Realizing the game, and I use that word lightly, was up, she handed the revolver to Betty Lou as a sheriff's car, and an unmarked vehicle came over the hill.

Tom Sutton stepped out of the first vehicle and came over to Carol. Her face was red, and she was crying. Tom shook his head as his deputy handcuffed her. The FBI agent showed Tom his badge and explained that Carol was being arrested for far more than an abduction. Hal was also being simultaneously detained at the local airport.

I was shaking with relief and the enormity of having escaped certain death. The final hurdle would be explaining this to Colin. Maybe death would have been a better solution. "I need to go. I need to change my underwear." I shrugged but as fast as an old lady could go, I ran to the edge of the woods and the pathway to return to my home and Luke.

As I approached the gate, both Luke and Colin ran toward me from the house. My relief was evident. We all hugged. Colin kissed me and hugged me while Luke enveloped us both from the side. "It's over, guys. I swear, I'm not stepping out of the house ever again without a guard. By the way, I promised Gabe and Betty Lou a full-ride scholarship for the baby and a five-star pony too."

Colin shook his head. "Darlin', I guess you can understand how disappointed I am after all of our discussions."

"Collie, I can explain." I felt so stupid. How could I have done such a foolish thing? He stared at me without even blinking.

"Try me." Colin's voice was strong and without any sign of sympathy.

"Um, maybe I can't. Is it Tuesday? If it isn't, we can pretend?"

Colin stared at me, and then a hint of a glimmer of a sliver of a smidgeon of a waver of the corners of his mouth told me I might be forgiven before I turn eighty—maybe.

Epilogue

The judicial system would run its course, but we would probably wait a year or more to know the outcome. Hal was also arrested for his part in the narcotics trade. Eventually, Hal and Carol's iconic barn burned to the ground. They were selling their plane and house to pay for their legal defense.

We decided to keep my cabin. We would maintain it and have it ready when my family visited. We were expecting a relatively large crowd for the wedding. Lauren Kennedy, the daughter of my deceased classmate, Rebecca Harper, already agreed to attend the wedding. She and her husband, Jim, would bring her father and her stepmother. Jodie decided to come with her husband. Colin offered to pay the flights for my entire Australian staff, but the rest declined.

My brother, Bill, would walk me down the aisle. Christy was feeling well enough to be the matron of honor. She wasn't out of the woods in her long battle with leukemia, but there was no way she was going to miss this event.

Now that fetish Tuesdays were a regular event, I began researching how to keep a marriage alive for us oldies. I need not have worried. Tuesdays were fishing nights. I usually feigned a bad casting technique, and Colin readily corrected my cast. We still practiced catch and release except for Tuesdays.

"Darlin' girl, there's no catch and release when it comes to you. You're my only catch and keep."

Colin started to put his hand under my shirt. Luke glanced over. "Grandpa!"

"Lukey boy, mind your line. I think you have a fish on."

Just one year, but again, God, I wouldn't say no to ten.

Acknowledgments

Many people helped in the production of this book. I would like to thank my initial and primary readers including, my sister Jane Gropp, Jeanie Olson, Jodee O'leary, Julie Laughton, Denise Piggott, and Dr. Sharon Spier with her vet's perspective. Critical input came from Candace Fox, who completed the final observations. Kimberley Hunt edited this book. David Blake performed his magic in the production. I would like to acknowledge Fiona Heysen for her cover painting. Her ability to capture the essence of these fishing stories brought this series to life. Once again, the reader needs to understand that this book was written while I was still practicing in South Australia. I now live and write from a log cabin with a trout stream in Georgia, USA. Life imitating art.

Elizabeth Woolsey DVM

Elizabeth Woolsey DVM grew up in post-war California. Sure she was the daughter of Roy Rogers, she spent her youth emulating him. Sadly, DNA evidence has proved her wrong. Thus, she followed in her other father's footsteps into equine veterinary practice. She subsequently migrated to Australia, where she  practiced equine veterinary medicine near Adelaide, South Australia, until her retirement in December 2020. She began writing about her experiences as a horse vet and published her first book, Horse Doctor An American Vet's Life Down Under in 2005. A few years before her father's death, she discovered a treasure trove of personal and historically significant letters. She knew this would make a great book not only for her family but also for WWII enthusiasts. She published Jack's War, Letters to Home from an American WII Navigator in 2015. While veterinary medicine has been her passion, fly-fishing, horseback riding, and writing occupy her leisure time. Her new books include stories about women in equine practice. Small Town Secrets: Horse Doctor

Adventures 2021 is her latest book. She now resides in North Georgia, where she follows her passions.

She loves to hear from her readers!
ewoolseydvm@gmail.com

https://www.facebook.com/elizabeth.woolseydvm

https://elizabethwoolsey.com/

https://amzn.to/3dPAoGc

Books by Elizabeth

Horse Doctor Adventure Books:
Horse Doctor Adventures **Small Town Secrets**
The Travels of Dr. Rebecca Harper Series
Book 1 A Matter of Time
Book 2 Troubled Waters
Book 3 Lauren's Story
Book 4 Past the Present

https://amzn.to/3DYs5lY

Catch and Release

Catch and Keep

https://amzn.to/3CdUraI

Also by Elizabeth Woolsey (Herbert)
Horse Doctor: An American Vet's Life Down Under
Jack's War: Letters Home from an American WII Navigator

Coming Soon
Horse Doctor Adventures A Man's Worth

HORSE DOCTOR ADVENTURES SMALL TOWN SECRETS

Chapter 1

All the signs were there. It was the end of a long, punishing drought. The rain signaled a change for many of us who relied on the land. It also coincided with an event that would change my life forever. It was the beginning of the end.

As I drove my vet truck in torrential rain toward the last call of the day, I phoned my friend to request an extension of her babysitting duties. "Hey, Jules, is this crazy or what? I've got one call to go. Can you stay any longer?"

"Two inches and counting, Carly." I heard Julie walking down the hall in our house. "I can stay, but it'll cost you."

"Inches and not millimeters. That's old school, isn't it? I'm sorry to do this to you. I called the hospital, and Dan's on a home visit. The receptionist didn't know when he'd be back."

"When's the last time you talked to your neighbor? An ambulance pulled up a few minutes ago."

"Oh, no. She has a cold. I hope she didn't fall."

"They don't call ambulances for colds."

"Dan saw her this morning. He never said anything."

Dan and I are living the dream. I'm a veterinarian, and Dan's an emergency-room physician. I come from a farming community and migrated from the United States to a small, rural town north of Adelaide, South Australia. At the same time, Dan's a city boy from Sydney. I followed the accent. We met at the university's emergency room, where Dan was doing his residency in the States.

I was finishing my internship in equine medicine at the university veterinary school. I sprained my ankle. It would be spectacular to say I'd been injured while wrestling a stallion. Sadly, in fact, I twisted my ankle while sliding in my socks on the freshly waxed linoleum in the corridor of the veterinary hospital. It was a regular competition between the large and small animal interns. Who could slide the farthest? The customary, late-night match followed the semiannual floor waxing on the old linoleum hallway.

I was transported over to the university hospital, where a young, redheaded doctor with an Australian accent was attending emergencies. "Hi, I'm Dr. Langley," was all I needed to hear. Forget his kind manner, above-average looks, and warm hands on my ankle. I was smitten by the accent.

Several days after the encounter, I saw him running in the local park. He acknowledged me with a wave as he and a few other men ran by me while I sat on a bench, throwing a ball for my dog, Buster. My heart didn't skip a beat. That's a ridiculous idea. My heart did increase in rate, and I'm reasonably sure there was a ventricular ectopic beat, which made me catch my breath. I waved, but soon he was gone. Buster replaced the ball in my lap, reminding me that my sole reason for living was throwing the ball for him.

s for dinner. Julie had fifteen or more years on me, but we bonded quickly. Julie's children were finishing school, and it was only in a pinch that I'd called her to ask if one of her daughters could babysit the girls for me today. Julie volunteered herself as her kids were sick, too.

"One hour, pinkie promise." I kicked up the windshield wipers. "Be glad you aren't out in this. It's really coming down. To hell with the drought. The rain gods must be feeling generous."

"Hey, Carly. That ambulance is still parked up across the road. Looks as though your babysitter might be headed to the hospital. Let me go suss it out, and I'll tell you what's going on when you get back."

"Oh, no. I hope she's going to be okay. I'll hurry. I hate for her to deal with this on her own." I felt responsible for Mrs. Miller's safety. I knew she depended on Dan and me both for physical as well as financial support. This was returned in spades with her care of our daughters. I worried that she was alone and ill. If something happened, I would never forgive myself.

Julie made sure I heard her addressing the girls. "Hey, girls. Want some sweets before dinner? We can watch some reality television while we eat ice cream and lollies." Julie laughed. She knew I was strict about snacks before dinner. They didn't watch television, except on special occasions. Our house had poor reception, anyway. However, I was going to hurry home before they were utterly corrupted. I would learn about Mrs. Miller when I returned.

I drove to the property, where three ranch horses were standing in the mud. One horse was holding his leg off the ground while pivoting on the sound limb. The owner was standing under the shelter, waiting for me. Jimmy Medika was a local Aboriginal station hand who lived in the town with his family. He worked on a remote station and was gone for weeks at a time. His wife worked at the bank, and the children were grown and in the process of moving out. Their youngest daughter was in her last year of high school.

"Hello, miss. Thank you for coming." Mr. Medika was particularly formal. "I think it's a hoof abscess. However, since I need to get back up to the station next week, I thought it was best to have you out."

The "station bred," bay gelding is a mixture of quarter horse and brumby. He was a kind horse, but his leg hurt. The pressure of an expanding, infected
fluid pocket under the hoof is like a blood blister under a fingernail. Froggy's digital pulse throbbed, and he jumped when hoof testers were applied to the inside quarter of his foot. When he jumped, he knocked me sideways. "Seems like we found it. I'll get a poultice and a sharper hoof knife, and we'll see if we can't get it open and draining. If we can release the pressure, you should be good to go in a day or two. How's his tetanus status?"

"All good, miss. Remember, he cut himself a few months ago. I still have leftover antibiotics."

"Don't use any yet, Mr. Medika. Wait until the abscess bursts. You might not require antibiotics, anyway."

"You can call me Jimmy."

"You say that every time, but you call me "miss" or "doctor." It goes both ways, you know." I smiled at him, and he grinned back.

"Maybe someday, miss." Most people called me by my first name, but he and a few others were still formal. I loved my clients, and they could address me as they chose.

I located the tract from the sole of the hoof to the probable abscess. However, because I didn't hit "pay dirt" or frank pus, I finished applying a poultice to Froggy's foot and left for home. I was soaked from the rain and cold. Feeling cold was entirely foreign. I was in heaven. I turned off the car air conditioner and opened the window. The steam was fogging up the windshield, so I had to turn on the defroster.

As I turned into the driveway, I noticed an ambulance and several emergency vehicles still parked at Mrs. Miller's house. I was alarmed. I raced up to my front door to avoid a new rain shower. Julie was inside, watching from the window.

"Dinner's finished. As a bonus, the girls are bathed and dressed in their nightgowns."

"Oh, consider yourself kissed. But, more to the point, what's going on across the street?"

The girls, who emerged from their rooms, ran over to me, which put a crimp in our conversation. Julie shrugged. "I've been waiting for you. Don't know. I didn't want to leave the kids. The ambulance has been there for an hour. It doesn't look good."

"Is that Kendall's car?" Kendall was our friend too. Kendall Bidwell was one of the four local cops. She was a legend in the area and was responsible for initiating several programs for our town's children. Her after-school programs appeared to be working to decrease crime. Rural towns had their share of crime partially due to a lack of kids' activities as they grew up. Alcohol and even drugs were a problem for young and old. Domestic violence was sadly prevalent in our town, as well. Dan often witnessed the resulting injuries with his work as an emergency doctor at the hospital.

Dan and I loved the rural life and the friends we'd met, but challenges still existed. The lack of support for our professional endeavors was one of many. Finding friends with similar interests was another. Dan played footy, and he made numerous friends through sports, but we craved intellectual stimulation. The positives outnumbered the negatives. My friends met my social needs. Both Julie and Kendall read books and were up to speed with respect to the current affairs of the world. Both had a wicked sense of humor, and neither was below taking on challenges. We formed a bond when the town mayor wanted to prohibit horses inside the city limits. As if....

The torrential rain continued. While I started to get the girls ready for bed and prepare dinner for Dan and me, Julie walked over to the cars parked out in front of Mrs. Miller's residence. Everyone was inside the house, and I watched Julie enter Mrs. Miller's home and retreat outside with Kendall. They talked briefly, and then Julie ran back to the house. She returned to our residence soaked.

"Kendall's not saying, but I know enough to say Millie's not babysitting anymore. The ambos and police are waiting for detectives to come from Adelaide before they move the body."

"You're joking." I almost said the F word, but I remembered the little ears listening and eyes watching every move. "Where the heck is Dan?" I picked up my phone to call him, but the battery had died. "What's going on over there?"

Julie was shaking from the wet and cold. "Don't know. Kendall isn't talking. She asked me how long I'd been at your house and if I'd observed anyone entering the Miller house."

"Had you?"

"Nope. The girls and I sat at the window, watching the rain all afternoon, and didn't see anything. Hey, I need to get back home. Just got a text from the sick bay, and supplies are required. Heading to the chemist. You want anything?"

"No. Thanks, though, and thank you for today, too. I guess I'll suck it up and start the kids in day care. I'm dreading the tidal wave of colds and viruses from the cesspool of immunologically naïve small children."

Julie laughed. "Welcome to motherhood. Better now than when school starts." She shrugged. "You can't protect them forever. It's a big dark world out there, and acquired immunity is the only way to survive."

"I guess. It's not the kids. It's me. I'll get whatever they bring home, you know."

"Ever the concerned, caring mother...."

"Yeah, I'm a bit of a fraud." I stared out the window and saw Dan's SUV roll into the driveway. "Here, he is."

As Julie walked down the steps and toward her car, Dan ran past and waved to her. I saw Julie point to the Miller house, enter her little red Kia, and pull away. Dan paused, stood in the rain, and gazed toward the Miller home, turned, and ran up the steps to our house.

As he entered, Dan was already soaked, yet he had a smile and tried to playfully hug me. I backed up and stuck my hands up. "Touch me with those wet clothes, and you're dead meat, mister."

Dan held up his hands in the arrested mode and smiled. I knew he was aware of what happened next door. "Terrible news. They're coming over to talk to me. Was I the last person who saw her? Carly, she was sick, but not that sick, and she was only seventy-two. I assume they'll do an autopsy. I know her husband died several years ago, and they didn't have any kids, but are there any other relatives?"

"I think she has a sister in Melbourne or Sydney." I could hear the girls calling their dad. I pointed to the bedroom where they both slept. "You're being summoned."

He stripped off his shirt and pants. I tossed him a towel and went to the laundry to get him a T-shirt and some sweats. "Can you read to them for a minute while I finish cooking our dinner?"

He grinned and went to the girls' bedroom. Our house was small and old. It boasted just two bedrooms and a small office. This was convenient when Dan's overbearing mother, Mira, visited. A night or two was all she could stand. It was exceptionally inconvenient when my mother wanted to come. Mom had traveled from Idaho twice. Our hide-a-bed accommodation didn't make her want to return anytime soon. We'd bought the house from my bosses when we moved to town. We decided it was more important to live near the hospital than in the country.

I wanted to raise the girls with animals. To date, however, we didn't even have a dog. Because bringing Buster to Australia was simply too complicated, he'd remained with my mother until he died last year. Well, if my twitchy uterus and timing were correct, we were going to finally make a move. I figured it was as good a time as any to inform Dan we might need to expand.

Julie's cooking was not as good as a Miller dinner. I purposely explained to Julie that I would cook for Dan and me. Mrs. Miller did it all. She regularly washed our laundry, kid wrangled, prepared our meals, and even grew a beautiful vegetable garden for us. I was sick, thinking of her dying alone in her house without someone holding her hand. It must have been quick. I was hopeful that her death was painless. Maybe she died in her sleep.

I poured a glass of wine for Dan and some juice for me. He noticed immediately and gave me "the look." He cocked his head to the side and raised his eyebrows. I smiled and nodded. Dan wrapped his arms around my waist and kissed me. "Are you sure?"

"Eighty percent. I haven't done a pee test, but I'm pretty confident. You have a lot to answer for, Danny Boy. You know what this means."

"A netball team."

"A new house." I was ready for this conversation.

"A second car." He grinned like a fool.

"Diapers and late nights."

"Nappy's darling, when are you going to start speaking like the natives?"

"A new wardrobe."

"Bigger breasts."

"A vasectomy."

"Tubal ligation. That way, you can meet with the milkman, and I'll never know."

"As long as he looks like Hugh Jackman."

"You win. I'll have the vasectomy." Dan took his glass, and we clinked them together.

"Well, early days, it can wait until he's born." I wanted to throw Dan a bone. I knew he would love a son.

"Or she. A softball team." Dan sipped his wine and grinned like a kid in a candy store.

"Have I told you that I love you lately?" God, I loved that man.

"Show, not tell. Isn't that what you learned in your creative writing class?" Dan smiled as he sipped his wine.

"I like your thinking, Danny Boy." While we both were happy about the possible pregnancy, we kept watching through the window at Mrs. Miller's house.

"What was she like when you were there?"

"Sick, but not dying sick. I can't believe she's deceased."

"Did she have any heart problems?"

"None. I was convinced it was merely a bad cold. I prescribed parac-etamol, a decongestant, and rest. I thought she'd be fine in a day or two. Do you have anyone to care for Casey and Faythe tomorrow?"

"Not yet."

Someone knocked at the door as we were finishing dinner. Dan was clearing the table, and I answered it. A plainclothes detective showed me his picture and placard that hung on a lanyard from his neck. "Mrs. Langley?"

I never bothered correcting the "Mrs." for the doctor. He probably didn't know I was a vet, anyway. "Yes, how may I help you?"

"I must speak to your husband. Is he home?"

"Yes, of course. I'll get him."

"Before you do, may I ask you some quick questions?"

"Certainly."

"I understand you employ Mrs. Miller, and she didn't come today due to her illness? And did you go to work or stay home today?"

"She's been sick for a few days. My friend Julie Chambers stepped in for me and was here all day. I was at work until six o'clock."

"I understand. Do you have a number for Ms. Chambers?"

I picked up my phone, which was still charging on the table next to the door.

"What's going on? Mrs. Miller simply died, didn't she? Is there something else? Is there something I need to worry about?"

"Probably nothing." He was scribbling Julie's name and number.

"What did you say your name was?"

"Detective Ronald Billings, ma'am. I need to see your husband."

Dan came around the corner from the kitchen, put his hand around my waist, and smiled at the detective.

"Dr. Langley?" The detective took a long, hard look at Dan, but then he smiled and laughed. "Danno, it is you. How are you? Still playing footy?" He reached out his hand and shook it warmly.

"Ronald McDonald, you dirtball. How the heck are you? How's Marci? How many kids? I see you met my better half. Carly, this is my classmate, Ronny, the guy I told you about when we stole my dad's car. I guess you've given up your life of crime and joined the other team."

The detective was laughing. "Yep, I play with the bad boys now. Hey, Danno, I need to take you down to the cop shop for a statement. It shouldn't take long."

"Just a sec. Let me get on some other clothes. Carly, if I'm not back in an hour, call our solicitor and try to raise some bail." We kissed. He patted my tummy, and he left with his old friend.

https://amzn.to/3CFhLhM

9 798987 963500